NIGHTWALKER

STORMWALKER BOOK 4

ALLYSON JAMES

JA / AG PUBLISHING

CHAPTER ONE

THE TINKLE OF A WIND CHIME WAS MY ONLY WARNING.

I popped my eyes open, staring at the dark ceiling of my bedroom, my heart drumming in thick, slow beats. The night was silence; no wind, no noise in the vast desert beyond my window. And yet . . .

My wards hadn't broken. No one magical had entered the little hotel I owned who shouldn't be there. My fiancé Mick wasn't there either, having driven off to New Mexico this morning on an errand he'd been vague about. After what had happened between us a few months ago, this worried me, but what had awakened me had nothing to do with Mick.

I lay in the middle of the bed on top of the sheets. July air from the open window touched my bare skin, but the night remained quiet.

Sleep started to overtake me. The hotel was peaceful within, the weight of the night soothing rather than frightening. Tension left my body, and my eyes drifted closed.

A grunt sounded softly in the darkness outside, followed by a twanging sound and a thump.

I was up and into my jeans and tank top before I made any conscious decision to move. I jammed on boots then forced my shaking fingers to make no noise unlocking the door outside my private rooms that led out back. I stepped in silence to the dirt and gravel outside.

The July night was heavy and humid—torpid, that was the word. No wind, no relieving rain, only heavy summer heat that hadn't quite dispersed for the night, patches of clouds dampening the stars overhead.

In that humidity I sensed two auras. One was human. The other was black and sticky and smelled of hot blood.

Nightwalker.

The human crouched under the juniper at the edge of the dirt parking lot. The noise had come from his direction, and as I tried to focus on him, I heard it again—a snap and a deadened twang that came from a high-pressure string and a trigger. Crossbow. Son of a bitch.

Someone was trying to slay my vampire.

The bolt missed. Ansel, the Nightwalker who slept his day sleep in my basement, ducked aside with inhuman reflexes, and the little missile brushed the wind chimes hanging outside the kitchen door. The chimes glistened with tiny sound, the noise that had awakened me.

I faded against the wall of the hotel and slipped around the corner of the building, keeping to the shadows. Once out of the shooter's line of sight, I scooted to the shelter of the squat cedars and juniper around my parking lot and used their cover to circle behind the attacker.

The night was too dark for me to make out the man's features, but his aura came to me clearly, red streaked with white. Violence boiled beneath his surface, but in a cold, contained sort of way.

Then there was Ansel. The slayer had him pinned down for the moment, but the moment the man's attention wavered from him, Ansel would be on him.

Ansel rarely did anything more dangerous than collect stamps and watch old movies, but I'd seen him let loose the Nightwalker inside him. *That* Ansel would rip off the slayer's head, drain the man dry, and walk away, off to go on a blood-lusting, Nightwalker rampage. Then I'd have to kill Ansel, and I really didn't want to. I liked Ansel. Sometimes it's hell being the good guy.

I went slowly, not letting a crunch of gravel or crack of twig betray me. I, the Diné Stormwalker, born and bred of this land, descended from generations of earth magic shamans, moved like smoke toward the tree that hid the attacker, stepped silently under its branches . . .

. . . and found myself staring down a crossbow pointed at my nose.

The man had *two* crossbows, one trained on me, the other still on Ansel. For one heartbeat I stared at the slayer—a wiry, tight-muscled man who'd seen fighting. The scars snaking across his face, arms, and shaved head told me that, as did the hard eyes that glittered at me for the second before he turned back to Ansel.

In the next heartbeat, I brought up a spark of my mother's brand of magic and made the bolt pointed at me implode. The man jumped, dropping the crossbow, and in that instant, Ansel struck.

Nothing moves faster than a Nightwalker. Ansel was across the lot before I could take another breath, smacking the slayer's second crossbow aside. In the next heartbeat, he lifted the man by the throat and slammed him against the tree.

The slayer fought back and fought dirty. A silver knife flashed and cut Ansel deeply. Silver doesn't kill Nightwalkers, but it does sting.

I tried to grab the slayer's knife hand, but he smacked me in the face with his fist. My head rocked back, and blood streamed from my nose.

I came up again, ready to crush him with another blurt of

magic, but Ansel peeled back his lips to reveal his narrow-jawed, animal-toothed, Nightwalker mouth.

"No!" I shouted. "Ansel. Stop!"

He completely ignored me. But once Nightwalkers latch on to their victims, they don't let go. Even if you cut off the Night-walker's head, his dead mouth has to be peeled away from the victim's flesh. Sometimes only the jaws remain when the Night-walker disintegrates, but even then, those teeth hold on and have to be cut out. Ask me how I know this.

The slayer had come prepared with a wooden stake, which I batted aside while I tried to pull Ansel away from him.

I might as well have tried to move a loaded semi with my bare hands. What I needed was Mick, my six-foot-six biker boyfriend with the blue eyes and dragon tattoos, who could shoot fire from his hands. So, of course, he wasn't here.

I could kill the slayer. I could gather a ball of Beneath magic and grind the man to atoms. If he'd been a demon or a skinwalker, I'd have done it already, end of problem.

But the slayer was human, and that changed the game. I had rules, I had scruples, not to mention gods to answer to if I killed innocent humans with the magic I'd inherited from my crazy, evil-goddess mother.

This particular innocent human was busy punching my face at the same time he tried to shove the stake between Ansel's ribs.

I tackled the slayer. My small body couldn't bring his down, but I at least deflected the pointed wood from Ansel.

The slayer tossed all five-foot-four of me aside and went for Ansel again. Ansel's mouth opened wide, the spittle that ran from his fangs glistening in the starlight. That mouth came down, forcing my choice. I gathered a ball of Beneath magic and threw it between them.

The magic exploded with the intensity of a small grenade, flinging Ansel and the attacker apart. Ansel landed on his back halfway to the hotel, and the attacker rolled through thorny grasses between the parking lot and raised railroad bed twenty yards away.

Ansel sprang to his feet. His eyes burned red in the darkness, his blood frenzy erasing every vestige of Ansel my antique-loving boarder.

I ran at him. "Go back inside! Back to the basement. Now!"

Might as well scream at a rabid dog. *Down, Killer. Bad boy!*

Far gone in the frenzy, Ansel sprinted around me faster than I could see and went for the slayer.

The slayer had already leapt to his feet and was sprinting for the abandoned railroad bed that led south into town. He scrambled up the bank, Ansel right behind him.

I scrambled after them, slipping and sliding in the gravel until I reached the hard-packed top where railroad tracks used to be. I ran down the bed, arms and legs pumping.

The slayer easily outpaced me, and Ansel, being a Nightwalker, was faster still, his lean, runner's body and long limbs closing the distance. I was too far away. I'd never stop Ansel, and the slayer still had his wooden stake.

I smacked Ansel with a snake of Beneath magic. The rope of it jerked his feet out from under him, and Ansel fell on his face. The attacker kept running.

Ansel was up and after him again in an instant. The all-powerful magical woman behind them panted and wheezed as she struggled to keep up.

My Beneath magic, mostly good for blowing things up or the direct kill, couldn't do subtle things, like make Nightwalkers sit down and be quiet, or stop humans from trying to stake my friends. If I could have used my storm magic, I might have done better, but I can't conjure storms—a Stormwalker can only use what nature provides, and tonight, nature was providing a warm, calm, starlit night. Mick had taught me some witch magic—protection spells, healing spells, defensive spells—but I needed sage or incense plus time to work the incantation, and I was fresh out of all those at the moment.

If I killed the human with Beneath magic, Coyote and other gods would make me answer for it. They'd made it clear in the past that fighting for my life and that of a friend was no excuse for taking human life.

So I smacked Ansel instead. Nightwalkers are hard to kill, and I'd apologize to him later.

Ansel stumbled and went down, tripped by my next snake of Beneath magic, but damned if he didn't spring immediately to his feet. I hit him again, and Ansel howled. The human slayer took advantage and ran like hell down the railroad bed, disappearing into the night.

I finally reached Ansel. He looked up at me with blood-crazed eyes, his mouth opening as he gauged the best angle of attack.

"Ansel! It's Janet. *Stop!*"

He couldn't care less who I was—he smelled my blood, and he wanted it. Fresh, tasty, human blood, right from the vein.

"Come on, Ansel," I said, putting on my friendly voice. "Let's go in. You can show me that new stamp you found, the one from Belgium, was it? Please, Ansel. I don't want to have to kill you."

Even talking about his beloved stamp collection didn't help. Ansel snarled and leapt for me, and I sadly gathered my magic to dissolve him into dust.

A dragon burst out of the sky. Black and huge, it dove for us with the precision of a fighter plane, a line of fire streaming from his mouth in a tight, efficient burst. I leapt backward as a ring of fire bloomed around Ansel, and then the dragon took down the Nightwalker by the simple, effective method of running into him.

Ansel crashed down the side of the empty railroad bed,

landing flat on his face in the dust and dried grasses of the desert floor. He lay unmoving, clawed hands still. The fire disappeared, and the dragon took to the sky, the hot draft from his wings stirring my hair.

The dragon touched to earth again some way away. The giant beast dissolved into darkness, and from that darkness walked a tall man with black hair, his arms covered with dragon tattoos.

He was naked but didn't seem to notice. I noticed plenty as he strode toward me on long, strong legs, his tight body shining with sweat in the hot night.

When he reached me he looked down at me with eyes of brilliant blue and flashed me the warm grin I liked so well.

"Hey, baby," he said. "Miss me?"

MICK CARRIED ANSEL OVER HIS SHOULDER BACK TO THE hotel, down the stairs to the basement, and to the room that Mick and my plumber Fremont had built this spring.

I had never trusted Nightwalkers as a rule, but I didn't mind Ansel, who'd been turned Nightwalker at the tender age of twenty-two when he'd been a British soldier captured in North Africa during World War II.

He'd been made a Nightwalker as a part of some bizarre Nazi plot, which Ansel said he never completely understood. Their plans for using Ansel had backfired when Ansel had turned on his makers, killing them. He'd escaped and spent the rest of the war sabotaging the hell out of the German army. They should have learned what my Wiccan hotel manager has taught me—whatever you dish out will come back to you threefold and smack you in the ass.

Ansel has always been pretty evasive about what he'd been doing between 1945 and the day he'd showed up at my hotel last winter, but he'd been quiet, grateful, and never complained, which put him a few steps above most of my other guests. He'd only given me trouble once, but he'd been caught in a hex. Not his fault.

Ansel had volunteered to sleep in the unfinished basement so he wouldn't take up a guestroom, but I didn't like the thought of him sleeping on the dank floor, despite his assurances that he'd survived far worse conditions. Mick and Fremont, with help from Maya, my electrician, had built him a comfortable, finished room with a bed, television, and a special cabinet for his stamp collection.

Ansel's gratitude had been immense, and he'd insisted on paying for the renovations himself. I had no idea where he got the money, but then Ansel had been alive for more than ninety years, and he'd obviously been good at putting a bit by.

Mick grunted as he dropped Ansel's inert body onto the mission-style bed. Ansel was out, but he wasn't dead. When Nightwalkers die, they deteriorate into disgusting bone, sinew, and what's left of their internal organs. Ansel was still whole; therefore, Ansel was still with us.

I fetched a gallon jug of blood for Ansel and a pair of jeans for Mick. Mick slid on the jeans but only in deference to Ansel, who was groggily coming out of it. Dragons don't mind nudity, and I don't mind Mick nude either. His body is a work of art, fluid harmony. Ansel, on the other hand, was quite modest and easily embarrassed.

I shoved the bottle of blood under Ansel's nose. He grabbed it with both hands, his Nightwalker mouth opening again, and he upended the plastic jug and poured the blood down his throat. A rational Ansel would use a glass and a coaster — *Standards*, he'd say.

He drank greedily. When he lowered the plastic bottle a long time later, the red had faded from his eyes, and his fangs had gone.

Ansel shakily reached for the napkin I handed him and dabbed at his mouth. "Cheers, Janet."

Cheers, I'd come to know, was Brit-speak for *Thank you*. "Better now?" I asked.

Ansel nodded. He started to close his eyes, ready to drop into his day sleep, but I shook him.

"Not yet," I said. "Talk to me."

He gave me a blank look. "About?"

Ansel could do innocent very well. He had hazel eyes in a handsome if rather long face, and thick light-brown hair with a natural wave. Girls in London must have fallen at his feet before he'd rushed off to war.

I sat down on the edge of his bed. "Tell me why the nice man with the crossbows and the stake was trying to slay you."

Ansel's smile, even with his bloodstained mouth, better suited the tall young soldier he'd been than the monster he'd become. "Oh, you know. With all the vamp books and movies out there, anyone who believes in Nightwalkers wants to try to slay one."

"Bullshit." I leaned closer to Ansel, looking him straight in the eye. "That slayer wasn't a wannabe Buffy; he was a pro. Tell me why was he after you."

Ansel's eyes flickered. "How should I know?"

Mick had pulled out the desk chair and straddled it backward, his strong arms resting on the chair's back. "Janet has a point. Hired pros don't appear out of the blue. Who's after you?"

Ansel snaked out his tongue to catch a last drop of blood. Mick sat quietly, but his dragon tattoos moved restlessly on his arms, their black eyes glittering. Ansel might be a deadly Nightwalker, but no one and nothing out there can be more terrifying than Mick when he decides to be all dragon. Ask me how I know *that*.

Ansel shrank into himself. He hugged his arms across his body and started to shake.

"Janet," he said in a voice so whispery I barely heard it. Nightwalkers don't have to breathe if they don't want to, and he wasn't putting breath into the words. "God help me, Janet, I think I killed her."

CHAPTER TWO

"*KILLED* HER?" I ASKED IN ALARM. "KILLED *WHO*?"

"Laura."

The name meant nothing to me. I hadn't met any Lauras lately, and Ansel had never mentioned her.

"Laura DiAngelo?" Mick asked sharply.

Ansel gave him the saddest nod I'd ever seen. I opened my mouth to question, but Mick shook his head at me, and I popped my mouth closed again. Fine. The Stormwalker is always the last to know.

Mick went on, "What did you mean, you *think* you killed her?"

"I mean don't remember," Ansel said. "A week ago, I woke up, lying facedown in the middle of the desert, blood all over me. It was night, but I could feel the dawn coming. I barely got to ground in time to escape the day. I'd started the evening with Laura, but she wasn't with me, and I couldn't remember what had happened to her. I called her when I woke up again the next night to make sure she was all right, and she didn't answer. She isn't at her house or her store, she hasn't returned my messages, no one has seen her, and I haven't been able to

find her." Ansel scrubbed his forehead. "Janet, I've been so
bloody worried."

For Ansel, the calmest and most understated of creatures I
knew, "bloody worried" meant he was out of his mind
with fear.

I'd never heard him talk about Laura DiAngelo, friend or
otherwise. I didn't make a habit of prying into my friends'
private lives, but I made an exception for Nightwalkers. Even
ones like Ansel, who are trying to stay off the human blood and
live as normal a life as possible, are extremely dangerous.
Having a Nightwalker in your basement is like storing a ton of
plastic explosives—perfectly stable until hooked up to a deto-
nator, and then . . . look out.

"Who is Laura, and why haven't you mentioned her?"
I asked.

"I ought to have. Sorry." That Ansel didn't tell me it was
none of my flipping business attested to his fear. "I met Laura
in Santa Fe. She has an antique shop there. In went in to look
at a few pieces—she keeps her shop open late during the
tourist season. We got to talking, and then we went out for
drinks." He shot me his boyish smile, the one that must have
floored all those girls in their high-heeled pumps in 1939.
"Don't look so surprised, Janet. I can be quite charming when
I put my mind to it."

I knew he could be. "So, you talked about antiques?"

"That and more. My family owned an antiques shop in
London before the war. Laura and I talked for a long time, before
the bar kicked us out. We became friends, and then we formed a
sort of partnership. She's a small dealer, nothing showy, but picks
up nice Native American artifacts here and there—genuine ones.
She rather roused the antiques bug in me again." He gave me
another smile. "I scour auction material online and tell her where
to go and what to buy. She sells it and shares the proceeds with
me. We've made a bit of cash; not much, but some."

"And that night?" I prompted.

"We met up in Gallup and went to dinner. She wanted to discuss something with me, a . . . project we'd been working on. Afterward, we got in her car and headed out of town. She took a turn and started driving north, onto the reservation, I think toward Shiprock. And then . . . I woke up near dawn in the desert with a headache and no memory of how I got there." Ansel sank back into his pillows. His face, which had picked up some animation while he talked, faded into hopelessness once more.

None of this sounded good. If Ansel had gone into his blood frenzy, he could have dragged Laura out of her car, fed off her, dumped her, and fled into the desert. In the dark, out in western New Mexico, there wouldn't have been many witnesses, if any at all.

I asked, "How did you get out of the frenzy? You have to have blood to sate it, right? Anyone you'd drained couldn't have been far away."

"Not unless I'd hidden the body before I passed out." A gruesome possibility. "But I was alone out there. I was terrified of the dawn and fled. I didn't stay to investigate. I spent the night underground, digging into a little cave I'd found in the side of an arroyo. I tried to go back to the spot when I woke up again, but I couldn't find exactly where I'd been. One stretch of desert looks like any other to me."

He looked so pathetic, stretched out between me and Mick, lean and boyishly handsome. I'd seen Ansel become a crazed killer, though. Whenever he was the Nightwalker, he showed a ruthless cruelty and a brutal sarcasm that cut as sharply as his teeth. That person was inside him, somewhere, and I hoped I never had to meet him again.

"Why the slayer?" I asked him.

"Laura's sister, Paige. She found out I was a Nightwalker. She's convinced I killed Laura, and she's probably right."

I exchanged a look with Mick. "Not many people believe in Nightwalkers," I said. "Did Laura?"

"Yes. She said that her research into history and antiquities has brought her up against many weird things. She guessed I was Nightwalker, and I told her my story. Laura promised to keep my secret, but Paige is a follower of the supernatural, it appears. Believes in Nightwalkers, Changers, angels, ghosts — everything occult. She's convinced I killed Laura, and now is sending slayers to kill me." Ansel dredged up a breath to let it out. "I'll go, Janet. When the slayer reports that you and Mick protected me, Paige will be after you too."

"You're not going anywhere," I said. "If this slayer puts out the word that you're being guarded by a dragon and a Stormwalker, they'll give up and look for easier pickings. No slayer's going to want to tangle with Mick."

"Unless he's a dragonslayer as well," Mick said.

I thought he was joking, but one look at Mick's eyes — which had started to turn dragon black — told me he wasn't. I lifted my hand. "One disaster at a time, all right? Ansel, how did Laura's sister figure out you were a Nightwalker? I don't broadcast the fact."

Ansel actually smiled. "People talk, especially about your hotel."

Good point. Gossip in the tiny town of Magellan put social networking to shame.

"Back to the night in question," I said. "How do you know you didn't run away from Laura when you felt the blood frenzy coming on? You might have decided to ride it out in the desert, where you couldn't hurt anyone."

"What about all the blood on my clothes? Besides, I smelled of her."

Not good. I wanted to believe there was another explanation, but it was looking worse and worse for Ansel. If he *had* killed this Laura DiAngelo, Mick or I would have to put him down. Friend or no, we couldn't let the bomb detonate.

Ansel knew it too. He squeezed his eyes shut again and began to shake. The poor guy was miserable.

Mick reached down and put his hand on Ansel's shoulder. "We'll find out what happened. Janet and I are on this."

I started to say that I couldn't guarantee success, but Ansel opened his eyes and looked up at us, so pathetically grateful, that I subsided.

"I have a photo of Laura in my nightstand," he said. "That's all I can tell you now. The sleep is coming."

His day sleep, he meant. Because Nightwalkers burned energy at an incredible rate when fully awake, they spent their days in hibernation. They *can* stay awake during the day, as long as they keep out of direct sunlight, but they remain groggy, crabby, and incoherent.

As Ansel drifted off, I rummaged through his nightstand drawer and found a picture of a young woman in hiking attire —shorts, T-shirt, hiking boots, her brown hair in ponytail under a baseball cap.

She had a wide smile in the sunshine, tanned arms and face, and pale circles around her eyes that showed she usually wore sunglasses. She looked like any other young woman out hiking the Southwest, though I'd never seen her before. I showed the picture to Mick, who studied it with interest.

Ansel was truly asleep now, the sleep of the dead. Mick covered him with a quilt and tucked the bottle of blood into Ansel's mini-refrigerator so it wouldn't spoil.

That was Mick all over—he'd knock you out to keep you from killing your friends then make sure you were comfortable for when you woke up.

～

MICK AND I WALKED UPSTAIRS TOGETHER. THOUGH I WAS tired and a little sore from the fight, I'd had a big adrenaline rush, and I needed to work off the energy.

I looked at Mick, fantasizing about peeling the tight jeans from his fine behind once we made it to the bedroom. I hooked one finger through his belt loop in preparation.

Mick, though, towed me to the front door and started unlocking the heavy thing, opening the hotel for the day.

This did not make me happy. Mick had been walking on eggshells around me the past couple of months. I'd thought we'd worked it out—what had happened this winter wasn't his fault, so there was nothing to forgive. I'd told him this. Repeatedly.

Should have been end of story, but Mick is a complicated guy. Plus, he'd been making mysterious trips, thankfully not long ones, that he wouldn't talk about. I worried about him like crazy when he wasn't around, but when Mick didn't want to say something, he was master at not saying it. He's about two hundred and fifty years old and has had a lot of practice.

"It's still early," I said, my finger finding his belt loop again.

"Why don't you go shower and take off for Gallup, and I'll prep for breakfast. You know Elena pitches a fit if the kitchen isn't set up the way she likes it."

"That can wait a few minutes, can't it?" *Your girlfriend's horny, Mick. Catch the hint.*

He gave me his heart-melting smile. Mick was a tall, broad-shouldered man with a hard body, currently wearing jeans and nothing else. I knew there was nothing else, because I'd watched him don the jeans over bare skin down in Ansel's room. His waistband rode low on his hips, showing me the glory trail that pointed downward from his navel.

As irritated as I was, I couldn't deny that Mick was sexiness wrapped in human form. Who could blame me wanting a little morning delight before I ran off to investigate a week-old possible murder?

Mick bent to kiss my forehead. "Trust me, Janet. We'd need longer than a few minutes." He touched my hair then turned away for the kitchen.

I put my hands on my hips and watched him go, filling my senses his bare back, fine ass under one layer of cloth, and the sharp-lined fire tattoo that ran across his lower back.

The vision would have to sustain me for a while. He ducked into the kitchen without looking back again, and I had to let him go.

In my bedroom, I ditched my clothes and showered, scrubbing off the dirt, blood, and sweat from the fight. I dried off, dressed, and walked out the back door to greet the sunrise — one thankfully empty of slayers, and of coyotes who liked to spy on me.

Not that I'd seen much of Coyote since his wife — his *wife*, the gods help us — had shown up. I liked Bear, what little I saw of her, but Coyote had made himself scarce.

What I did see outside was my new Harley gleaming in the morning sunlight. Mick had brought it out of the shed and parked it at my back door while I showered.

Mick, now with a shirt and boots to go with the jeans, came out of the kitchen. I gave him another full glance. The black T-shirt clung to his body, and I knew he was still commando under the jeans.

"Come with me," I said. "You're good at this."

Mick could be a more clearheaded thinker than I was — most of the time. When he got mad, though, all bets were off. He was a dragon and thought like a dragon, which meant, *If it pisses me off, crush it.*

"One of us needs to stay," Mick said. "Ansel's vulnerable in his day sleep, and the slayer was human, which means our wards won't keep him out. And . . ." Mick looked up at the two stories of square brick hotel rising behind us. "If there's a price on Ansel's head, who's to say that one of your other guests isn't a slayer? I'll stay and keep watch and fill in Cassandra and Elena when they get here."

Cassandra, my hotel manager, was a witch of incredible power, in addition to being a damn good hotel manager. She'd

understand the need to protect Ansel until we knew what
was up.

I wasn't as certain about Elena, the temperamental cook.
She too was a powerful witch, but in a different way, having
access to incredible Apache shaman magic that had pooled for
about a century. She didn't much like Nightwalkers, though.
She was good about stocking blood for Ansel, but she'd made
it known she didn't approve. Elena could go either way on the
Ansel question, and might decide to give aid to the slayers.

However, Elena liked Mick—one of the few people she did
like—and Mick would better be able to persuade her to help
than I could.

Mick kissed me good-bye, a lingering kiss that made me
want to push him back inside the hotel and lock the door. But
he straightened up, told me to watch myself, and waved me off.

Not that riding out into the dawn on my new, dark blue
Softail was a bad thing. I'd wrecked my last Harley, a Sport-
ster, this past winter, by falling with it into a two-hundred foot
sinkhole. The thing had shattered, and all that was left now fit
into a shoebox. Mick had bought me the new one after he'd
assessed that I'd had time enough to grieve for the old one.

I started the Softail and closed my eyes to enjoy the throb
under me. My previous bike had rattled my bones no matter
how much I'd tuned it, but this girl was smooth as silk. Mick
had tucked a pair of gloves onto the handlebars, and I drew
them on, fastened my helmet, lifted my feet, waved to Mick,
and glided out of the parking lot.

I rode north, up through Flat Mesa toward the I-40. With
any luck, Sheriff Jones would still be curled up next to Maya
Medina in his house in Flat Mesa and not out watching for the
first opportunity to pull me over. Not because I'd done
anything wrong, but because he could. In Hopi County, Sheriff
Nash Jones was God.

Whether Jones was still home or striding in early to work,
I made it through the quiet streets of Flat Mesa unharassed,

and continued to Holbrook. The early morning was cool, a breeze moving the dry grasses. North of me, the land was pink and gold with the rising sun, thin red buttes poking from the desert like fingers into the morning.

In that direction lay home—Chinle and Many Farms—but I needed to go east, on the freeway that would take me along the edge of the Navajo Nation, to Gallup where Laura and Ansel had dined.

I wished Ansel hadn't fallen asleep before he'd given me more than Laura's name and her photo, but at least I had that. I could ask connections in Santa Fe to tell me what antique store Laura owned, and Ansel could fill me in on more details when he woke up.

Ever thoughtful, Mick had filled my gas tank. The freeway was quiet this early, and I smiled as I leaned into the bike, riding into the rising sun.

About an hour later, I rode between straight-sided cliffs, an ancient river valley, and into Gallup, a town upon which people from the Navajo, Zuni, and other Pueblo nations converged to trade, shop, eat, sleep, pass the time of day, and sell things to tourists.

I'd been an art photographer before I'd decided to restore the hotel in Magellan, and I still sold the pictures I took of the Navajo Nation and the deserts around Magellan through a shop run by a man called Jeff Benally on the main highway in town. Jeff was always up on gossip. He'd be able to tell me if Ansel had come to town to have dinner with a white woman from Santa Fe—and probably what they'd ordered, what time they'd left the restaurant, whether they'd left together, and which direction they'd been heading.

I started to take the exit to town—Jeff and his wife never minded me dropping by—and discovered I couldn't move the handlebars. At all. The bike was still going seventy miles per hour, but the handlebars were locked solid.

I tried to lean into the turn, to slow down and glide off the road, but nothing happened. Alarmed, I yanked the bike toward the road's shoulder, and the bike yanked back.

I hit the brakes, which did nothing. I tried throttling down. Nothing. I cut the power, but the bike roared to life again under my hands. *What the fuck?*

The motorcycle took off, me clinging on to its back like a spider. The speedometer climbed to seventy, eighty, ninety, a hundred.

The bike flew on east as the sun climbed, Mount Taylor looming in the distance, but I was closing that distance fast. Leaping off the motorcycle at a hundred miles an hour would only kill me, and smacking the bike with magic might destroy it and me along with it.

A voice chirped to my right, a piece of magic mirror custom ground by Mick into my side mirror. "Oh, girlfriend," it said in its drag-queen drawl. "What's going on?"

"Tell Mick!" I shouted. The wind tore away my words, but the mirror heard me.

"Can't," it said.

"Can't? What do you mean *can't*? You have to. You're supposed to obey me."

"Can't," it repeated. "Sorry, sugar."

The mirror—the original of which was hanging in the saloon at my hotel—was magic-bound to obey me and Mick, and no one should be able to take that obedience from us. The idea that someone or something had done it scared me even more than my out-of-control bike.

The bike glided around eighteen wheelers, RVs, and cars without me doing a thing, taking me east at breakneck speed.

Not surprisingly, I picked up the attention of the local police. A state patrol car got on my tail, and another one going west tore through the island between the east- and westbound lanes and pulled in behind me. Nothing I could do. I put my head down into the wind, and the cops kept pace behind me.

At the turnoff to the 371 toward Farmington, my motorcycle swerved onto the off-ramp, squealed around the corner at the end of it, and headed north. The cops were right behind me. A tribal police SUV swung in ahead of me, trying to cut me off, but my bike kicked in still faster. The motorcycle rocked back, front wheel rising into the air like a rearing horse, me hanging on in terror.

The bike came down and sped forward, swerving around the tribal SUV and tearing on up the road.

The Softail dodged onto a narrow road after Crownpoint and headed east then north again on a rough, unpaved road. My bike banged through ruts and holes without stopping, me gritting my teeth and clinging on as best I could.

The state patrollers in their sedans got left behind, but the Navajo cop was still on me. This road was supposed to be impassable for passenger cars, but the cop had a high-clearance SUV, so he'd be fine. Or, if not, and I got him stuck in a wash, he'd only bust my ass even harder.

I finally had an idea where we were headed, though. About forty miles up this road lay Chaco Canyon, a mysterious place with deep history, and an aura that made me crazy. The huge structures at Chaco had been built a thousand and more years ago, and the pueblo people who lived in them had also constructed wide roads that led nowhere. New Agers claim the roads are landing strips for aliens; Navajo stories say that the peoples who lived there built the roads for races against a god. Whatever the theories, the place has the weight of magic and the ages.

The first time I'd gone to Chaco Canyon, years ago by myself, I'd screamed and ridden away before I'd been five minutes into the monument. The weight of the place had nearly crushed me, its magic tearing through my body so hard I was sick for days.

The second time, I'd been with Mick, and he'd helped temper my reaction. That time, I could pause to appreciate the beauty of the place, but I'd still had to rest for a while afterward.

For whatever reason, my motorcycle now wanted to take me straight into the heart of Chaco Canyon, my sensitivity to auras be damned. It sped me through the gates and tore toward the ruins, never mind the parking areas and not-yet-open visitors center. I raced between the canyon walls, and the houses and kivas there, and out onto one of the ancient roads.

There the Softail spun out, dumping me in the dirt before landing on its side. The engine cut out, and all was quiet.

CHAPTER THREE

I LAY FACEDOWN, HURTING ALL OVER. THE RISING SUN gently touched my bare arms, stinging on cuts and abrasions, my helmet the only thing keeping my face from the dirt.

Now that I wasn't flying through it at breakneck speed, the aura of Chaco Canyon descended upon me full force. Sensory data from a thousand and more years pressed on me, the eons rushing together to crush me as I lay there. Blood ran from my nose, but I couldn't lift my hands to dislodge my helmet.

My head pounded as though I had a five-day hangover, and my body began to thrum in time with the vibrations of the place. I swore I started to compress, flattening out against the land as though I'd ooze into it and vanish, becoming one more mote in the fine layer of dust.

Over the humming in my ears, I heard the tribal SUV skid to a dusty halt and its door open. Booted feet hit the ground, then the cop strode cautiously but quickly for me. I knew without looking that he'd drawn his gun, approaching me with textbook precision.

He stopped in front of my head, then when I didn't move, he leaned down, dragged my helmet from my head, and started checking my body for injuries. I lay there, stunned, and let him.

I could tell he'd been a cop for a long time, because he checked me quickly and competently, without trying to grope me or hurt me. He checked my bones for breaks and my head for contusions, then satisfied that I wasn't too badly hurt, he rolled me onto my back.

I looked up into the face of a middle-aged Navajo cop, one with a large, flat nose and an even flatter scarred face. His hair was very black, no gray in sight, but his face bore lines of experience, and his eyes were hard. He'd seen a lot on his years patrolling the huge reservation, and he obviously wasn't impressed with me.

"You all right?" he asked.

"Not really." My voice was a croak.

He looked me over, taking in the blood on my face plus the bruises the slayer had left when he'd punched me. The cop slid broad fingers around to my back pocket, pulled out my wallet, and plucked out my license. "Janet Begay," he read.

"That's me," I mumbled.

He tucked the license and wallet into his pocket, then hauled me to my feet. I suppose he was being nice to me by not putting me in handcuffs, but I couldn't have fought off a mosquito at the moment. No storms were around to help me, and using Beneath magic in this place could be suicide. One spark might leave a hole a mile wide and have geologists and meteorologists scratching their heads for centuries to come.

The cop holstered his gun and marched me with him to his SUV. He opened the back door, stuffed me into the seat, thrust some tissues at me so I could mop up the blood on my face, and slammed the door again.

I was locked in, behind a grill. I touched the tissues to my nose, wincing as more blood flowed out. The cop's identification in the front showed him as Frank Yellow from Farmington, his ID photo stiff and unemotional. Now that I was secure, the cop got into his front seat and ran a check on my driver's license and the motorcycle's registration.

Minutes passed, he not hurrying through the procedure. He had all day, his movements said, to figure out what was going on with me.

I glanced out the windows at the ruins, the canyon walls thrusting up from uneven land, the stillness immense. My skin prickled all over, my scalp tingling as though I'd washed my hair with minty shampoo. Last time I was here, Mick's presence had dampened the aura which rendered me barely able to breathe or think. I'd survived my last trip here because of him, and I had to wonder if I'd survive this one.

At the same time, I needed to know why I'd been brought to this place. Someone or something had possessed my bike to drag me here. To do what? To find something? Laura?

Frank wasn't ready to let me go, though. He looked at the readout from his police computer, checked a few more things, then made a phone call and chatted to the person on the other end.

He finished the call, put away his phone, and studied me in the rearview mirror for a long time, as though trying to understand what I was from my face, my eyes, and my bloody nose. When he spoke, he took his time, a Navajo man who'd learned how to get things accomplished with slow patience.

"It seems you were a real worry to your folks when you were younger. Started a couple of fires, ran away from home."

Under his calm stare, I wanted to squirm and apologize for my entire childhood. It hadn't been easy when my Stormwalker powers had started to manifest, which turned out to be a picnic compared to what had happened when I'd figured out I had Beneath magic in me too.

"Not on purpose," I said. "Except the running away part. But I always went back home." That is, until I turned eighteen and lit out, trying to get away from who and what I was.

Frank returned his placid gaze to me. Deceptively placid. This man wasn't stupid.

"Any reason you decided to break a clean adult record with some criminal speeding this morning?"

My bike got possessed and decided I needed to visit some ancient ruins?

I always tried honesty first, in case it worked. "My bike got stuck in high speed. I couldn't slow it enough to ditch it until I got here."

"You try turning off the engine?"

"Yes." The annoyed tone of my voice conveyed I wasn't lying. "Maybe the gods wanted me out here for a reason." Whatever that reason, they were certainly beating me over the head for it.

"That might be," Frank said. "Doesn't mean I won't give you a ticket for reckless driving and excessive speeding."

Just my luck. A man who was spiritual but not superstitious. He probably wasn't happy with me blaming the gods for my predicament. But who else could I blame? If Coyote had something to do with this, I'd . . .

Well, I didn't know what I could do to him. Nothing ever seemed to work.

Frank was reading my record again. "I've met your dad."

"Yeah?" Pete Begay, my poor, innocent, gentle dad, stuck with a crazy daughter like me.

"One of the sisters of my clan is marrying him," he said.

I didn't gasp, press my hand to my heart, or exclaim that it was a small world. The Diné might make up one of the largest tribes in the United States, but when I was in this part of the country, I could never *not* run into someone I knew, or who knew someone I knew, or who was related to someone I knew.

When the man said *sister* he meant *cousin*, as Anglos term it. It wasn't unlikely that a cop from Farmington would be related to the woman from Farmington who'd agreed to marry my father.

Gina Tsotsie would become my stepmother this autumn. I'd met her this spring, a woman taller than my slender father, quiet but strong. I'd not had a chance to truly get to know her yet, because every time I went to Many Farms, there was either a melee of people at my house, or my father and Gina had gone off to Farmington to visit her family.

"She is the daughter of my mother's sister," Frank said, clarifying. "Do you want to stick to your story of your bike malfunctioning?"

"Not so much a malfunction as a possession."

Another skeptical look in the rearview mirror. "The gods or demons aren't to blame for everything we do, you know."

"Not always in my case."

"My cousin told me about your family's shaman ability. Don't shame it by using it to cover up for your mistakes. I'll let you off with a warning this time, but don't let me catch you speeding like that again, family or no family."

Once again, I was being blamed for the weird things that happened around me, out of my control. But I kept my annoyance to myself. Frank could have hauled my butt to jail and called my dad. "Thanks," I said with sincerity.

He slid his bulk out of the front seat, opened the back door, and helped me out again. "I'll take you and the motorcycle to Gallup or Farmington and let you call someone from there. I don't want you riding home."

I hadn't thought he'd let me back on the bike. But I didn't want to leave Chaco Canyon just yet. I needed to find out why I'd been brought here—what entity had bothered to yank me up the road and across the desert to dump me into the middle of it?

Would whatever wanted me here possess Frank's car if I tried to leave? Or hurt Frank in some way? I couldn't risk that. I needed to stay, as much as the canyon's aura was coating my skin like thick oil.

Before I could open my mouth to suggest that I call my

boyfriend from the visitor's center instead and wait for him there, Frank stiffened, his gaze focusing on the ruins behind me. Like an animal that scents danger approaching, he went still, unmoving except for the breeze stirring strands of his hair.

I turned and followed his line of sight. I saw the natural walls of the canyon, the tumbled rocks and walls of the ruins. Everything stood stark in the morning light as they'd stood for a thousand years. The ancient road, smooth and straight, running to nowhere, lay empty except for my motorcycle lying forlornly in the middle of it.

"What?" I whispered.

"I don't know," Frank said, his words murmured so they wouldn't carry. His hand was on the butt of his gun, but he didn't draw. "Spooky out here."

I tried to find a hint of what had alerted him, but I couldn't feel anything apart from the intensity of the place, which I didn't dare touch more closely. The thousand years of people living, working, praying, and fighting piled upon the canyon like layers upon layers of paint. Gods had been here, and humans, and the demonic. One more demon, human, or god wouldn't put a dent in what I already felt like whips all over my skin.

After a long moment, Frank eased his hand from his gun. "Come on. Let's get your bike into the SUV."

"What did you think you saw?" I asked as I followed him across the dirt back to the motorcycle.

"Don't know. Someone poking around where he shouldn't be."

"People camp here. Could be an early hiker."

"Maybe . . ." Frank glanced at me, his eyes went flat again, and he walked to the motorcycle.

"Aren't you going to check it out?"

Frank turned back to me, easily and neutrally, as he'd been doing everything else. "Why do you want me to?"

I wasn't sure. Frank needed to get out of here, before he got involved in anything concerning me. A demon might toss Frank aside as collateral damage in order to get to me.

Then again, perhaps the entity had only wanted me to follow Laura's path. Ansel had said they'd taken the highway north toward Shiprock—had Laura meant to come out here? Driving all the way to Shiprock, then to Farmington and back south to Chaco Canyon gave a regular car better roads than the way I'd come.

On the off chance, I took Laura's photo out of my pocket and held it out to Frank. "Have you ever seen her?"

Frank's eyes widened, and he snatched the picture from my hand. "Where did you get this?"

"You recognize her, then?"

"What do you know about her?"

Frank was a good cop—he wouldn't give up anything about Laura until he knew who I was and why I had this picture.

"I'm looking for her," I said.

"Why? You a friend? Relative?"

"I'm looking for her . . . for a friend. I'm kind of a private detective." Unpaid, doing favors for people when they were at their most desperate.

Frank didn't change expression, but his eyes managed to radiate disapproval. I probably shouldn't have said *private detective*. My grandmother always had the same reaction. "What friend?"

"Client confidentiality," I said, pretending I used the phrase all the time. "This friend is worried about her and asked me to find out whether something supernatural had happened to her."

"Because you're a shaman?" he asked, voice ringing with skepticism.

"Something like that. I can sense psychic residue."

His look said, *Don't bullshit me*, but he decided to nod. "That why you were riding out here this early in the morning?"

"I was heading this way, then my bike brought me here. I can't explain it, but I'm thinking I was brought for a good reason. Will you let me look around?"

Frank's eyes narrowed as he studied me. I couldn't read minds, but I didn't have to be telepathic to see that he knew I wasn't telling the whole truth. He didn't believe in my so-called ability, and he wondered if he shouldn't arrest me. Maybe a night in jail along with a psychiatric evaluation might straighten me out.

"Please," I said. "If something's happened to her, we should find out what. Maybe I can help."

I tried to sound helpful. I knew Frank had read my entire record, which said *Troublemaker* with a capital T. But that was all in the past, which I'd put well behind me. Right?

Could my innocent look convince him, or the fact that my dad was such a nice guy and we were about to become family?

Frank assessed me, the man not impatient, arrogant, or surly. He knew his job, he knew right from wrong, and he understood the gray area in between. Some people grow wiser as they grow older, and middle-aged Frank was one of them.

"Tell me everything you know about her," he said.

Again, I decided to go with as much truth as I could. "I know she owns an antique store in Santa Fe, that she was driving this direction after having dinner in Gallup a week ago. She'd been talking to my friend about something she'd found, but she never said what."

"This friend was with her?"

"He doesn't know what happened to her," I said.

"Was he with her?"

Frank had the stubbornness of deep water. "He had dinner with her in Gallup. You'd probably find that out anyway." At this point, I had to veer from the truth. "But she drove off and left him, and he hasn't seen her since."

Frank just looked at me, his gaze going all the way down inside me. I'd never met anyone who could stare at me with such unmoving exactness, no one human anyway. Mick could do it, and now Frank Yellow.

"She was camping out here," he said.

The words were flat and uninflected, but I read in them that he was prompting me for whatever information I could give him.

"Camping?" I asked.

"In the campground over there." He pointed to the east of the ruins. "She told a couple other campers she was driving down to Gallup to meet someone." He looked at me again. "She never came back. Witnesses in Gallup say she ate at a diner with a slim white man with brown hair. She never made it back here." More staring deep inside Janet. "I'd be interested to find this slim white man and ask him a few questions."

"Mind if I look at the campsite? I might be able to pick up something."

Frank kept staring at me, his dark eyes glittering in the morning sunlight. I could imagine tough criminals facing him across an interrogation table and wilting more every second.

He also struck me as a guy who'd use any resource he could no matter how bizarre to get to the bottom of a matter.

"I'll take you there," he said. "But you stand next to me all the time and you touch nothing. Understand?"

I raised my hands. "Got it."

He nodded once and turned back to the SUV. He wasn't doing me a favor, his broad back told me. He was milking a source.

Frank loaded my bike into the back of his SUV, a strong man who didn't need any help. He let me sit in the front seat while he drove me back across the ruins to the main road and around to one of the camping areas.

"It's a hike from here," he said, setting the break and turning off the engine.

I was still sore from my fall, but I clumped along after him, down a trail, through a dry wash, and along another fairly flat mile to the camping area. Part of the site had been cordoned off and emptied of campers' gear, but the dirt was filled with footprints, too many for individual sets to be distinguishable.

A few tents had been erected in the far part of the campground, and campers were already up, eating or pulling on big backpacks to hike out. They went early, because the summer day would get blistering hot, and rains could come in the afternoon to fill the washes, stranding anyone on the wrong side of them.

Frank took me to the corner of the campground. Whatever tent had stood there had been removed, along with Laura's gear, leaving only the stake holes in the ground and burned out ash in a fire pit.

I'd wished I could hold something that had belonged to her, but I made do with standing inside the four points of the stake holes and closing my eyes. To make it look to Frank like I was doing something, I raised my hands, palms down, over the place her sleeping bag would have been.

At first, I felt nothing but the same blinding, pounding presence that had been beating on me since I arrived, grinding through me like a toothache.

My problem with ancient sites is that I don't see auras from only the last few days. I see them through the ages, some bright, some faded, all overlapping until they swirl like a vortex in my head. This campsite wasn't as overwhelming as the ruined pueblos, but I felt a wave of humanity from the builders who'd laid the first stones to the last vacationer from Ohio.

I tried to concentrate. Many people had lain here over the years in this very spot, men and women, talking, laughing, sleeping, having sex.

But the young woman from Santa Fe had been the only one

abducted. I sucked in a breath when I saw it—not the incident itself but her fear.

Stark terror, rising up like blackness in the morning. I sensed her struggling and saw the aura of what she struggled with.

The stench of blood, the black outline of fear —Nightwalker.

But overlapping the Nightwalker aura was another aura, which sent my heart pounding. Sharp, fiery, with a bite of hot ash.

Dragon.

CHAPTER FOUR

FRANK, OF COURSE, WANTED TO KNOW WHAT I'D SENSED. I couldn't very well tell him I suspected that Laura had fought not only a Nightwalker, but a dragon, one whose aura was very much like my fiancé's.

"Um," I said. "Not much. Are the campers sure she never came back?"

He gave me his keen stare. "They're sure. The campground was crowded that night. Plenty of witnesses. Why?"

Because I'd sensed Laura being dragged from here. The campers might have missed seeing her return from her dinner in Gallup, or maybe she'd gotten back here very, very late.

But . . . if Ansel had been with her, what had happened to him between the time he'd blacked out in the car and Laura fighting him in the campsite later? If Ansel had gone into blood frenzy he most likely would have killed her right there in the car, not ridden with her the many, many miles to Chaco Canyon. At some point, he'd left her and woken up alone in the middle of the desert.

And a dragon had most definitely disturbed the campsite.

The auras had been left at the same time. Dragon, Night-walker, and Laura had been there together that night.

I seriously needed to talk to Mick.

I CONVINCED FRANK TO DRIVE ME BACK OVER THE RUTTED road and down to Gallup. He left me with my now silent motorcycle at a large coffee shop that had just opened up, where I and a mixture of Indian and white travelers ordered breakfast.

From there I called Mick on a payphone—I could never find my cell phone when I needed it—told him what happened, and asked for a ride home. Mick's voice went rough with rage when he heard about my possessed bike, and said in clipped tones that he was leaving immediately.

I'd have an hour and more to kill before Mick arrived, so after consuming a breakfast burrito way too fast, I walked a few doors down the street to Jeff Benally's store. He wasn't open yet, but he was there, saw me, and let me in. He wrote me a commission check for a few photos he'd sold since he'd sent the last one, and I took it gladly. Running a hotel was expensive.

"I need more," he said. Jeff was a large Navajo who wore plenty of turquoise and silver, a walking advertisement for his store. "I can't keep your pictures in stock."

I hadn't sent much more lately than the few photos I'd taken of Canyon de Chelly in the snow last winter. I thought of the sunrise I'd just seen at Chaco Canyon and decided it would be a good place for my next shoot, if I could dampen my reaction to the place long enough. Plus it would be a good excuse to go back out there and look around.

"Soon, Jeff. You can't hurry art."

He gave me a grin. "Sure, Janet. That's what they all say."

Mick pulled to a stop in front of his door, in a truck with

Fremont Hansen: Plumbing and Fix-It on the side. Fremont wasn't with him, for which I was grateful, because Fremont could talk, talk, and talk some more, and I wasn't in the mood right now.

Mick pulled me into a hard embrace outside the shop, with Jeff looking on interestedly, then stood me back and checked me over for bruises and abrasions. Satisfied that I wasn't as near death as I sometimes had been in the past, he lifted my bike into the roomy truck bed and drove us west into Arizona.

I told him the whole story, slowly and with more details than I'd been able to convey on the phone, ending with me standing in the campground, taking in the aura.

Mick listened to me without interrupting, and when I'd finished he said, "Hmm."

"That's it?" I asked as his eyes flicked between road and speedometer as he drove around an eighteen-wheeler. "I'm carried off by my possessed Harley and sense that Laura was abducted possibly by a Nightwalker, possibly by a dragon, and all you can say is *hmm*?"

"It's interesting."

"Not the word I used. My language was more colorful."

Mick moved his strong hand to rest on my thigh. "The fact that you're all right is what's filling my mind, Janet. The rest of it—the bike, the abduction, the missing woman—all that is noise."

I suddenly wished we weren't in a pickup racing at eighty down the freeway. Mick's blue eyes darkened, and he gave my thigh a warm caress.

"Did you hear what I said about sensing she might have been taken by a dragon?" I asked.

"Yes." Mick calmly drove on, but his eyes changed from blue to deep black. "Do you know which dragon?"

"I couldn't tell. I was hoping you would know. What is this dragon business you keep going out to the compound for?"

"Nothing to do with abducting antiques dealers from Santa Fe."

I waited, but it was clear he wasn't going to tell me. I kept my temper in check and asked, "Do you know who could have done this?"

"No. But I'll find out."

"You know, if you turn this truck around, we can be at the compound by this afternoon," I said.

Mick kept stubbornly driving west. "No way am I letting you near the dragon compound again. They tried to hold you hostage before, and there's nothing to say they won't again. I can get there faster on my own, and I'll interrogate a certain obnoxious dragon out there until he gives me some answers."

"You mean Colby? I was thinking more of Drake."

Drake was the assistant to Bancroft, one of the dragon council, which consisted of three dragons who pretty much ruled dragonkind. Drake's position as Bancroft's eyes and ears gave him a lot of power but also meant that Drake did whatever dirty deed Bancroft didn't want to handle himself.

Colby, on the other hand, though a troublemaker, was not an evil bastard. He inked his human body like a yakuza, lived to harass Mick and other dragons, and was currently serving a sentence at the dragon compound for some crime he hadn't told me about. Probably hadn't genuflected to his dragon highness Bancroft fast enough, or something.

I conceded that Mick should approach Colby alone, because he was right—the dragons didn't like me. I was not the most popular person at the dragon compound that rested high on a cliff outside Santa Fe.

Mick took the turnoff at Holbrook and drove us back south through Flat Mesa to my hotel at the Crossroads. By the time we rolled through the dirt parking lot, the tourists were up and wandering about, taking pictures of the view, the hotel, and—after I stepped out of the truck—me, the Navajo woman who ran the place.

Mick unloaded my motorcycle, saying he'd check it over before he started contacting dragons and getting them to talk. He pushed it toward its shed while the guests snapped pictures until they'd had enough and headed out for their destinations of the day.

Inside the high-ceilinged lobby, Cassandra had fixed her steely gaze on a woman who jabbered at her over the counter. Cassandra wore her usual work attire—raw silk business suit, hair in a sleek bun. No one would put her down as the most powerful witch in the western United States, but she was.

More powerful than the woman gesticulating to her—Heather Hansen, dressed in flowing clothes, multiple pendants, and lots of bangles. Heather owned the local New Age store, which sold incense, jewelry, tarot cards, books, and plenty of souvenirs from Magellan and its vortexes. Our vortexes weren't as famous as the ones in the red rocks of Sedona, but ours were more deadly. Not many people knew how deadly.

Heather and Cassandra were arguing, Cassandra in her understated way, Heather with hands on hips and determination in her eyes.

"It's too dangerous," I heard Cassandra say. "You'll be messing with forces beyond your control."

"That's why I want you there," Heather said. "You're a much better witch than I am." She said this with envy, but it was the truth. "I need your help. Janet, you too."

"Help with what?"

Cassandra gave me a dark look. "Heather wants to have a séance."

"Oh?" I asked, understanding her alarm. "Why?"

What most people think of as séances—mediums, dark rooms, candles, supplicants holding hands around a table—are harmless nonsense. Most are hosted by fake mediums out to impress people.

Real séances are dangerous. Cassandra wasn't kidding

about forces that could be unleashed by a weak witch—demons, dead witches who should stay dead, and other bad things, always waiting for a gateway to open.

I doubted Heather could deliberately open a path herself, but she might accidentally. Though she was more the nature-lover variety of witch, Heather did have some magic in her.

Heather answered me. "I have a client whose sister has been killed, but she has no proof of the culprit. She wants to ask her sister in person what happened."

Three guesses as to who the sister was. Heather suddenly had my interest.

"The dead are notoriously unreliable witnesses," I said cautiously. "Nine times out of ten, they have no idea what happened to them."

"I tried to tell her that," Cassandra said. "Nine times out of ten, you don't even get the person you are trying to reach. A demon or someone else waiting to cross over sees the opportunity and rides in on your pathway. Like a hitchhiker. A demonic, slash-your-throat and spit down your neck hitchhiker."

Heather waved this away with a soft clinking of bracelets. "I've done hundreds of séances, ladies. I'm very good at finding connections for people. This will be simple. Paige will talk with her sister, and we'll be done."

"Paige?" I asked, pretending to be casual.

"She came here from Santa Fe. Her sister disappeared, but Paige is sure she's dead."

The bite of uneasiness in my stomach turned into a melee, which didn't sit well with my breakfast burrito. "I'll come," I said, ignoring Cassandra's anger. "Where and when?"

"Tonight at Paradox," Heather said. "Eight thirty. I want to make sure it's fully dark."

A person could hold a séance any time of the day or night with the same result, but people are attracted to the dark and spooky. I don't know why. I like safety, friends around me who can kick some serious ass, and no demons.

"Good." Heather beamed. "I wanted to let you know, Cassandra, as we are the only true witches in town."

Cassandra gave her a cold stare, but she was businesslike enough to realize she shouldn't piss off the person who constantly recommended my hotel to her tourist customers. *If you want the full Magellan experience, visit the vortexes, shop at Paradox, and stay at the Crossroads Hotel,* Heather would tell them.

"Then I thank you for telling me," Cassandra said. Fortunately for her, the phone rang, and she said, "Excuse me," and turned away to answer it.

As I walked Heather to the front door, she said, "Don't take this the wrong way, Janet, but leave Mick at home. I don't want him scaring away my guests."

Heather was afraid of Mick. She had no idea that Mick was a dragon—she thought he was a biker, a Hell's Angel, maybe, and she was more afraid of bikers than she was of dark forces. Not very smart, but understandable. The Crossroads Bar across the parking lot attracted some pretty scary-looking humans.

I agreed I'd come without Mick, and Heather left, mollified.

I needed to question Ansel again, but there was nothing I could do about that until he woke up, so I went to question another being I needed to interrogate.

At least all seemed to be in order in my hotel this morning, thank the gods. Elena was chopping vegetables with vigor in the kitchen, the two new maids were busy cleaning upstairs, the brochure rack was full, and the plants were watered. The saloon was well stocked to open this afternoon, complete with cracked magic mirror hanging over the bar.

The mirror had come with the hotel. I'd found it upstairs in the dusty attic soon after I'd moved in, after Mick and I had awakened it with a burst of Tantric magic. The crack in it had come later, after one of the harrowing adventures that made me question my wisdom in opening a hotel.

Because Mick and I had woken it, the mirror was now bound to obey both of us unquestioningly. The fact that the mirror had been able to disobey me on the road made me more than uneasy.

The mirror appeared to be asleep. I shook its frame, the glass tinkling, and was rewarded with a sleepy, "What?"

"What happened out there?" I demanded. "I told you to contact Mick, and you said you couldn't. What did you mean, you couldn't?"

"I mean I couldn't, honey," it said, the mirror coming more awake. "*Something* was keeping my mouth shut. Oh, girlfriend, it was *terrible.*"

I didn't like the sound of that—something or someone that could make my magic mirror immune to my commands had to be deadly powerful. Magic mirrors were highly magical talismans, and as annoying as this one could be, it had proved its worth more than once, saving my life and Mick's several times over.

"Janet," the mirror said. "Take me with you to the séance. *Please?*"

"No," I said immediately. I could see the trouble *that* would bring.

"I can make spooky noises," it said. "You know, lend atmosphere."

"The people such a thing might impress wouldn't hear you anyway." Those without magical ability can't hear the magic mirror at all. I envied them. "And I thought you were asleep during that conversation."

"Maybe, maybe not."

"Forget it. You're not going."

"Fine," the mirror said grumpily. "Séances are crap anyway. It wasn't a person," it finished.

"Sorry?" I blinked at the non sequitur.

"On the bike, sweetie. I didn't sense the presence of another mage. Not a person."

"A spell then?" I asked.

"But someone has to cast the spell, don't they?"

Someone did. I left the magic mirror, disquieted.

I went in search of Mick, who was tinkering with my bike near its shed behind the hotel. His only greeting was a quick look at me before returning his gaze to his socket wrench, but Mick could smolder me to ash with just a glance.

He had very blue eyes, the color of which had caught me when I'd looked up into them the night he'd taken my virginity. That had been after I'd tried to kill him with my storm magic, which he'd let crawl all over his body before he'd dispersed it and laughed at me.

"I can't find anything wrong with this bike mechanically," Mick said as he put aside his wrench, wiped his hands, and straightened up.

He mounted the bike, which looked small under his big frame, and started it up. It purred like it should. Mick lifted his feet and drove across the parking lot, me watching, waiting for the motorcycle to turn wild and race off with him.

It did nothing so dramatic. Mick circled the big dirt lot I shared with the Crossroads Bar and came back to me. He turned off the engine and remained straddling the bike. "Everything's fine."

"The magic mirror said it wasn't a live being that possessed it," I said, and related the brief conversation. I also told him about Heather's séance.

Mick listened to it all with a serious look on his face, and gave me the *hmm* again.

"Your conversation is not very helpful this morning," I said, folding my arms.

Mick didn't rise to my irritation. "I know you don't want Ansel to have killed her," he said quietly. "I don't either." He gazed across the lot into the wide desert. A light breeze moved the air, bringing with it the scent of dust and the lingering exhaust from my bike. "But people like us sometimes have to make the decision to do something about the danger, even if we don't want to. Even if it hurts."

I knew what he was really talking about. "Like you being ordered to kill me if I turn into an insane killing machine?"

"Yes." He returned his gaze to me. "Except I can't do it anymore. I can't hurt a hair on your head." Mick reached over and touched said hair. "You're too much a part of me now."

His hand was warm, but I resisted melting into his touch. If I did, I'd drag him off to bed get nothing else done today. "If I turn into an insane killing machine, I give you permission to stop me," I said. "I don't want to hurt anyone. Least of all you."

"I won't be able to," Mick said. "Not anymore. You know my true name. That has tangled me up with you more than I can begin to understand. Killing you would probably kill me too."

My heart squeezed with worry. "Gods, Mick, don't say things like that."

"It's true." His fingers moved to my jaw. "You hold me in thrall. And at the same time, you belong entirely to me."

I swallowed the lump in my throat. I wasn't certain how I felt about being Mick's possession, and lately he'd become even more protective. I, who'd fought tooth and nail for my independence, had difficulty belonging to anyone. I had to admit, though, that if I had to belong to someone, Mick wasn't a bad choice.

He caressed my cheek again, then he gave me his usual hot smile. I rose on my tiptoes, bracing myself on his wide shoulders to press a kiss to his warm, strong lips.

The sweet moment was interrupted by a cell phone. His, not mine. Mick set me gently on my feet, answered it, listened, and said, "Sure, she'll be right there."

"I'll be right where?" I asked as he hung up. "Who was that?"

"Barry. He wants to talk to you."

Barry owned the Crossroads Bar across the lot. "He called *you*?" I asked, puzzled. "Why didn't he call me? He knows my number."

Mick looked at me with tolerant amusement. "Where's your cell phone, Janet?"

My hand went to the holder on my belt to find it empty. I remembered I'd had to use a payphone in Gallup to call Mick earlier, and I had no idea where I'd left the damn thing this time. I was hard on cell phones. I either lost them in stupid places, or they got crunched during my adventures. The magic mirror was a more reliable communication device between me and Mick anyway.

"I don't know," I had to say.

"It's probably in Ansel's room," he said. "Or in the refrigerator. Hope it's not in a potted plant this time."

"That only happened once." I hadn't retrieved it before the maid had watered the plant . . . a couple of times. "Does Barry want to talk right now?"

"He said as soon as you can. I'll look for your phone." Mick dismounted the bike, touched my chin, and kissed my lips again. "I just like the look on your face when I tease you about it."

I liked the look on *his* face when he teased me. I returned the kiss with some heat then took myself across the parking lot to the Crossroads Bar.

Barry's bar had been in business far longer than my hotel, which had stood derelict until I'd had the whim to buy the place and open it. My hotel had a saloon, but that was more for tourists and guests who would be way out of place in Barry's biker hangout.

The Crossroads was a real bar, dark inside with a long counter, barstools chosen for their function not beauty, pool tables, and tables and chairs that had seen better days. Barry carried every kind of liquor a person could want, but mostly he sold beer. He had no magic, and he wasn't fond of serving the magical. If I hadn't ridden up here the first day on a Harley, I doubted he'd have spoken to me at all.

Barry had opened his doors a half hour ago, but he had only two customers—a man from Flat Mesa who came there regularly to hide out from his wife, and a tough-looking youngish guy I'd never seen before.

I slid onto a barstool and watched Barry put away clean beer mugs.

"Guy over there says he wants to talk to you." Barry jerked his chin at the tough-looking man. "Find out what he wants and make him go away. I don't want any trouble, understand?"

I understood. Barry's bar had gotten busted up in a raid earlier this year, and while Sheriff Jones had done the raiding, it had happened, indirectly, because of me.

"Got it," I said.

Barry gave me a dark look but let me go. I walked to the tough-looking guy's table and sat down. He was drinking beer from a bottle, holding the bottle with battle-scarred hands.

"I'm Janet," I said.

He looked me up and down, his eyes pale blue against tanned skin. He'd buzzed his blond hair so short it was only a golden sheen on his head.

"You're guarding the Nightwalker," he said.

Oh, perfect. I hadn't met a slayer in years, but today I got to chat with two of them.

"My Nightwalker is harmless," I said. "He drinks cow blood from a jug."

"That's not what I hear. And there's no such thing as a harmless Nightwalker. They're vermin, and vermin need to be exterminated."

"Well, this one's off limits. He's under my protection."

The look the slayer skimmed over me told me he wasn't impressed. "What are you? Witch?"

"Stormwalker. Not the same thing." I could have boasted

that my boyfriend was a dragon, but dragons weren't too keen on people knowing they existed. I hadn't forgotten Mick's mention of dragonslayers, which I had not liked.

"Whatever you are, this is a courtesy visit," the slayer said. "There's a bounty on the Nightwalker, and I intend to collect it. So take some advice, sweetheart. Clear out of my way, and you and your boyfriend might just stay alive."

If he expected me to cower in terror, he didn't know anything about Stormwalkers. I rested my elbows on the table and regarded him calmly. "Who set the bounty?"

His disgusted look told me he'd expected better of me. "Like I said, this is a courtesy visit. I'm the best slayer in the country, and I'll go right through you to get to the Nightwalker if I have to." He leaned toward me around his beer. "Be a shame to see someone as hot as you be sliced down the middle."

His aura showed me no magic in him whatsoever—he was as mundane as Barry. But I didn't need to read his aura to know that he was a hard man, an experienced fighter, and had killed in the past—Nightwalker, human—he didn't much care about the difference.

"Yeah, that would be a shame," I said. "You might want to know that someone else tried to collect the bounty this morning. Man with two crossbows. He came up against me, and he ran away."

What might have been a smile creased the man's mouth. "I know the slayer you're talking about. He's good at running away. Me, not so much." He pulled a card from a pocket in his vest and slid it across the table to me. "If you want to negotiate, you text me."

I left the card where it was. "How many other slayers have come to town looking for the bounty? Am I going to have a Slayer Fest on my hands?"

The hint of smile again. "A couple others, but they're pussies. I'm the one you have to worry about. You're a sweet little thing, and I thought I'd spare your boyfriend some grief. If you and he get out of the way and let me through, no one will get hurt."

"Except my Nightwalker."

He shrugged. "That's the whole point."

I looked at the name on the card. "All right . . . Rory. Thanks for the warning. I'll keep it in mind."

"You need to take this seriously, honey—"

Rory's words cut off with a startled noise as he looked at something behind me. I turned to see what had made him choke.

A large woman had moved quietly to our table. I hadn't seen her come in, which was odd, because she was definitely noticeable. She wore traditional Navajo garb—a long dark skirt and velvet shirt, squash blossom turquoise necklace, and turquoise and silver rings and bracelets. She was tall and wide, but the word *fat* never occurred to me when I looked at her. Bear was big and formidable, but she held a timeless beauty in her unlined face and fall of thick, jet-black hair.

"This man smells of death," she said in her low, rich voice.

CHAPTER FIVE

"HE'S A SLAYER," I SAID TO BEAR. "OCCUPATIONAL hazard."

"You should come away from him."

"I agree." I rose and snatched up Rory's card, not because I'd be texting him, but because it contained his full name, and I planned to find out everything I could about him.

I put my fists on the table. "Let me explain something, Rory. My Nightwalker's off limits. Spread the word. And get out of the bar. Barry doesn't like you."

The slayer wasn't looking at me. He had his full attention on Bear, trying to figure out what she was and whether he should be afraid of her. His eyes told him *harmless woman,* but I knew his gut was screaming at him in primal terror.

I could have told Rory he had plenty of reason to fear her. Bear was a goddess, one of the oldest, almost as old as Coyote, though I wasn't certain. She, like Coyote, was a shifter god, and what she shifted into was a giant grizzly bear. Rory was feeling the basic instinct to flee from danger, like all little animals did from giant predators.

Bear only looked at him. Rory took a quick drink from his

beer bottle, wiped his mouth, threw down a tip as he got up, and quickly walked away from the table and out. Bright sunlight flashed through the dark bar as he opened the door and then vanished. Barry gave me a nod of thanks then went back to wiping beer mugs, his worry over.

I LEFT FOR THE SUNSHINE OUTSIDE WITH BEAR. THE DAY'S temperature had climbed to over a hundred, and my skin prickled with the heat.

"You gave the slayer something to think about," I said. We watched Rory mount a motorcycle and head out down the highway toward Winslow. He never looked back. "Thanks."

"He's not wrong about Nightwalkers, my friend," Bear said. "And Ansel might have killed this woman."

That Bear knew all the details didn't surprise me. If she hadn't figured them out by herself, she would have gotten the story out of Mick.

"I want to hear Ansel's side before I hand him over to a slayer," I said.

"I too have come to like this creature who calls himself Ansel. I will not let a human slayer come near him."

No, she'd let me finish him off if need be. If Ansel had to be slain, best leave it to a friend, right?

I blew out my breath. "Why did you come to the bar? Were you looking for me?"

Bear gave me a slow nod. "Cassandra told me you were going to a séance tonight. I would like to attend with you."

I shot her a grin. "You won't find Coyote that way, you know."

She didn't smile in return. "This has nothing to do with my game with Coyote. And I have found him, several times. No, I want to know about this woman who is missing, and the sister who thinks her dead."

I wondered at her interest, but I didn't deny I'd feel better at a séance with a powerful goddess by my side. If Heather did manage to let anything through the ether, or worse, out of one of the vortexes, I had no doubt that Bear could handle it.

"I don't see why not," I said. "Heather likes a show, so the more the merrier."

We reached the hotel's front door. I stopped, looking it over in surprise, then I warmed with anger.

I'd replaced the door, made by an artisan in Santa Fe, not long ago. His first door had been destroyed in one of my many adventures. The second one he'd finished was as nice—the wood was old and well-polished with age, the aura of it deep and resonating with contentment.

White chalk marks now snaked all the way up one side of the door and halfway across the top of the frame, signs I didn't recognize. They weren't Wiccan symbols, nor were they glyphs.

They also weren't magic. Mick and I warded this hotel with invisible sigils, and these markings hadn't touched those, nor did the chalk vibrate with any kind of spell. Also, they hadn't been here when I'd opened for the morning.

"What the hell?"

I looked at Bear, but she was eyeing them with the same puzzlement.

Mick opened the door, as though he'd seen us coming. He'd donned chaps and motorcycle boots, ready to ride off again east to talk to dragons.

"Slayers' marks," he said. He frowned as he ran blunt fingers over the symbols. "It's how they communicate with each other. Marks the abode of a Nightwalker and tells whether they've been successful in the kill. In this case, no."

"They're using my hotel doorway as a bulletin board?"

"It's both a brag sheet and for safety. They sign in before they go on the kill, in case they need someone to pull their balls out of the fire. It's like signing in with park rangers before you hike a long trail."

I clenched my hands, my anger tasting sour. "You know a lot about slayers. Dealt with them before, have you?"

Mick looked away. "Let's just say we've tangled."

"You tangle with a lot of things."

"I've been around a long time. The way to deal with slayers' marks is soap and water. I'll have Julia or Olivia wash them off." He named my two maids, cousins of Maya Medina, my electrician. They were young and working their way through college, and had agreed to work for me despite all the stories about the weird shit that happened in Janet's hotel. They were local and therefore inured to weird shit by this time.

"I bet that rat bastard in the bar did these before he gave me his friendly warning." I hadn't paid any attention to the front door on my way to the bar, having walked around from the back.

Bear skimmed her hand above the marks, sunlight catching on the silver of her many rings. "Mmm. Not a nice message."

"You can read that?" I asked.

She nodded without conceit. "The translation is simple." Her fingers floated above the marks as she read. *There is a Nightwalker in this house. I claim him. The kill extends to those protecting him.*"

My anger boiled to compete with the afternoon heat. "He has balls."

Bear gave me a grave look. "Do not dismiss the threat because he is only human and has no magic. Humans have killed most of the magical things in this world. Look around you."

She had a point. So many vastly powerful beings tried to best me and Mick that I sometimes forgot to take the smaller threats seriously. But if I hadn't been awakened by the wind chimes last night, Ansel might have been a smear on my back porch this morning.

I went inside, calling to Olivia to please go soap off the doorframe. She looked irritated and said a few choice words in Spanish to whoever had made extra work for her. She was related to Maya all right.

Bear had vanished by the time I came back out, but I was no longer shocked at the way she came and went without warning. She had much in common with Coyote, who'd she claimed, to my vast surprise, was her husband.

Mick straddled his big bike, which he'd brought around front, preparing to leave. I closed my hand over his where his rested on the handlebar.

"You can't interrogate Drake on the phone?" I worried about him every time he went to the dragon compound, though the dragons had more or less promised not to touch him. But if anyone could bend rules, it was a dragon.

"Better to talk to dragons face to face," Mick said. "Trust me."

"It's not face to face I worry about, but flame to flame."

He chuckled like I was joking. I wasn't.

He leaned down and kissed me. I touched his cheek, wishing he'd stay, but also knowing I had to stop hovering around him, babying him. He was a grown dragon. I had to let him go.

I kissed him again, didn't miss his promising look, then he started up the bike and rode out of the parking lot.

I'd almost lost him this winter, forever. Paranoia was a bitch.

THE REST OF THE DAY PASSED UNEVENTFULLY, EXCEPT FOR the crap that goes along with running a hotel. Clogged drain in room Four. Loose tile in the hall. A pair of low-level witches complaining about the noises in their bedroom, which turned out to be the magic mirror teasing them.

Those with minor magic can hear *something* when the mirror makes noise, and it plays things up by moaning and screeching like special effects in a low-budget movie. The witches could hear only muffled sounds, but I, of course, got the full force when I walked into their bedroom. The magic mirror was channeling through the mundane mirror over their dresser, wailing and moaning like a stage banshee.

I didn't want to let on that I had a magic mirror in here. Even the weakest witch can use one to her benefit, but the mirror's current owner has to die before it can be used by the successor. Never believe that deters a mage who really wants a mirror.

I positioned myself in the middle of their bedroom, raised my hands, and shouted the magic words: "Would you shut *up!*"

"Aw, come on. Don't ruin it for me. Let me have my fun."

"I banish thee, evil thing," I said loudly.

"Make me," the mirror said, and made a raspberry noise.

The witches held each other while I walked closer to the wall on which the mirror hung. I said in a low voice, "If you don't stop it, I'll tell Mick to flame you."

It was tough to kill a magic mirror, even to melt it, but Mick's fire could make it suffer for a while. I'd seen Mick hurt it before.

"Oh, that is *so* not fair."

"I don't care about being fair; I'm trying to run a hotel. You have a cushy place here. Don't wreck it, or I'll toss you out with the trash."

The mirror went silent, and I held my breath. It was supposed to respond to my every command, but the mirror constantly figured out ways around that when it wanted to.

"All right." The mirror heaved a sigh, which made the glass rattle. "I'll shut up. But I'm not withdrawing from this room. They're a couple, and no way am I not watching that."

I knew I shouldn't be disgusted with an inanimate object, but the mirror was a complete pervert. "If they complain again, you're out of here." I turned to the two young witches, who watched me in awe and admiration. "The demon was trying to come in through the mirror," I said. "I've banished it for now, but just in case, you might want to put a blanket over the mirror at night."

They nodded, eyes wide. Behind me the mirror said, "Aw, now that's just *mean*."

Tough. I ignored it and walked out.

ANSEL HADN'T WOKEN BEFORE I LEFT FOR THE SÉANCE, BUT I wanted to hear what Laura's sister had to say. I'd shake Ansel's story out of him when I got back.

Cassandra drove me and Bear—who'd showed up again as we were leaving—to Magellan two miles south of my hotel, Cassandra's look still disapproving. When she dropped us off at Paradox, I thought she'd admonish me to be careful, but she said nothing. Cassandra put her car in gear and drove on toward the apartment she shared with her shape-shifter girlfriend.

Rows of wind chimes whispered as we entered the store, letting in the warm summer wind from outside, the air inside layered with the scents of incense and sage. Trays upon trays of crystals glittered in the central aisles, and one wall was covered with books on every topic from places to visit around Magellan to spells using sex energy to ways to communicate with the dead.

Heather stretched out her bangled hands as she rustled forward. "So glad you could come. Is this your friend called Bear?" Heather bowed and a said a few words in mispronounced Diné.

Bear accepted the greeting graciously. "*Ya-at-eeh*, friend of my friend." In the traditional way, Bear didn't use Heather's given name—names had power, and using a name could draw demons to that person. The younger generations didn't always pay attention to that, and my grandmother called me by name plenty, but Bear did it as a courtesy.

Heather, looking pleased, led us to the back of the store and through a beaded curtain to a short passage that ended in a French door, which led to fairly large private room. Heather's store was one of the oldest buildings in town, originally built of brick, and shored up with plaster, wood, and cement over the years. The walls bowed, patches of new brick were mixed with old, and the wooden floors squeaked and sagged as we walked on them.

This had been a rancher's house, way back when, and supposedly haunted. Heather had purchased the abandoned building and fixed it up, much as I'd done with my hotel. She'd wanted the place for its atmosphere. I'd wanted the hotel so I could have something of my own, a permanent place that was part of me.

Heather's research had told her that the ghost that haunted her store was a child called Pearl, who'd died of a fever when she'd been about ten. Poor kid. That Pearl had existed, I believed—town records confirmed it. The story that she haunted the store was a load of shit.

There aren't any ghosts. What people think of as ghosts is usually psychic residue, which some people, me included, are good at detecting, whether they know they have the ability or not. The psychic aura can be strong, especially around places of violent death, but it's not a ghost. Nightwalkers and Changers are real, but ghosts—no.

Heather, however, believed in Pearl as hard as she could. She waved at a corner in the hall as she led Bear and me into the back room. "You can go to bed now, Pearl. I know you don't like séances, but it's okay. I won't ask you for help tonight. I put your dolls in your trundle bed upstairs."

Bear and I exchanged a glance. There was absolutely

nothing in the corner, not a presence, not a psychic residue, and definitely no ghost.

A table had been set in the middle of the room with chairs drawn up to it. Candles clumped in the middle of the table, their thick fragrance battling with the incense that snaked from holes in a wooden incense burner.

Another woman was already seated at the table. Her features and her dark blond hair told me she was Paige, Laura DiAngelo's sister.

Heather introduced us, but Paige didn't seem interested or impressed with us, even when Heather told her I was a powerful magic user. I took the seat next to her, and Bear sat next to me, composed as usual. Bear spread her large hands on the table, her turquoise bracelets clinking.

"A few more are coming," Heather said. "Not long now."

The few more were my plumber, Fremont Hansen, and his cousin, Naomi Kee who was now married to my oldest and closest friend, Jamison. With them was Naomi's deaf daughter Julie.

Naomi greeted me with her usual big smile as she took the seat across from me. Fremont said a warm hello and took the chair across from Bear.

Fremont believed himself a great mage in the making. He did have a little bit of natural magic, enough to get him into more trouble than he knew how to get out of. Then he came to Janet Begay, his local Stormwalker, to pull his balls from the fire. Fremont loved séances and ghost lore, so I wasn't surprised to see him there.

But Naomi and Julie, no. Naomi had once been the biggest Unbeliever I'd ever met—though she'd changed that status when she'd married the shape-shifting Jamison. Even so, she was skeptical about most of the woo-woo magic our town was famous for, and ninety percent of the time, she was right.

"I didn't think this would be your scene," I said to her.

"Heather invited us, and we were curious," Naomi

answered. Julie, who had sat down next to her and across from Paige silently signed to me: *Séances are a bunch of crap.*

I bit back a laugh as I signed back the way she'd taught me. "I know."

"The sun is completely down now," Heather announced, shutting the French door behind her. "I think we can begin. Paige, did you bring the things?"

Heather took the seat at the head of the table, and Paige began fishing items out of a tote bag—a photograph, a bracelet, and a hat. Heather gathered them in front of her, put her open hands on top of them, and closed her eyes.

The aura of the belongings floated around Heather's fingers like dust motes, a tint of warmth from the missing Laura.

Heather shivered. "She's trying to get through."

Fremont leaned forward, his balding head shining under the lamplight. He had soft brown hair that he kept cut short and the warmest brown eyes I'd ever seen. "You can feel that?" he asked.

"Yes," Heather whispered.

Heather had less magic in her than Fremont did, but both were responding to the faint psychic buzz that clung to Laura's things.

Heather let go of the bracelet, hat, and photo, arranged the lit candles around them, then instructed us to hold hands.

I took the ice-cold hand of Paige in my right and Bear's warm, strong one in my left. Bear gave my hand a little squeeze.

Heather turned out the lights and sat down with us, telling us to close our eyes.

I'd prepared myself for an evening of Heather moaning and then talking extensively to her Native American spirit guide, who didn't act or speak like any Indian I'd ever met. Heather had a great imagination and conjured things so real to her that she convinced herself she had extensive powers. It made her happy, and she truly believed she helped people, so I let her enjoy herself.

I was therefore unprepared when the windows in the back of the room burst open, and an Arctic wind rushed through the close room, stirring my hair and rattling the blinds.

"Ah," Heather said, in an excited whisper. "She's here."

CHAPTER SIX

THE TEMPERATURE TODAY HAD TOPPED OUT AT A HUNDRED and three, and while the desert cools down pretty rapidly at night, the balmy seventy-five degrees outside now was a long way from the icy air that poured in on us.

Half the candle flames went out. Bear jumped, her eyes as wide open as mine. I looked out the windows, but saw nothing but a strip of dark desert and a strand of streetlights about a mile away.

"Laura?" Heather asked.

She alone had her eyes closed—the rest of us were trying to figure out what was going on. I looked around for special-effects machines. I'd once watched a movie being made in New Mexico, and they'd faked everything—wind, sunshine, snow, rain . . . even when it was raining. The director had wanted to control every detail.

The machines had fascinated me, and the techs had showed me a lot of stuff. That was back when I'd been traveling the country with Mick, us carefree on our Harleys. He'd known the technical director on the film, who'd let us hang out with him on the movie location. Mick had known everyone, I'd thought, and I'd been starry-eyed in love with him.

I was still in love with him, with fewer innocent stars but more strength. Some things are better second time around.

"Are you there?" Heather asked.

The wind picked up again, and the rest of the candles died.

"Are you there?" Heather called.

"Yes!"

The voice echoed through the room, and everyone but Heather swiveled heads trying to see who'd spoken.

I am here. Softer now, a woman's voice, a bit muffled, with both a touch of anger and sorrow. *Paige, have you come?*

"Laura?" Paige's hand clamped down on mine so hard that I clenched my teeth. "Where are you?"

In a better place.

"Then it's true. He killed you?"

Heather's eyes remained firmly closed, her body rigid.

Yes, sister. He murdered me. He drained me of blood and left me to die.

"The Nightwalker?"

I thought he was my friend. A long, despairing sigh. *Avenge me.*

"I will," Paige said, still crushing my hand. "I'll get him for you, Laura. Do you understand?"

Yes. Another sigh, this one relieved. *Avenge me, sister. Avenge me . . .* The voice drifted away.

"Wait!" Paige called. "Laura, don't leave me . . ."

Julie frantically tapped her mother's shoulder and pointed out the open windows. All of us except Heather and Paige craned to look. I froze, astonished.

A white light whirled out in the desert a foot above the ground, the wind kicking up dust and giving it an eerie glow. I'd seen light like that swirling above vortexes, but there were no vortexes in this part of Magellan. Vortexes are ancient things—they don't just form—so this wasn't a new one.

The light danced, back and forth, back and forth. I couldn't help thinking it was making fun of us.

And then, everything stopped. The light vanished, the wind died, the voice was gone. The seven of us were left sitting in the dark around a table in a windswept room, the only light coming from faint starlight outside.

Heather jumped to her feet and switched on the overhead light, a triumphant smile on her face. The rest of us blinked at the sudden glare, Paige shaken, Fremont fearful. I extracted my hand from Paige's grip and rubbed it.

"Wonderful!" Heather said. "I've had the spirits speak *through* me, but never out loud like that."

"What was that light?" Fremont asked. "Outside, behind you. Did you see it?"

"No." Heather looked disappointed, then she shrugged. "Probably the manifestation of Laura's spirit. I ward this shop very well, so only the voice got through."

Bear and I exchanged a glance. She agreed with me—the voice and the light had been two different things. The voice and the wind had definitely been fake, though I didn't know how Heather had done it. The light, I wasn't so sure.

Paige started pulling Laura's things back toward her. "I know now what I need to know. Laura is dead, and the Nightwalker *you* are harboring in your hotel, Ms. Begay, killed her."

"You don't know that at all," I said hotly.

"She never called Ansel by name," Fremont pointed out. "She could have meant another Nightwalker. Ansel's a decent guy. You know, when he's not under a hex."

Paige's voice was thick with anger. "He killed her. I want him to pay."

"Now, hang on," Fremont said, getting to his feet. "What do you mean, *pay*? You have to prove it was him first."

"You heard her," Paige said. "Laura told me to avenge her." She jammed her sister's belongings into her big purse. "Thank you, Heather. This was worth it."

Without saying good night, she slung her purse over her shoulder and stalked out of the room. We heard the shop's front door bang a few moments after that.

"Great," I said, getting up. Following the dictates I'd learned as a kid, I pushed in my chair. "She'll have every slayer in the country running out here for the bounty. Mick and I can't fight all of them."

"Nightwalkers are dangerous, Janet," Heather said, walking past me in a whiff of patchouli. "I've never been easy with you letting him live in your hotel."

"I'm more dangerous than any Nightwalker, Heather. Trust me."

I walked out into the cool night with Naomi, Julie, and Fremont in time to see Paige peel out of the dirt lot in a small sedan. Bear had already disappeared, but this didn't surprise me. Like Coyote, she came and went as she pleased.

"I'd give you a lift home, Janet," Fremont said, starting for his truck. "But I have a date." He winked.

"With who?" I asked in alarm. Fremont had the propensity for going out with entirely the wrong women—magical femme fatales—to dire consequences. I've had to extract him from disastrous relationships more than once.

Fremont's grin flashed in the darkness. "It's Olivia Medina."

"Oh." One of Maya's cousins, who was a harmless human being. Hmm. A Medina going out with a Hansen. The world might cease revolving.

Fremont drove away south, and Naomi offered to give me a lift home. I accepted and climbed with Julie into the big truck in which Naomi hauled around nursery plants for her business. As Naomi pulled around the strand of big cottonwoods that lined the parking lot, I saw to the north an orange light, the definite flicker of flame, and black smoke rise to blot out the stars.

Only two things lay in that direction — Barry's bar and the Crossroads hotel. One of them was on fire.

"*Shit!*"

Two fire trucks rushed past us, and Naomi turned onto the highway to follow them. I couldn't help pressing my feet to the floorboard as Naomi drove the twisting road north out of town.

"If the slayers are trying to burn Ansel out," I said, "I'm slaying *them*."

Naomi shot me a glance. "You said something about slayers inside. What do you mean by slayers?"

Julie watched my mouth, reading my lips interestedly as I explained. "Bounty hunters who kill Nightwalkers. The bounty on Nightwalkers is temptingly high."

"Who puts a bounty on something no one believes in?"

"Lots of people. Pissed off mages, families of Nightwalker victims, families of the Nightwalkers themselves. Who wants a vampire in the family?"

Naomi shook her head. "Poor Ansel."

"Some Nightwalkers do deserve to be staked," I said. "But why the fuck are they burning down my hotel?"

"Almost there." Naomi didn't admonish me for swearing in front of her daughter, not that I'd have noticed at the moment.

Naomi's truck flew through the parking lot of Barry's bar — the bar intact — and pulled up behind the fire trucks. The bar had emptied, bikers standing outside in the motorcycle-filled lot to watch the flames eat into my hotel. Red lights flashed from the north on the highway, Flat Mesa responding to the call as well.

I leapt from the pickup before it stopped moving and sprinted toward the commotion.

My saloon was on fire. The high-ceilinged saloon had been an add-on to the three-story, nearly square hotel back in the 1920s. It jutted out from the rest of the hotel and had its own outside entrance as well as one from the lobby. Carlos, the bartender, in his white shirt and black pants, stared morosely at the saloon, hands on hips.

My guests and hired help had gathered on the west side of the hotel. I scanned the knot of them, about twenty people in all, but I didn't see Ansel.

I did hear the magic mirror screaming inside. The sound reverberated through every mirror in the hotel, winding up to a shattering frequency. I could hear it even in the mirror on my motorcycle around the back.

I couldn't do anything for it. It might be terrified, but an ordinary fire wouldn't destroy the mirror. It would have to tough it out for now.

If this was an ordinary fire.

The firemen were unrolling hoses and getting on with their business. "What happened?" I yelled at Carlos.

He only spread his hands. "*No se.* Everything was fine, and all the sudden, the roof exploded into flames. I ran like hell."

"You all right?"

Carlos nodded, swallowing. "Yeah, I'm okay. We got everyone out."

"Ansel?"

He shot me a startled look. "I don't know."

I left him, sprinting around to the back of the building. Acrid smoke poured into the night, stinging my throat. I saw another clump of people gathered on top of the empty railroad bed, and I ran for that.

Mick broke away from the group and met me at the bottom of the bank. Before I could demand he tell me what had happened, he cupped my face in my hands, his eyes filled all the way across with black. "You all right?" His voice was fierce.

"Fine. What—?"

My word choked off as Mick yanked me into his arms and held me in a breath-stealing embrace, his lips finding mine in a savage kiss.

He released me and rearranged his look of raw worry to a grim one of anger. "Ansel's still inside," he said. "He refused to come out."

"Is he crazy? If that fire reaches him, he's dead."

"He said he *might* be dead if he stays inside, but he *will* be dead if he comes out. I didn't argue with him."

"What the hell does that mean?"

Mick took my hand and helped me scramble up the six-foot, soft-sided bank of the raised railroad bed. On the top, where ties and rails used to be, was a flat stretch about four feet wide that ran for miles, used now as a hiking trail.

On the summit stood Elena my cook, and a tall, black-haired man, stark naked, with the tattooed ends of dragon wings rising from around his shoulders up his neck.

"Drake!" I snarled, starting for him. "You flamed my hotel? Please, let me kill you."

Mick seized me from behind and lifted me off my feet. Drake looked me over with quiet dark eyes. His long black hair was loose in the moonlight, he obviously having recently shifted from being a dragon.

"I need the Nightwalker," he said to me in his cool voice.

"Too bad. What did you have to do with abducting Laura DiAngelo? Where is she? Is she dead?"

"I did not abduct her, she is not dead, and I insist you bring me the Nightwalker. Surrender him to me, and I'll stop the fire."

His answer told me he knew all about Laura and much more about what was going on than I did. "Ansel's my friend," I said. "And if Laura is alive, it means he didn't kill her." That fact both relieved and confused me, though relief was buried way down on my list of emotions at the moment.

"Even if Ansel did not kill *this* woman, he's murdered in the past," Drake said. "He's drained humans of blood and left crushed bodies in his wake. He must make restitution. Give him to me."

"Since when are dragons interested in standing up for humankind? What do you really want, Drake?"

"I want the Nightwalker," Drake said in a hard voice.

Elena stepped up to Drake. At first glance, Elena Williams, an Apache from Whiteriver, looked like a harmless middle-aged woman, plump in body, a habitual frown on her face. She wore her hair pulled into a tight bun, and her attire, as usual, was white polyester pants, a bright print top, and white sneakers.

She was also the conduit of generations of Apache shaman magic. She made a mean tamale pie and had a temper as sharp as the knives she kept honed in my kitchen.

Drake looked down at her without worry—big mistake.

"The Nightwalker is under my protection," Elena said. "And if that fire gets into my kitchen, my next dish will be roasted dragon wings."

Drake looked puzzled. "You would defend a Nightwalker? I'd thought he would be anathema to your people."

"I haven't asked my *people*," Elena said. "but he's done no harm to me. Or to you. Dragons don't care about how many humans Nightwalkers drain. You Firewalkers care about no one but yourselves."

I couldn't have put it better myself. Drake pretending he wanted to kill Ansel to avenge human victims was a big, fat lie.

"You have to give us more than that," Mick said to him.

Though Mick hadn't spoken until now, he hadn't let me go. I stood in the circle of his arms, his chest hard against my back.

Mick wasn't just being affectionate—he held me because he didn't trust me around dragons, with good reason. My Beneath magic was clamoring to come out so I could whack Drake fifty feet backward. He was *burning down my hotel*, for the gods' sake.

"The Nightwalker has something I want," Drake said impatiently.

"What?" Mick asked.

"He stole it, he and that woman. She doesn't have it, so he must. Bring him to me."

Ansel had stolen something from the dragons? Ansel hadn't mentioned dragons in his story about Laura and finding antiques for her, but then, Laura lived in Santa Fe, and the dragon compound on the cliffs near there probably had immeasurable treasure stored in it. Dragons liked to hoard.

Mick let go of me, but it was to move me behind him so he could face Drake full on. "Unless you have proof, the Nightwalker is under my protection."

Drake started to growl. "Once you bring him out here, I will make him reveal where the object is. That will be proof enough."

Dragon logic. Then again, Ansel's day sleep this morning had come upon him a little too conveniently. I seriously wanted to interrogate him myself.

"Leave the Nightwalker to me," Mick said. "If he has stolen something belonging to the dragons, I'll let you know."

Fire danced in Drake's hands, rage glittering in his eyes. "This is not your business Micalerianicum. I don't care what kind of general you are, or how bravely you fought in the war. My task is to get the object back, and I intend to use any force at my disposal to do it."

Behind us, the firemen were struggling to put out the flames, arcs of water shooting into the sky. But dragon fire burns ten times hotter than a normal fire, and there would be no saving my hotel.

"Mick," I said, forcing my voice to be calm. "*Please*, let me kill him."

"Bring me the Nightwalker," Drake repeated with more force. "And I'll spare the rest of your abode. That's all you have to do."

I stepped out from behind Mick. "Do the words *fuck you* mean anything to you?"

Drake's eyes burned red, and a big ball of fire danced

between his hands. He tilted back his head and shouted a word into the night.

I had no idea what he said, but Mick apparently did. He was past me, going for Drake before I could draw a breath.

Drake threw the fire at him. I yelped, but the fire hit a wall of flame that Mick had thrown up in front of him. Drake's fire struck Mick's wall and flowed harmlessly around him, leaving him untouched in a bubble in the middle.

I grabbed Elena and pulled her well out of the way as Mick let fly his fire at Drake. Drake defended with his own flame wall, and then both dragon-men disappeared into fire and smoke, the inferno competing with the already wild one of my saloon.

An orange-red missile zoomed out of the night from the east, coming in on us with swift precision. I recognized it as a dragon, and I knew *which* dragon, but instead of touching down, he headed for the hotel, rising above it in a cloud of darkness.

The darkness hid him from the people below, but I the magical being could still see him. He hovered above the hotel proper, his dragon sides expanding as he drew a long breath.

"Colby!" I screamed. "No!"

Colby let out his breath. Fire belched out of his mouth, streaming through the blackness of the night, aimed directly at the main part of the hotel.

My hard work, the year and a half of my life, the place I'd carved out for myself, was about to be swallowed by dragon flame.

Elena reached out her plump and work-worn hand, skin covered with little burns and nicks from her work in the kitchen. She chanted a word under her breath.

As I watched in astonishment, a glassy light flowed up from the base of my hotel and oozed around it. Colby's fire met the glasslike bubble around the hotel walls and dispersed.

Elena's face, touched by the firelight, was calm, even

serene. If I'd performed that feat, I'd be panting and exhausted, crazed with power and trying to stop myself blasting Colby out of the sky so he'd fall on Drake.

Colby somersaulted in midair and came for us, dragon wings sending a hot wind to whip my long hair into my face. He landed out in the desert with another *whap* of dragon wings, and a dark mist obscured him.

When the mist cleared, Colby the man was jogging toward us, his all-over inked body an interesting pattern in the darkness.

I ran at him. "Colby, you—"

Colby raised his big hands. "Before you start yelling at me, Janet, I'm bound by dragon law to obey that asshole for another five months. Drake gives me the command to flame your hotel, I flame your hotel. I'm a loaded gun, and he's allowed to point me and shoot."

He'd stopped my words, but my anger didn't die. "What the hell for? Why is he doing this?"

"Because he wants that Nightwalker. Don't ask me why— no one tells me a damn thing."

Colby was a big man, as all dragons were, his body tattooed all over, his hair as dark as his dragon eyes, though his human eyes were light blue. I was still boiling in rage, but Colby wrapped his big arms around me and lifted me off my feet in a crushing hug.

"Janet, sweet baby, it's been too long."

"Put me down, you idiot."

Colby thumped me back to the ground but didn't let me go. "Hey, just because Micky and Drakey are battling it out doesn't mean we can't catch up on old times."

I struggled away from him, trying to see what was going on with Drake and Mick. They'd battled before, but Drake was formidable, and this time they were more evenly matched.

Mick was punching Drake in the face behind the flames,

which made me feel slightly better, but then Drake raked fiery hands down Mick's chest, burning flesh.

I couldn't take it anymore. I reached down within myself to find my Beneath magic, but before I could touch the coil of gleeful power waiting for me, a gunshot sounded not ten feet away.

I yelled and clapped my hands over my ears. Colby spun around, and even Elena jerked her attention from the hotel.

Sheriff Nash Jones marched up the bank of the railroad bed. Red and blue lights flashed from the top of his new SUV, parked as close to the railroad as he could put it, white spotlights glaring through the night. The light glistened on his short black hair and also on the shotgun he carried in his hands.

Nash said nothing to me, Elena, or Colby, but moved past us to the dragons. He slung his shotgun over his shoulder, reached right in through the fire, grabbed both men, and yanked them apart.

Mick cut off his fire instantly as Nash let them go, but Drake shot out another flame to whirl around Nash. Not to kill him, I saw, but to try to drag him off his feet.

The fire covered Nash all right, as he stood unmoving. Nash lit up like a halo, a being surrounded by St. Elmo's fire. Then the flame imploded, rushed into the depths of Nash's body, and winked out.

Drake stared at him in astonishment then moved his gaze to the shotgun Nash aimed directly at his chest.

CHAPTER SEVEN

DRAKE AND NASH HAD MET BEFORE, AND NEITHER HAD
thought much of the other then. They were too much alike,
dragon and man, both with sticks up their asses.

Drake's naked state didn't faze Nash. Nash had once been
the biggest Unbeliever in Hopi County, but during the past
year or so, he'd become used to seeing grown men standing
around unashamedly nude after they'd shifted. He held his
shotgun steady, looking unwaveringly down its barrel
at Drake.

"Whatever is going on here, you don't belong," Nash said
in a voice as sharp as winter wind. "Take yourself back to your
big house in New Mexico, and don't interfere in our business."

Colby barked a laugh. "Oh hey, I'm enjoying this."

"You too," Nash said. "I don't mind arresting both of you,
so you can leave, or you can spend the night in my lockup."

"I want the Nightwalker." Drake's body was covered in
bruises and burn marks, but the fight hadn't defeated him. "He
has stolen from us."

Mick said firmly, "And I'll question him about it." He was
bruised from the fight as well, but barely breathing hard. "I

told you, if he's stolen from the dragon compound, I'll bring back whatever he's taken."

Drake did not like that at all. The stick wedged even higher in his butt, and his dark eyes went ice cold. Usually, Drake enjoyed letting minions do work for him—not that Mick was in any way a minion to Drake—and the fact that he didn't want to delegate meant that Drake wasn't too pleased for Mick to find out what Ansel had taken.

Drake gave Mick an evil stare. "If he has it, you bring it to me. No one else. Understand?"

"I'll let you know what I find out," Mick said evenly.

Drake had to be satisfied with that. He turned his back on us and walked away, no goodbyes, no parting shots. His body faded into darkness, and from that darkness, a black dragon rose into the sky.

Colby watched him go then turned back to me. "See you, Janet." He balled his fists and tapped them to mine. "Don't be a stranger. *Please.*"

He jogged down the east side of the railroad bed in Drake's wake, shrouded himself in darkness, then shot into the air as soon as he became dragon, winging his way after Drake. He was spellbound to Drake and the dragon compound by magic —he couldn't simply fly off in the other direction.

Nash shouldered his shotgun. "Where is Ansel?" he asked Mick. "If he did take something, he'll have to relinquish it."

I didn't answer, preferring Mick and me to take care of this, but Elena said, "He's in his room in the basement. He's hiding there."

"Elena," I said in dismay. "I thought he was under your protection."

"He is." Elena raised her hand again, and the magical barrier she'd put around the hotel receded and vanished. "But only from the Firewalkers. I don't like Firewalkers, Mick excepted. I also don't like thieves. Or Nightwalkers."

She started to walk away, but I stepped in front of her, a

dangerous thing to do. "If you could protect against the flames, why didn't you do it in the first place?"

"I didn't get a barrier in place in time when the dragon first flamed it," she said, studying me calmly. "I was taken by surprise. And it's a defensive shell, not a fire extinguisher. My magic isn't all-encompassing."

Finished, Elena stepped around me, climbed back down the bank and walked away. The saloon fire was out now, defeated by more mundane means, white smoke drifting into the darkness.

"Nash," I began.

Nash turned his gray-eyed stare at me. "Don't piss me off, Janet. I've had a hell of a day, and it ends with me hearing your hotel is on fire."

"We took care of it," I said.

Nash studied the smoldering remains of my saloon. "Sure, I can see that. Now, I'm going in there to talk to Ansel."

Mick stepped in front of him. "I'd rather you didn't."

Nash had come to respect Mick, one of the few people he did respect, but he didn't waver. "I had a woman in my office today, hysterically claiming that her sister had been abducted and killed by a vampire. Now your dragon friend wants a piece of your Nightwalker, not to mention the dragon tries to burn him out. All that makes it my business."

Mick didn't move. "If Ansel has stolen any dragon secrets, I'll have to ask you to be bound to silence. There are things we can't afford to have humans know."

"I'll think about it." Nash moved around him, his badge glinting in the starlight, and headed for the hotel without waiting for us.

I didn't like any of this, but no one had asked my opinion. *My* hotel had gotten fried, and Ansel was there on *my* sufferance, but did my dragon boyfriend or pain-in-my-ass sheriff think of any of that?

Ahead of us, Nash broke into a run. After he paused step,

Mick did too.

I didn't see what had startled them, but I figured it couldn't be good, so I hurried after them. Mick could run like an Olympic sprinter, and he passed Nash and reached the hotel first, me panting to catch up.

A crossbow bolt flew out of the darkness at the back door and thunked into Mick's chest. Mick flinched from the blow but didn't stop. I doubled my efforts and reached Mick in time to see him pull the long bolt from his chest and drop the blood-coated thing on the ground.

The slayer who'd fired it stared at Mick in amazement, then he found Nash's shotgun in his face. "Drop it," Nash said in clipped tones.

The crossbow followed the bolt to the dirt. The slayer—not Rory, but a new guy—raised his hands, then scowled when Nash twisted his arms behind his back and clipped handcuffs onto his wrists.

"What are you doing?" the slayer asked in amazement.

"Arresting you for assault with a deadly weapon," Nash said.

"I didn't hurt the guy." He jerked his chin at Mick who still stood upright, in spite of the bloodstained hole in his T-shirt.

"It went pretty deep, actually," Mick said. "I have to go."

I knew what he meant. Mick could withstand bad injuries, but only if he turned into a dragon to heal himself.

Without further word, Mick kissed the top of my head and walked away from us, disappearing into the desert. I watched worriedly, but he vanished almost at once, and I turned my attention back to the slayer.

"There's a Nightwalker in there," the slayer said. "Do you understand what that means? A *vampire*. He'll suck you dry and crush your bones. You want him to get his teeth into this little lady here? He'll rape her before he drains her. That's what they do."

"She can handle herself," Nash said dryly. "Assault and

attempted murder are assault and attempted murder. I don't give a crap whether it's against a human being, a Nightwalker, or something in between. You have the right to a defense attorney. Good luck finding one who believes vampires are real."

The slayer looked outraged, as though he thought Nash should be on his side. Maybe law-enforcement officials elsewhere — the ones who believed in the supernatural, that is — did assist slayers, but this was Nash. He ran his county like Captain Bligh of the *Bounty*, and Nash hated vigilantes.

Nash half pushed, half dragged the slayer across the gravel to his waiting SUV and shoved him into the back. Then he perched in the driver's seat to call in the arrest or whatever, leaving me relatively alone.

The slayer had left chalk marks on the doorframe, advertising his intent. I rubbed them off and went inside, leaving the door unlocked for Mick's return.

The stench of burned saloon was sharp, but the hall and my private rooms held no smoke. Maybe Elena's shield had kept out the smoke, maybe the solid wall between the saloon and hotel had. Whichever, I was grateful.

I went into the bathroom and washed my hands, surprised but thankful the water was still on. The saloon ran on a different set of pipes, but I wouldn't know the extent of the plumbing damage until Fremont went over it.

The mirror reflected my face smeared with dirt and blood, a hunk of hair singed where I hadn't leapt away from Drake and Mick's fire battle fast enough.

I touched the mirror with one damp finger. "Are you all right in there?"

No answer. No wailing or dramatic moaning, no screeching obscenities. The mirror might have gone dormant to preserve itself, or it might be sulking.

I dried my hands, caught up one of my lantern flashlights, and went to check on my next patient. The firemen were moving around the saloon, and my guests were still out front —

the firemen wouldn't dare let them back in until they were certain all was well.

No one saw me slip through the dark doorway marked "Private" that led to the basement. I didn't flip on the light as I went down, fearing to short out something and start another fire.

I used the flashlight to make my way down the stairs to the basement, a place which never failed to give me the creeps. We'd cleaned it out and repaired it after the last fiasco, putting in fresh drywall over the brick and studs. Maya and I had painted it a nice ivory that went well with the brick floors. It still gave me the creeps.

One room down here was for maintenance—the generators, water heaters, circuit breakers, and so forth. A smaller room in the very back was locked with a padlock. Elena, Mick, I, and no one else had the keys. Behind that door lay a pool of very powerful magic—shaman magic had been poured into it and built up over generations. I had no idea why an ordinary door, purchased at a hardware store in Winslow, would keep it contained, but Elena had assured me that this was the case.

The third door, on the other side of the large open area at the base of the stairs, now contained Ansel's bedroom. I walked to it, shining my flashlight into the corners. Though Mick and I had warded this place well—and I could see the faint shimmer of our marks on every beam—I knew better than to let down my guard.

"Ansel?" I called before I reached his door. "Everything should be all right now, but I need to talk to you."

No answer. I opened the door, finding the light on—so the electricity did still work. I'd taken one step inside before I realized that I'd just made a big, big mistake.

A slender hand with the strength of angels clamped around my neck, and I was slammed into the wall next to the door. I looked up into Ansel's red-tinged eyes, his lips pulled back from long, nasty fangs.

"Hungry," he said.

"Ansel!" I shouted.

"Shut up!" He shook me, his hand cutting off my air. "I'm sick to death of your grating, whining voice. I'm going to bathe in your blood."

"You didn't kill Laura," I struggled to say. "She's alive."

For a split second, sanity flickered into his eyes, the brown of the mild-mannered Ansel returning. For a second. Then the Nightwalker reemerged.

"You're good at lying. I hope you kissed your lover goodbye."

He opened his mouth. Nightwalkers, when they are about to kill, elongate their mouths into long, narrow maws, like wolves—all the better to eat you with.

I worked a spark of Beneath magic into my hands, the spinning white ball the size of a marble. Ansel hadn't fed on human flesh in a long, long time, and I knew he wouldn't be sated with my blood alone. Once he got human blood inside him, he'd go on a rampage. All those people milled around upstairs—Mick was away healing himself, and Cassandra had gone home long ago—no one to protect them.

"I'm sorry, Ansel," I said. "I always counted you as a friend." I brought up my hand to flick the ball into his heart.

A plastic jug full of red liquid was thrust between my face and Ansel's. I gagged on the stench. Cow's blood. Lots of it.

Ansel slackened his grip on my throat just enough for me to twist out of it. I turned around, panting, and saw Elena holding under Ansel's nose the jug of cow's blood Mick had put into Ansel's mini fridge.

I held my breath, and not just because of the smell. Last spring, we'd offered the blood-frenzied Ansel cow's blood to calm him down, and he'd spit it out in rage. He'd gone into blood frenzy that time because of a spell, though, whereas earlier tonight he'd gone into it fighting to survive. This time he'd woken up both hungry and in fear of his life again.

Ansel glared at the bottle. Elena, unperturbed, pinched his nostrils between her fingers and poured blood into his mouth.

The blood flowed out again, all over Ansel's nice gray button-down shirt, but he closed his mouth and swallowed. Elena upended the jug again, and this time, Ansel held still while he drank. And drank and drank. He gulped down most of the jug's contents before he closed his eyes and took a step back.

His mouth returned to normal, and when he opened his eyes again, the brown of the antiques enthusiast regarded at me.

"I am so, so sorry, Janet." He wiped his mouth with a shaking hand and glanced with dismay at his ruined shirt. "Perhaps you should let the next slayer take me."

"No," Elena said before I could speak. "We will not."

She screwed the lid onto the jug and put the jug back into the refrigerator. She went into the bathroom, ran some water, and came out with a damp cloth, which she handed to Ansel so he could wipe his hands and face.

"Thanks, Elena," I said.

"I won't accept your thanks," she said. "There is much more going on here, and *you* need to find out about it." She pointed a plump finger at me. "Keep your thanks until we are done." Her finger moved to Ansel. "A Firewalker is willing to burn down your haven around you to make you give him something. Slayers are leaving their marks on the doors and trying to break in to kill you. People are holding séances to try to find out information about you. Women are thought dead and then aren't. You must now tell us everything."

"I think you'd better," I said.

Ansel conjured up a sigh that sounded as though it came from the depths of his long, lost soul. "Oh, Janet," he said, looking more sorrowful than I'd ever seen him. "What have I done?"

CHAPTER EIGHT

"YOU TELL ME," I SAID.

Elena rummaged through Ansel's closet, which contained a neat row of button-down oxford shirts, polo shirts, suit jackets, and slacks. Even his casual jeans were folded neatly on shelves.

The clean shirt Elena picked out was a tasteful maroon polo. Ansel, always modest, ducked into the bathroom to change.

When he came out, having hidden the bloody shirt in his laundry hamper, he looked almost like a normal human being, except for his too-pale complexion and his haunted expression. He sat down on the desk chair Mick had straddled earlier and put his hands on his knees.

"Janet, I'm sorry. I heard the things I said to you. I . . ."

I held up my hand. "Blood frenzy. It happens. I'm more interested in what Drake wants, and why you were willing to risk burning to death to not give it to him."

Ansel nodded, looking wretched, a far cry from the brutal Nightwalker who'd been about to suck me dry.

"Laura and I . . . We've done something bad, but for a good reason, I think." He spread his long fingers. "You don't know much about me, do you, Janet? That's why I'm so grateful for your compassion in letting me stay here."

Elena spoke before I could. "You mean you're grateful for more than a place to hide from the sun, don't you?"

Ansel nodded. "I told you that, before the war, my family owned an antiques store, which unfortunately perished in the Blitz. What I didn't tell you was that my father was the greatest confidence trickster the antiques world had ever seen. Well, one of the greatest. The business, unfortunately, is rife with thieves."

"Did you follow in his footsteps?" I asked. That would surprise me. Ansel was always so careful and polite, but then again, his air of guilelessness would help him be a good con artist.

"I didn't approve of what my father did. He'd cheat people out of fortunes. He'd tell an elderly widow that her houseful of eighteenth-century silver was worthless but that he'd pay her a little more than they were worth because he was compassionate. Then he'd turn around and sell off the whole collection at great profit to himself. Or he'd hire a forger to copy a unique piece of furniture and sell both the original and the copy to two different buyers in two different countries as the real thing. Easier to fool people in the days before you could look up your purchase on the Internet and find out there were six others just like it."

I'd sunk to sit on the bed while Ansel told his story, but Elena remained standing, arms folded. She wasn't a very tall woman, but she didn't need height to be intimidating.

"You must have had an interesting upbringing," I said.

Ansel looked embarrassed. "I did, yes. I knew how to run a swindle and run it well by the time I was twelve."

I squeezed my eyes shut for a moment. "Please don't tell me you ran a swindle on the dragons."

"I had no intention of doing anything with the dragons at all. I swear to you, Janet. I'm not that foolish."

"Then what happened?"

He waited a moment, studying his hands. Nightwalkers, when they don't pretend to breathe, can go entirely still, and Ansel sat as still as death.

"Laura has a small store, but she's well-known in her field. Buyers come to her from all over the world, especially those wanting Native American art and artifacts. People contact her and tell her what they want, and she finds it for them."

"And you help her," I said, "knowing the business as you do."

"I've kept my hand in over the years," Ansel said, looking modest. "Computers make it easier, though there's no substitute for holding a thing in your hand and examining it. Internet photos — any photos — can be doctored by anyone with a laptop and affordable software."

Elena broke in, her voice quiet but holding the force of ages. "What did you agree to help this woman find?"

Ansel looked up at her, shamefaced. "A pot. An ancient one."

I stood up. "Please tell me she didn't go out to Chaco Canyon to dig up a pot."

The theft of Native American artifacts was a continuing problem. Non-Indians didn't understand why they shouldn't go dig up all the thousand-year-old pottery and other things buried in places like Chaco Canyon or Homol'ovi, or even out in the canyons around Magellan, and sell them to museums or private collectors for a stack of cash.

Most Indians, on the other hand, regard the pottery as sacred relics from their ancestors, which should be left undisturbed. They feel about it like a non-Indian might feel about someone going to a churchyard and digging up their great-grandmother to sell her bones and whatever jewelry she'd been buried with. Federal laws, with prison sentences attached, were on the books to discourage pot hunting, but it still goes on.

But there's an even better reason not to desecrate the dead. Not only is it macabre, it's dangerous. There's no telling what kind of god or spiritual force is guarding the dead—you could have a ton of evil trouble on your doorstep for even moving a potsherd. Gods and goddesses are not necessarily *nice*.

"No," Ansel said quickly. "This particular pot has been circulating for a long time."

"Then why was Laura hanging out in Chaco Canyon?"

Ansel shrugged. "I'm not really certain why. I'm piecing much of this together myself."

And why had Laura been abducted from there? And where was she now? Drake needed to answer questions, and I had some ideas about how to make him talk.

"Anyway," Ansel said, "Laura was approached earlier this year by a collector in Santa Fe who was looking for this particular pot. Laura and I started the research, learning all about the type of pot it was and where we might find this particular one. A few months later, Laura called me, uneasy. The collector who'd hired her was pushing her to find the pot, offering to pay more and more money if she hurried it up. When she had to say we were still looking, he started threatening her. It can take years to locate a piece and buy it, and clients understand that. But this man was adamant."

"Why does he want it so much?" I asked.

"Why, indeed?" Ansel said. "I continued to look for the pot, while Laura began researching our client—discovering everything she could about him. We found the pot, by the way. It was at a private museum in Flagstaff. Laura notified the client, he transferred the money, and we bought it."

Elena scowled at him, and I balled my fists. "So you have it," I said. *"Ansel."*

Ansel held up his hands. "No, I don't. This is what I do not understand. Laura took it, not me. I never had charge of it, and she delivered it to the collector."

"Wait." I rubbed my temples. "Why are we talking about

swindles if you bought the pot and gave it to Laura's client? The deal is done."

"We did swindle him," Ansel said in a quiet voice. "The museum wanted two hundred thousand for the pot. I bargained them down to one hundred and fifty. But we agreed to tell the client that we bought it for the whole two. He paid up, and Laura and I split the fifty grand between us. That on top of Laura's commission. Normally I'd never dream of doing something like that—but if you'd met the man . . . When Laura didn't find the artifact fast enough, he threatened to put her out of business, threatened to ruin me—he doesn't know I'm a Nightwalker. He lives in a big house, surrounded by riches, and is the most tight-fisted miser I've ever met. The things he said to Laura . . . We decided that he could afford to give us a little more money for what we had to put up with."

I could understand myself giving the guy a little kick in the balls, but I'd also learned that such people could be dangerous. "Did he find out?"

"No. At least, I don't think so. But something is very wrong. I'd already sent most of my money to my family in England—I like to help them out. Laura called me last week, all excited, and said she'd done something else. She said she knew she should have told me, but she was afraid of getting me involved, and that I'd understand. She didn't want to tell me on the phone. We agreed to meet in Gallup where we could talk. When I got there, Laura was scared. She was sure she'd been followed. She convinced me to leave with her. And then . . . that's where it all goes fuzzy. We were driving, and I must have gone blood frenzied for some reason. I don't know why. I'm sorry, Janet, that's all I can remember."

"Why'd you keep this to yourself?" I asked. "I might have been able to help you sooner, *before* the slayers came calling."

"Told you that I'd killed my girlfriend in a blood frenzy?" Ansel asked, eyes wide. "You would have thrown me out of here, at best. At worst, you and Mick would have decided that you needed to kill me. Don't think I don't hear your conversations about that."

"I'm sorry," I said. "Ansel, what you don't understand is, I know exactly what it feels like to be an out-of-control killing machine. That's when you need your friends the most. To stop you."

"Perhaps. But I'm a Nightwalker. You at least can be a potent magical force for good in the world. I'm nothing but a bloodsucker, no good in me at all. I was created to be a weapon, to kill without remorse. Our situations are a bit different."

"We could get into a big, long argument about that, but right now isn't the time. Drake told me that Laura was alive, but that he didn't know where she was. Are you sure you have no idea what she meant to tell you? About the pot? About the client? About Chaco Canyon? She was driving in that direction, and she was camping up there."

"What I do know," Ansel said, "is that she didn't give me anything—not the pot or any other artifact, no money, nothing. When I woke up in the desert, there was just me. Getting to shelter was my only concern at that point. I have no clear idea of where I was, as I told you. Somewhere in northwestern New Mexico is about as specific as I can be."

"We need to find her." I stated the obvious, but sometimes, it has to be stated.

"The Firewalkers are convinced you have this pot," Elena said. "Why is it important to them?"

Ansel spread his hands. "As I say, I have no idea."

I believed him. Dragons could be annoyingly cryptic, and I planned to shake a few things out of them. Starting with Mick, who'd gone to the dragon compound today to find out why I'd sensed dragon at Laura's campsite. We hadn't exactly had a moment to talk.

But Ansel knew things too. "Who was the client, Ansel?" I asked. "The one so anxious to get this piece of pottery?"

"His name is Richard Young."

"Oh, Ansel," I said, blowing out my breath.

Even I had heard of Richard Young, a man who owned a large chunk of the businesses in Santa Fe and Albuquerque, who lived in a vast house on a hill above Santa Fe with a view people would pay millions for. The man was powerful and influential. And, some whispered, a criminal, or at least, he had criminal connections.

"We can't always choose our clients," Ansel said. "If they have the dosh, we don't ask too many questions. Antiques dealers are always in need of an influx of cash."

Which he sent off to his family in England. I couldn't help admiring that. On the other hand, Richard Young was not the best person in the world to try to rip off.

"Thank you, Ansel," I said. "For being straight with me. I'm going to try to find out what the dragons know and see if we can track down Laura. This might be easily solved." *Sure.* "The big question is—if Laura's fine, what was that stupid crap with the séance? Whoever faked it told Paige that Laura was dead and needed to be avenged."

Ansel looked perplexed, so I quickly filled him in about the séance at Heather's and the "message" from Laura.

Elena looked disapproving. She, like Cassandra and my grandmother, didn't like séances. I had the feeling I'd get a phone call from Grandmother soon.

"She must have faked it," Elena said. "The sister. So she'd have justification for hiring these slayers to kill Ansel. She might believe her sister is dead but not be able to prove it."

"You will tell Paige she's all right?" Ansel asked.

"First call I make." Second call, I meant. For the first I wouldn't need a phone.

I told Ansel to stay in tonight, to be safe, and he nodded. He'd have his DVD machine cranking out classic movies in no time.

He looked so unhappy and guilty as I started to leave that I came back and gave him a hug and a kiss on the top of his head.

Quick ones. Ansel smelled like blood, his aura had my magic screaming, and he was dancing too close to blood frenzy for any lingering touch.

I left his room, and Elena marched upstairs behind me, heading off to check her kitchen for damage. Whatever she found, I was sure the dragons would hear about it. Loudly.

The firemen were still in my saloon, trying to decide what had started the fire. *Lightning* was one man's speculation. The fire was completely out, wisps of smoke drifting in the night breeze.

"Can I go in?" I asked a guy in his oversized yellow suit, still wearing his hard fire hat. He was one of the Salas family, related to Magellan's Assistant Chief of Police. Emilio Salas himself was outside in the parking lot talking to the other firemen.

Emilio saw me and came walking up with his usual energy. "You know what happened, Janet?"

"I wasn't home," I said, sticking to the literal truth.

"A couple of your guests saw a fireball come out the sky, and the place went up. Heat lightning is what will go in the report. A freak of nature."

I'd be sure to tell Drake he was being listed as a freak of nature. I wanted to watch his face when I said it.

"Am I allowed in?" I asked again.

"If you want to take a quick look right inside the door, you can," the fireman said. "But don't go all the way in, and don't touch anything. There's a lot of glass fused to the floor and what's left of the tables."

Glass. I ducked past him and stepped inside the saloon.

It was a complete wreck. The long wooden bar, barstools, and tables were nothing but a pile of black lumps. The walls still stood, but they were black all the way to the tin ceiling, which had buckled and melted under the volcanic heat of dragon fire. Dragons were born in volcanoes, and the room looked as though one had erupted inside it.

The glass the fireman mentioned had come from the rows of glasses that had hung above the bar, the bottles of wine and liquor that had lined the shelves behind it, and the windows that had imploded.

The magic mirror hung above the bar in its usual place, and I relaxed a little. It was still intact.

The frame had warped and half melted away, but the frame wasn't part of the mirror. The magical part was the glass itself, the silver backing it, and the ton of spells a long-ago mage had poured into it.

The face of the mirror was black. I couldn't tell from the doorway whether it was filmed with soot, or whether the darkness was inside the glass itself.

The fireman was standing right next to me, and so was Emilio, so I couldn't very well launch into a conversation with the mirror. But I risked one question.

"Are you all right?"

Silence. The mirror didn't respond, not even with a tinkle of broken bits.

Emilio's big hand landed on my shoulder. "I know it's hard, Janet. But it will be all right. Fire chief says the saloon's structure is still sound, so get on to your insurance company and start clearing things up."

Emilio Salas was a cheerful sort, always optimistic, in spite of his job, and in spite of living in the weirdness of Magellan all his life.

He patted my shoulder again, his work done, and went to the kitchen to see if Elena was good. Emilio was one of the few people Elena liked—maybe because sorrow, sarcasm, and anger bounced off him and didn't leave a mark. Emilio seemed to absorb negativity like Nash absorbed and annulled spells.

The fireman told me my guests could come back in, but of

course, the saloon was off limits. He'd told me to have someone board up the door right away.

I went back outside to the clustered guests to find that Cassandra had returned. She'd already handed around coffee and was talking to everyone about their options, whether they stayed here or moved to another hotel.

With Cassandra was her girlfriend, Pamela, a tall woman with black hair in a tight braid and wolf-gray eyes. Pamela was a Changer who could become a wolf. And like a wolf, she was insanely protective of Cassandra, who was, in Changer terms, her mate.

I was happy that Cassandra had someone to keep her safe, but Pamela sometimes decided that Cassandra should be kept safe from *me*. A Changer thinking someone threatened her mate was a dangerous thing.

"Who did this?" Pamela asked me in a low voice. She had her arms folded and regarded me with coldness.

"Dragons," I said.

Her eyes flickered. "Mick let them?"

"I wouldn't say he *let* them. But don't worry, they'll pay."

One way or the other. Pamela returned to helping Cassandra calm the guests—though why Pamela thought *she* could calm anyone, I didn't know. I went inside and into my office, opened the desk drawer, and took out one of the shards of broken mirror I kept in there.

When the mirror had been broken, Mick and I had pried pieces out of it to carry with us or keep stashed around the hotel in case we needed them. Mick and I could communicate through the mirror over long distances much better than we could on cell phones. The mirror never hit a dead zone.

I took the piece of mirror out of the leather bag in which I kept it, carefully laid it on the desk, and peered down into it.

CHAPTER NINE

DARKNESS. THE MIRROR HAD GONE BLACK ALL THE WAY across, as though this piece had burned along with the others.

The mirror didn't answer me when I again asked if it was all right. I even apologized to it and told it I'd take the damage out of Drake's hide.

Still nothing.

I stroked the surface of the mirror, but I didn't even get a shiver of delight or a string of lewd comments.

I was cold with misgivings as I put the mirror shard away. The thing drove me crazy with its drag-queen drawl, sexual suggestions, insane laughter, and stupid jokes. On the other hand, it had saved my life several times over. Without the mirror, I'd have been very definitely dead a while ago. But not only would losing a magical talisman be bad for me, I'd miss it.

Magic mirrors could be repaired. The trouble was, any mage strong enough to repair a magic mirror would also be strong enough to kill you for it.

I had hoped that the mirror would be well enough for me to use it to spy on the dragon compound. Last year, when I'd been taken to the compound, the mirror had told me how to finagle the shard so it could look through all the mirrors in the dragons' mansion. I'd discovered later that the mirror had maintained the contact so it could look into the dragon compound any time it wanted.

Mostly the mirror enjoyed watching the human houseboy, a buff twenty-something called Todd, strip for his showers. But I sometimes used the mirror myself to keep track of what was going on with Bancroft, Drake, and their cronies.

I'd have to wait for Mick before I could talk to the dragons. He was the only one who could get me in contact with the compound without me being fried. But Mick was taking his time out there while he recovered from the crossbow wound, and I started to worry about him too.

I called Heather Hansen, listened to five minutes of her distress about the fire—she'd seen something dark in my aura, she swore it, and she was so sorry she'd been distracted by the séance and hadn't warned me. I let her run down—she did truly feel bad—and then I asked her for Paige's phone number.

She gave it to me readily, telling me it was so nice of me to help with Paige's sister. Heather offered her services as medium to me any time I wanted them, gratis. Perhaps I'd like to speak to my deceased mother, to tell her I was all right?

I managed to give her a polite answer before I hung up. The last thing I needed was Heather trying to conjure the spirit of my evil-goddess mother. She might show up.

I called Paige and got her voice mail. I left a message, urging her to call me, telling her I'd had word that her sister might be fine and well. With any luck, Paige would call off her slayers until she found out what I knew, but I didn't hold my breath. The slayer marks had been cleaned off the doorframes —I hadn't seen any new ones as I'd run around outside, apart from the ones made by the slayer Nash had arrested. Maybe they'd think Ansel had perished in the fire and give up. Hey, it could happen.

I helped Cassandra settle the guests who were staying into

their rooms again. She offered to spend the rest of the night here, and because we weren't full—we'd just lost a hiking couple to the motel in Magellan—I put her and Pamela in the usual room they took when they stayed overnight.

Emilio, who was hanging out in the kitchen talking to Elena and eating the mess of chilaquiles she'd decided to whip up, cheerfully said he'd sent for some of his nephews to come over and board up my doors and windows.

They arrived soon, along with Maya Medina, who did my electrical work. Maya eyed the damage from the lobby as Salas's four nephews started hammering.

Maya had the kind of figure that managed to make even jeans and a simple pullover top look sexy. She had lavish curves and a nicely formed behind, her blue-black hair fell in gorgeous waves down her back, and her eyes were the color of strong coffee.

Sheriff Jones loved this woman, though he didn't always like to admit it—he pretended emotion was what happened to other people. Maya loved him back with fierce intensity and didn't care who knew it.

I'd inadvertently walked in on Maya and Nash once when they'd been *in flagrante,* and I'd seen vividly that Nash was both a virile man and an enthusiastic one. I'd also kissed him when I'd been high on storm magic and needed the magic siphoned off. Mick hadn't been around to help me calm down, and Nash with his magic-sucking ability had been right there. Unfortunately, when I get too storm-crazed, I don't have a lot of control, and inhibitions are blown away.

But the seemingly cold Nash made it clear to all that he preferred the volatile Maya. Maya had actually softened him a little and he her, though you'd have to know them very well to be able to tell.

"How do you do it, Janet?" Maya asked, hands on hips. "I get this place into better shape than anywhere else in town, and you go and destroy it. Every time."

"I'm a victim of circumstance," I said. "Not my fault."

She gave me the skewering look that only Maya could manage. "It never is."

"Think you can fix it?"

"Of course, I can fix it." She trailed off into mutters. "I'll never get out of this town, not when I have to repair your hotel all the time."

"I thought you were living in Flat Mesa with Nash."

"Same difference."

She still owned a house in Magellan, though, with a nice garden and painfully neat interior. Nash had lived like a bachelor for a long time, and Maya was disdainful about the state of his house. Something they needed to work out.

Finally Salas's nephews finished closing off the saloon. Cassandra and I worked a spell to rid the rest of the hotel of lingering smoke, seal off any bad gasses that might have collected in the saloon, and sweeten the air. To the scent of sage and sandalwood, I went to bed.

It was three a.m., and still no Mick. I looked out windows, hoping to see a dragon winging his way home across the desert. Given our history, I went a little crazy when I didn't know where Mick was. I knew, though, that I couldn't keep a leash on him. Our relationship would never make it if I tried to do that.

The hotel was silent now, the guests and Cassandra in bed, the spectators gone. When I'd gone down to the basement to look in on Ansel—who'd been enjoying a viewing of the original *Thirty-Nine Steps*—I discovered Elena sleeping on a folding cot near his room, like a guard dog. She'd been sound asleep when I passed her, but I had little doubt she'd awaken if another slayer went down there after him.

I didn't think I'd sleep again with so many things on my mind, but I was out by the time I pulled up the covers.

I awoke to a sensation I couldn't mistake. Mick's mouth on

me between my legs. The wild friction of it brought me to a half-awake state, to a place of joy I never wanted to leave.

He'd stripped the sheets from my sweating body, and now he lay on the lower half of my bed, my legs over his arms. I made a sound between a gasp and a moan. "Welcome back," I said.

Mick smiled up at me, his eyes hot and blue. Not black, not his dragon eyes, which was good for now. Mick the man was enjoying me, and Janet the woman lay back and let him.

He worked on me, his mouth talented, until my body was rising to his mouth. The coming was good. Black and purple lights danced at the edges of my vision, my body one point of squeezing ecstasy.

When I collapsed, trying to catch my breath, Mick pulled me up to him, him on his knees on the bed, me with legs locked around him.

I loved watching Mick have sex with me. He would gaze straight into my eyes, his so blue, his face relaxed, his skin damp.

He wasn't a quiet lover though. "Janet, you're a fire in my heart. It burns me when I'm not with you."

My replies weren't as poetic. We crashed down onto the bed, me on my back, his big body weighting me into the mattress.

He finished, and everything went still.

We ended up with me on my side, Mick cradling me back against his chest. I loved moments like this. I thought I could stay forever curled into the curve of him, Mick's arms around me and protecting me from harm.

The world didn't work that way, but for now, I could bask in his warmth and let the world go to hell. And hope it didn't, not literally.

"It's what dragons do," Mick said quietly, drawing light fingers across my throat.

"What's that?" My words were barely coherent.

"Curl up around each other, male and female, to keep warm after mating. It's our most vulnerable time."

"I can see why. I'm weak as a kitten."

He kissed my shoulder. "No, you're not. You're strong, my Janet. That's why you can take me. I saw your strength the night I met you."

"After I tried to fry you," I said. "And then you ate the lightning and laughed. I was pretty sure I was dead."

"My way of telling you I liked you. I took you out for Mexican right after, didn't I?"

I smiled. "And then seduced me." I remembered walking into the hotel room in Las Vegas with him, knowing what we'd do there. I'd been both excited and scared to death.

I'd fallen in love with him that night—as much as I'd pretended I hadn't—fallen hard.

Had never really fallen out again.

"Couldn't help myself," Mick said, his voice tickling my ear. "You were the sexiest woman I'd ever met."

"Since most of your women were dragons, I'm not sure that's a compliment."

Mick kissed my shoulder again. "I've been alive a long time. But the moment I saw you, my whole world changed."

He knew how to melt my heart. I rolled over, kissed him, and we made love again, slowly this time, face to face. I loved looking into his so-blue eyes.

We slept again afterward, and when we woke, the sun was coming up. Mick lay next to me, facedown now, with the covers halfway up his legs. I sighed in relief. I'd woken up too often without him.

While we lay in the early sunlight, I filled him in on what Ansel had told me while he'd been off healing himself. Mick's skin was whole and smooth now, only a little scar on his chest to show for it, one too near his heart.

Mick's eyes flicked to black then back to blue as I went

through the story. "I think we need to have a talk with Richard Young from Santa Fe."

"And the dragons," I said with vigor. "I want a word with Drake. By the way, I've never had a chance to hear what you found out from them. You know, before Drake decided to set fire to the hotel. Please tell me it was nothing you said."

"I never saw Drake. I spoke directly to Bancroft. He doesn't know where Laura is, or what she was doing at Chaco Canyon, and I believe him. He seemed surprised I thought he'd know."

"Drake's playing a game by himself, maybe?"

"Maybe." Mick's frown deepened. "Mmm."

"What?"

He shook his head, lifted my hand on which I wore the silver and turquoise ring he'd given me, and touched his lips to the ring. "We're going to have to work to figure this out, which means less time I can spend in bed with you."

My body warmed. "Then I say let's find Laura as fast as we can, punch Drake in the nose, clear Ansel, and go back to bed."

Mick shook his head in mock anger. "I'm sacrificing way too much for them."

"I agree."

We both rolled out of bed, me stretching, Mick standing naked in the sunlight and watching me stretch.

"Seriously," I said. "You need to kick Drake's ass for burning down my saloon."

"He'll pay for the damages, believe me." Mick reached for the jeans he'd left on the floor. I loved watching him bend over for his clothes.

"Mick," I said as he slid on the pants and began zipping and buckling. "What else did you do at the dragon compound? Something to do with why you've been going out there so often lately?"

He didn't look at me, which was a bad sign. Pretending to

have trouble with his belt buckle, Mick said, "Dragon business. I'll tell you in time."

Dragons lived so long that *in time* might mean five years from now. "I'm not trying to be nosy. You know why I worry."

"I know. You have good reason." He finally looked up at me, his expression unreadable. "But I will tell you, when I'm ready. On this—you're going to have to trust me. It's complicated."

Everything about my relationship with Mick was complicated. Worth it, but complicated.

"Do you trust me?" he asked, watching me for my answer.

"Oh, I trust *you*. I don't trust the rest of the dragons or anyone else magical out there who wants to kill you or enslave you."

"You hold my true name, Janet. As long as you do, no one else can touch me." He brushed one finger across my cheek. "The only one who can destroy me now is you."

I looked at him in sudden terror. "Oh, great."

His eyes warmed with his grin, and he kissed my parted lips. "I'm not worried."

Good for him. "You said last night that there were dragonslayers as well as Nightwalker slayers."

"That's true. But dragonslayers are few and far between. Most humans aren't stupid enough to go up against a dragon. Those who are . . ." He made a movement like he was scattering dust. "*Aren't* any more."

"Natural selection at work?"

Mick laughed. He kissed me again, picked up his shirt and went out, no doubt to find a giant breakfast. Sex always made him ravenously hungry.

I showered, noting that Mick had worked healing spells on me while we'd enjoyed ourselves. My cuts and bruises had faded to mere shadows.

I dressed and went outside my back door to perform my morning ritual of scattering corn to the rising sun. A few local rabbits watched me, waiting to dive in and grab the morsels, as did a crow perched high in the juniper.

I waved at the crow. Might be Grandmother, manifesting to watch me, or just a crow. Either way, didn't hurt to be friendly.

I caught sight of movement on the railroad bed. Just a flash, but it was a coyote's tail, the coyote dashing down out of sight into a wash.

Then I heard a roar.

Dust rose into the air from the top of the railroad bed, kicked up under the feet of a giant grizzly. The bear was far larger than a normal bear, its fur rippling brown and golden as it ran with startling grace across the railroad bed and down into the desert beyond. Dust hung in the air in its wake. It roared again, and the howl of a coyote answered it.

I hurried to the railroad bed and scrambled up it, half curious, half worried. I didn't often get to see Bear in her grizzly form, and I wanted to watch Coyote try to evade her. He wouldn't be able to, I knew it in my bones.

The grizzly easily gained on Coyote as he loped through the dry wash and up the other side. The morning light flashed on the bear's brindled coat as she leapt, crashed into Coyote, and dragged him to the ground.

I started to laugh. Coyote should know better than to try to run from his wife.

Coyote shifted to his man shape, a big, muscular Indian male, well-formed in all areas. At the same time, Bear rose into her human female form, tall and formidable, breathtakingly beautiful.

My laughter cut off as Bear raised her hand. In it was a long, brutal-looking knife that had appeared out of nowhere. As I watched, my eyes getting wider, she plunged the knife straight down into Coyote's heart.

CHAPTER TEN

I FOUND MY FEET MOVING, FASTER AND FASTER, CARRYING me down the side of the railroad bed and through the warm morning toward the scene of the carnage.

I sprinted through the dry wash and up the other side. By the time I came out from behind a screen of scraggly cedars, Bear was gone. Completely gone—no sign of her bear lumbering into the desert, or her in human form walking away.

Coyote lay on his back on a flat stretch of ground, still human, a huge knife protruding from his chest.

The knife looked odd, very plain and obviously old, but nothing like I'd ever seen before. As I dropped to my knees I saw that the inch of blood-soaked blade sticking up was made of stone—not flint or obsidian, but ground stone like granite. The handle was made of the same stone and wrapped with a strip of leather.

I noticed this distractedly, because what I saw mostly was Coyote, his breathing labored as blood poured from his wound.

"Janet." His voice was barely a sigh. "You weren't meant to see this."

"But why did she do this? *Why?*"

I liked Bear. I hadn't been able to get to know her as well as I'd wanted, because I'd been busy in the five or so months since she'd arrived, and she, like Coyote, tended to disappear for long stretches of time. Even so, I'd found her to be patient, kind, and full of practical wisdom.

Not the type to pull a huge stone knife out of the air and viciously thrust it into her husband.

But this was Coyote. Coyote was a god, a seemingly inde-structible god. Earlier this year I'd thought him dead, but then he'd been fine. He'd laughed at me for worrying.

Bear was a goddess—did that make a difference? Gods could kill each other, while mortals couldn't make a dent in them.

"What can I do? How do I help you?"

"Take the knife out."

I reached for it. If this was some bizarre god game with god rules, maybe taking out the knife would restore him.

As soon as I touched the handle, the knife dissolved and disappeared. I snatched my hand back, a dark tingle snaking up my arm.

The wound didn't close, Coyote didn't spring to his feet and laugh, or tease me for worrying. He lay gasping, his lifeblood pouring out of him, his eyes clouding. He could no longer see me.

I pressed my hands to the wound, trying to stop the bleed-ing. He couldn't stay here. I needed Mick to take him off some-where to heal him—anywhere. Maybe even a human hospital could help him.

"Don't try to move," I said. "I'll get Mick."

Coyote grabbed my wrist with a bloody but still strong hand. "No. Nothing you can do. This is between Bear and me."

"Why would you let her do this? I don't understand."

"It's her right." Coyote gave me a smile, his eyes as warm as ever, even glazing over in death. "One thing you *can* do."

"What? Tell me."

"Kiss me. Legends say that a maiden's kiss can heal a dying god."

"I'm not a maiden."

"I'll risk it."

Coyote's hand tightened around my wrist. He tried to reach for me, but he fell back, weak.

I knew he wasn't faking this. I'd seen people die before, and Coyote was dying. No way he could survive all the blood streaming from his chest.

What the hell? I leaned down, reflecting that I'd always liked his big, handsome face, which always seemed to be in need of a shave.

I pressed a kiss to his warm, parted lips.

Coyote thrust his tongue hard inside my mouth, taking command. His lips banged against mine, teeth scraping. No gentle good-bye kiss for Coyote.

I was about to smack him and call him a fraud, when his head fell back again, striking the ground with an audible thud.

Coyote was still alive, but he wasn't healing. More blood gushed from his wound, and his skin was cooling, his face taking on the ashen gray tinge of death.

"You shit, don't you dare die." Tears clogged my voice. "I can't do this without you."

Coyote gave my wrist a little squeeze. "Yes, you can." He spoke in the Diné language, making my tears come all the more. "You're so strong, little one. Stronger than all of us. You'll need that in the time to come."

"Don't you go all cryptic on me and then die. Hang on, Coyote. You're a *god*."

"Even gods have their limits. Remember that. I . . ."

He drew one breath to say something more, then he stopped. Just stopped. Stopped breathing, stopped moving, and his eyes went blank.

"No! Quit messing with me. Stop it."

I shook him. My hands were red with his blood, and I

rocked there, shaking him, yelling at him to open his eyes and tell me this was a big joke.

He didn't. A beam of the rising sun touched him, and his body rippled with light. Then he dissolved into stream of thousands of tiny light and dust motes that sparkled under the sun for a moment, and then they too were gone.

I was kneeling alone in the dirt, sobbing, hands and shirt covered in blood, the warmth of the desert floor soaking into my knees.

I DON'T REMEMBER HOW I MADE IT BACK TO THE HOTEL, BUT I found myself there again, stumbling in through my private entrance and right into Mick.

He took a step back and stared down at me, then he grabbed my wrists and turned up my gore-soaked hands.

"Janet, what happened?" He shook me, his voice harsher than I'd ever heard it. "What happened?"

"It's not my blood." I sniffled, then told him all of it. "He's gone."

"He might not be. He's Coyote."

"I thought of that. But Bear's a goddess, and what if the rules are different?"

Mick stared at me a moment longer, then he dragged me close, blood and all. "Baby, I'm so sorry you had to see that."

I was sorry too. I couldn't erase the picture of my friend Bear rising up like an earth elemental and striking her knife into Coyote's heart.

Mick kissed me gently on the lips. "You go get cleaned up and have some breakfast. Elena's going all out for everyone this morning."

I nodded. I didn't want to shower; I wanted to grab Mick and run away with him, somewhere a long way from hotels, vortexes, dead gods, dragons, Nightwalkers, and my burned-down saloon. This spring, Mick had taken me to Hawaii, the Big Island, where we'd stayed in an old ranch house on the side of a mountain, riding down to the beach whenever we felt like it, lying in our big bed on cool sheets all day when we felt like that. He'd flown me to his lair, on an island not far away, and showed me his paradise.

We'd only been able to stay in Hawaii a week. I wanted to go back there for a year, or better still, kick around the world with Mick like we'd done years ago, when I'd first fallen in love with him.

My shoulders weighted, I slogged into the bathroom, undressed and took another shower. When I was clean again, I found Mick in the kitchen with Elena.

Elena had indeed cooked a big spread—everything from eggs with chiles and spices to flatbreads, corn pancakes, and fluffy syrup-dripping puffed apple pancakes that my guests loved. I looked at it all and felt sick.

Mick made me eat. He hadn't mentioned Coyote's murder to Elena, and the look in his blue eyes warned me not to. He plunked me down at the kitchen table, dumped a mess of chilaquiles and corn pancakes onto my plate, and rested his hip on the table, watching to see that I ate it.

I gulped it down with the aid of Elena's thick black coffee. Elena paid no attention to me, busy filling plates for the horde of workers that had showed up to start tearing up my saloon.

"Drake sent them," Mick told me before I could ask. I figured my insurance company had nothing to do with it—days would pass before they even sent out an assessor. "He's paying for all the damage."

"Did you talk to him last night when you were out healing?" I asked, eating another corn pancake, the knot in my stomach easing a little.

"I did." His eyes twinkled. "How did you know?"

"Because otherwise he wouldn't have sent someone out this

fast," I said. "Or he would have conveniently forgotten about it."

"No, he wouldn't have. Whatever you think of him, Drake has honor. He lives by a rigid code of it. I admit I pushed him a little to have people out here first thing."

I laid my fork on my empty plate. "Well, thank you for that."

"While they have things in hand," Mick said, "you and I can ride out to New Mexico and visit to Richard Young."

Elena stopped chopping and held up her knife. "Who is he?"

"A rich man who might have some answers for us," Mick answered.

"I don't trust rich people," Elena said, resuming her torture of a bell pepper. "They don't understand the importance of day-to-day work, of talking to people like they're people. They hide in their fancy mansions, afraid to come out, afraid people might take all their money away if they ever leave."

I watched her plump hands working to viciously gut the pepper. "Are you speaking from experience?" I asked.

"When I lived in Manhattan, I worked for rich folks who shut themselves up in penthouses on top of buildings, living in decadence you can't imagine. They liked to show off their Apache cook, so I saw a lot of the rooms and their guests. Parasites living off the hard work of others."

But the anger with which she moved from the pepper to an onion told me that her anger was personal, not general. Someone had outraged her more than by simply existing in decadence.

But I wouldn't hear the story today. Elena closed her mouth into a tight line, which told me she was finished talking. In fact, her eyes had a dangerous flash, and I sensed that the kitchen was closed.

Mick took my plates to the sink while I slipped out of the room.

I looked in on the saloon, where workers in hard hats were prying down burned beams. I found the foreman and asked him to have the mirror taken down and moved into my office.

He eyed the mirror skeptically. "I don't think you can save that. Best get a new one."

I agreed that the mirror, its frame half-melted, cracks radiating out from a hole in the middle of the glass, looked beyond repair. But the foreman couldn't know what finding a new one or repairing this one entailed. I doubted Drake would foot the bill for that.

Besides, I owed it to the mirror to take care of it. I told the foreman that it was a family heirloom and to cart it to my office anyway. He shouted for two men to come and lift it down.

I supervised the move, hovering like a mother with her hurt child as two men carried the mirror between them across the lobby. Mick joined us. I cleared space in my office, and Mick helped the men set down the mirror and lean it against the wall.

The mirror was still smoky black. I studied it a while, hands on hips, before Mick covered it with a sheet he'd brought from the linen room and gave its frame a little pat.

"Ready?" Mick asked me.

"Sure." Action was better than sitting around here looking at the wreck of my mirror and thinking about Coyote's death. Was he dead, or wasn't he? Were the shimmering motes I'd seen his soul disappearing back into nothingness? And dead or alive, why had Bear killed him?

Too much for me to take in right now.

I headed for my Softail in the shed, but Mick stopped me. "Ride with me."

I rubbed my arms. "Storms are coming. You want me on the back of your bike when that happens?"

There weren't many clouds overhead, but I could feel the tingle that meant the weather, always changeable around here, was building to something big. Yesterday I'd seen clouds over the San Francisco peaks to the west, but nothing had come down to the plateau. Unusual in this season, when afternoons could bring storm after storm.

Today, on the other hand, clouds were already gathering to the north, over the Navajo and Hopi Nations, west over Flagstaff, south on the Rim, and far to the east. By the time noon rolled around, thunderheads would be swirling around us, and I'd want to soak up their power.

"I can handle your lightning, remember?" Mick said with a hint of his smile. "And I'd rather you not be on a motorcycle that ran away with you before."

He had a point. Not that I minded snuggling in behind Mick to enjoy the ride. Mick rode a big bike, which gave me a nice space to sit and wrap myself around him. The bike throbbed under me, Mick was warm in front of me, and my heart lightened the slightest bit as we headed out.

Santa Fe is about three hundred miles from Magellan, five hours or so, give or take weather, road construction, traffic, and how often I have to stop for the bathroom.

It was a glorious summer morning, perfect for a long ride. The road unrolled in front of us, flat as Elena's corn pancakes for a time, then running past low cliffs as we entered the old river valley around Holbrook and beyond. On the other side of Gallup, in New Mexico, the rise of Mount Taylor, one of the four sacred mountains of the Diné, towered to the north and east.

We passed the turnoff I'd been forced to take toward Crownpoint. I held my breath, but Mick's motorcycle kept going, obeying Mick.

We came out of Navajo country and flew on by the pueblos of smaller tribes, ancient cultures that had existed long before Europeans had ever heard of this place. Along some stretches, except for the black ribbon of freeway and its caravans of eighteen wheelers and RVs, the landscape looked the same as it must have those thousand and more years ago.

Storm clouds gathered out here too, for now mostly hugging the mountain ridges to the north and south. Behind us, in the Chuska Mountains on the Navajo lands, the sky started to turn black with rainclouds.

After a time, Albuquerque loomed out of the desert with its glittering buildings and huge mountain behind it. Mick took the loop of freeway that headed north, and we were out of the town before we even got properly into it. The freeway climbed. And climbed, and climbed, taking us on to higher mountains and lowering storms.

Mick leaned into the ascent, his powerful bike passing cars, SUVs, and trucks that struggled up the long, steep hill toward Santa Fe and Taos beyond it. The air cooled, mercifully, but the sky darkened to slate gray, thunderheads climbing high over flat curtains of rain.

I loved it. When the first lightning strike hit the ground a mile from the freeway, I whooped.

I resisted calling to the lightning bolt, because I'd only short out the bike's electrical system, or maybe blow up the gas tank. Mick could survive that and pull me to safety, but he'd be pretty pissed off if I wrecked his Harley.

I held myself together while we climbed to the seven-thousand or so elevation of Santa Fe. Mick left the freeway behind and started winding through the city's streets.

Richard Young lived in a hilly part of the town, his house the last in a secluded neighborhood of residences that hid behind walls, gates, and tall foliage. Young's home had a big stucco wall around it pierced by tall wooden gates, reminiscent of a hacienda of old. Piñon pines and dogwood lined the wall on both sides, creating a tall barrier between Mr. Young and his neighbors.

Behind Young's property, mountains rose against the sky. A tiny dusting of snow coated the tops like powdered sugar, despite the fact that this was July. The storm clouds were densest there, a wall of gray surrounding the green. The air was cool, soothing, smelling of rain and pine, and the slight odor of electricity.

Mick pushed a button on a speaker near the gate. Through an intercom, he proclaimed who he was and said he had an appointment.

First I'd heard of this appointment, but I didn't argue. One of the wooden gates opened in silence, powered by an electronic control somewhere in the house. Mick rode us through, and the gate closed as silently behind us, its lock clicking into place.

I didn't like that. The walls were high, about ten feet, and those wall-hugging trees towered another twenty over that.

I took heart that I was with a dragon, who could fly, and though the driveway between the walls was narrow, Mick wouldn't mind breaking down stucco and concrete with his dragon body. Even if the walls had been reinforced with iron rebar, they wouldn't be able to withstand a dragon who really wanted to get out.

The path to the house wound through a landscaped garden, complete with a little stream and a wooden bridge spanning the stream. The gardeners had planted native trees and shrubs, which meant they thrived in high altitude and could survive brutal winters and arid seasons. This being high summer, most of the bushes and flowerbeds were in full bloom, a riot of scarlet, blue, violet, and yellow.

Should have been idyllic. I found it sinister. The garden screamed *look, don't touch—don't even linger.* The back of my neck itched, and I was fully aware of the security cameras that trained on us as we walked.

The front door was opened by a lackey as well-groomed as the garden. His tie was very tight, his expression tighter. The lackey looked us over in our jeans and motorcycle chaps and didn't bother to hide his disdain.

"Mr. Young will see you in his library."

Lackey walked away without further word, expecting us to

follow. Since neither Mick nor I knew where the library was, we did.

The dragon compound not far from here was a truly old Spanish-style house, with narrow corridors, stairs tucked into niches, and few windows that mostly overlooked the courtyard. Young's house was new and modern, built within the last decade. We walked through a massive front room with a ceiling that soared three floors above us, with floor-to-ceiling windows bringing in the mountains. A ponderous iron chandelier hung from a thick chain from the planked ceiling high above.

Carved, old-Spanish chairs stood about the room, along with a wooden couch covered with cushions. But most of the floor space was taken up with long glass cases, and inside them lay a vast stretch of Southwestern Indian history.

Most cases held pottery, but I found one that held a line of carved fetishes, another filled with beaded jewelry from hundreds of years ago, and another showing a collection of obsidian knives, carved from hard, volcanic leavings. Wall cabinets held larger pieces of pottery, some broken, some pieced back together, a few intact.

Many tribes were represented here—Navajo, Hopi, Acoma, Zuni, and tribes from pueblos scattered through this part of New Mexico. These things were *old*, not what Indian artists now crafted to sell to tourists or in museum shops.

I'd have known they were old without even looking inside the cases, because of the auras of the things. They cried out to me, some strong, some barely shadows. These things had been handled by people, some only a few times before they'd been broken or lost, others handed down through generations for hundreds of years.

Their history shrieked at me, making me dizzy. Though Mr. Young's living room might not hold the weight of ages of Chaco Canyon, my stomach still roiled. The things here were alone, lost, far from where they were supposed to be.

My feet dragged, my body slowing. Mick put his hand under my elbow and guided me along after the lackey, his warm strength comforting. I swallowed my nausea and moved with him the best that I could.

Lackey took us up a flight of stairs and along a gallery that overlooked the room below. At the end of this was a huge, heavy, wooden door, which opened without noise, silent like everything else in this house.

Silent on the surface. The auras continued their clamor in my head, which only built as we walked inside the library.

The man who must be Richard Young rose from behind a desk. He was in his sixties and as nattily dressed as his lackey. On a warm summer day in New Mexico, in his own home, the man was wearing a suit and tie.

The narrow, high-ceilinged room was lined with glass cases against white walls, high windows near the ceiling letting in light and a glimpse of the storm clouds. The pieces in the cases, I noted with a quick glance, were larger and more intact than those downstairs. I also saw more gruesome things—among the knife blades were bones, human ones, mostly fingers or whole hands, and in one was a line of shriveled skins with long black hair attached to each.

The rattling vibrations in my head increased tenfold, light and dark auras shimmering everywhere and distracting me from why we'd come.

Almost. A young woman turned from the glass case at the far end of the room, behind Young's desk, and stopped me in my tracks.

She was not Laura DiAngelo. This young woman had silky black hair that hung straight down her back, eyes as dark as mine, and Apache Indian features. She grinned at me, her white teeth flashing as I stood there gaping.

"Hey, sis," Gabrielle said. "About time you got here."

CHAPTER ELEVEN

"GABRIELLE." NOT A BRILLIANT THING TO SAY, BUT THE only thing that came out of my mouth.

Gabrielle Massey is my half sister. Sort of. We share a mother, the one from Beneath, who'd instilled in both of us her blinding powers of evil.

Stormwalker magic — earth magic — from my father's side of my family, grounds me against the crater-blasting Beneath magic that wants to come out and play at the slightest provocation. Stormwalker magic is my failsafe. Gabrielle doesn't have one.

To say she's dangerous is an understatement. At the moment, she was more or less contained — or supposed to be — by my watchful Grandmother, my dad, and my many aunts. Why Gabrielle was here, not in Many Farms, my home, I had no idea.

I kept staring at her, ignoring Richard Young who came around the desk to shake Mick's hand.

A second lackey had entered with a silver tray loaded with bits of food, followed by a maid with a bottle of wine and glasses on trays. These two faded away, and the first lackey poured the wine and carried it around to all of us.

I took the offered glass of cool white wine, my gaze still fixed on Gabrielle. She lifted her glass to me in silent toast then drank a good mouthful.

Young's attention was all for Mick. "You come highly recommended, Mr. Burns," he said. "Mr. Bancroft has quite the reputation as a collector."

I jammed my wineglass against my lips to stop my questions. Mick had obviously fed the man some line of bull and dragged Bancroft's name into it.

I didn't like white wine, but I dumped a gulp into my mouth. Then I admitted that this wasn't bad — the expensive stuff, I gathered. But between the shaking auras and Gabrielle's presence, even the smooth wine couldn't calm my rebellious stomach.

Young signaled to the lackey. The lackey set down his tray, turned smartly, and exited through a door behind Mr. Young's desk.

"I hope you don't mind that I brought in another expert to authenticate the pot." Young nodded graciously at Gabrielle. "I thought two heads would be better than one."

Mick had taken in Gabrielle without a change in expression, but that didn't necessarily mean he'd known Gabrielle would be here. Mick was just good at not giving away his emotions.

We sipped wine in silence, while Gabrielle continued to shoot amused looks at me, until the lackey returned with a large, latched box.

Lackey set the box on a table made of wood so old it shone with age. The lackey unlatched the box then stepped back and let Young open its lid.

Inside the box lay a pot. It was a simple vessel with a flat bottom, its sides bulging into a pleasing swell. That swell flowed back in to the pot's mouth, which was a near-perfect circle about four inches across.

I knew how these pots were made, though I'd never mastered the art myself. Clay was rolled into long snakes that were then coiled around and wrapped one on top of the other, the final shape finished by hand. No potter's wheel had made this.

The potter had then painted a line of bears and tortoises marching around the outside of the bowl—not realistic animals, but abstract, square-lined ones. Jagged patterns like lightning interspersed between tortoise and bear. For a finishing touch, black waves ran around the lip of the vessel's mouth, every line perfect. The colors were simple—white, rich brown, black, and red.

Once the pot had been fired, it had taken on a hardness and sheen that was enduring. The colors had faded a bit from time and weather, but they were still beautiful. This bowl, as lovely as it was, would have been used for a practical purpose —to store grain maybe. Useful beauty.

I couldn't, however, discern from which tribe it had originated. Ansel said he'd found it in Flagstaff, which meant it could have come from any of the tribes in a line from the tiny valleys around the Grand Canyon all the way east through Arizona and southern Utah to the pueblo tribes of New Mexico. There were plenty of ruins in the cliff-sides around Santa Fe.

Young handed white gloves to Mick and Gabrielle and donned a pair himself. Apparently, I was the only one who wouldn't be allowed to pick up the pot, because a pair wasn't handed to me. Whatever story Mick had woven didn't include me playing an expert.

Mick pulled the gloves over his big hands and carefully accepted the pot from Young. They made a strange pair, the slim, medium-height Mr. Young, with his brushed suit and carefully trimmed gray hair, and Mick, tall, massive, with black hair every which way and in his biker clothes.

Mick held the pot as carefully as he would a newborn baby. He turned it around in his hands, examining every line, every minute crack, while I sipped wine and watched.

Mick passed the pot to Gabrielle, who took it just as gently. I expected my zany little sister to do something like smash the pot against the wall and laugh, maybe blow out all the glass in the cases with her magic to prove she could.

But it wouldn't matter even if she did dash this pot against the nearest wall, because it was a fake.

Gabrielle lifted the pot to her eyes and examined it as Mick had. She was no expert, I was pretty certain. She was only copying what Mick had done, but she did it very well.

"It's a fake," she announced.

Young blinked at her. "What are you talking about?"

Mick glanced at me for confirmation, and I gave him the barest nod.

The thing had no aura, or very little anyway. It was beautiful, a work of art, but it was no antique. This pot had been made recently, within the year, at a guess. Age can be faked to the naked eye, but not to the inner eye of someone who can see auras. A broken pot in the case behind Young, the pot's design barely discernible after all these centuries, carried far more vibrations than this vessel did.

"She's right," Mick said. He reached to take the pot from Gabrielle, who surrendered it willingly. Mick lifted the pot to his nose.

Then his expression changed. It was just a flash, his eyes going from blue to deep, dragon black. They shifted back again before Young could see, but I'd caught it.

I moved closer to him and looked at the pot in his hands. I saw it then, or rather, smelled it—the faint tinge of Nightwalker. And I knew which Nightwalker.

Young's expression went from that of a smooth-faced, wealthy man showing off a treasure to a man realizing he'd been conned. And beneath his shock and anger, I saw stark fear.

Fear?

"That can't be right," he said. "Check again."

Mick shrugged and set the pot back into its case. "It's not more than a few months old at best. If you tell me who sold you this, I'll do what I can to have them prosecuted, and possibly get your money back."

Young's chagrin changed to anger. "No," he snapped. "You tell me that this pot's real and sign a paper to prove it."

Mick looked at him in surprise. "I thought you were willing to let me tell you whether you'd been sold a fake. You have been."

"You don't understand. It doesn't matter what I bought. You have to declare that it's real."

I could tell Mick was dying to know why. I was too. The only one calm and smiling like a smug cat was Gabrielle.

Mick said, "I wouldn't maintain much of a reputation if I signed off on a fake."

Mr. Young's hand dipped into his suit coat and came out with a small pistol. "Perhaps I haven't made myself clear," he said.

He pointed the pistol not at Mick, but at me.

I hate guns. They're unpredictable, deadly, terrifying. Anyone can point one at another person and shoot him or her dead, a life taken in the blink of an eye.

To a Stormwalker or a Beneath magic user, guns just get in the way. They are as liable to blow up in our hands as they are to be of any use as a weapon.

A twenty-two was now aimed directly at my chest. I didn't raise my hands, as movies teach us to do. I had a glass of wine in one hand, the other folded across my stomach, and I didn't much feel like moving.

Thunder rumbled outside. Close. The storm was at last rolling down out of the mountains to engulf the town.

Mick's smile spread across his face. "You might not want to do that," he said to Young.

"Yep," Gabrielle said. "Janet can be a real bitch."

Young's gaze flicked to me, and he really looked at me for the first time. He took in that I was Indian, a biker chick, and had the remnants of bruises on my face from my fall in Chaco Canyon plus the tussle with my Nightwalker. I saw him note the singed piece of hair I'd had to cut away. He didn't look impressed.

"I dictated a letter in anticipation of our appointment," he said to Mick, the pistol not moving. "All you have to do is sign it. I promise not to kill your girlfriend, but I do guarantee that I can put her in the hospital. Your choice. Sign, or watch your lady here rely on a feed tube for a while."

The gun was cocked, loaded, and I could tell by Mr. Young's eyes that he'd pull the trigger. And that he knew the difference between shooting to wound and shooting to kill.

"Maybe you should look at the letter, Mick," I said.

"Maybe I should." Mick's voice was rumbling, the dragon edge coming into it. He knew the storm meant that I could take care of myself, but he was dragon, and I was his mate. Every one of his instincts was telling him to flatten Young and put me out of danger.

Young nodded at his lackey, who wasn't fazed in the slightest that his employer had pulled a gun on one of his guests. Lackey went to the desk and returned with a thick piece of stationary paper containing two typed paragraphs. I saw Mick's name at the bottom of the page, with a line for his signature.

Mick took it, and I craned to read. The top paragraph was a note from Mr. Young explaining that he'd employed Mick Burns, an expert with a string of qualifications from different museums around the country, to authenticate the pot. I'd love to know whether those qualifications were true. The second paragraph said that Mick stated he'd examined the vessel and found it to be real.

"Who's the letter for?" I asked.

Young glared at me but spoke to Mick. "Just sign it."

Lackey moved to Mick's other side and handed him a pen. Lightning flared outside the high window, closer now. The lights inside dimmed, and a roll of thunder scooped its way through the room, rumbling on and on and on.

Sparks snapped to my fingertips, which I hid by balling my hand into my stomach.

Mick studied the greeting. "Someone called Pericles McKinnon. Interesting name. Never heard of him." He glanced at me. "Janet?"

"Nope. I wonder why Mr. Young is so afraid of him."

Young's lips tightened. "Sign the damned letter or your girlfriend bleeds."

"Who is he?" I asked Young. "Why is it so important he thinks the pot is real?"

Gabrielle broke in. "Because Mr. McKinnon probably paid Mr. Young a gob of money for it already, and he might get testy if he thinks Mr. Young is trying to hand him a fake."

"Then Mr. Young should have had it tested before he bought it," I said.

"I *did*," Young said. "That DiAngelo bitch and her boyfriend had it authenticated, and so did the museum in Flag. It was real then. I swear it. But McKinnon told me I'd better be absolutely sure. When you called wanting to have a look at the pot, I decided to ensure that it would be deemed real, no matter what. So sign this and make him happy, all right?"

"If you've been duped, why should McKinnon be pissed off at you?" I asked. "Give him his money back, and Mick will make sure you get yours returned. What's the deal?"

Gabrielle laughed, a sunny sound in the gloom. "I bet

McKinnon wants the real one for more than its value, or the fact that it's pretty."

Gabrielle, my crazy little sister, could be astute. Or else she knew more about this pot than she was letting on.

"Your entire collection is pretty illegal," I said to Young. "I can't believe you're rubbing it in the faces of two Indian women, all the while trying to woo us with good wine. The feds can put you in prison for pot hunting, and all this—" I waved my hand at the glass cases "—is pretty much evidence."

Young's face went chartreuse, and he shoved the pistol at me. "Shut *up*. You've just made sure you're dead."

Lightning cracked outside, and all the electricity went off. Gray light from the high windows glinted on the glass cases, and the next lighting strike glared against them all.

Perfect.

Young pulled the trigger. At the same time, I grabbed the lightning and all its reflections around the room and directed it at the pistol.

"Down!" Mick roared.

Gabrielle dropped flat, and Mick followed her to the ground. Even the lackey hit the floor with the swiftness of a man used to dodging gunfights.

The pistol exploded. Young screamed as he dropped it, or tried to. Lightning crawled up his body and wrapped him in a blanket of white arcs.

Arcs that I controlled. The lightning didn't touch his body —it flowed around him, its deadly charge kept from contacting his skin by me and my whims.

The thunder kept rumbling, strike after strike of lightning landing outside. Mountain storms could be hell on earth.

"Who is Pericles McKinnon?" I asked him.

Young continued to scream. The lackey on the ground leapt to his feet as several more equally well-dressed lackeys burst through the door. All were armed.

"Oh, now," Gabrielle said. She flicked her fingers, and

every single one of Young's bodyguards cum servants hurtled toward the ceiling. They fired wildly at us, but their bullets stuck in midair as though they'd hit a wall of gelatin.

"Gabrielle," Mick admonished her.

"What? You want bullets ripping through you?" Gabrielle's eyes widened. "I promise I won't kill them. Much."

I made no such promise. I was angry, both at Young for assuming he could manipulate Mick, and at a certain Night-walker skulking in the basement of my hotel. The slayers might find only a pile of sinew and dust when they finally caught up to him.

"Who is McKinnon?" I directed my question upward to Lackey Number One, the one who'd let us in. His body was pressed against the ceiling, his face white in the gloom.

"Not sure," Lackey said in a choked voice. "Some badass Mr. Young agreed to get the pot for. Don't know why he's so scared of him. He's a little dude."

"Unless he's some kind of powerful magic being." I looked at Young. "What is he? Nightwalker? Shaman?" I didn't say *dragon*, because dragons were happy if not too many people knew they existed—as dragons, that is. If McKinnon was Drake under an assumed name, I'd smack him.

"I don't know," Young managed to say. "But he does some powerful shit. More powerful than what you're doing."

That hurt my feelings. Right now, I was pretty hot stuff. The entire force of the storm filled me and made me stronger than anyone in this room. A ball of Beneath magic waited deep in my core, there if I needed it. I could hold onto the earth magic of the storm and roast the entire place with the ball of Beneath magic. Nothing could stop me, not even Mick, and Mick knew it.

I borrowed Gabrielle's idea and lifted Mr. Young off his feet. Higher and higher Young rose, still wrapped in the light-ning. His pistol, on fire, burned his hands.

"Why does this oh-so-powerful mage want this pot?" I

asked. "The real one, I mean. If he's a mage, he'll know it's a fake as soon as he sees it. I knew as soon as you opened the box."

Mick answered. "But Mick Burns will have authenticated it. Not Young's fault if he didn't know it wasn't real. The mage still gets mad, but he goes after me instead, to find out what I know, and to kill me if he wants to make himself feel better."

I shoved Young a little higher. "Hmm. I'd like to see that fight."

"No, you wouldn't," Young said down to me. "McKinnon will kill you in a cold minute. All of you. Doesn't matter how much lightning you play with."

"I don't know," I said. "See, I'm not *playing* with the lighting—this is me being nice. I'm not letting it touch you. Where can we find Mr. McKinnon?"

"I don't know."

I shoved Young upward until his back slammed against the smooth, plastered ceiling. "Where was that?"

"I swear to you, I don't know. He gets in touch with me when he wants me. I don't know where he's from."

I believed him. Powerful mages didn't hand out business cards with their addresses printed on them. The problem with being a powerful mage is that other powerful mages are always ready to go after you. Mages can steal each other's powers, usually when the first mage was dying.

I'd met an ultra-powerful mage this past spring. He called himself an ununculous—no, *the* ununculous, the only one in the world. Emmett Smith had gotten the position by killing the previous ununculous. He'd made no secret of the fact that he'd murdered his way to the top, absorbing and stealing the magic from the mages he'd killed along the way.

"Why does he want the pot?" I asked.

"For spells," Young said. He looked pathetic stuck to the ceiling like a bug in a spider's web. "Don't ask me what kind. He just said he needed it for spells."

Which made me want to have a good look at the original pot. Magic could cling to artifacts from the past, building up over time—like a sword from the European middle ages, or an ancient Native American pot, or my hotel basement. I suspected that the vessel known as the Holy Grail had started as a simple table cup from ancient Rome, which by the Middle Ages had contained vast magic, building quietly year after year.

Such artifacts are hard to find, because they're powerful enough to hide themselves. They aren't sentient, exactly, but they somehow obscure themselves from the naked eye, or even the magical eye. The Holy Grail must have been picked up and tossed aside hundreds of times. After millennia of trying, no one has ever found it, have they? Claims in novels and movies notwithstanding.

All of which made me suspicious of Ansel's story that he'd found the pot after such a brief search. Something smelled.

Something really did smell. Young. He was on fire.

My speculations had only increased my rage. Young's clothes were singeing, and the odor of burning wool curled inside my nose.

"Janet," Mick said warningly.

I wasn't allowed to hurt and kill people with my magic. Dragons and Hopi gods would appear out of the mists to stop me, by my death if necessary.

So not fair. I whipped the lightning away from Young. His face and hands got a little burned in the process, and he screamed. Oops.

I also let him fall. Mick shot a look at Gabrielle, who gave him a stubborn glare back. At the last minute, she rolled her eyes and cushioned Young's fall with a bubble of Beneath magic, the same kind that held the bullets suspended in midair.

Young hit the floor with a loud thump. Well, Mick hadn't told her to make the landing soft, just not lethal.

I still had all this lightning in my hands, with nowhere to

go. The Beneath goddess in me wanted me to crash it into Young and his lackeys, killing them for the petty criminals they were. I knew damn well Young hadn't come by all the stuff in his house honestly.

The auras of the artifacts both here and in the giant room below continued to knock at me. Ancient pieces, wrenched from where they'd been buried, torn from the people who'd been buried with them. Angry, lonely, and scared, they yearned to return to the places from which they'd come.

I brought the lightning back to me, gave it a little spurt of Beneath magic, and let it loose on all the glass cases.

The doors shattered, one after another, and the tops of the floor cases smashed in one long, spectacular crash. The lightning whipped through objects inside — pieces of history, pieces of lives. My Beneath magic nudged the auras, and they rose, black and angry, seeking vengeance.

CHAPTER TWELVE

EACH POTSHERD AND ARTIFACT HAD ONLY THE SMALLEST OF auras on its own, but put every tiny piece together, and they filled the room. The lackeys on the ceiling screamed as bullets of darkness, like tiny shards of glass, tore at their faces.

Young got to his feet, swaying. "No! No, what are you *doing*?"

The auras from the floor cases shot into the air. First came the pottery shards, then knives, bones, and finally the blackest auras from the shriveled skins. They swirled around each other, faster and faster, taking on the force of a tornado, then they threw themselves at Young. The man threw up his hands as the gathered spirits of his beloved collection descended on him.

The windows high above us exploded. Mick hit the floor, dragging Gabrielle down with him.

I laughed with my power. I'd awakened a thousand years' worth of rage, the rage of captives finally turning on their captors. My storm magic fed the artifacts the power of the earth in which they'd rested, and the Beneath magic gave them the nudge they needed to be deadly.

Wind blasted through the open windows, and with it came hail. Round stones of ice cascaded over the remnants of the cases, splintering wood, shattering the last of the glass.

Mick got under one of the heavy tables, Gabrielle huddling next to him. My breath fogged in the freezing cold air. The hail struck me, nicking my skin and staining it with blood, but I didn't feel a thing.

The next lightning strike came right through the window. Fat and white, it blew me down the length of the room and slammed me into the door. The ceiling sprouted a giant hole, and the beams and smooth plaster slowly buckled and fell inward.

The ceiling carried the lackeys down with it, and buried Young. Ripped wiring crackled, and pipes spewed water. The lightning bolt had gone right through the floor, and acrid smoke came up through the hole in the carpet.

I could no longer feel my body, and could hear nothing after that explosion of sound. I seemed to be on the floor, but had no recollection of falling there.

Men were crawling out of the wreckage, only to find the whirling black auras of ancient anger dancing before them. Blood flew as the tornado of rage whipped into them.

"Janet!" Mick's shout sounded from somewhere in the maelstrom. "You have to stop it!"

I had to try a few times before my voice worked. "I didn't create the lightning strike. It's a storm. Nature."

"You're attracting it. This whole house could come down. Shut it off."

He made it sound so easy. Like all I had to do was snap my fingers, and everything would go away.

I wrapped my arms around my chest, but I was still numb, no sensations in my body. I could move but that was about it.

The lightning struck again—not this room, but somewhere else in the house. The explosion shook the whole building, and fire leapt into the sky.

If the lightning had hit a gas pipe, we'd be in big trouble. Still I couldn't move.

I needed Mick. He could steady me, but he was all the way across the room under a table.

I closed my eyes, trying to find the calm core within myself, as the koshare—a Hopi clown—had taught me. Mick and Cassandra also had been teaching me more about Wicca magic, about the importance of grounding and centering so the magic didn't twist me into nothing.

The problem was, I'd been practicing these meditations in the cool calm of evening outside my back door. Easy to ground myself when I knew Elena was cooking something delicious in the kitchen, my guests were down for the night, and Mick would be waiting for me inside.

Now I had the full force of a high-desert storm dancing around me, plus the collective magic of ancient objects I'd awakened, hot and ready to kill.

I couldn't anchor myself by focusing on my breathing, because I couldn't feel anything in my chest or hear anything above the shriek of wind. Same went for my heartbeat. If I hadn't been aware of being aware, I wouldn't know I was alive.

I closed my eyes, shutting out the sights of men bleeding from a thousand razor-like cuts, Mick's bulk folded under the table, Gabrielle beside him, for once being sensible and taking cover. I needed to focus on an image, one that would calm me and stop the crazed laughter in my brain.

Mick's hard face and warm blue eyes usually did it for me, but the image that sprang instantly to me was Coyote, dying while I watched.

His expression had been one of release and relief. Also surrender. I'd never seen Coyote give up, and so readily.

He couldn't be gone. He was a god. And yet, his last breath had held finality. Then he'd dissolved, floated away on the wind.

He'd have wanted that. Traditional Navajo were afraid of

dead bodies and their lingering ghosts. Coyote would not have wanted to upset people by leaving remains.

Tears filled my eyes and spilled down my cheeks. A shudder went through me, and then I felt my heartbeat, which *hurt*. My chest burned and ached, and my throat shut up tight.

I thought about the big man with his wicked smile and lewd jokes, and his eyes so warm. I thought about how he dressed in his jeans, cowboy boots, and button-down shirt and hung around the center of Magellan, playing Indian for the tourists. He'd tell stories, some outrageous, some sad—of the gods and of the tribes who'd populated the area for centuries. He was especially good with kids, dialing back his off-color humor for them. Julie Kee, in particular, adored him.

Julie. I'd have to tell her.

I pressed my arms tightly over my stomach and let sobs wrack my body. Even if Coyote had managed to save himself, and he wasn't really dead, being a god, there was no telling whether I'd ever see him again. He came and went—sometimes, he'd told me, for centuries at a stretch. At least he'd kissed me good-bye.

"Janet."

Mick was beside me. I opened my eyes. Thunder still rumbled, and lightning flickered, but farther away now. The storm had rolled on, naturally, down the valley.

The auras were gone. The hail had softened to rain, which was now pouring in through the broken roof. The soaked floor was littered with Young and his lackeys, all bleeding, all groaning.

Mick gathered me into his arms and pressed a kiss to the top of my head. "That's my girl," he whispered.

≈

THE STORM STILL SHOOK ME AS MICK HELPED ME STUMBLE

from the house, back to his bike, which stood wet but unharmed at the bottom of the driveway.

I needed release, my skin crawling with the aftermath of lightning. Mick knew it, because he kept his arm around me as we walked out, his big body shielding mine.

Mick knew the best method to draw off the residue of the storm and keep me from having one of my bad magic hangovers. Unfortunately, it involved a private room, a large bed, a long stretch of time, and no clothes.

Right now I was in a neighborhood halfway up a mountain, the neighbors coming out to see the storm damage. Sirens sounded as emergency vehicles raced into the neighborhood to make sure the fire didn't spread.

Plus, we had Gabrielle with us. She walked along beside Mick as we made our way down the driveway, her black windbreaker slung over her shoulder. Mr. Young apparently had sent a car to bring her to his house, so unless she stole one from the garage, she had no transportation back into town, or wherever she'd come from.

She was all for stealing a car from Young, but Mick stopped her, telling her we didn't have time to deal with bailing her out of jail when she got caught.

"What are you doing here, anyway?" I demanded when we reached the bike. The electricity to open the gate was still off, but Mick solved that problem by wrenching the thing open with his big hands. "You're supposed to be at Many Farms with Grandmother, driving her crazy instead of me."

Gabrielle looked at me with wide, innocent eyes. "Who do you think sent me? Ruby heard about Young buying this old pot, and she sent me here to see if it was real."

I stopped. "Grandmother sent *you* to find an artifact that might possess magic great enough to interest a strong mage? She sent *you*?"

"Don't keep saying it like that, Janet. Yes, she trusted me. Well, all right, she's pretty sure that what Young bought was a fake. And she asked me to get a picture of it, so she could look at the markings." She grinned. "But I went one better."

Gabrielle carefully swung her jacket around and opened it. Inside lay the fake pot Young had bought from Laura.

"It survived the storm somehow," Gabrielle said. "So I grabbed it while Young and his boys were feeling sorry for themselves."

"And when Young comes after you for taking it?" I demanded.

"It's fake. What does he want with it? Now he can tell his big, bad mage Pericles that it was stolen by two Indian chicks and a biker dude."

"Then Pericles comes after *us*," I said.

Gabrielle hefted the pot. "So? We can take care of him. Aren't you interested in what this pot does?"

I was. So was Mick, I could tell. And so was my grandmother.

I snatched the pot from her. "I need to talk to Ansel. And find Laura. She must have the original."

"I say we find this mage," Gabrielle said. "Make him tell us everything."

My sweet, innocent little sister. She was pretty, with her round, soft face, her dusky skin and shining black hair, her body's curves showed off by her cropped top and jeans, the kind of outfit I liked to wear.

My eyes narrowed. She wasn't just dressing like me — those were my clothes. She'd taken them out of the dresser in my bedroom at Many Farms. Gabrielle had more on top than I did, and she was stretching out the shirt in a bad way.

"Have you ever gone up against a mage, Gabrielle?" I asked.

"Sure. I won."

"A truly powerful, unstoppable mage? It's not that easy."

"Mages have earth magic. I have goddess magic. Goddess magic always wins."

"No, it doesn't," I said. "Mick, can you take her back to Many Farms? I'll rent a car or something, or ask Maya to drive out here and get me. I want to take a look at Laura's antique store before I leave."

Before Mick could answer, Gabrielle said, "Ruby and I are staying in Santa Fe. Just give me a ride to our hotel, Mick."

She grabbed my helmet and swung herself onto Mick's big bike without waiting for his invitation.

"Grandmother's *here*?" Grandmother, who didn't like to leave Many Farms or the Navajo Nation for any reason had come to a city as large as Santa Fe? With Gabrielle no less. Grandmother's exception to her rule of never traveling far from home was my hotel, and she only went there so she could find out what I was up to.

"She wasn't about to let me that far off the leash," Gabrielle said. "Hurry up, Mick. I'm hungry."

"I'll take her," Mick said to me, getting on the bike. "You going to be all right?"

He meant because of the storm. The aftermath was still crawling through me, and I needed to let off steam, but there wasn't much I could do here and now. I nodded.

Mick looked at me in concern, but he knew that we had to contain Gabrielle before we worried about me. "You have your cell phone?" he asked me. "I'll call you when I'm done, and we'll meet to check out the store."

"Nope," Gabrielle said. Her voice rose as Mick kicked the bike to roaring life. "Ruby says I'm supposed to bring you to see her, Mick. She wants to talk to you. It's important, she said."

~

THEY LEFT ME WITH THE FAKE POT. I TOOK OFF MY JACKET as Mick roared off, Gabrielle giving me a cheerful wave, and wrapped the pot in the jacket, hiding it. Of course Gabrielle had left it with me, stolen from the rich Mr. Young, with police coming up the hill in the wake of the fire trucks. She'd think that was funny.

I did my best to look like an innocent bystander as I walked away down the block. Gabrielle wearing my clothes had one advantage—I heard a neighbor's gardener telling a policeman he'd seen a biker and his black-haired woman ride up to the house, and he'd just seen them ride away. I'd been wearing a helmet, and so had Gabrielle. I had my jacket off now; she'd put hers back on.

It was still raining, so I bent my head and just kept walking.

For once I'd remembered to bring my cell phone, and it actually worked, so I called a taxi when I reached the main intersection at the bottom of the hill. A sandwich shop, new and clean, stood next to a gas station, everything shiny new for this wealthy neighborhood.

I was hungry and still shaky, and I ordered a sandwich and ate it while the rain pattered down. I wondered exactly what Grandmother wanted to talk about with Mick, and I knew neither would tell me unless they wanted me to know. Who knew how long I'd have to wait for them to be finished, and where Mick would have me meet up with him after that.

In irritation, I crunched the house-made chips that came with the sandwich. They were good. I should tell Elena to consider making some—not that she ever listened to my culinary suggestions.

The taxi arrived as I finished eating. I threw away my sandwich wrappings, took my soft drink with me, and told the taxi to take me to a corner in the heart of Santa Fe near the train station.

I'd looked up the location of Laura's antique store after Ansel had told us about it. It lay on an innocuous side street lined with older shops; some of the shops had been little bungalows, now converted into stores or offices.

Laura's shop was a regular store front with glass windows and a glass door. *Laura's Treasures*, she'd called it, proudly lettered, with a logo of the right-angled design that was on the flag of New Mexico.

The shades were pulled down tightly over the windows and door, with a Closed sign hanging askew on one of the windows. I continued walking down the block without pausing, went around the corner, and walked up the alley behind Laura's street.

The shop owners had nicely labeled their back doors, so that anyone making deliveries in the alley could find the store they needed. It was dark and raining, and I had to use a little glow light from my residual storm magic to read the signs on each door before I found Laura's.

The same little bit of storm magic allowed me to open the lock without trouble. I let myself into the store and quietly closed the door behind me.

I didn't dare let too much light flare in here. Anyone seeing it would assume *burglar* and call the police. The store did have small emergency lights above the front and back doors, and those tiny glows would have to be enough.

I waited until my eyes adjusted to the darkness then walked through the store, taking my time. The shop was pretty typical—aisles of locked glass cases for the expensive things, the cheap junk lying about on shelves. Not that Laura had much in the way of cheap junk. She stocked a few obvious souvenirs—T-shirts and sweatshirts, jars of red and green chile salsa, and chunks of polished rock with *Santa Fe* or *Bandelier* or *New Mexico* printed on them.

The rest of the store was filled with Indian pottery and jewelry, most made by artists and artisans in the pueblos that surrounded Santa Fe, interspersed with a few Zuni and Navajo pieces. Some were new, but most were antiques, made decades ago by talented craftsmen and craftswomen.

Laura didn't have a cash register, but she had a credit card reader that was tucked away out of sight. No ledgers. I found a printer and a space for a desktop computer or laptop to rest next to it, but no computer or laptop.

Laura might have taken the computer home every night. The computer or laptop would have all her transactions stored on it, and I itched to see them.

If Laura were proclaimed dead, who would get all her belongings? This store? Her sister, Paige? I thought about Paige at the séance, very convinced that Laura was dead. She'd had a photograph of Laura and a bracelet, and Laura's hat. Where had she gotten those? Laura's house?

But Laura was alive, if Drake told the truth. Why then, hadn't Laura tried to contact Paige? I'd been assuming Paige herself had faked the séance, but could it have been someone else, wanting Paige to go on thinking Laura was dead? And why?

Next to the back door of the shop was another door that opened to a stairwell, which had wooden stairs leading up and concrete stairs leading down.

Laura might have locked her laptop into an upstairs office. I had an office in the third floor of my hotel, where I kept information I didn't necessarily want guests or the maids to stumble upon. Nothing sinister, just private.

I was also intrigued at what might be downstairs. A potter's bench? An array of paint ground from clay and natural dies? Various chemicals for aging things? Was Laura a professional forger, or had this pot been a one-time deal, or had Laura farmed out the forging?

I had taken two steps down the concrete staircase when I knew someone was in the basement. The aura of the other person was subtle—or well hidden. In either case, I hadn't sensed him or her when I'd entered the shop. Usually I wasn't so oblivious, but I'd had no idea until the faintest tendril of the aura tickled to me on the stairs.

As I halted in the shadows, a thin light flashed once, pale

white like an LED light, but it didn't bob like a flashlight in someone's hands. I heard a tiny clink, then a footstep.

I sniffed, but I didn't smell Nightwalker or dragon, or even skinwalker or Changer. Whoever was down there was human.

I moved silently down three more steps. From there I could see that the staircase opened into a large room that ran the length of the store upstairs. A light hung steadily from the ceiling, a lantern maybe, or another emergency light.

I sent a bit of residual storm magic into the room, delicately probing.

And met a wash of magic so strong it lifted me off my feet, carried me over the stair railing in a rush of blackness, and slammed me without remorse to the floor.

CHAPTER THIRTEEN

I LOST HOLD OF THE JACKET-WRAPPED POT, WHICH ROLLED free of the cloth. Hands caught my shirt and dragged me up, up, and up in an impossibly strong grip.

I looked down at a man who wasn't big, but his muscles were heavy. He was balding, like Fremont, but unlike Fremont, he had eyes that were hard, glittering, and had long ago lost every bit of warmth they might ever have possessed. I dredged up the remnants of lightning that still itched beneath my skin and threw it at him.

The man's eyes went black, voids of evil. Those eyes sucked in the lightning, fast, faster. Electricity sparkled across his retinas, turning them white, then the man blinked, and the lightning was gone. I could only hang in his grip and gape at him in terror.

"Stormwalker," he said, as though both puzzled and amused. "Who sent a *Stormwalker* after me?"

"No one sends me anywhere," I said, trying to sound tough. "Who are you?"

"It's not here," he said. "I've already looked."

"The pot you mean?" I tried to act as dignified as possible

while hanging in midair from hands I couldn't wrench away. "You must be Pericles."

Pericles transferred one of his hands to my throat. "And who might you be?"

"A Stormwalker, like you said." Not that I could talk very well with him squeezing my larynx. "But a little more than that."

Coyote was dead, and Mick couldn't blame me for using Beneath magic to save my own life. I let a ball grow in my hands, prayed I had enough connection with the storm to not blow up the building and the ones around it, and shot the magic into his face.

Pericles dropped me. I landed on my knees, gasping for breath, my kneecaps smacking the stone floor with an audible crack.

Pericles danced backward, flailing against the Beneath magic that covered him like napalm. I felt sick. I'd meant to disable him to keep him from killing me, but Beneath magic has a mind of its own. Burning someone alive . . . slowly . . . wasn't the kind of thing I wanted to think myself capable of.

Then, as I watched, the Beneath magic solidified around his body like molded glass, cracked into a thousand shards, and fell from his body. The shards tinkled like broken icicles on the floor, and then vanished.

Pericles stood up and faced me, while I still struggled, on my knees, to breathe.

"Impressive," he said to me. "Nice bit of magic working." He really did sound impressed.

I could barely speak. "Why do you want the pot so much?"

"You mean this pot?" The fake pot zoomed out of the dusty corner to which it had rolled and danced in midair in front of me. "The fake Richard Young was going to foist off on me? Before you burned down half his house? I laughed about that."

"Word travels fast." I wiped away something that tickled my lower lip and found blood on my hand.

"I have spies everywhere. Remember that, little Stormwalker. You're not bad looking. Want to work for me?"

"No."

"I'd pay you a shitload of money." Pericles looked even more like Fremont now, face bland, arms folded, not going anywhere in a hurry. "You'd be able to do anything you wanted, have anything you wanted, have any*one* you wanted. As long as you show up with your storm magic and . . . whatever that was . . . whenever I need it. Put out the occasional blow job, and we're good."

"No," I repeated.

"What are you? Navajo? I could use a Native American to find me more artifacts. The tribes hide away the best ones. Pretend it's all secret and their heritage, but they just don't want mages who'd know what to do with them to get a hold of them. Am I right?"

"I'm not working for you," I said. "Pericles. Is that really your name?"

"My parents had a strange sense of humor. No, I didn't kill them for it—they're living in comfortable retirement in Tucson. I visit them every once in a while, and my father talks about his golf game. I have a good life, Stormwalker. Lots of money. Don't you like money?"

"To a point."

He snorted a laugh. "Your choice is—you work for me, or I try to kill you. I say *try*, because Stormwalkers aren't weak, and you have a little sting in your tail. But I'll keep at it until you're dead. Not only that, I'll put out the word to everyone who works for me to try to kill you. A lot of people work for me, so they'll be coming from all sides."

"I'll take my chances."

My bravado, unfortunately, wasn't anything more than bravado, and Pericles knew it. The man was strong—he'd thrown off my Beneath magic like it was nothing. Not many could withstand it. The only one I'd ever seen stare at me without blinking when he got a full dose of my magic was Sheriff Jones, who sucked up all magic and never felt it.

Pericles had felt it, but he'd destroyed it with a spell of his own.

But then, if he were so powerful, why was he looking for an artifact to help him out? Objects could be laced with incredible magic—the same way the magic mirror had been—but Pericles didn't seem like the type to need a boost.

"What is it about this pot that makes it so popular?" I asked.

Pericles shrugged. "If you agree to work for me, I'll tell you. I'll even ask you to help me find the real one for me. Want to satisfy your curiosity?"

"You seem plenty capable on your own. What do you need the pot for?"

He laughed, still relaxed. "I collect things. And people. I like having all the magic users and little shamans on my payroll. A good job and cushy living keeps them from getting ideas about moving up the mage food chain and ousting me. By *ousting*, you know, I mean killing."

"Not all mages kill each other," I said. "Most know it can take a lifetime to learn about the powers they *do* have." I still didn't know everything I could do, despite the guidance of first my friend Jamison, then Mick and Coyote.

"Ambitious mages kill each other," Pericles said. "Trust me."

I thought again about Emmett Smith. *He* qualified as an ambitious mage, and he'd slaughtered his way to the top. I guessed that Pericles aspired to be the next ununculous. There was only ever one at a time.

"I'll have to try to make it on my own," I said.

"Last chance."

"No." I readied more magic, my body aching all over. "You're kind of sleazy."

Pericles finally lost his smile. He gestured at the pot that dangled beside my face, and it exploded into fragments, sharp pieces slashing my skin. I threw up my hands to fend them off, and Pericles sent a wave of darkness at me.

The darkness held cold and death and the screams of helpless things, things from which the magic had sucked all power. Now it wanted mine.

I desperately blocked the black wave with Stormwalker-laced Beneath magic. The deadly wave hovered in front of me, making me weak and sick, then it reluctantly dispersed. The tendrils that touched me before it dissolved froze my skin, leaving behind little burned patches.

The backlash of his magic mixed with mine was like a dam bursting, except instead of concrete and water, a flood of chaotic power poured through the basement.

The wave swept up everything in its path. It lifted me from my feet and threw me backward with the force of hurricane winds. I crashed into a workbench, smacked my head on something hard, and went to sleep.

I WOKE SURROUNDED BY THE AURA OF DRAGON.

Dragon aura is fiery with a hint of smoke—sweet-smelling smoke, not oily like a furnace. I think I fell in love with Mick's aura before I realized I loved the rest of him, even before I knew he was a dragon.

I reached up, hand landing on a muscular arm, and I smiled.

"Wakey, wakey, Janet."

I popped my eyes open. Mick would never say something as asinine as *Wakey, wakey.*

The overhead light was on, and by it I saw that the muscular arm was covered with tattoos. Completely covered, wrist to shoulder.

Colby grinned down at me as he hoisted me to my feet. I

landed against his solid chest, and he steadied me with his arms around my back, in no hurry to let me go.

Lines of tattoos emerged from the neck of Colby's T-shirt, climbing his throat to his chin. Every part of his body was inked, except his hands and face. And I do mean every part.

I pulled away from him. "Where's Mick?"

"Is that any way to greet a friend? I saw that look of disappointment when you realized it was me, not Mickey. Hurts, Janet. That really hurts."

"If you're here," I said when I found my breath, "where is Drake?"

"Tossing the place upstairs. He told me to look down here. Imagine my surprise when I found you out cold on the floor." Colby pressed a loud kiss to my forehead. "Mickey's about to take the town apart to find you. He told us to keep an eye out."

"Yeah, I'd better call him." I rubbed the back of my head, my brain still not working right. "Drake won't find anything up there. I already looked."

"You're probably right, but you know Drake. Stick shoved firmly up his ass. Has to go over every inch of ground, even if he's done it before."

I reached for my cell phone but found empty air in the little holster. The phone must have flown out when I hit the floor. "If Drake has searched here before, why is he doing it again?"

"Because he got wind that Pericles had come back here. Drake hauled ass—his and mine—to get here, but he was too late. Peri was gone."

"Then why search?"

Colby rolled his eyes. "Because he's *Drake*. He's convinced that if Pericles came back here, there was something to find. Drake says he'll figure out what Peri took based on what *isn't* here this time."

"Logical." I rubbed my head again.

"Yeah, well, that's Drake. Mr. Logic."

I pushed Colby out of my way and started hunting for my

cell phone. "You two knew all about Pericles, the wonderful mage. Why didn't you tell me? Why are you telling me now?"

"Well, you know about him now, obviously. He get what he was looking for?"

"I don't think so."

I spotted my cell phone under a worktable and stooped to retrieve it. The phone wasn't a phone anymore, but a melted mass in my hand. "Damn."

"Looks like he fried it," Colby said. "Lots of other stuff too."

Our magic backlash had been bad, but Pericles must have blasted the place with fire as well before he left. The tables were marked with black streaks, glass and plastic containers had melted, and curios had been reduced to small piles of ash. Whatever Laura had been working on, sitting at one of the worktables, had been smashed to powder.

Pericles had tried to burn the room behind him. For some reason—maybe my residual magic, or maybe because he thought I might be useful later—the fire had burned out instead of building into an inferno. I went cold.

"I'm glad you found me," I said, heartfelt.

"Any time, sweetie. Does this mean I get a reward?"

"No way," I said.

"Damn. I'll keep trying until you dump that fire lizard you call Mickey."

"*I* don't call him Mickey. You do." I dropped my useless cell phone to a table. "Help me with this."

I bent to the floor and started gathering the shards of the pot Pericles had broken. Colby picked up a piece and stared at the pattern. "Where the hell did you get this?"

"Richard Young."

Colby tossed the piece onto the table next to my melted cell phone. "It's a fake."

"I know. And you've just revealed to me that you know about the real one."

Colby shrugged, unembarrassed. "So why do you want this one? If it's fake?"

"Because it's handy to have a replica of what I'm looking for, for when I shove people up against the wall and question them. Like I want to do to you. This is what Drake was after the night he fried my hotel, wasn't it? The real one, I mean?"

"Yep. You sure your Nightwalker doesn't have it?"

"No, I'm not sure. But that doesn't mean I'm letting your dragons have him. Ansel and my hotel are off limits."

"Not *my* dragons. Don't insult me, Janet. I'm a prisoner here. A victim."

"Right. You never did tell me what you did to get yourself into so much trouble with the dragon council."

Colby lifted his hands. "It was a big misunderstanding."

I glared at him, but he wasn't going to budge. Never mind. I'd get it out of him later.

"Help me put this back together." I rummaged in the metal cabinets that hadn't melted, searching for glue. "And call Mick before he hurts someone looking for me."

"Demand, demand. I can't do everything at once."

"Call Mick, then."

"I don't have a cell phone."

I bit back some bad words. "Then start sorting pieces, and I'll make Drake call him."

Colby lost his grin and lowered his voice. "I didn't alert Drake that you were down here. We need to keep it that way. He's mad at you for the way things went at your hotel. When I say *mad*, I mean he's in a killing rage."

"He's mad at *me*?" My voice started to rise, and Colby frantically waved me quiet. "He's the one who set fire to my hotel."

"I know, but he's pissed off because you wouldn't turn over the Nightwalker to him. It's dragon law that creatures of evil aren't allowed to walk free. Nightwalkers are creatures of evil —dragons are creatures of good."

"Since when?" I snapped.

"Let me finish. In Drake's worldview, you should have given him the Nightwalker without argument. Drake would have found out what Ansel knew, then fried him. End of Nightwalker problem. You defended Ansel, an evil being, and you're letting him live in your basement. Plus, you defied Drake, and he doesn't like that."

"Too bad."

"It *is* too bad." Colby looked more serious than I'd seen him look in a long time. "Drake's hot to arrest you and take you prisoner, like he did me, for violating dragon law. Mickey would try to defend you—you being his mate—but Drake would take it to court."

"You mean up before the dragon council? But I'm not a dragon."

"No, but you're a dragon's mate. They can't kill you without going through Mick—and trust me, they don't want to go through Mickey—but you'd do time in the dragon compound. But hey, it wouldn't be so bad. We'd be inmates."

I growled under my breath. How easy my life had been when I hadn't believed in dragons. Now I was beleaguered by them.

Dragons were the most arrogant creatures in the universe. They didn't trust me, and they'd assigned Mick, long ago, to watch me, to kill me if I ever got out of line.

Mick had told them what they could do with themselves, but Drake and his master, Bancroft, still thought I needed that restriction. And I couldn't blame them. I was pretty dangerous, after all. But that didn't mean I'd sit still and obey their rules.

I dumped the rest of the shards I'd gathered to the table and slammed the bottle of glue down in front of Colby. "Start repairing," I said. "I'm going to talk to Drake."

Colby grabbed my arm. "Haven't you heard anything I've said? Drake will arrest you. That means *bind* you, not have a chat over an interrogation table."

"He can try."

Colby studied me, concern in his brown eyes, then he released me, letting his grin return. "In that case, can I watch? Please?"

I tapped the glue bottle. "Glue now. Watch later."

"Aw, you're no fun."

I patted Colby on the shoulder, grateful to him even if he was a shit, and marched upstairs.

CHAPTER FOURTEEN

DRAKE HAD OPENED THE BOTTOM OF A CABINET AND WAS ON his knees pulling out the contents—flattened boxes, paper, little foam popcorns, and shredded paper. The popcorns and paper had scattered across the tile floor, but I don't think Drake cared about being neat with Laura's things.

He was fully dressed in a black suit, his black leather duster draped over the counter. He and Colby must not have flown here—they wouldn't have taken the time to dress again. Drake had probably insisted on bringing the limo.

The store's lights were on, Drake unconcerned if anyone saw him. I remembered how, during my stay in the dragon compound, the police had been suspiciously deferential to Bancroft and Drake, instead of arresting them for kidnapping me. If the Santa Fe cops caught Drake turning over an antiques store, they'd probably apologize for interrupting him and leave him to it.

I cleared my throat.

Drake's head whipped around, but he only lost his composure for a second. Then he was rising to his feet, smooth as butter, dark threads of a binding spell streaking for me before I could so much as say hello.

I countered the spell with my very last spark of storm magic, which then went out. The binding spell regrouped and came at me again.

I quickly pressed a bubble of Beneath magic out around me —a trick I'd learned from Gabrielle. The binding spell hit it and bounced back toward Drake. He snapped off the spell with a flick of his fingers, the black threads disappearing.

"What's so special about the pot?" I asked him. "And why couldn't you explain before you burned down my saloon?"

Drake lowered his hand, as cool as ever. Did he look ashamed for vandalizing my hotel, terrifying my guests, burning off a piece of my hair, and destroying my magic mirror? Not in the slightest. "Council orders," he said. "Those same council orders forbid me to tell you any more than you already know."

I sent him a smile, not a nice one. "Come on, Drake. I thought we were friends."

His look told me he wondered where I'd gotten that idea. "Council orders are that I bring you in for harboring a Night-walker. Nightwalkers are deadly, Ms. Begay. It doesn't matter if some of them pretend to reform. As soon as they let down their guard, they go into a blood frenzy and become killing machines. You know that."

I did know that. I'd had my share of encounters with blood-frenzied Nightwalkers, up to and including Ansel last night.

"I agree," I said. "And if Ansel gets out of control, both Mick and I know it's our duty to kill him. But Ansel is trying. Being Nightwalker isn't his fault. He was turned against his will."

"That makes no difference." Drake's eyes were dark like a starless night. "Nightwalkers lose their humanity the instant they are turned. That's why there's nothing left but blood and sinew when they die. The human being they once were is gone."

"Since when do you love humans so much?"

"I don't. But I also don't like to see humans slaughtered like animals. As I have. Believe me, it's a terrible, terrible thing."

The quiet horror in his expression wasn't feigned. Drake was a tight-ass, but he wasn't completely cold.

"Tell the dragon council that I'm protecting Ansel," I said, "whether they like it or not. That means I'm willing to take full responsibility for him. If he screws up, I kill him. Even if I can't, you know Mick will. The dragon council will have to live with it."

"My orders are to bring you in," Drake said, stubborn. "And find the pot and take it out of the world."

"What's so special about it? It has magical abilities—I get that—but what does it *do*? Enhance magic? Protect the mage? Sing sea chanteys while you're working tough spells?"

I watched his reaction as I spoke, and I realized—Drake didn't know. He'd only been told the pot was dangerous and had to be found.

I knew that, like Nash, Drake was a straight-up guy. He liked rules and regulations, believing they'd been put in place for a reason, and strove to abide by them. If Drake said he wanted to protect the world from the pot, he meant it.

However, I didn't trust the dragon council he worked for an inch. I'd seen what they could do—what they thought they were entitled to do. I didn't want a vessel filled with magic anywhere near Bancroft, leader of the dragon compound in Santa Fe, or even Colby, as warmhearted as he could be.

Dragons might decide that the pot was too dangerous for humans to use but not for dragons. Dragons could be perfectly trusted to know what was best, their rationalization would go. They loved power, and they didn't mind using people, gods, supernatural beings, and even other dragons to get more of it.

"I don't know where the real pot is," I said.

"Your Nightwalker does."

"I don't think so. He's as baffled as I am by all this."

Drake shook his head. "He stole the woman."

"You mean Laura?" I went through what little I knew in my head. "I looked over her campsite. I saw the aura of Nightwalker there, but also of dragon. That dragon was you, wasn't it?"

"Not me," Drake said, giving me a little shake of his head. "Colby."

I paused for one surprised heartbeat, then turned around and yelled down the stairs, "Colby! Get up here!"

Colby barreled up so fast that I knew he'd been listening on the stairs.

"I heard," Colby said as I opened my mouth to tell him what I thought. "It wasn't my fault." He pulled at imaginary threads on his chest. "Binding spell, remember? I have to do what the dragon shits order me to do."

"I know, but you couldn't have told me?"

"What part of *binding spell* don't you understand? They tell me to go to the campground and fly off with a cute human blond woman—and by the way, don't tell anyone, especially not Janet Begay and her boyfriend Mick—and I have to do it. To the letter. Now that you know, my lips are loosened. But now that you know, there's nothing left to tell."

"What about Ansel? Was he there?"

"When I got to the campsite? No. When I grabbed Laura, yes. He came out of nowhere. Blood frenzied, strong as . . . well, as strong as a Nightwalker in a blood frenzy. I fought him hard—that boy is damn fast. I tried to fry him, squash him, grab him, drop him. Nothing. He moved like lightning. I finally chased him off, but by that time, Laura was gone."

"Gone where?"

Colby shrugged, looking unhappy. "Just gone. She wasn't stupid enough to sit around waiting to see who won the fight over her. She ran off into the night, and it was hellacious dark out there. I flew around looking for her, but nothing. By sunup, I had to leave before anyone saw me as a dragon, but I never found her." He shot a look at Drake. "Don't think that didn't get me into trouble."

"The Nightwalker must have taken her," Drake said. "It's the only explanation. She ran while Colby and Ansel fought, then Ansel caught up to her and spirited her somewhere. There's nowhere to go out there."

That was true. The Chaco Culture monument was surrounded by a whole lot of nothing. Beautiful nothing, but miles and miles of open country. A human woman, especially one unused to the open desert, was unlikely to survive a hike across that country, not in the dark, and not in daylight when summer temperatures rose into triple digits.

Therefore, either Laura was dead in the desert, and Heather's séance really had conjured her spirit, or Ansel had found her and taken her to safety.

Ansel had said he remembered nothing until he'd awakened alone, and I believed him. The blood frenzy erased whatever part of him was Ansel the stamp collector, turning him into an evil fiend. That didn't mean, though, that Ansel hadn't hidden Laura somewhere safe and simply couldn't remember where.

"Damn it," I said softly.

Mr. Young had accused Laura of switching the pot on him. If he was right, that meant that the one person who knew where the real vessel lay was Laura. And if Colby and Drake were right, the one person who knew where Laura was, was Ansel.

If my Nightwalker didn't start talking to me, I'd slay him myself.

I needed to go home, and I needed to do it quickly, or I'd have to wait another day for Ansel to wake up. Riding back with Mick on his motorcycle would take too long, even as swiftly as Mick drove. We wouldn't reach home much before dawn.

Albuquerque, an hour from here, had an airport, but any flight that could put me in the middle-of-nowhere Arizona would have to go through Phoenix or Denver, with a connection that would get me only as far as Flagstaff. There'd be another hour or so drive after that to Magellan, and the last flights to Phoenix and Denver had probably already left Albuquerque anyway. A passenger train from Albuquerque heading west did stop at Winslow, only thirty or so miles from Magellan, but only once a day. I'd likely already missed it, and a train might not get me to Winslow any faster than riding with Mick down the freeway.

"Move," someone said.

I knew that voice. Small but stentorian. My grandmother, Ruby Begay, barged through the front door of the shop to plant herself in front of a startled Drake.

My grandmother, as usual, wore long skirts and a dark blouse. Most Diné women these days donned traditional garb only when dressing up for an event, but Grandmother lived in her traditional clothes and didn't care who thought her old-fashioned. I saw that she'd taken the time to put on her turquoise and silver rings and a necklace as well. Anyone who came across her would be impressed, which was the point.

"Firewalkers are nothing but trouble." Grandmother leaned on her cane, turquoise-clad fingers gripping it tightly. She looked Drake over with her crow-dark eyes, the glitter in them of a creature who could be both wise and deadly.

Behind my grandmother came Gabrielle and Mick. Drake looked pained. "I was trying *not* to alert the street to our presence," he said.

News to me. But I agreed with him that a bunch of people walking in the front door of a closed shop might attract attention.

"It's not here," I said around everyone to Mick.

Mick wasn't listening. He pushed past Drake and Colby to me and caught me by the shoulders.

Mick didn't ask whether I was all right. He studied me with his dark blue eyes, looking deep down inside, examining me for hurt, relaxing when he found none. He brushed his hand over the back of my head where I'd hit the table, and tingling healing magic itched through my scalp. The lingering pain went away, blessed relief.

"How'd you know I was still here?" I asked him.

"I enhanced the GPS chip on your phone with a little magic." Mick traced a circle on the base of my neck with his thumb. "When the signal went dead, I came to its last known location."

The look in his eyes told me that when the signal had gone, his fears for me had kicked in.

I tried to lighten the moment. "Don't tell me my grandmother rode with you on the back of your motorcycle."

Mick gave me the smallest of grins. "She bullied a taxi driver into following me."

I imagined the taxi had shot away once they'd reached the store, the poor driver happy to escape.

Gabrielle had darted around us and down to the basement, and now she emerged with the pot, pasted back together, more or less, by Colby.

"I'll take that," I said. I wanted to wave it under Ansel's nose and demand to be told what he'd done with the real one.

"No, *I* will," Grandmother said.

"It comes with me," Drake said.

"No." Mick gave Drake a quiet look across the room, his eyes black, and Drake snapped his mouth shut.

"Why is everyone so hot to have it?" Colby asked. "It's not the real one."

"To keep others from using it to dupe more victims," Drake said.

Mick kept looking at him. "That's not why the dragons want it. You want it because you don't want anyone else to know the real one is loose."

"The Firewalkers can't ever have it," Grandmother said.

I broke in. "I want it so I can get answers out of people without having to explain what I'm looking for. The fake pot has one magical power that I'm going to use — getting people to talk about it."

"Which is why I instructed Gabrielle to take it," Grandmother said. "I don't *want* people talking about it."

"Mick and I can keep it safe," I said.

My grandmother humphed. She was master of the *humph*. "A fine job you've done so far. You've gotten your hotel ignited, your Nightwalker nearly killed, and you've lost the real pot."

I didn't bother answering. Any argument that if I'd known what was going on in the first place, I could have prevented much of this, would run against the stone wall of her stubbornness.

I took the pot out of Gabrielle's hands, and to my surprise, she let me. She gave me a wink and said, "I'd rather have the real thing."

"Gabrielle," Grandmother said sharply.

"Big sis is right," Gabrielle said. "This one's harmless, and besides, if Janet uses it as a decoy, people can chase it around and not the real one."

No one in that room looked happy, except maybe Colby, who didn't want to be involved in the problem at all.

"What does the real one do, Grandmother?" I asked, resting the pot against my hip. "It's magical, yes, but in what way?"

"I don't know." Grandmother looked troubled. "I need to find out. That's why I want it — so I can ask the shamans about it. Ones I trust."

Grandmother trusted about two people on the entire planet, and neither one was me. I set the pot on a counter, took Mick's cell phone from his belt, turned on the photo function, and snapped a picture of the vessel. I turned the pot around and took pictures from all angles, including the bottom and the inside.

I handed the phone back to Mick. "Mick will email these to you."

"I don't like computers," Grandmother said. "They suck every bit of common sense out of anyone who looks at them. Your father likes the laptop you gave him." Her look told me she'd consider any lack of sense on his part from here on out to be my fault.

"Mick will email them to Dad, then. Right now, I want to get my hands on Ansel."

"I will go with you," Grandmother said. "I, too, want to talk to your Nightwalker."

I shifted in impatience. "Fine, but we have to go *now*."

"I'll fly you, Janet," Colby said. "Promise to hold you nice and snug."

I said no. I might, any other time, trust Colby not to drop me, but while he was under the binding spell to Drake, Drake might order Colby to use the three-hundred and more miles of empty desert to rid the dragons of a pesky Stormwalker.

"We all go," Drake said. "I too want a word with the Nightwalker, as you know."

"Stop!" I grabbed Mick's cell phone again. "Let's do this the easy way."

I punched numbers. Almost instantly, Cassandra answered in her crisp tones, but I heard worry in her voice.

"It's Janet. Would you go down and tell Ansel I want to talk to him?"

Cassandra dropped the hotel-manager facade. "He's not here, Janet." The worry escalated, unusual for Cassandra. "He went just after dark. Yes, I tried to stop him, and no, I couldn't. He threw off my binding spell like it was a cobweb, and he was gone. Where are you? I've been trying to call you for hours."

CHAPTER FIFTEEN

ANSEL'S DISAPPEARANCE FOMENTED ANOTHER ARGUMENT, which Mick ended. He'd stood quietly through most of our discussion, but now he took the pot firmly away from me.

"Janet and I are returning to Magellan. Drake, tell the dragons to stop pursuing. Ruby, this is dangerous—too dangerous even for you. Let Janet and me handle it."

"*I'm* dangerous, Firewalker," Grandmother said.

Mick acknowledged this with a nod. "True, but no mage gets to be the caliber this one is without leaving a trail of bodies in their wake. They con and kill their way to the top. He'll use you, and he'll use your family. I'd hate to see Pete get hurt."

Grandmother was very protective of my father—we all were. I'm not sure Dad appreciated our protectiveness all the time, but he was vulnerable, and my grandmother knew that.

"Don't smarm me, dragon," she said to Mick. "If this mage finds the real artifact, you know none of us will be safe."

"Yes, but Janet and I can meet him in battle. You can't."

"Don't be so sure of that. I'm not an old woman cowering in the corner."

"Especially not with me to protect her," Gabrielle put in.

Grandmother turned to Gabrielle, and for a split second, her eyes filled with compassion. "I am the one protecting you, child."

Gabrielle opened her mouth to argue, then she went still. She looked away from Grandmother, her gaze resting anywhere but on one of us.

Drake rumbled in his throat, his eyes sparking red fire. "I don't take orders from you, Micalerianicum. You might be a decorated general, but I work for Bancroft."

"Who can't be allowed access to this kind of magic." Mick met Drake stare for stare. "Which means I fight you."

Drake didn't like that, but he didn't flinch. I'd seen a battle between them before—not the little one of last night, but a true dragon-to-dragon, all-out fight—and it had been nasty. I, for one, did not want to witness another fight like that.

Colby, on the other hand, wasn't shy about expressing his views. "Don't catch me in the middle of this shit, Mickey. If you fight him, I'm under this stupid binding spell, which means I'd have to join him to stop you. And I know you'd kick my ass. So if you plan to fight Drake, could you please wait five months, six days and . . ." Colby looked at the ceiling as he calculated. "Three hours and forty-five minutes."

"I'm flying Janet back," Mick said, ignoring him. "Ruby, would you make sure my bike is somewhere safe for the night? I'll send someone for it tomorrow morning."

"Oh, let me," Gabrielle said. "I'll take good care of your ride, Mick, I swear."

Colby chuckled. "I like her, in a weird sort of way."

"Come on, Mick." Gabrielle held out her hand for the keys.

Mick handed the keys to my grandmother, and Gabrielle scowled at him. "Ruby's right," she said. "Firewalkers are the most arrogant sons of bitches ever to come out of the earth. Just for that, I'm frying it." She started for the front door.

"No, you won't," Mick said calmly. "It's warded. Don't be a brat."

Gabrielle turned around and beamed a big smile at him. "You are such a shit. I always wanted a big brother, even if he is a dragon." She started for the door again, but as she passed Drake, she stopped and turned to him. She took a slow look at him, roving her gaze over his still body.

Drake was handsome as a human, with dark hair, sloe-black eyes, and swarthy skin. He was also tall and well built, with an athletic body. His suit, tailored for him, enhanced what he had rather than hid it. Because I'd seen him naked, I could safely say that Drake could make his own pinup calendar, and women would pay good money for it.

Drake also had no idea that he was attractive. Absolutely no sense of it at all. His arrogance didn't come from self-adoration.

Gabrielle ran her finger down his dark silk tie, pressing between his finely defined pectorals. "You, my friend, are *hot*. You ever want a vacation from that compound of yours, you come and find me."

She let her fingers go down, down, *way* down, while the rest of us watched in a kind of stunned fascination. Gabrielle skimmed her touch all the way down past Drake's belt to rest for a fraction of a second on his fly. Then she turned and walked out of the store.

Drake had jumped when her fingers had brushed his cock through his trousers, and now he stared after her in amazement. My grandmother snorted her disapproval, and Colby threw back his head and laughed.

"Damn. That was worth my captivity to see. Okay, maybe not, but thinking about it will make the time go by faster."

Drake scowled at him. He made for the door, catching up his leather coat. "Colby," he snapped.

"My master calls." Colby leaned down and kissed me

noisily on the cheek. "See you, Janet. If you need me, you know where to find me."

Grandmother was in a hurry to go after Gabrielle, but before she left, she addressed Mick, not me. "I trust that you'll take care of it."

Mick nodded. "I will."

She made another *humph* noise, and started out the front door.

"Take care of what?" I called.

Grandmother turned around. "Mick knows. Go find that pot, granddaughter. It's very important."

She was gone. Not in silence. I heard her remonstrating with Gabrielle to get away from the motorcycle, then start haranguing Drake to give them a ride back to their hotel and to take Mick's bike as well.

Mick grasped my elbow and turned me around. "Time to go."

"Take care of what?" I asked him.

Mick kissed me on the mouth. He steered me out the back and down the alley. I had to be quiet back here, damn him, and he knew it, so no more questions.

WE HAD TO WALK A LONG WAY TO FIND A SPACE BIG ENOUGH for him to change to dragon. We ended up beyond a railroad switchyard, in a deserted area among sidings. Railroad cars old and new lingered here, waiting to be hooked to an engine and carried off to a new destination.

Mick calmly undressed and gave me the care of his clothes and the glued-together pot. Then he kissed me again, jogged away into the darkness, and became dragon.

Mick's dragon was gigantic, black and gleaming in what was left of the moonlight. His eyes were black and golden, pupils tinged with red. He brought his great scaly head down to my level, the heat of his dragon body engulfing me.

I was never sure what to do with Mick in this form. He was still my Mick, but his dragon was a precise and deadly killing machine, and dragons did not have a lot of mercy in them. I couldn't communicate with him—I could talk, but he couldn't answer in words. I couldn't yet understand the snarls and roars dragons used, and the nuances of their body language was way beyond me.

However, when Mick closed his talons around me, he was gentleness itself. He lifted me without moving a hair on my head and cradled me against his warm chest, sheltering me from the night.

That was fine, but as soon as he launched himself from the ground, my stomach pretty much stayed behind, and I had to fight my screams. Think of the scariest, most stomach-churning ride at an amusement park, and then multiply that by about a hundred and fifty. That's flying with a dragon.

Mick shot across the darkness, dragon wings pumping in the night. I huddled against his chest, clutching everything I was trying to carry, and tried not to think about the hundreds of feet of empty space between me and the hard ground.

Happily, nothing happened to make him drop me. Mick held me competently, even keeping me warm, and we landed a few hours later in the desert behind my hotel, the railroad bed between us and the Crossroads.

When I say *landed*, I mean Mick dove for the ground with the force of a cannonball. At the last minute, he reversed, bringing his hind feet down, his great wings spreading like sails.

He touched down with a *whump*, but when he leaned to lower me, again it was with every tenderness.

I stood up, unkinking my stiff limbs and trying to catch my breath. Mick glided away into the darkness, shifted, and came walking back, my tall man replete with muscles and dragon tatts.

"You okay?" he asked when he reached me.

I handed him his clothes. "Dragon is not the most comfortable way to travel."

"Sorry." Mick sounded sorry. "But we needed to get here fast."

"I know. Any sign of a runaway Nightwalker as we flew?" Not that I thought there would have been.

"Didn't see any," Mick said.

I started to walk toward the hotel, but Mick drew me back. One arm full of his clothes, he wrapped the other around me and kissed me on the mouth.

His healing magic entered me through the kiss. My legs stopped trembling, and my stomach settled down.

He released me, dressed, and we walked together back to the hotel.

Cassandra was locking the doors for the night, though she planned to stay, not knowing how long I'd be absent. Pamela was there with her.

"I don't know where he went," Cassandra said before I asked. "Even Elena couldn't stop him. Ansel wasn't blood frenzied, just determined."

Mick and I went downstairs to Ansel's room to hunt for any clue to where he'd gone, but we came up with one big nothing. Nothing specific, anyway.

Mick stood in the middle of the tidy chamber, his blue eyes taking in everything. "He's gone to try to find Laura."

"I figured," I said. "The dragons thought Ansel had Laura, and I bet Ansel thinks the dragons have her. If he breaks into the dragon compound . . ."

"He hasn't," Mick said. "I would have heard."

"You mean he hasn't *yet*."

"Colby will tell me the minute he shows up. They know

Ansel's under my protection, and that if they kill him, they have to mess with me."

"Doesn't mean they won't kill him and take their chances," I said unhappily. "We need to find him."

"I'll search. You need to rest and eat something."

"I had a sandwich before I went to Laura's store."

Mick came to me. "And a fight with a bad-ass mage, who knocked you out and nearly killed you." He looked down at me, the raw pain in his eyes erasing his habitual calm. Here was a man who felt deeply, with emotions I couldn't begin to understand.

He smoothed my hair with a hand that shook a little. "He could have killed you, Janet. He didn't have to leave you alive. And I wouldn't have been there to stop it."

"I was still walking the storm," I said. "And he couldn't have gotten past my Beneath magic in the end. He's strong, but not my evil mother strong."

Mick exhaled, and at the end of it he pressed his lips to the top of my head. "You don't get it, do you? It's all I can do not to drag you out to my island and keep you there, safe from Nightwalkers, dragons, your goddess mother—from everyone who ever tried to hurt you. I want to so bad, it's killing me not to."

"Is that your dragon instinct?" I asked. His eyes had gone black now, without a hint of blue, his hand resting against the side of my head, strength there but contained. "What would I do all day on your tropical island?"

"Whatever the hell you wanted. I wouldn't give a shit. You'd be safe."

"I'd be bored. Your island is nice, but I can only drink so many Mai Tais on the beach. I'd start hankering to see my dad, my friends, the Diné lands . . ."

"And I wouldn't care," he said, his voice on the edge of a growl. "I fight against my instincts every day. I want to keep you safe, but I also want you to be happy. I know I can't have both. So I hold back." Mick put his other hand on the small of my back, grip firm, no holding back there. "I force myself to let you live in your world. I watch over you and work the wards on this hotel, but I know it's not enough. Will never be enough. I can't ever truly keep you safe out here, and *I can't explain to you how much I hate that.*"

My mouth opened as I listened. His words were grating, the dragon in him looking out from his black eyes.

Mick had always been protective, but I'd had no idea he fought himself not to be as protective as he wanted to be. I knew that if he chose to sweep me up and keep me sequestered on his island, he could do it, and I'd have a hard time fighting him. He could have done it tonight.

"I'm not good at being confined," I said, my voice faint. "I never have been. I'd end up trying to kill you to get away."

"I know that. I also know I could stop you. I almost did before."

"That was different." I put my hands on his chest. His heart was beating rapidly, the skin beneath his shirt hot. "You had me in a place where I couldn't fight back." In a cave full of scary petroglyphs that tried to feed off my boiling evil magic.

"I know," he said. "I manipulated you there, because I knew I'd have the advantage. I'd do the same thing again, this time to protect you. The only reason I don't . . ." Mick stopped and drew a breath. "I don't because . . . I love you."

His eyes switched to blue when he said it. My throat went tight. "I love you too, Mick."

"You still don't understand. Dragons don't love."

"What are you talking about? You love." Mick loved —fiercely.

"No, dragons obsess. We hoard, and we defend what we hoard. We mate to produce offspring, which we also possessively defend. All dragons know that another dragon's one weak point is his lair."

"I thought it was the true name."

Mick shook his head. "No dragon will reveal his true name to another dragon, even accidentally. But the lair can be found, can be attacked. We'll defend it to the death. Not because we love it, but because it's *ours*."

"And now I'm yours."

"Yes." The dragon black returned to his eyes. "If what I felt for you was desire alone, it wouldn't be so hard for me. I'd lock you away and be done with it. I'd own you, keep you—end of story. But for some reason, I've decided I want you to be happy. It hurts me when you aren't happy." Mick let out a breath. "This . . . this *need* . . . is new."

And strange to him. I thought about the times Mick watched me with a look I couldn't decipher. He'd study me as though trying to figure me out, to understand why the hell I did the things I did.

I hadn't realized he was battling himself, torn between wanting to bury me in his comfortable prison and letting me walk around free and happy, but in severe and constant danger. He went through this dilemma every day.

I ran my hands up Mick's chest again, brushing my thumbs over the hollow of his throat. "When you start leaning toward sequestering me, let me know. I'll help you fight it."

"No guarantees that you can."

He took my mouth in a long, slow kiss, one that said that if we weren't trying to find Ansel and figure out the secret of this pot, he'd have me on Ansel's mission-style bed in a heartbeat.

Instead he released me, his eyes changing to blue again.

I knew he was right that fighting him would be tricky. While Mick wasn't affected by my storm magic, my Beneath magic was a little different. Dragon magic was the magic of this earth, magic forged in the inferno of volcanoes. Beneath magic came from the worlds that existed before this one, where gods held power, and humans were few. Beneath magic was different from earth magic—in some ways more powerful, and in some ways less.

Mick, though, was resourceful enough and strong enough to compensate against my Beneath magic. I'd never won a contest of magics against him, and I never wanted to have to.

We wouldn't find Ansel by standing here talking about our bizarre relationship. After another bone-searing kiss, Mick led me back upstairs, where Cassandra was busily looking over the glued-together pot. While Mick ducked into my office, saying he needed to make a few phone calls—and probably to calm down from our little talk downstairs—I approached Cassandra and leaned my elbows on the counter.

"Do you know what that is?" I asked.

She shook her head, still studying the patterns. "I've never heard about anything like it, or anything about these designs. I could look it up, but . . ." She set down the pot. Pamela picked it up, turning it in her hands, but she didn't look enlightened either.

I finished Cassandra's thought. "But if you ask about it on your Wiccan network, you'll alert other mages to its existence."

"Exactly. Witches and mages are always looking for something with which to enhance power. From what you've told me, a lot of people seem to want it. I'd be careful who finds out about it."

"Have you heard of Pericles McKinnon?" I asked.

"Yes." Cassandra looked at me so sharply that Pamela set down the pot and stepped closer to her. "He's cunning and mean," Cassandra went on. "And powerful. Why?"

"Like Emmett Smith powerful?"

"Not as strong as Emmett, but close. Pericles makes it no secret that he'd love to push Emmett out of power."

I nodded. "He said as much to me."

"Why don't we just let Emmett have at him, then?" Pamela asked. "Pesky mage problem solved."

"The enemy of my enemy?" I mused. Pamela had met Emmett too, and her wolf had wanted to chomp on him. I'd love to have let her. "If Emmett kills Pericles for us, then we'd have to worry about Emmett trying to get his hands on this pot. The last thing we need is an all-powerful mage going for more power."

"I'll try to see what I can find out without alerting anyone," Cassandra said. I knew she could, since she was one of the most resourceful and efficient people I'd ever met. "Laura must have known more about it than she let on, even to Ansel."

"Which is why we need to find her."

Mick came out from my office, which was still dark. He hadn't bothered turning on the light in there. "I've asked people around town, but no one's seen Ansel. But I'm going to scour the ground for him. Eat something, Janet."

"Not here," Pamela said. "Elena's closed the kitchen. And locked it. I want a snack, but I guess I'll have to go hunt a rabbit."

"Not if you're sleeping with me, you're not," Cassandra said briskly. "That's why the Goddess invented all-night diners. Both of you go. Eat."

WHICH WAS HOW PAMELA AND I ENDED UP AT THE DINER IN Magellan. Pamela actually going somewhere with me said a lot for her hunger. We rode our separate motorcycles but walked into the diner more or less together and sat at the counter next to each other.

I had to admit that Mick had been smart to prescribe dinner. Lifting a hot, juicy burger with all the fixings to my mouth made me realize how hungry I was. Fighting all-powerful mages, arguing with Drake and my grandmother, worrying about Gabrielle searching for a magical artifact, and flying back from Santa Fe in a dragon talon gave me a hearty appetite.

A guy in a jeans jacket with a chunky silver wristband slid

onto the empty stool next to me. He took up a lot of space and shoved his big elbow into me when he opened his menu.

I looked over to tell him to be careful, then half my burger splatted back to my plate, bathing me in droplets of ketchup.

The guy was Indian, with a long black braid, a wide, handsome face, soul-searching brown eyes, and a white-toothed grin.

"Hey, Janet," Coyote said.

CHAPTER SIXTEEN

"HOLY FUCKING SHIT!"

My voice carried. Conversation dipped, and every head in the place turned to me. Parents glowered in disapproval, and I think a baby started to cry.

Then everyone gave one another looks that said, *It's just Janet,* and returned to eating.

Coyote sat there smiling at me. As though Bear hadn't stabbed him with a stone knife made by the gods, as though I hadn't watched him die in the desert and disappear into swirling dust. He looked whole and unhurt, his black button-down shirt unwrinkled, his hair neat in its braid. The cowboy hat he liked to wear rested on the empty stool beside him.

He was there, solidly, but I recalled another night I'd sworn he'd been sitting next to me at this very counter, only to learn he'd been riding in Naomi Kee's pickup at the exact same moment. No one in the diner had seen him but me.

I swung to Pamela, but she'd left her seat and was making her way to the ladies room, so I waved down the waitress who wandered along the counter, coffeepot in hand.

"Jolene," I said. "Someone is sitting here beside me, right?"
I pointed.

Jolene stopped, smiled, and filled the cup Coyote pushed
toward her. "Hi, Coyote. Been a while."

"You do see him, then?" I asked.

Jolene gave me an odd look as she refilled my cup, but she,
like everyone else in Magellan, was pretty convinced I was
crazy. "Yes. I see Coyote, the storyteller. He comes here a lot.
Are you feeling all right?"

"Fine." I picked up my coffee cup and dumped half the
burning liquid down my throat.

Jolene winked at Coyote. "Giant cheeseburger, rare, and a
mess of fries, right?"

"You got it, sweetie."

Jolene turned away, putting a little wiggle in her hips.
Every woman flirted with Coyote.

Then again, Coyote could be deluding Jolene as well. I
reached over and pinched his wrist, hard.

"*Ow!* Hey, Salas, you saw that, didn't you?"

Emilio, still in uniform but trying to enjoy his dinner at a
booth behind us, looked up. "Give it up, Coyote. She's with
Mick." The other diners either chuckled at the exchange or
ignored it completely.

"You know, if you're into it, Janet, I'm game. We'll ditch
Mick and have some fun. Or he can come with us. I know you
two like a little of the rough stuff."

"Will you stop that?" I said in a fervent whisper. "What the
hell is this? You died. I watched you die. Was it a trick? Did
you think it would be funny to put me through that? I should
kill you myself."

Coyote lost his grin. "No, that was real. Bear killed me."

"Seriously—what the fuck is going on?"

"It's a test. For me. We've been doing this for millennia.
How else am I going to prove myself to her?"

"Prove yourself?"

"All women need to know their guy is sincere."

"By letting her *kill* you?"

"Yep."

"This is crazy."

Coyote tore off the ends of five packets of sugar and streamed them into his coffee. "I know your grandmother told you stories about Coyote when you were a kid, the clean ones anyway. If you don't know what I'm talking about, it means you weren't listening."

"I was seven. My mind wandered. Give me a break."

Coyote tore open another five packets of sugar and dumped those into the coffee as well. He picked up a spoon and stirred noisily. "Bear and I go for a while without seeing each other. Decades, sometimes centuries. Then I get the hankering to be with her, so I let her know where I'm hanging out." He picked up his cup and took a noisy sip. "She comes to find me, but before I'm allowed to touch her, I have to pass her tests. Sometimes it's feats of strength, sometimes it's letting her kill me. Several times."

"*Several times?* Are you insane? Or is she?"

He shrugged and drank more coffee. "It's a challenge, Janet. We enjoy it. Let an old married couple play some love games."

"But if she loves you so much, why put you through that?" And put *me* through that? "Why don't you just buy her flowers? Or jewelry. We like jewelry."

Coyote pressed his broad hand to his chest. "Because I'm *Coyote*. I love the ladies. I sleep around. I pull wild pranks. Bear has to know that, when I call her, I'm not just bored, or want to use her for something. She's not going to let me touch her until she's sure that I really, *really* need to see her. Not that I just want some." He grinned. "She has to know it's not just a booty call."

"Either you truly love her, or you're even crazier than I give you credit for. Why else would you do that?"

Coyote took on a fond look, and his eyes softened into an affection I'd never seen in him before. "She's an amazing woman. Totally worth it. Besides, have you ever been with someone who can turn into a bear? It's like nothing you've ever experienced, and it's something you'll never forget."

I snatched up my messy burger. "You could have told me," I said between my teeth. "You could have told me you'd come back to life, instead of letting me grieve like that."

"Oh, hey." Coyote took one of my ketchup-stained hands and pressed it between his. "Sweetie, I didn't think you'd grieve. Not for me."

"Of course I would. How stupid are you?"

I had tears in my eyes. Coyote's smile had completely vanished, his look concerned. "I'm sorry, Janet. I didn't realize. And anyway, when I was lying out there, I wasn't sure. Bear knows how to kill me permanently. One day she might destroy the last of my life essence, and I'll be gone forever. I also never know how long it will be before she bothers to bring me back. It's a kind of trust thing between us. I'm showing I trust her by putting my life into her hands. Literally."

"Gods, it's like an S&M relationship taken to the bizarre." I wiped my eyes. "Anyway, why didn't *she* tell me? I thought Bear was my friend."

"She doesn't like to talk about her personal life, particularly her relationship with me. Not her fault you happened to be taking your morning stroll while we were courting."

"Courting? You're both out of your minds."

"We're gods," Coyote said patiently. "Comes with the territory. Aw, thank you, sweetheart," he said as Jolene shoved a platter in front of him filled with the biggest burger the diner made plus a mountain of thick, golden fries. "This looks great. Being dead makes me hungry."

"I know how you feel," Jolene said, topping up his coffee. "When I got out of bed this morning, I could barely find the bathroom. Never right until I have coffee inside me."

She cheerfully walked away, and Coyote dug into his burger.

I'd lost my appetite. "Are you going to sit there and eat like nothing happened?"

"Yep," Coyote said around bites. He glanced at my plate. "You going to finish that?"

I pushed it at him. "I can't believe I was grieving for you. What a waste of time."

Coyote put down his burger, wiped his fingers, and laid his hand on mine. "Did you truly grieve? Are you sure?"

"Of course I'm sure! How would I not be sure?" I thought of how torn up I'd been after his body had vanished, and I wanted to smack him.

"I appreciate that," Coyote said. "I really do." He looked straight into my eyes. "I won't forget."

"Good." I poked at my own burger, but I didn't want it anymore. I plucked a fry or two from his plate and ate them. "When you're feeling less hungry, I need to ask you about something."

"What's that?"

"Eat, then come with me."

Coyote grinned, his lewd look back. "I like the sound of that."

I didn't bother with an answer.

Coyote didn't hurry. He ate his burger and fries, bantered with Jolene, waved at and talked to other diners, and downed the other half of my burger. Pamela finished her dinner without saying much and left without me, not being too fond of Coyote. She didn't like to stay away from Cassandra long either.

Coyote finally finished and pushed both plates away. He actually paid for his meal with a crumpled twenty instead of foisting the bill off on me or some other gullible person in the diner.

I took him outside and to my bike, unlocked one of the

saddlebags and pulled out my wadded up coat, which I'd wrapped around the pot. I unfolded the coat, baring the pot for Coyote's scrutiny.

Under the weak lights of the diner's parking lot, the vessel looked as ancient as it was supposed to. The crumbling paint, faded bear and tortoise designs, and even the cracks where Colby had repaired it, made it look old and valuable.

"Where did you get this?"

Coyote's voice was harsh and cold, all trace of teasing or affection gone.

I gave him a startled look. "From Richard Young, a collector in Santa Fe. *He* got it from a woman named Laura DiAngelo, who's an antiques dealer, and Ansel, my Night-walker. The collector thought he was buying an ancient Indian pot, and instead they gave him this and hid the real one."

Coyote took it from me. He turned it around in his hands, his expression fierce. "Where did they find the original?"

"In a museum—a private one in Flagstaff."

"Where did *they* get it?"

"I have no idea."

"You need to find out. Now. Then destroy this thing."

I stared at Coyote as he shoved the pot back at me. "It's only a replica."

"Doesn't matter. They'll be coming for it. They'll take this from you because it points to the real thing—it tells the world what it looks like. They won't care if they have to kill you to get it, or how rough they are when they tear the knowledge of it from you."

Coyote rarely showed his anger, but he was showing it now. All trace of the affable storyteller who high-fived kids and swapped greetings with people in the town square had been replaced by a towering man with burning eyes. Coyote the god had returned.

"Who are *they*?" I asked. "What am I fighting this time?"

"Everyone who's ever wanted power. The mages, the skinwalkers, Nightwalkers, dragons, Changers, the gods. Destroy this copy, find out how the museum in Flagstaff got the original, and then find the original and bring it to me."

I couldn't stop staring. "You're saying that every magical being in existence could start a free-for-all over a *pot*?"

"It's not just a pot. It's a vessel of the gods. Full of power. Anyone who possesses the real thing could have unlimited access to magic, which means unlimited power. Whoever gains it can kill all other rivals, or start a magical war that scorches the earth. They could open the vortexes and let loose the evil Beneath. They could shake apart the world."

Not good. Not good at all. "If this vessel is so dangerous, then why am I just now hearing about it?"

"It was supposed to have been destroyed. Tossed into the volcano that's now Sunset Crater to be buried between the layers of this world and the one Beneath. And it turns up in a museum in Flagstaff." He snorted. "Humans will stick *anything* into a glass case and charge admission to see it."

I held the pot out to him. "If all magical beings will try to kill me to get to it, why don't you destroy it for me?"

Coyote raised his hands and took a step back. "Because I'm a god. I can't be found near the thing. Even a replica. Or the other gods will strike."

"So *I* have to do all the dirty work?" I asked angrily. "Figure out where it came from and where it is, all by myself? And if you can't be found near it, why should I bring you the real one?"

"Because I'm strong enough to make myself destroy it before I'm tempted by it. No one else will be. *No one.* That's what you need to understand."

I lowered the pot, which, though light, seemed to drag down my arm. "Laura—and maybe Ansel—knows where the real one is. Wait, that means *Ansel* already wants this thing?"

"Ansel has rendered himself powerless to live among you in peace. He likes you and trusts you. But if he could have unlim-

ited magic at his disposal, if he could gain revenge for everything that's been done to him, and no one could stop him. . .
What do you think he'd do?"

Dismay was pouring over me, followed by a good dose of
alarm and anxiety. "Shit."

"You must keep it away from him. Even if Ansel thinks
he'd doing the right thing by hiding it, he won't be able to
resist it for long." Coyote held me with a hard look. "When I
said *no one* is strong enough not to be tempted, I meant it.
Including Mick."

My heart sank. "I can't do this without Mick."

"Mick has a lot to worry about, including convincing a
Stormwalker that she wants to spend the rest of her life with
him. Mick's one of the top dragons. Think what he could do
with a talisman that built up his magic into a powerhouse."

"Mick also has a load of common sense. He's worried about
the real pot falling into the wrong hands. We've already had a
run-in with a mage." I told him what had happened with
Pericles.

"You see?" Coyote said, not sounding very surprised. "It's
started. The sooner you find the pot, the better."

"Oh thanks. And anyway, what about me? What happens
when I get my hands on a vessel of the gods, full of magical
juju? I have volatile Beneath magic in me, and I'm sure the
Stormwalker side of me wouldn't mind a boost either. I have a
lot of scores to settle."

Coyote's grim expression fled, and he relaxed into a smile.
He closed the space between us, cupped his hands around my
face, and pressed a kiss to my forehead. "Because you're Janet.
You're the only one I trust."

My mouth popped open. "Me? Why?"

"Because you grieved for me."

I blinked at him a few times, Coyote's callused hands warm
on my face. "That makes no sense at all."

"Yes, it does. Find the vessel for me, sweetie. And don't let anyone else get their hands on it. At all costs." He released me and settled his jeans jacket against the breeze that had sprung up. "Oh, by the way, get your magic mirror fixed. You'll need it."

I wrapped the jacket around the pot and tucked both into my saddlebag, locking it again. "You toss off these impossible tasks like they're nothing. Find the real pot before anyone else does. Fix the magic mirror. Like I can snap my fingers, and all this will just happen."

I found myself talking to an empty space. Coyote was gone, nothing but the prints of his cowboy boots left in the dust where he'd stood.

"And I *hate* when you do that," I said, but my words died on the rising wind.

∼

WHEN I GOT BACK TO THE HOTEL, PAMELA WAS THERE, lounging against the counter in my lobby while Cassandra finished her spreadsheets for the day. Pamela's long body, comfortable in jeans and boots and tank top, matched the rangy look of her wolf.

"Mick called for you," Pamela said when I walked back in, the pot still wrapped in my jacket. "He said he wants you to meet him on the 40 a few miles east of Holbrook. He'll flag you down."

"What's wrong?" I asked in alarm.

"He didn't say," Pamela said. "I just took the message. Cassandra was too busy to answer the phone."

She never moved from leaning back on her elbows, but her annoyance that she had to wait for Cassandra to finish for the night rang clear. Pamela liked her alone time with Cassandra, and didn't want one minute to go to something else.

"Cassandra, if you have time, do you know a mage—one I

can trust—to fix the magic mirror?" If Coyote said it was important, it was important.

"Problematic," Cassandra said without looking up.

Always a problem telling other mages about a magic mirror. They'd all want it. Like the feeding frenzy Coyote said would happen with the pot.

"Well, any ideas you have, I'm willing to hear," I said.

Pamela flashed me another look, becoming more possessive of her mate and their time together by the second. I decided to leave them to it. I gave the fake pot to Cassandra to put into the safe, then ducked down the hall to my private rooms to use the bathroom and wash the ketchup from the corners of my mouth before I left to find Mick.

My route, as always, took me through Flat Mesa. I obeyed the slow speed limit through and around the little town, because I knew Nash had trained his deputies to happily write me a ticket for going one mile per hour over and demand the fee be paid before I left town again.

As much as I throttled back my bike though, a sheriff's SUV pulled in behind me. Lights flashed, and he was pulling me over.

When Sheriff Jones hopped out of his SUV and walked to me, I took off my helmet and pointed at my speedometer. "Thirty-five," I said. "Not thirty-six or thirty-four. If you changed the speed limit, it's not posted."

"I didn't pull you over for speeding," Nash said. "I pulled you over because you're a witness. Or maybe an accessory."

"Witness to what?"

Nash stood calmly in the glare from his headlights, minus the sunglasses he habitually wore during the day. The lights brushed over his close buzz of black hair and made his eyes a clear gray.

"To murder," he said. "What else?"

CHAPTER SEVENTEEN

I WENT ICE COLD DESPITE THE BALMY WIND BLOWING OVER us. "What murder? Who? When?" I thought about Ansel pushing his way out of the hotel past two powerful mages, and tried to stem my panic.

"A man with a crossbow," Nash said. "Found dead on the side of the freeway not half an hour ago. He's pretty torn up."

Crossbow meant slayer. Maybe normal people enjoyed running around in the desert after dark, shooting at things with crossbows, but I doubted it. The question was, which slayer?

"How am I a witness or accessory?" I asked. "Half an hour ago, I was leaving the diner in Magellan. Plenty of people can attest to that. Jolene. Pamela. Even Coyote."

Nash didn't look impressed. "A man with a crossbow was seen running down the railroad bed heading away from your place yesterday morning. Then there was that vigilante I arrested who was after Ansel. I'm sure there were more incidents." He gave me his cold stare. "You knew about these attempts, and you didn't report them."

"Because this is supernatural stuff—Mick and I handle that."

"This is where we disagree," Nash said. "I want to know everything that goes on with you. Why are these hunters hot and bothered enough to try to kill Ansel? Is he going crazy again?"

"I hope not." I prayed not. My Nightwalker had rushed out into the night, Cassandra and Elena unable to stop him, and now a slayer had been killed.

"This have anything to do why you drove at top speed into New Mexico two days ago, and why you and Mick went back there this morning?"

I figured Nash would know all my comings and goings. I wouldn't be surprised if Frank Yellow had called him after he'd released me. I imagined their conversation — Frank: *You know about this woman?* Nash: Yeah, she's trouble. Leave her to me. I'll keep her in line.

I hadn't wanted to bring Nash into this, but I knew he'd find out sooner or later.

I told him the story, as I knew it, up until now. I didn't mention Ansel's fear that he'd killed Laura, now groundless, because Laura was still alive. I also left out the part about me destroying Young's house and his collection. I'm sure that incident had made it onto a police report somewhere, and Nash might already know, but I didn't want to talk about it.

Nash listened — with no reaction, just his stare — and I don't know whether he believed all I told him or not. He wasn't one to accept facts without checking them out.

"Let's get up to the scene of the crime," he said when I finished. "I'll be right behind you." He made it sound like a threat.

I sedately rode the rest of the way out of Flat Mesa and up the highway to Holbrook. That town was already buttoned up for the night, and we didn't meet much traffic as we wended through it and drove up onto the freeway.

We rode about five miles east on the 40 before I saw Mick

and his big bike, and state police cruisers as well as county sheriff's cars, lights flashing, on the shoulder.

This stretch was out of Nash's jurisdiction, but the state police sometimes called him for his opinion, because Nash had a good reputation for thoroughness. He also wasn't competitive about who caught the bad guy. As long as someone got locked up somewhere, he was happy.

Nash turned on his cop lights as he eased his SUV over, and I pulled up alongside Mick. I yanked off my helmet. "What happened?" I asked him.

Mick steadied my bike as I killed the engine, got off, and hung my helmet on the seat. "I smelled him out there while I was looking for Ansel," Mick said. "A Nightwalker did this, Janet."

I looked at him in disquiet. "You're going to tell me you haven't found Ansel, aren't you?"

"Haven't found him—yet."

I hated this more and more. "Was the scent Ansel's?"

"Couldn't tell. Too much dead slayer. I think it's the slayer you fought a couple mornings ago, the first one."

I remembered the guy sticking a crossbow in my face while he fired the other one at Ansel. Now he was a heap of bone and flesh on a stretcher being carried to the waiting ambulance. Poor guy. Dying by Nightwalker was not a good way to go.

"Come and look at the scene," Nash said to me before he climbed down the gully on the side of the road and headed for the lights in the desert.

Recent rains had filled the dry washes, and though the water had receded, the ground was still slick and muddy. By tomorrow afternoon, unless another storm rolled through, the land would be bone dry again, but for now, I had to slosh through mud and wet grass.

A generator-run light had been set up where Mick had found the body. We were about thirty yards from the freeway and well hidden by dips in the land and overgrown brush.

The lights fell on flattened grasses stained with blood. Quite a lot of blood. The very young state police trooper who'd been left to watch over the scene kept trying not to look at it.

The slayer hadn't died that long ago. Maybe a few hours, not more, and Nash said that the medical examiner had agreed. The blood had congealed on the grasses but hadn't been washed away yet.

I was aware of scavengers gathering around the perimeter of our light—tall turkey vultures unworried by our presence, and coyotes that yipped and snarled in the darkness. They wouldn't find much when we left the scene to them, but they smelled the blood, and they were hungry.

I knew without asking that Nash had brought me here to examine the aura of the scene. The psychic residue was already coming to me—violence and fear, desperation, terror, and then pain, horrific pain, followed by a blank.

I was already shaking before I stretched out my hands over the kill site and closed my eyes. Mick's bulk beside me reassured me somewhat, but I was still queasy.

I saw the aura of the slayer himself—faint, yellow, no rage in him. He'd hunted Ansel because he'd wanted the money and thought Nightwalkers were vermin. He was like a glorified rat catcher.

The Nightwalker aura was there too, black with orange streaks, smelling of blood and death. And fear. I saw fear in the aura, a Nightwalker thinking he was about to die.

Which posed the question. Did Ansel kill the slayer in blood frenzy? Or fight in his nice guy persona, in fear for his life?

I opened my eyes. "I don't think Ansel did this."

"Why not?" Nash asked. "The man was trying to kill him. Ansel fought back, went into his Nightwalker rage, and killed him."

I stared down at the torn-up grass. "Too much blood," I said. "Nightwalkers drain their victims completely. Once they start feeding, they can't stop. Ansel goes into his blood frenzy because he wants blood, not just a kill. He might break apart the corpse afterward, but by then it's dried skin and bones."

The trooper, who'd turned to watch me in curiosity, looked shocked and sick. First body, I suspected.

Mick said, "Janet's right. Too much blood."

"But a Nightwalker was here," I said. "Maybe the slayer tried to kill Ansel but Ansel got away."

"Or whoever killed the slayer took Ansel," Mick said.

Nash looked skeptical. "Who else would want to kill a vampire bounty hunter besides a vampire? Vigilantes are tough. They don't go down easily, and this guy didn't even get a chance to fire his weapon."

"A supernatural killer then," I said. "Let me look around."

I didn't want to walk beyond the circle of light where the coyotes and the birds waited to scrounge for whatever they could get. But the aura of death and Nightwalker was so strong that if a third person had been there, his or her aura had been masked.

I made myself walk a perimeter of about twenty feet, Nash and Mick with me. Mick was right beside me, his aura smoky black shot with red. Nash was with me too, but his aura was a blank. Always was.

I didn't find anything else. I felt the tiny auras of the vultures and coyotes, plus snakes also attracted by the warm smell of blood. Beyond that, nothing. The fight had been intense in that one spot, but no one else had wandered out here.

After a time, I gave up and shook my head. "Sorry."

Nash let out his breath. "Not helpful. What are you getting, Mick?"

"She's right. I don't smell anything other than what happened at the fight."

"Mmm." Nash stood looking around, but it was clear he

didn't see anything or sense anything either. "I'm interested in talking to your friend Ansel. Find him and bring him to me."

"Get in line," I said.

Nash had turned to walk back to the crime scene, but he swung around again. "No—bring him to me first. It's important."

Without letting either of us answer, he walked on toward the lights.

I looked at Mick, and he looked back at me, his eyes black in the darkness. "Do you have *any* idea which direction Ansel went?" I asked.

"East." Mick slid his hand down my arm and locked his fingers around mine. "He must be trying to find out where he left Laura, and figure out what he was doing at Chaco Canyon."

"Chaco Canyon," I repeated. "That keeps cropping up. There was some reason I was taken up there in the first place."

"I say we find out."

"It's a long way from here."

"Not if I fly."

I shivered. "Not that I don't appreciate seeing you naked as often as possible, but I still haven't recovered from the trip back from Santa Fe."

Mick's teeth flashed in the darkness. "I'll make it up to you."

His way of saying, *Suck it up, Janet.*

I let out a sigh. "As long as we can leave our bikes some-place safe."

WE LEFT THEM IN THE PARKING LOT OF THE HOPI COUNTY Sheriff's Department. No one in their right minds would steal anything from Nash's parking lot, and if they weren't in their right minds, Nash would lock them up and explain why they needed to be.

I walked with Mick back out of town and into the desert where he could change to dragon.

As Mick lowered his head to look at me, I reflected that I was always stunned that this sinuous black, gigantic dragon was *Mick*. He wasn't a cold lizard—his scales were warm and satiny, a pleasure to touch. I rubbed my hand under his eye, which I knew he liked, and he rewarded me with a rumble, like a colossal cat who's decided to purr.

I'd become more used to Mick like this over the past year. I was comfortable enough to press a kiss to the end of his nose before he lifted me in his talons and tucked me against his chest.

I closed my eyes as he took his dizzying leap into the air, and kept them closed while he took off across the night.

We made it to Chaco Canyon fairly quickly, Mick landing on his powerful back legs, wings spread. He carefully set me down, and I rubbed my arms, catching my breath, while Mick changed back to human form.

Dragons shift a little differently from Changers and other shapeshifters. They cause a black mist or cloud to form around their bodies, and from this emerges either the dragon or the human. I asked Mick about it once—was the darkness the magic that made the change? Or a side effect of the magic?

Mick had blinked at me and said he didn't know. Which meant he didn't care. It worked, and it wasn't important to him. If it *had* been important to him, Mick would have been able to tell me every single detail about it, probably more than I ever wanted to know.

Mick came walking out of the cloud, human-shaped once more. He didn't bother with the clothes I'd once more carried for him, but there was no one out here to see him. He took my hand, and we walked together to the ruins, which lay silent under the moonlight.

The layers of auras began to pound at me, but Mick's hand in mine both kept me steady and served as a conduit to the little bit of healing magic he trickled into me.

If we hadn't been looking for a Nightwalker, possibly in a killing frenzy, in a dark place sacred to the gods and full of ancient auras, I'd like this. My boyfriend walked tall by my side, we were alone in a night of beauty, and we were in love.

But our lives were such that the best places for us to look for romance were generic hotel rooms, far from anything magical and anyone who knew us. Moonlit walks among ruins only meant potential trouble.

Mick at least pulled on his jeans before I showed him the campsite where Laura had disappeared. The campground was open again, but few people were here tonight. A place where someone had recently been abducted made all but the hardiest curiosity seekers shy away. By day, fine; staying here overnight, no.

The aura of the fight between dragon and Nightwalker had faded further, but Mick nodded at me, smelling what I'd sensed. We knew that Laura had gotten away from Colby and Ansel, but not where she'd gone.

We tried to find her trail into the desert. The terrain was tough, it was dark, and I stumbled over rocks and scrub. Mick walked more steadily on his bare feet, which wasn't fair, but he was Mick.

"There," he said.

He started walking ahead of me, picking a trail for me across the uneven ground. Moonlight highlighted his straight back down to the flame tattoo that rode across his hips, right above the jeans' waistline.

Now he stopped and pointed into a crease of wash that cut across our path. I heard coyotes rustling in the darkness, watching us.

Mick walked unerringly to a place in the soft wall of the

wash where someone had been digging. Not an animal—the marks were too regular, made by a trowel or small spade.

I crouched down. Someone had dug a hole and covered it back up again. Mick sank back on his heels and gingerly began scraping the dirt away. Out here in the cool darkness, any hole probably contained a snake, either one sleeping or one waiting to feed, so Mick moved the dirt very carefully.

A snake did lay coiled in this hole about an inch beneath the surface. Mick said a soft, sort of hissing word I didn't understand and lifted out, by its neck, five feet of rattlesnake. The snake slid its body around Mick's arm, but gently, touching as though getting to know him.

Mick carried the snake a few yards down the wash and released it. "Good hunting, my friend."

"He a cousin or something?" I asked Mick when he came back.

"She," Mick corrected me, deadpan. "No relation."

"You speak reptile?"

Mick gave me a modest look. "Learned it at my mama's knee. Now let's see what she was guarding."

Nothing. When Mick cleared out the hole, we found it empty. But the aura that burst out like a comet when Mick cleared away the last of the rocks and dirt smacked me hard and sent me backward onto the rocky ground.

CHAPTER EIGHTEEN

"IT WAS HERE."

I lay on my back, gasping for breath. The residue of whatever magic coated the pot entangled me in its net like strands of live wire. My heart jerked, then raced, as though someone had just defibrillated me.

Mick was instantly at my side, the moonlight showing the concern on his face. He helped me back to my feet with strong hands. "I feel it too."

"It's not here now," another voice broke in. "Neither is she."

I knew the voice, and when the aura that had knocked me over receded a little, I could feel him too. Tall and lanky, his brown hair shining in the moonlight, his clothes blood-free, Ansel stopped a few feet from us and gazed at us with mournful eyes.

"Ansel," I said in relief. "You all right?"

"If you mean, am I blood frenzied, then I can safely say I'm not." Ansel gazed at the dark opening in the bank of the wash, the pent-up aura still plenty strong. "I've been searching for something that points me to her."

"What about the slayer?" Mick asked.

"Which one?" Ansel gave him the ghost of a smile. "I'm losing track of them all."

"The one Janet and I scared off two mornings ago," Mick said. "He's dead on the side of the 40, near Holbrook."

Ansel's eyes widened in surprise. "Dead?" His astonishment was replaced by alarm when he looked at our expressions. "You think by me? No. I was nowhere near Holbrook tonight. I hitched a ride with a guy who was going through Snowflake and St. John's. Then another guy out to Gallup. Then I walked."

Nightwalkers could move fast, covering miles in a matter of minutes. Nightwalkers don't need to breathe and don't get tired. As long as the sun isn't around, they're stronger than any human athlete could aspire to be.

But that meant that not only could Ansel have gotten here quickly on foot, he could have made a detour to kill a slayer.

"How did you know to come here?" I asked him. "To this spot."

"Laura talked about hiding the real pot in or near Chaco Canyon. *Taking it home,* she said. But I wasn't sure exactly where she had in mind, so I didn't lie to you when I told you I didn't know what she meant to do that night. We decided it was best that way—plausible deniability. But now that she's disappeared, I have no way of knowing what she did with the pot. Did she take it from here? Or did someone else?"

I pushed around Mick. "You held out on me, Ansel. You told me that the swindle with Young was that you made him pay fifty grand more than he needed to, and you and Laura split it between you. You said nothing about hiding the real pot and giving Young a fake. Explain to me why you didn't tell me."

"Because it's bloody dangerous!" Ansel, my quiet boarder, cried out into the night. "I wanted you to leave the pot alone. I thought you'd interrogate the dragons or find out they had it. I thought they must have grabbed it. And maybe Laura too." He gestured wildly at the open hole. "I know you must feel that. And that's from a place the pot rested only a short time. Imagine what would happen if that got into Young's collection, what effect it would have on his other things? And imagine what would happen if the mage Pericles got hold of it."

"You knew about Pericles?" I asked, my temper rising. The pot's aura was doing things to me, stirring up the nastier side of my magic. My fingers twitched, my magic wanting to strike out at Ansel and make him cower.

Ansel folded his arms over his chest, as though protecting himself from me and my rage. "Laura and I knew that Young wanted the pot for another client. We dug around until we found out who. Young has acquired things for Pericles McKinnon in the past, and the more I learned about Pericles, the more worried I became. I decided it was important that Pericles didn't get his hands on this pot, and Laura agreed. So we decided to give Young a replica."

"Who made it?" Mick asked. "Who could you trust for that?"

"Laura did." Ansel's voice took on a note of pride. "She's an excellent forger."

"Except that you can't fake magical properties," I said. "Any magical being knows instantly that your copy is a fake."

"Yes, but *Young* didn't know, and that was the point. He never saw the real pot—we sent him photos from Flagstaff— and we delivered the replica to him. He couldn't tell the difference. We figured that by the time Young handed the pot over to Pericles and they found out it was a fake, the real one would be long gone, out of Pericles's reach. Or it was supposed to be." Ansel glanced at the hole again. "Laura said she'd hide it, in a place even the gods couldn't find it."

"We found it," I said. "Without much to go on."

"No, you found where she *started* to hide it," Ansel said. "Obviously, Laura decided to find a better place." He scanned the moonlit world around us, letting out his breath in a conjured sigh. "Or the dragons got it from her. I wish I knew where she was."

Mick rumbled, "If Laura is all right, wouldn't she try to contact you?"

"I don't know. That's why I think the dragons must have her. Or maybe she believes it better if she lies low. I'm dangerous, after all."

Standing with his hands in his pockets, his expression sad, Ansel looked about as dangerous as an unhappy puppy. But then, I've seen puppies rip things to shreds in the blink of an eye.

Drake and Colby had claimed they didn't know where Laura was. Ansel claimed not to remember what had happened the night she disappeared. Paige wanted to convince us with the faked séance that Laura was dead, and I think she believed it, which meant she didn't know where Laura was either.

Either Laura was perfectly fine and in hiding, or someone like Pericles had found her, or she truly was dead.

Where would someone like Laura think herself safe? Not with her sister, obviously, but I wanted to talk to Paige. She could give me a better sense of Laura, where she might go if she was in trouble. Paige hadn't responded to my message that Laura might be alive, and apparently slayers were still running around the county, searching for Ansel.

I looked around the dark night, the sky brilliant with stars. I wished I could stop the madness and lie on my back to stargaze with Mick, but it was not to be.

Mick had gone back to the hole again and crouched down next to it, talking to Ansel over his shoulder. "If Laura came up here after she left the restaurant in Gallup with you, what happened to you? She couldn't dig out this hole with such care with you in a blood frenzy."

"I wish I could remember," Ansel said.

"We could try to hypnotize him," I said to Mick. "Have him take us through that night in his memory."

"Not sure that would work with a Nightwalker," Mick said. "But I have an idea." He cast Ansel a thoughtful glance, and his eyes changed from blue to dragon black.

"What are you thinking?" I asked. "I'm pretty sure I'm not going to like it."

"Ansel doesn't remember what he does in his blood frenzy when he's calm and sated. But he might remember once he's in a blood frenzy again."

My heart squeezed. "I was right. I don't like it."

Ansel raised his hands. "Gods, Mick, you don't want me to deliberately go Nightwalker. I've been doing it too much lately, and I don't have a blood supply with me. I'll attack you. I'll drain you. I'll kill you and Janet both."

"Not if I'm a dragon, you won't. I can easily crush a little Nightwalker who gets out of hand." Mick opened and closed his broad fingers.

"But how will you bring me out of it again if you don't let me drink? I can only calm down if I have blood."

"We'll take you home and pour bottled blood down your throat," Mick said.

I thought Mick a little too certain this would work. When Ansel went into his frenzy and craved blood, the nearest blood-filled human would be me. Sure, Mick could stop him, but would Ansel have time to take a good bite out of me first?

But Mick's smile was pure dragon, showing me the cool beast that lay behind the warm man I loved. His eyes glittered with that unstoppable curiosity, the determination that could move glaciers. When a dragon wants to do something, there's not a being on earth that can slow him down—except another dragon, and then only maybe.

Ansel kept his hands up. "Can we try another way? I don't like what I am when I become Nightwalker. I'm . . . cruel."

"Not your fault," I said. "You make up for it when you're

not the Nightwalker. You know, you're a very strong person for being able to keep it at bay almost all the time."

I had no idea if that were true, but Ansel looked slightly appeased. "If you truly think I can tell you something useful . . ." He spread his hands. "But the minute I go insane with the blood need, please kill me. Please. I can't face the thought of waking up and seeing what I've done to my dearest friends."

Dearest friends. The guy really knew how to go for the heart-strings.

"Trust me, Ansel," I said. "I'll make very sure you don't kill us."

Mick rose to his feet, brushing the dust from his jeans, eager to start.

He and I coordinated what we'd do. We left the wash, walking another mile or so to put more distance between us and the Chaco campsites and ruins. We didn't want to be too close to other humans when all this went down. Ansel and Mick moved rapidly, me jogging to keep up with them as we made our way down a little-used dirt road, into the heart of nothing.

At least, many people would call it nothing. I called it the real world, where no buildings, paved roads, or fences marred the natural beauty of the landscape—just miles upon miles of unbroken land. I knew that eventually we'd come to another highway, a pueblo, a town, a city. But here in the heart of Indian country, the land was vast.

When we reached a point where Mick thought we'd be safe, he told me to stay with Ansel while he walked off from us into the darkness.

I heard a rush and a roar, then the downdraft of Mick's wings engulfed Ansel and me like a hot summer wind. He skimmed by us, silent as darkness, then he soared straight upward, a giant dragon shape black against the stars. I craned my head to watch him as he wheeled back and forth for the pure joy of it.

Mick loved being a dragon. Having to hide his true nature most of the time must be hell for him.

Mick swooped by again. I was so engrossed in watching him that I didn't notice until too late that Ansel had sidled away from me. By the time I spotted him, he was sprinting off into the darkness.

"Ansel!"

He didn't respond. I guess he'd decided at the last minute not to participate in our little experiment.

No one could outrun a Nightwalker. I started after him, but I knew there'd be no way I could catch him.

Correction—no one could outrun a Nightwalker but a dragon. Mick swept downward, plucked the fleeing Ansel up out of the desert, and flew back to me.

By the time Mick deposited Ansel at my feet, Ansel's Nightwalker had taken over.

"Delivering me straight to a snack?" Ansel said. "I take it back, Mick, old friend. I like this scheme." His voice had become smooth, charming, entirely unlike the soft-spoken Ansel who'd introduced me to *Kind Hearts and Coronets.*

Ansel took a step toward me, and Mick's large front foot landed in front of him. Ansel laughed, but Mick remained crouching next to us, a giant mass of watchfulness.

"So," I said to Ansel. "Tell us about the night you met Laura in Gallup."

"That night. Ah, that night." Ansel smiled at me, showing his elongated teeth. Nightwalkers didn't have sexy little fangs like they did in fiction—Ansel had the mouth of a monster. "It was a special night. Mmm. Laura and I had sex for the first time."

Wind blew across the desert, bringing some coolness but also dust. I coughed. "Are you sure? I didn't know Night-walkers could . . ."

"I assure you, love, we're fully functional. If your pet dragon wasn't here, I'd show you."

"No, please don't." I waved my hand at his Nightwalker body. "Tell me you went to her as Ansel, not . . ."

"Ah yes, Ansel. Poor, timid chap, finally got his leg over. He's in love. Can't imagine what got into the fellow. Oh, yes, I do. That bloody pot."

"With its magical properties."

"Roused old Ansel out of his antiquities and stamp-collecting mania. I never thought anything could do that. But Laura smiled that cute little smile at him, and he was gone."

"Then what happened?"

"What happened was, I thrust my little man into her sweet, tight—"

"I meant *after* that. Shit, Ansel."

"*After* being at it like rabbits for two hours and more, we went out to dinner, and discussed what we should do with the pot. The whole time the magic of it was hammering at me, waking up my blood need. I wanted to eat everyone in the restaurant. The wimpy me told Laura we'd better get out of there, so we went out to Chaco Canyon so Laura could hide the pot. Somewhere between here and there, I managed to bury the part of me that's Ansel and become what I truly am. Then the dragon came."

"Colby." I fit the pieces together. "Drake sent Colby out to snatch the pot from Laura, and she ran off while you fought him." Something still wasn't right. "But when I saw the auras, I saw Laura struggling with a Nightwalker, sensed that she'd been abducted. I now know that Colby didn't snatch her. So it must have been you."

"No, I was fighting that fucking dragon. I knew I wasn't going to win that fight, but I slowed him down enough to give her time to get away. The Nightwalker you sensed trying to grab her must have been the other Nightwalker."

Mick came alert, shoving his face closer to us. I saw in his eyes the same amazement and rage I felt.

"*What* other Nightwalker?" I shouted.

CHAPTER NINETEEN

Ansel looked annoyed. "The one chasing Laura. I got him away from her before the dragon swooped in, and he ran off. He must have been the one who killed the slayer on the freeway, because I certainly didn't. I wouldn't be so hungry now if I had. I'd have drained him."

Perfect. This was just effing perfect.

"Do you know the Nightwalker? Who is he?"

"I don't know every Nightwalker in the universe. But I think this one is working for Laura's sister."

"Laura's sister? The one sending slayers after you, because she says you killed Laura?"

Ansel's grin widened. "Ironic, isn't it? How do you think Paige knows about Nightwalkers? I got Laura's blood on my clothes, because he'd cut her a bit when she tried to get away from him. When I fought him off, and Laura disappeared, the Nightwalker probably told Paige about me and assumed I'd killed or taken Laura. She sent the slayers after me, but to slayers, one dead Nightwalker is as good as any other. The slayer must have gone after that Nightwalker and got ripped open for his pains."

Mick raised his dragon head and scanned the open desert. I was suddenly aware of all the empty space around us, and the shadows. "All this time I thought the only Nightwalker I had to worry about was you."

Ansel spread his hands. "Sorry, sweetheart. I never remember what I do or who I meet in my blood frenzy. I wonder why Nightwalkers who can control the frenzy don't remember? Maybe we think that if we remember the horrors, we'll be so remorseful we'll kill ourselves. Must be survival instinct."

At the moment I didn't care. "All right, so you fought off the Nightwalker, Colby let you go when Laura ran away, and you lost Laura. What did you do then?"

"Went after her. Poor little thing wasn't going to last long on her own with dragons and Nightwalkers searching for her. Didn't find her though. Sun was coming, and I went to ground. Literally. Had to hide out in a cave. The sleep finished the blood frenzy, and I woke up Ansel, baffled and bewildered as usual. He's always been a twat."

I didn't know what a *twat* was, but I could guess. "I like Ansel," I said.

"Of course you do. He's weak, and you can control him. You're fond of people you can control. Like him." He jerked a thumb at Mick, whose neck cranked around as he scanned and sniffed the desert around us.

"I'm fond of people who aren't trying to kill me every second."

"Exactly." Ansel's eyes were red as he looked at me around Mick's talon. "Speaking of that, I'm hungry. Give us a taste, sweetheart. I've told you this delicious information, so how about I have a little snack on you? From your groin, maybe? There's a nice thick artery there."

Ansel was fast. The words were barely out of his mouth before he was up and over Mick's claw, mouth open to that terrifying animal maw, bone thin hands outstretched for my throat.

In the next second, Mick grabbed him, tore him off me, and slammed him on his back to the ground. Ansel's head thumped against a small boulder protruding from the dirt, and he went limp.

"Thanks, Mick." My words came out on my next exhale.

Mick backed away into the darkness, and with a crackle of bones and flesh became human. He walked to Ansel, crouched down, and flicked back one of Ansel's eyelids. "He'll be out for a while."

I was still shaking, the fight-or-flight reaction of Ansel's attack whirling inside me. My logical brain said that everything was okay; my primitive brain told me to run and keep going.

"We need to get him home. Blood . . ." I put my hands on my knees.

Mick touched me, and a tingle of healing magic trickled beneath my skin. "Thank you," I said again.

I liked his fingers caressing my neck, but I straightened up and wiped the sweat from my face. "By the way, how did you get Ansel to go frenzied? He was fine when he ran off. You flew him back, and he was blood crazed."

Mick chuckled. "Ansel's afraid of heights. When we were a couple hundred feet up, I started to open my claw and scared the shit out of him."

WE MADE IT BACK TO THE HOTEL JUST AS DAWN BEGAN spreading its fingers to the east. Summer clouds streaked the sky, the sunrise staining the undersides a brilliant fuchsia.

Ansel had been out for the entire flight, and now Mick dressed again in the clothes I'd carried for him, took Ansel downstairs, and put him to bed. Ansel sank into his day sleep without regaining consciousness, which for now, was fine with me.

I had a million things to do and think about, but exhaustion from the long day and night caught up with me. I said good morning to Cassandra—or thought I did—then stumbled to my bedroom, spread my arms, and fell facedown across my bed. A pit of darkness opened up under me, and I didn't fight sliding into it.

When I woke, I was alone—no Mick—disappointing. The best way to wake up was to find myself snuggled back into him. I always felt safe, warm, like nothing could ever harm me.

A side effect of the mate thing, maybe? I didn't know. I enjoyed the illusion of safety whenever I lay with him, because it was the only feeling of safety I ever got. I'd take it, because I knew that as soon as we got out of bed every morning the danger would come. It always did.

My clock told me it was a little after eleven. If I were a normal person, I'd spend the day going over details of the hotel with Cassandra and Elena, talking to my dad and Gina about their wedding, and conferring with the contractors, and Fremont and Maya about how the saloon rebuilding was going.

Instead I grabbed a giant muffin from the breakfast buffet in the lobby, climbed onto my bike, and rode into Magellan to Heather Hansen's woo-woo store to ask her more about Paige. Heather looked up from helping tourists purchasing a map to the vortexes and waved to me.

"Hey, Janet. *Ya-at-eeh.* Janet is Navajo," she explained to the interested ladies in hiking clothes. "She was here for our very successful séance the other night. We contacted the spirit of a woman's sister. It was amazing. Wasn't it, Janet?"

"Yes," I said carefully. "It was pretty amazing."

The women looked at me as though surprised I could speak English, but Heather's enthusiasm impressed them.

While I waited for Heather to finish at the register, I

became aware of another presence in the store. I walked quietly across the creaking floor to the book section, where I found Bear perusing a book on Hopi pottery.

"It is a ritual we have been performing for centuries," Bear said without looking up from the book. "When we first met, I would not let him into my hogan until he proved his worth to me."

I leaned my arm on the shelf next to a book called *Tantric Rituals Throughout the Year.* "A tough way to prove himself."

"We are gods. It is not the same." She closed the book, her bracelets clinking as she placed it back on the shelf. "Humans give each other gifts or exchange tokens. Gods show they are willing to sacrifice themselves, or what they love, for the other. When Coyote first tried to force his way into my life, he loved nothing better than himself."

"And now?" I asked. The Coyote I knew cared for people —Julie, Mick, the residents of Magellan, and even me.

Bear smiled, the corners of her eyes crinkling. "Now we enjoy the game."

"Rough game."

"Coyote is so difficult to hurt that he gets cocky. Our game reminds him how to be humble."

"Humble? Coyote?"

Bear's smile grew. "As I have heard young humans say, humble-*ish*."

I shrugged. "You two do what you want. I'll stay out of it."

Her wise eyes told me she didn't believe my indifference. "I know it was very hard for you to see. I am sorry about that. But Coyote and I will have our little courtship, and then I will leave again."

"Oh," I said, suddenly unhappy. "No, don't. Stay a while."

Bear watched me a moment, then she gave me a grave nod. "I will think on it. Did you come here today, like me, to puzzle out what happened at the séance?"

"I'm trying to find out where Paige is living, but sure, I'm interested in that séance. What have you found out?"

Bear glanced to the front of the store, but Heather was still talking with her customers. Bear led me down the short hall in the back, opened the door of the séance room, and led me around the table to where Paige had been sitting. She lowered her large body to a crouch, her skirts spreading, and she pointed under the table.

I got down on my hands and knees beside her. The wood on one of the struts of the table had been slightly gouged and splintered, and a sticky piece of duct tape clung to it.

"A small device was taped there," Bear said. "Something that could make us hear Laura's voice?"

"A digital recorder, sure." They could be tiny but loud, with good-quality sound. "All you need is a recording of her voice and voice software—you cut out the sound waves of each word and paste them back in a line to make a sentence. Play the file back on a digital player, having it say whatever you want it to say." One of my nieces had showed me that. "Add a little muffling effect so it sounds like she's whispering from the spirit world, which might also cover up any inconsistencies in her speech pattern. And as I remember, Paige asked Laura all the questions, and her voice faded before Heather could say anything."

Bear leveraged herself up from the floor and went to the window that had blown open. "I think Paige has not had the time to come and retrieve her props. She was able to tear away the recorder before she left, but she did not have a chance to get this."

Bear pointed out the window. I saw a heavy spring and what looked like a small gearbox, plugged into an outside outlet. "What is that?"

"I believe it is used to open garage doors. She had a remote control in her pocket or perhaps also taped under the table, and pushed it to make the window open. There was wind last night, so she only needed to open it a little before the wind took over."

"What about the cold breeze? It's pretty easy to open a window, but make the summer wind feel like winter?"

Bear looked amused. She beckoned me to follow her back down the short hall and around a corner to the small bathroom. A customer looking at the books stared when both of us walked into the one-toilet bathroom together and shut the door behind us.

An air conditioner rested in a space cut in the wall above the toilet. The sagging wall around the opening had cracked long ago, letting in light from the summer morning.

Someone had fixed a thin, flexible hose into the air conditioner's grill. Bear showed me how it snaked outside through one of the cracks around the air conditioner, then bade me follow her back to the séance room where she opened the back window.

I leaned out. The bathroom and this room shared a wall, and I could see the AC unit sticking out. The tube wound down the wall and had been fixed under the window with more duct tape.

"Paige was the first to arrive, that night," Bear said. "I would guess she asked to go to the bathroom to prepare herself. She turns on the unit, setting the thermostat as low as she can, closes the door, goes to the private room, tapes the digital machine under the table, and is sitting quietly when the rest of us enter."

"And she probably had put the motor and the pipe in place, maybe in the dark before she came in, or the night before," I concluded. "If Heather heard any noises, she'd assume it was the ghost of the little girl she thinks haunts here."

"The window opens, the cold air streams in, and we hear Laura's voice."

"Crude props," I said.

"But we weren't expecting them. You and I both thought

we'd see, hear, and feel nothing. Small illusions can be deceptive."

That was true. I'd watched magicians in Las Vegas lounge acts perform simple tricks without stages, lights, costumes, and special effects. They'd used their quick hands, distraction, and patter to disguise what they did. These people had no real magic, only their wits, and I loved watching them, trying to catch how they deceived me. I never could.

"That is the true reason humans hold séances in the dark," Bear went on. "Easier to fool us when we are all holding hands and have our eyes closed."

"Julie knew it was a trick," I said.

"Julie is a perceptive little girl."

"What about the lights in the desert? Did she fake that?"

"No." Bear looked out the window at the bright sunlight, the huge sky, and the wide land beyond the town. "I think that was true magic. From a vortex maybe. Or a mage working magics at the same time."

Another thing I'd have to discover. I turned away from the window and the bright heat of the day. "The question is—do we tell Heather?"

"She seems very excited by her success."

We looked at each other, both debating whether it would be kinder to tell Heather the truth or to let her believe she'd conjured the voices of the dead.

We left the séance room without a word, but we'd both drawn the same conclusion. Let Heather have her moment.

I took advantage of Heather having no customers at the cash register to ask her if she'd tell me where Paige lived. I could have obtained the same information from someone like Emilio Salas, who knew everything about everyone in town, but I didn't want to alert the police to the fact that I wanted to talk to Paige. In light of Laura's disappearance, Salas would feel obligated to report to his chief.

Heather willingly gave me the address, telling me that Paige had rented a small house in Magellan.

When she told me *which* house, a chill went through me. The house Paige had rented was one belonging to the Magellan's Chief of Police, where his daughter Amy had once lived. I'd investigated a supernatural crime there, trying to find clues to Amy's disappearance. I realized that, in a small town, with few places available for short-term rent, Paige couldn't have had much choice, but the fact still unnerved me.

Bear and I left the store as Heather turned to new customers, then both of us sneaked around the store to the tall desert grasses in the back, and dismantled Paige's setup. That a woman of Bear's bulk could move without sound or drawing any attention at all fascinated me. She was much better at stealth than I was.

We quietly returned to the parking lot and stashed Paige's accoutrements in my saddlebags. Bear declined my offer to let her ride behind me before I even said it, saying she'd meet me at the house.

I turned down the road to the McGuire's rental, passing Maya Medina's small house with its neat garden full of summer flowers on the way. The last house on the road that dead-ended into desert was as pretty and charming as I remembered. I'd avoided this place since I'd finished the investigation, though there was no real reason I should. There was nothing wrong with the house itself.

Bear waited for me under a large cedar that split the yard between Paige's house and the one next door. I didn't waste time wondering how she'd arrived before me.

I parked my bike, took the accoutrements out of my saddle bags, and walked with Bear to the house.

When Paige answered the door, I shoved the stuff at her and said, "Nice try. Where's your pet Nightwalker?"

CHAPTER TWENTY

PAIGE COULD HAVE WASTED TIME PRETENDING SHE DIDN'T know what we were talking about. Instead she hugged the evidence of her crime to her chest and settled for a glare.

"He's not here," she said. "Where's yours?"

"Why do you want Ansel dead so much?" I countered.

"Why do you think? He killed my sister."

"He didn't," I said. "I told you—I left you a voice mail. She was still alive when he lost sight of her."

Bear stepped past us and into the house, but Paige's outrage was all for me. "I heard your message. If your Nightwalker told you that, he's lying. Laura is dead, and that filthy Nightwalker killed her. He sucked her dry and dumped her body somewhere."

Out of the corner of my eye, I saw Bear wander slowly around the small living room, stopping in front of every table and shelf, looking over the ornaments, photos, and curios—some belonging to the McGuires, some belonging to Paige.

I didn't need to concentrate on auras to scent Nightwalker. He'd be in his day sleep now, but he was near, probably in a back bedroom with windows shielded against the sun.

"Why did you think Ansel killed her in the first place?" I asked. "Did you have evidence, or did someone just tell you that?"

"If she's not dead, then where is she?" Paige ignored Bear, facing me as though she considered me the bigger threat. "All I know is that my sister met a Nightwalker for dinner in Gallup. The Nightwalker came back, and Laura didn't."

"That's all true, but Ansel didn't kill her," I said. "He's been searching for Laura too, trying to help her."

"Of course he'd tell you that. Who is gullible enough to believe a Nightwalker?"

"You are, apparently," I said. "Why are you letting him stay with you?"

Paige made a noise of exasperation. "All right, since you know everything. He's a friend. No, a boyfriend. Before he was turned. He's the one who told me you had a Nightwalker living in your hotel, and that he'd become friendly with Laura. He told me he found Laura and Ansel in Chaco Canyon. My boyfriend—Bobby—was trying to rescue Laura and bring her back to me, but Ansel was too strong and ran him off. Ansel is much older than Bobby. Apparently they get stronger with age."

Rescue Laura, my ass. "You don't seem very stunned that your old boyfriend is a Nightwalker. You're amazingly calm, in fact."

"He's been staying with me for a year. Trying to fight the blood frenzy and live normally. Like you claim yours is."

Bear turned around. "You're lying."

Paige blinked. "No, I'm not. He really is trying."

"I meant about everything," Bear said. "How about some truth? Or would you like me to tell it for you?"

Paige studied Bear with new worry. "What are you talking about?"

Bear waved a large hand at a table of framed photographs. "You care enough about these photos to have brought them with you. Friends, your parents, your boyfriend—before he became Nightwalker, perhaps? None of your sister."

"I packed in a hurry. I grabbed what I could."

"A person in a hurry would have left all these home," Bear said. "You came here intending to stay a while, and you brought what you treasured in case you didn't go back. Why don't you like your sister?"

"I like her fine. I mean, she's dead, isn't she? I didn't want her picture—I didn't want to be reminded."

I wasn't much for keeping photographs myself, but I knew that people found comfort in the photos of loved ones, living or dead, so they could remember them every day. I, for instance, kept a photo of my dad on my desk and a copy in my wallet so I could look upon his face whenever I wanted to.

"Not getting along with your sister is nothing to be ashamed of," I said. "I don't get along with most of my family, except my dad. Not many people have pictures of me among their most treasured things."

"All right, so we weren't best friends," Paige said in a hard voice. "That doesn't mean her death doesn't bother me. And that the Nightwalker shouldn't die for it."

"You faked the séance to convince me she was dead so I'd hand Ansel to you. But Ansel's a nice guy, and he's as worried about Laura as you are." My eyes narrowed. "Or maybe you're not as worried about *her* as much as about what she'd found?"

Paige stared at me a moment, her pale eyes round. She looked a bit like Laura, but less tanned, less energetic. Maybe living in the shadow of Laura's success as an athletic, pretty, and successful businesswoman had embittered her, or maybe it was more complicated than that. Family dynamics always were.

"Get out of my house," Paige said.

It was Chief McGuire's house, but I didn't argue. Bear turned and walked out the door without another word. I had to have a parting shot.

"Your Nightwalker killed one of the slayers. If word gets out about that, Bobby will be on top of the slayers' to-kill lists. They won't care that he's under your protection. Slayers hate Nightwalkers, period. They're in it for more than just the bounty."

Paige matched me stare for stare, my warning not striking fear into her heart. "One of the slayers I hired will get through, and Ansel will die. Even if my sister is still alive, it's his fault she got messed up in everything she's messed up with. I'm not calling off the slayers."

I gave her a nod. "All right then. I know where you stand. Mind if I just say hello to your Nightwalker while I'm here?"

I spun away and was down the hall before Paige could stop me, to the door at the end, where the Nightwalker aura was strongest. The door wasn't locked and gave way faster than I thought it would.

I half-fell into the room, but it was empty. The window blinds were down but the slats were open, letting in streaks of sunshine that landed across the bed. The sheets were rumpled, a man's clothes lay on the floor, but nobody, human or Night-walker, was in the room.

The Nightwalker's aura was. He'd been here and, by the number of clothes on the floor, he'd staying here a while. If I hadn't been avoiding this side of town I might have sensed him, but I hadn't come down this street in a long time, at least not since Paige had moved in.

Paige watched me from the doorway, her arms folded, looking a bit smug. I pushed past her. "Tell Bobby to come see me when he shows up again," I said, and I left the house.

∽

BEAR WAS NOWHERE IN SIGHT BY THE TIME I GOT OUTSIDE. I looked up and down the street and out into the desert, but I didn't see her.

The land was heating up for the day, shimmers of warmth rising from the flat desert east of town. Nowhere did I see the bulk of Bear either striding along or waiting for me. She'd gone again.

I started my bike. Paige's Nightwalker had gone to ground somewhere else today, and my chances of finding him weren't great. Nightwalkers are excellent at hiding themselves during the sun hours. They know they're the most vulnerable then and trust very few with their secret hideaways.

I didn't have time to go running around all over Magellan and beyond hunting another Nightwalker. I had a young woman and an artifact to find, then I had to figure out a way to destroy the pot before Pericles got hold of it.

On the other hand, I didn't need to hunt a Nightwalker myself when there were so many others out there eager to do it for me.

I rode to the diner, took a booth in the back, ordered lunch, and pulled out a now-creased business card. I remembered that my cell phone had been reduced to melted slag, and asked Jolene if I could use the kitchen's phone. It was cordless, and she brought it to me with my milkshake.

I dialed the phone number on Rory's card. He'd told me to text him, but he'd have to put up with hearing a human voice.

"So the bitch who hired me is harboring a Nightwalker too?" Rory asked. "What is wrong with people in your town?"

I started to explain that she wasn't from my town, but let it go. "Can you find him?"

"Find him, stake him, behead him. If you want me to dispose of the remains, it's an extra fee. What's the bounty?"

Probably more than I could afford. "You wouldn't do this for the satisfaction of ridding the world of another Nightwalker?"

"Nope. Slaying is dangerous work, and I want to get paid. Then there's wear and tear on crossbows, clothes to replace the ones I ruin when I make the kill, crossbow bolts, wooden stakes . . . All that plus my risk of the Nightwalker biting, draining, or turning me."

"Fair enough. How about five hundred?"

He snorted. "How about five thousand?"

I gripped the phone. "I don't need you to kill him. I need to talk to him first."

"Capturing a Nightwalker alive is even harder. That will cost you another grand."

"Are you kidding me? I don't have that kind of money."

"Tell you what—you let me have *your* Nightwalker so I can collect the bounty on him from Paige, and I'll give you a discount."

"No," I said firmly. "Bring me that other Nightwalker, and we can talk."

"If I capture him alive, and you don't pay up, I'll just let him kill you."

Rory hung up.

I sat staring at the phone until Jolene brought me my burger. "Bad news, Janet?"

"No." I sighed and handed her the phone. "Just asshole men."

Jolene laughed. "Can't argue with you there." She took the phone, her backside swaying in her tight capris as she stopped on the way to refill Salas's coffee cup.

I ate the burger, lost in thought, trying to decide my next move. I hadn't brought the fake pot with me today, but I wanted to ask my friend Jamison Kee about the markings. What Jamison didn't know about the pueblo peoples who'd filled this area in ages past, not to mention the legends of all the tribes of the Southwest . . . No, there was nothing he didn't know.

I finished, paid, and slipped Jolene a tip. I said hello on my way out to Salas as he lifted his chicken sandwich. I liked Emilio—he was one of the few people I knew who wasn't underhanded or didn't have his own agenda.

I left the diner to talk to another man who wasn't under-handed. Jamison Kee, from Chinle, one of my closest friends, had been the first person outside my immediate family to become aware of my Stormwalker powers. He'd not only acknowledged me as Stormwalker, he'd taken the time and trouble to teach a scared teenaged girl how to handle her powers and not be too afraid of them.

At the time, he'd been a storyteller with shaman abilities—that was before he'd found out he was a Changer.

Jamison was also an artist, a sculptor. One day he'd been working on carving a mountain lion out of a hunk of sand-stone, when he'd became a mountain lion himself—a real one. Scared the shit out of him.

Terrified he'd hurt Naomi and her daughter, with whom he'd been living at the time, he'd taken off to Mexico to find a group of Changers he'd heard about. They'd taught him about being a Changer—after torturing him a while, for his own good, they'd said—and he'd finally escaped them and returned home.

Jamison had an artist's studio behind the house he shared with Naomi and Julie, Naomi now his wife. Naomi owned and ran the plant nursery that fronted the highway, and their house lay behind that.

When I pulled into the nursery's lot, Naomi stood next to a flatbed trailer full of trees in big wooden planters and talked animatedly with one of the guys who worked for her. I waved but didn't stop, going on through to the private drive, where I parked and went in search of Jamison.

From the sounds coming from the hogan-like shed behind the house, he was in there sculpting. I debated disturbing him—the creative fire isn't something that can be turned on and off like a faucet. Jamison's creative work was worth giving him his solitude.

Julie came out of the house, a big smile on her face. "Hello, Janet." Her hands made the sign as she spoke.

"What's Jamison working on?" I asked, turning to hang my helmet on my bike. Then I felt stupid. Sometimes I forgot that, in spite of medical technology, Julie couldn't hear well enough to make out my words, especially at this distance, without reading my lips. I had to be looking at her to talk.

"He's working on a piece of basalt," Julie said before I could repeat the question. "He's excited about it."

Apparently, she *had* been able to figure out what I was saying. Good. She wouldn't have to gently remind me this time. "Do you think he'll mind if I interrupt? It's kind of important." I used sign language with the last words, showing her how much I'd learned.

Julie laughed, her face lighting up. "It's all right, Janet. You don't have to sign. I can hear you. Perfectly, in fact."

CHAPTER TWENTY-ONE

My mouth dropped open in shock. Julie kept looking at me, her smile telling me she enjoyed seeing me jerked out of my presumptions.

Then the enormity of her announcement connected in my brain. *Julie can hear.*

I ran at her in joy, lifted her off her feet, swung her around, and kissed her cheek as I set her down. I was not usually one for impromptu demonstrations of affection, or even touching anyone without their permission, but this was a special occasion.

"What happened?" I asked excitedly. "Did you have surgery? Is this a new kind of implant? What?"

"Nothing like that." Julie's speech still slurred a little—she'd learned to say the words when she couldn't hear the click and stop of every consonant. "Jamison did a spell."

"Jamison . . ." I stopped in a different kind of shock. "Did a spell . . ."

My elation blew away on a cold wind, the heat of the summer day gone.

There was no way that Jamison, as much as I cared for

him, could have performed a spell of that magnitude. Changing a person in a profound way—giving the blind sight, the deaf hearing, or making a paralyzed person walk again—was complicated magic that took intense power, experience, and skill. I couldn't have done it, and neither could Mick. The ununculous, Emmett Smith, might be able to—*might*—and only if he had help.

Jamison Kee, artist and storyteller, didn't possess this kind of power. Jamison's shaman abilities had been enhanced when the Changer in him had surfaced, but they were still nowhere near enough for a spell of this level.

Julie nodded happily, oblivious to my growing horror. "He did it the day after the séance. He asked me and Mom not to tell anyone right away, and then to say it had been a medical procedure, but you can know. You're practically family."

Oh gods, Jamison, what have you done?

I turned away from Julie, who started to look puzzled. "Janet? What's wrong? I thought you'd be happy."

I was. Or would have been. As it was, fear overrode any kind of gladness for Julie. I didn't answer her as I headed at a run for Jamison's studio.

JAMISON KEE, A TALL, NICELY MUSCLED DINÉ WITH A mesmerizing voice, wore only a T-shirt and shorts as he worked with hammer and chisel in the summer heat. The shirt was sweat-soaked and stuck to his finely honed back, and the shorts bared legs of power and light chocolate-colored skin. His long hair hung in a tight braid down his back, and he wore goggles to protect his eyes.

He tapped the chisel in careful strokes into the black rock on the sculpting stand, not looking up when I ran into the hogan. The sculpture was in early stages, but a feathered wing already emerged from the basalt, and I could tell that it and the rest of the bird would be beautiful.

"Jamison," I said.

The chisel slipped, and Jamison swung around. The goggles hid his eyes, and his face was flushed from the heat.

The quiet-spoken, good-hearted Jamison I knew growled, "Son of a bitch, Janet. I'm trying to work."

"Where is it?" I demanded.

"Where is what?"

I slammed the door behind me. "You know what I'm talking about. There's no way you are magical enough to do what you did with Julie. Are you crazy? Or just stupid?"

His mouth firmed, Jamison displeased, not ashamed. "I only did the one spell."

"Who was the person who told me that when you deal with forces of magic, the first thing you have to learn is control? *Total control.*" I was speaking the Diné language, angry. Gods, I sounded like my grandmother. "We have to resist the temptation to play god, and first be reasonable and thoughtful. Who told me that? Oh. I remember now. *You!*"

Jamison dropped his tools and ripped the goggles from his face. "I told you. I did the one spell. One. The most important one."

"Shit, Jamison. How long have you had the artifact?"

He didn't even try to deny it. "A week, I think. Yes, I got it a week ago."

"Where did you get it? From Laura DiAngelo? Someone else?"

"Laura brought it to me. She said she didn't trust anyone but me."

Laura. A week ago. She must have managed to get away across the desert from Chaco Canyon after all, and she'd sought out Jamison. And then went where?

"How did she even know you?" I broke off. "Oh, wait . . ." Jamison Kee, historian and storyteller, familiar with legends from the Four Corners area and beyond, would be a fantastic resource to an antiquities dealer who needed to know the location and value of a certain historic pot.

"I told Ansel where it was," he said, confirming my guess. "Ansel and Laura brought me drawings Richard Young had given her of the pot he was looking for. I told Ansel I'd seen a pot like it in Flagstaff. I swear to you, I had no idea what it was, or how powerful it was, until Laura brought it to me for safekeeping."

"No, because if you'd known how dangerous it was, you would have told me or Mick at once, so we could rush up to Flag and destroy it. Right?"

"What do you mean *destroy it*?" Jamison's flush drained away. "You can't destroy it. It's our heritage."

"Yes, I can. It's fucking dangerous."

"One spell—I told you, that's all I did. I promised myself I'd never touch it again after that."

"Sure. That's how it starts."

Jamison balled his strong, sculptor's hands, dusted with black grime. "Show some faith in me, Janet. I've been a practicing shaman since I was in junior high. I know all about talismans and temptation. But you can't blame me for what I did. If something like this came into your possession, the first thing you'd do would be to make life better for someone you love. You know you would."

"That's not the point!"

"What *is* the point then? What's the point of having all this magic if we can't heal Julie with it? You think I can be handed something with that much power and say, *Sorry, Julie, you'll have to go the rest of your life not being able to hear, because Janet will be pissed off if I help you?*"

He was breathing hard, sweating from the heat outside and the closeness in here. His dark eyes held a wildness I'd never seen in him before, and on top of the wildness, guilt and defiance.

There was no way Jamison could best me in a magical fight. I could slash him down with Beneath magic if I dared to, take the pot, and walk away.

Jamison knew that too. His defiance grew, and I saw him think about the fact that with the artifact, maybe he *could* best me.

I reached for no magics, because Jamison was talented enough to sense that. "This has nothing to do with Julie," I said. "Some very bad people are after this vessel. For one, a mage who's vying to be the most powerful in the world and doesn't have any scruples about how he gets that power. For another, dragons who will stop being polite when they get impatient, and simply take what they want. For a third, a Nightwalker—not Ansel, but one who's struck down and killed a slayer, a human being. That's only the beginning. When the rest of the powerful magical beings of the world figure out you have the pot, they'll come down here for it, and they won't care who they have to kill to get at it. You. Naomi. Julie."

"What about you?" Jamison asked me, his voice harsh. "You're one of the powerfully magical. How do I know you haven't come to take it for yourself?"

"You don't. But who has a better chance of surviving a fight over it? You, or me?"

"If I have the pot, I can survive anything."

My friend Jamison had the best heart of anyone I knew. The man I faced had violent insanity in his eyes. He'd touched the power; he'd learned what it was like to have intense magic surging through every part of him, had felt the joy of making something wonderful happen with it.

"Remember when you first found me?" I asked. "I was sitting on a rock on the edge of Canyon de Chelly, with lightning striking around me. I was so scared, and at the same time, so excited that I had this uncontrollable magic in my body. Remember what you said to me? You said—*The magic is not you. You are you, and the magic is part of your whole.* So now I'm telling you, Jamison —this magic isn't you."

"I said a lot of dumb-ass things when I was younger. I'm not letting you take the pot away and risk that Julie will go back to being deaf. Do you think I can do that to her?"

He pulled off his T-shirt as he spoke. When I saw his skin, my eyes widened. Jamison's flesh was scored with hundreds of little cuts, now scabbed over, crisscrossing his chest, abdomen, sides, and I assumed his back as well.

"Shit, what happened to you?"

"When I did the spell, dust from the pot flew up and started cutting me all over. Hurt like hell. But I kept going, and I got through it. And Julie is cured."

"Gods, Jamison, you didn't *stop*? What if the magic had done something to Julie? You *never* touch an unfamiliar magical device without knowing exactly what it wants as payback. You should have called me and asked me before you did this."

"No, because you would have tried to talk me out of it, like you're doing now. A thousand shallow cuts won't kill me. I'm a Changer. I heal quickly. I'm the perfect person to use it."

"The pot made you think that—"

Jamison snarled. "What the hell do you know about it? You didn't know anything about this vessel until other people started looking for it. *I'm* protecting it. I deserve a little reward for that, and you can't tell me that Julie being able to hear isn't a giant reward."

"Jamison, stop it—"

"Is that your argument? Stop it, because Janet knows about everything?" He struck his chest with his gathered fingers. "You don't understand about *this*, or about ordinary people. I was wrong about the magic not being who you are. You glow with magic, and if it left you, you'd die. I'm made of magic. This is what *I* am."

As he said the last, his body distorted, his hands becoming

paws, his face elongating into a mountain lion's muzzle. His eyes turned dark yellow tinged with red, and the rest of his clothes fell from his body.

I had an instant to see his ears go back flat and his mouth open in a fang-bearing snarl before he leapt at me, several hundred pounds of enraged wildcat ready to kill.

I scrambled away from him, but Jamison's leap caught my side, and we went down to the floor, him on top of me. I fought, but my human strength was nothing to his mountain lion's.

His grappling claws bit deep, shredding my shirt and drawing blood. His fangs snapped closed an inch from my skin. I held him off, but I wouldn't be able to for long. Mountain lions are tough, and Changers are larger than natural wildcats. He was strong, and he was furious.

As we thrashed around the floor, Jamison's huge back caught his sculpting stand. The thing teetered, and the chunk of black basalt he'd been working on came down.

I rolled desperately, managing to separate myself from Jamison. The basalt piece hit the floor between the two of us. The intricate wing Jamison had almost finished broke off, shattering into several pieces.

I was sure the loss of his artwork would shake Jamison back to himself, but the red eyes that turned to me didn't give a shit about art. The beast wanted me dead.

I scrambled to my feet, trying to get to the door, but Jamison was on me again. Claws raked my back as I went down for the second time.

My Beneath magic wanted to rampage. I could stop Jamison, as I'd stopped the slayer from shooting me and Ansel, but I might kill Jamison. I'd had to use all my willpower to keep the burst of Beneath magic tiny when I'd blown up the crossbow bolt. I hadn't been angry then, or fighting for my life, just annoyed at a human.

If I hit Jamison with the magic, I'd kill him. I'd try not to, but I couldn't guarantee it. I had no storm with which to stabilize myself—the magic would be raw and pure, like Gabrielle's.

I closed my eyes, trying to tamp down the white ball that rose inside me into something less than lethal. I needed to knock out Jamison, nothing more.

But the evil goddess buried within me, the she-witch I battled every day, surged up in fury, wanting to *kill*. The same wildness in this hogan that was calling to Jamison started calling to me. The Beneath magic rose into incandescence, the power of it searing my hands.

"Jamison!" Naomi's voice rang through the slammed-open door, the heat of the desert sweeping in with her.

I opened my eyes. The sudden sunlight hurt my sensitive retinas, but I saw Naomi in the doorway, sighting down the tranquilizer rifle in her hands. Julie peered around her, her eyes wide with terror.

"Jamison," Naomi said again.

I fought down my Beneath magic, but the stuff glowed and pulsed, building up into a wild ball of lightning in my hands. It wanted me to slam the magic into Jamison, to watch him burn and writhe like Pericles had, except that Jamison wouldn't be able to shrug it off.

"Naomi!" I screamed. "Shoot him!"

The tranquilizer gun popped. The dart hit the mountain lion right between his shoulder blades, missing my hand by an inch.

Jamison gave one final snarl of rage, then his eyes clouded over, and he collapsed, unconscious, right on top of me.

I pushed at him, jiggling on my elbows and hips, trying to squirm out from under several hundred pounds of limp mountain lion. Jamison heaved a little sigh in his sleep. His wildcat receded, and I had Jamison, my best friend, stark naked on top of me, with his wife and stepdaughter standing over us.

Naomi leaned the tranq rifle against the wall, reached down, and rolled Jamison off me with gentle compassion. I sat up, panting, shoving my hair from my face. My hands came away covered in blood.

Jamison, one of the most modest men I knew, lay sprawled on his back, his privates out for everyone to see. Julie, the sensible girl, snatched up one of the tarps he used to keep his work covered, and draped it over him.

Naomi didn't try to help me up. She let me sit on the floor, breathing hard, as I fought my magic back down again.

"Janet," Naomi said, her eyes soft. "Thank you."

"For what? Enraging the nicest guy in the world so he'd turn into a mountain lion and attack me?"

"For not killing him. I know you could have. You might have had no choice."

I shuddered, swallowing bile as I forced the white magic buzzing in my body to *go away*. It trickled off slowly, angrily. "Yeah, well, it came close."

Naomi smoothed Jamison's hair back from his face, her love for him plain to see.

Julie picked up the sculpting stand and the basalt, grunting a little as she lifted the stone back into place. She picked up the pieces of the broken bird's wing and gazed at them mournfully. "He was making this for me."

"Julie, I'm so sorry." I scrubbed my face, finding more blood. "Tell me what happened," I said to Naomi. "Were you here when Laura brought the pot?"

"She showed up in the middle of the night," Naomi said. "Jamison went down to meet her, but I followed him. I didn't know who she was—Jamison hadn't met her face-to-face before—but she was terrified. She gave him this thing, wrapped up in a leather bag, telling him to keep it secret. Then she was gone."

"That's it? You didn't ask any questions?"

"She didn't give us a chance. She said she couldn't think of anyone else she trusted besides Jamison, and that we were to tell *no one*, including you. She said it was dangerous for anyone to know about it—especially you. Jamison promised, and I promised too. I'm sorry."

Explained why Naomi had shown up at the séance. She'd wanted to know whether Laura was truly dead, or at least why her sister thought so. Julie had seemed oblivious to everything at the séance, which meant she hadn't known about Laura and the pot until Jamison performed the spell the next day. Naomi should have said something about Laura to me then, but if she'd thought she was helping Jamison, I understood—reluctantly—why she'd kept silent. I didn't agree with her, but I knew that with Naomi, Jamison and Julie always came first.

"After she'd gone, Jamison took the pot out of the bag," Naomi said. "It looked like typical pottery to me. Antique and valuable, yes, but not dangerous. Jamison carried it out here and locked it up. I couldn't figure out why Laura was so worried about it. The pot had sat up in that museum in Flagstaff for years—why wasn't it dangerous then?"

"Hidden in plain sight," I said, speculating. "No one working for the museum or visiting the museum was magical, I guess. Or magical enough. No one knew about it until Pericles hired Young to start poking around looking for it."

"Jamison didn't talk about it. I got busy with the nursery— it's one of our busiest seasons—and I didn't notice that Jamison was spending so much time out here. I figured he was doing a new sculpture. I know how he gets when he's excited about a new piece of art, and I leave him alone.

"Then yesterday morning, Jamison called us to the hogan and told us he'd found a spell he wanted to try. He didn't say what the spell was for, but he said that Julie alone could be there for it. I was supposed to wait outside. But I didn't like how Jamison looked—his face was almost gray, and his eyes kept going yellow, like his mountain lion's. I didn't know what was wrong. So I refused to leave."

"Wise," I said.

Julie broke in. "Jamison got mad at Mom. And Jamison

never gets mad. But she wouldn't go. So finally Jamison did the spell with us all in here."

"At first, it didn't look any different than any other shaman spells I've seen him do," Naomi said. "I like when Jamison lets me watch him do magic. It's soothing, peaceful. But this spell scared me. Jamison went into a trance—when he meditates or lets his magic take him, he usually is very calm and relaxed. This time, I could tell he was in pain. The designs on the pot started moving, and then little tiny shards rose up out of the pot and swarmed him. I tried to push him out of the way and maybe break the pot, but he opened his eyes and yelled at me to get back, that I'd be hurt if I did that."

"I was scared," Julie said. She sat down cross-legged between Naomi and Jamison, resting a comforting hand on Jamison's inert shoulder. "It was so powerful. But I didn't run. I didn't want to leave Mom and Jamison alone with that magic." She rested her other hand on her mother's knee.

"Jamison finished the spell," Naomi said. "And the shards cutting him flowed back down into the pot. He was exhausted, but all right. And then Julie started screaming. I thought she'd been hurt, that maybe the shards had attacked her somehow."

Julie smiled sheepishly. "I was scared. All the sudden, sound started pouring into my ears, like it was beating at me. I never realized the world was so *loud*." The smile became one of pure happiness.

"Naomi," I said, trying to finger-comb my hair. "Where did Jamison look up this spell? I know he doesn't have spell books lying around." Jamison was a shaman, and his knowledge of magic came from oral tradition. "But he couldn't have known how to do this without some research. Please tell me he didn't look up spells on the Internet."

"Yep," Julie said. "He asked me to show him how to use the search engines. He borrowed my laptop and was at it for days."

I groaned. "Oh, Jamison, my stupid old friend."

"He was trying to help me," Julie said, defending him.

I climbed painfully to my feet. "Do either of you know where the pot is? You need to give it to me."

Both Naomi and Julie nodded without asking me to explain why. Julie picked up a key ring from Jamison's now-ripped shorts, went to his supply cabinet, unlocked it, and pulled out a leather-wrapped bundle.

Julie said as she brought it to me, "You're worried that if he searched the Internet for such a powerful spell, any astute mage would find out, right? They'd know Jamison wasn't a powerful mage himself and wonder why he was searching for these spells. They'd guess he'd found some way to enhance his power. And this mage you yelled at him about would be looking for people who'd found some way to enhance their powers. Right?"

I took the bundle. The strength of the pot inside jolted a shock through me as hard as any lightning strike. What I'd felt come out of the hole where Laura had started to bury it was nothing compared to this.

"You're smart, Julie," I said, my throat tight.

"You okay?" Naomi asked, worried.

"No. This is . . . bad. Which is why I'm taking it away."

I headed for the door. Naomi got in front of me. "Janet, if you hide the pot or find some way to destroy it, what will happen to Julie? Will the spell die without the pot?"

My chest hurt as I struggled to breathe. Julie watched me quietly. She'd been handed a piece of the world she'd been denied all her life, and now I had to tell her she might have to let it go again.

"I don't know," I had to say. "I'm sorry. The spell might fade as Jamison's power does. Or it might be permanent. I just don't know."

Naomi nodded once, her throat moving. She'd watched her daughter lose her hearing once, long ago. Now she might have to do it again.

"Take it, Janet," Julie said. "I don't want this if we lose Jamison for it."

"I'm sorry," I said again.

"Will Jamison be all right?" Naomi asked, still in front of me.

I looked down at him slumbering so peacefully on the floor. "I hope he wakes up the Jamison we all know and love, but I don't have any idea what this thing does, or what residue it leaves. Watch him. Call me, or call Mick, if he doesn't come out of it."

Naomi nodded. Her eyes held a bleakness that I hated.

I clenched my teeth against the rising magic of the pot, pushed past Naomi, stepped into the hot afternoon, and got the hell out of there.

CHAPTER TWENTY-TWO

As soon as I walked out and stashed the artifact in my saddlebag, I felt the eyes of the supernatural world upon me.

The driveway behind Naomi's house was empty, the workers in the nursery moving with the slow ease of men doing physical labor in the heat. None of them looked my way.

I started up my bike and slowly rode down the drive back toward the road. One of the workers raised his hand in farewell. I made myself wave back, everything normal.

Sweat trickled from under my helmet as I rode along the highway through town. Magellan looked no different than usual—the lunch crowd at the diner was thinning out, people going back to work, tourists fanning out to hike to the vortexes or along the old railroad bed. RVs rocked ponderously past me, summer vacationers on their way to view the next natural attraction.

All the while, the pot screamed to me. Its aura rose around me like a bubble shot with red and blue flame, muting the rest of the world, broadcasting its whereabouts to everything magical.

It couldn't be broadcasting, though. Jamison had kept it hidden in a cabinet in his studio all week, and the magical hadn't swooped down upon him to grab it. I hadn't felt a thing, and I'd been looking for it. No one had found it in Flagstaff either, where it had sat for years.

Then again, the pot hadn't yet been in the hands of anyone as magical as me. Normal humans ran the museum; Laura wasn't a mage; and Ansel, though he was magical by nature, couldn't actually work magic. Jamison had power, but nowhere near the kind of power I could draw.

I had to stash it somewhere. But while I ran through ideas for where to take it, the artifact called to me.

Part of me wanted to know why it had been made and how. The other part of me was busy imagining all kinds of ways I could use the pot to make myself powerful beyond imagining.

I realized now that the artifact singing away in the cabinet while I'd fought Jamison had enhanced my Beneath magic, which was why I hadn't been able to damp it down as I had when fighting the slayer.

The Beneath magic was now throbbing and humming through me, not having subsided in the least. Crackles of it moved through my body, popping in my ears. The magic leaked out through my fingers, contacting the handlebars and lighting up the bike in electric arcs.

If I didn't contain the magic, I was going to fry myself. My beautiful new Softail would be a melted heap on the highway, and I wouldn't be in much better shape.

The bike sped on, fed by power. I checked my rearview mirror, hoping no police decided to try to pull me over. I was afraid of what I'd do to them if they did.

My right-hand mirror—the one with the piece of magic mirror in it—was still dark. The mirror still hadn't recovered from the fire, or it had buried itself too deep to be reached.

And I suddenly knew exactly how to fix it.

Yesterday, I'd worried about hunting for a mage powerful

enough to bring the mirror back to life, yet trustworthy enough
not to try to kill me and Mick to steal it. Today I knew with
clarity that I didn't need another mage.

All I had to do was—

"No!" I yelled it out loud, clenching the handlebars to keep
myself from reaching for the mirror.

If I healed the mirror, Cassandra and Mick would know
instantly—the loudmouthed thing would make its presence
known in every mirror and every shard in the hotel. Neither
Cassandra nor Mick would take long guessing how I'd done it.
The surge would be so strong that the dragons might sense it in
their compound, through the mirrors my mirror had pene-
trated there.

The dragons would fly straight for me, and if Pericles had
an eye on them, he'd follow. And then there was the Nightwalker Paige harbored. He wouldn't be up during the day, but
he'd be coming for the pot as soon as he woke. Why he or
Paige wanted it, I didn't know, but magical talismans could
cause a feeding frenzy.

Then the artifact told me exactly how to deal with Pericles,
dragons, and the Nightwalker. In one of the visions it gave me,
I saw myself holding the pot in one hand, while building up a
ball of my goddess magic in the other. The vision showed me
Pericles rising higher and higher on a vortex of my magic until
he was a speck in the sky. Then the magic disappeared, and
Pericles fell down, down, down to splatter across the ground.

The goddess in me laughed.

Thunder rumbled behind me and spread to fill the land. A
glance into my good rearview mirror showed blue-black clouds
building up on the southern horizon and racing toward
Magellan.

The artifact explained that I'd no longer have to wait for
storms to form to use them—I could create and build them
myself.

The first icy balls of hail fell on me as I sped out of

Magellan toward my hotel. Traffic dried up and disappeared as I left town, and I raced toward the Crossroads alone.

Sheets of rain mixed with hail fell with the intensity only a desert storm can bring. I could barely see the road through the hail and the mist boiling up from the hot pavement. Hailstones crashed against my helmet and beat on my exposed body.

A sensible motorcyclist would stop and wait for the wave of rain to pass. I kept going. I needed to reach the hotel . . .

And then what? At my hotel I had Cassandra, a mega-powerful witch and her Changer girlfriend. Then there was Elena, an Apache shaman who guarded a huge pool of magic in my basement. And of course, the Nightwalker. Even the two low-level witches who'd stayed on after the fire would sense the aura of this pot, and if things went as expected, they'd fight me to get it.

Coyote's words came back to me: *When I said no one is strong enough not to be tempted, I meant it. Including Mick.*

I trusted Mick. I trusted him with my life.

I thought of Jamison, one of the good guys, and the madness I'd seen take over his kind eyes. He'd been using the artifact to help Julie, and he'd fought me to protect her. Good motives, and still it had driven him to kill.

Mick was a stronger person physically than Jamison, and he had far stronger magic. I'd also seen what Mick could do when magic turned him against me, and I never wanted to see it again. The fact that I held his true name *might* stop him, or the pot might tell him exactly how to wrest the name back from me and be free.

The aura from this thing was already sliding under my skin, urging me to call down the storm and mix it with my Beneath magic. If I did that, I'd be unstoppable. The Hopi gods and Coyote had warned me they'd crush me if I used my powers to hurt or kill, but too bad for them. I'd be too strong for them to stop me.

In fact, I'd be the strongest magical being in the world.

The ununculous? Ha. I'd stand toe-to-toe with Emmett Smith and blast him out of existence. And then I'd go find Bear and tell her what I thought of her horrific game with Coyote.

No. I bit back a scream. I'd been down this road before, and it hadn't ended well.

My hotel was in view. I gunned the bike, flew past the now-wet Crossroads, and kept on toward Flat Mesa.

Ten miles of open road lay between me and the next town. Ten miles of lightning, hail, and driving wind, while the artifact called me to link my powers with it and make myself invincible.

I was babbling to it, begging it to stop, when I roared into the parking lot of the Hopi County Sherriff's department fifteen minutes later.

I didn't want to open my saddlebag and pick up the leather-wrapped vessel. I didn't want to touch it, even with the layers of my riding gloves and the bag between me and it.

I started sobbing, but I made myself open the hatch and reach inside. I couldn't risk leaving the pot out here even for a minute—if Pericles or Drake had been following me, they'd grab it as soon as I ducked inside.

The vessel's power beat on me. I stumbled from bike to front door, not having the strength to close the saddlebag. The pot howled at me, calling me a coward, making my mind start whispering words of power to bring it to life.

"No, no, no, no, *no!*"

"Janet?" Deputy Lopez looked up from where he was taking particulars from a large but dispirited-looking biker. "You all right?"

"No!" I flung my helmet to the counter as I crashed my way behind Lopez and down the hall, not stopping until I reached the door marked, *Nash Jones, County Sheriff.*

Nash never locked his door, so I burst inside, praying he was there. He was, and he got to his feet when I ran inside, drenched and wild-eyed, clutching a dirty leather bag to my chest.

Nash swept up all the folders on his desk and slammed them onto his filing cabinet, not because my crazed entrance scared him, but because he wouldn't want me to get his beloved paperwork wet.

I dumped the leather bag onto the middle of his desk. "Pick that up. Please."

Nash stared at me with his winter-gray eyes. "Why?"

"*Please!* Damn it, Nash, just do it!"

Nash regarded me with stone-faced suspicion, but finally he reached down and touched the top of the bag.

The noise of a thousand screams filled my head, winding up into piercing shrieks. I covered my ears and yelled with them.

Nash continued to pin me with his flint-hard gaze, but he finally opened the bag, frowned into it, reached inside, and pulled out the pot.

Tiny shards of pottery—white, black, and red—leapt from the vessel and flew up to surround Nash. The instant before they hit his skin, they stopped, hovering in midair like a swarm of indecisive bees. Then they reversed, flowing back to the surface of the pot. I heard the click, click, click as they fell into place, then the pot went dormant.

The voices ceased. The hail, which had been grating on the window, died away to a soft summer rain.

I fell into a chair and pressed my hands to my aching head. "Thank you," I whispered. "Thank you."

"Want to tell me what this is?"

Nash scraped the bag away from the pot and set the pot on top of it.

It was a perfect match for the fake. Ansel had been right to call Laura a talented forger.

The real pot had the same slightly rounded bottom, the wide flare of the sides, the perfect pull in to the opening, plain without a lip. The inside of the pot was black, the outside white with red and black designs—the tortoise, the bear, and lines representing lightning.

Made of clay common to this region, it had been built up by hand, baked, and painted, the designs unique to the potter's clan and family. Then it had been infused with god magic, making it a hundred times more magical than most mages could ever hope to be.

Now that the pot's aura wasn't beating on me, I could appreciate its beauty. It was very old, but the colors were still vivid. The designs had softer and more curved lines than newer pottery, which could be sharp and abstract. Care and skill had gone into the pot's making. And power. Lots and lots of power.

I couldn't know whether the magic had gone in as the woman potter had formed the vessel or whether the power had been added afterward. I only know it had fixed on me as a being with goddess magic and had wanted to teach me to do amazing things.

It had recognized the powerful magic in Nash, but too late had realized the nature of that power.

Nash was a negative—a magic null. Even the most immense magics in existence were cancelled out when Nash touched them.

"Janet?" he prompted, and he didn't look patient.

I sighed and told him everything that had happened since I'd left him next to the dead slayer on the 40, ending with Coyote tasking me to destroy the pot.

"Easy enough," Nash said. "I have a hammer."

"I don't think it's that simple. I'm guessing breaking it or even grinding it to powder wouldn't stop it."

"Then how?"

"I don't know. I need to talk to Coyote."

Nash drew the bag up around the pot again and closed the

drawstring mouth. I could still feel the faint hum of its aura, but Nash's negation was keeping it from tearing at me.

"I'm guessing you want me to keep this," Nash said, sitting down again, the wrapped pot on the desk between us.

"Yes. With you, at all times. Never let it out of your sight. Bad people want to get this."

Nash sat straight in his chair as always, hands resting lightly on the desk. "Bad people, who?"

"Powerful mages like Pericles McKinnon. The Nightwalker who killed the slayer up on the I-40. He's an old boyfriend of Paige DiAngelo, by the way."

"Is he?" Nash's eyes took on a gleam of interest. He loved arresting people.

"Careful with him. He either wants this pot for himself to make him stronger, or else he's working for Pericles. He has a lot of people on his payroll."

"How do you know that?"

"He told me. When he was demanding me to come work for him too."

"And you said . . ."

"I said no." I folded my arms over my wet shirt, shivering as more water dribbled from my hair. "Of course I said no. He's creepy."

Nash didn't praise me, but I could tell he was pleased with my answer. "Where can I find Paige and her Nightwalker boyfriend?"

"In Amy's old house. Paige is renting it."

Nash's gaze flickered. Bad memories there. Nash had been engaged to Amy once upon a time . . . long story.

"Maybe Emmett Smith," I went on. "If he hears about it. You remember him."

"Hard to forget. Not the happiest time of my life, me locked into your hotel with you and your friends. I got thrown across a room."

"Pericles wants to knock Emmett off his throne, and

what better way than with an artifact full of god magic? Pericles certainly will come for it. But you being you, he can't kill you with spells, no matter how powerful he makes them."

"True," Nash said. "But he can kill me in other ways. He can shoot me, stab me, beat me to death, poison me. . ."

I lifted my hand. "Yes, all right, I take your point. But you're Nash. I can't see you letting someone get close enough to kill you."

"I won't." Nash said it without boasting. He didn't have to. "I can't take this home, not with Maya there. I won't let her be hurt by someone trying to get to me or this thing."

I gathered my long hair in my hands, and another rain of water splashed to his linoleum floor. "She won't like it if you don't go home."

"No, she won't."

We both went silent a moment, imagining the furious whirlwind of Maya when she found out Nash couldn't come to her because he was babysitting an old pot for me.

"Tell her you're having sex with me," I said. "She'll be so busy hunting me down to kill me, she won't have time to get near the artifact."

Nash didn't crack a smile. "I'll tell her the truth instead. Meanwhile, you find Coyote and figure out how to get rid of this thing as fast as you can."

"That was the plan."

"Good." He glanced at his paperwork, then back at me, clearly wanting me out of there.

I didn't want to go—it was calm in here, peaceful even, despite the pot's presence. Nash's null field always had a soothing effect on my crazed magic.

He gave me an icy look when I didn't move, but I knew that underneath that ice —somewhere —was the man Maya had fallen madly in love with.

I pulled myself to my feet, aching all over, and headed for

the door. "Thanks for understanding. Not out of your sight, remember."

"I heard you the first time." Nash lifted the pot and held it loosely in his hands. "Tell Lopez to get back here with a mop and towels."

~

THE STORM HAD DIED TO A FLOWING RAIN WITH THUNDER around the edges by the time I reached the parking lot again. I put my helmet back on, my hands shaking with exhaustion and release.

But I wasn't finished, not by a long way. I needed to find Coyote and ask him how on earth I was supposed to destroy the pot when I couldn't even get near it.

Coyote had said it was supposed to have been thrown into Sunset Crater back when the mountain had been a live volcano. Now Sunset Crater was a black, inert cinder cone surrounded by lava flows, rivers of rock frozen in time.

If an active volcano was the only thing needed, I could always take the pot to Hawaii, to the Big Island, and toss it into the bubbling volcano there. But then, maybe the god magic specific to the San Francisco peaks was important. Hawaii had its own gods, with their own agendas, and who knew what they might do with a vessel full of power?

Best to search for Coyote. I still didn't have a cell phone — not that Coyote always answered — so I decided to ride back to the hotel. Bear might have returned there, and despite their bizarre hide-and-seek game, she probably knew exactly where Coyote was.

I rode on, more fatigue hitting me with every mile. I nearly missed the turn into the hotel, my eyes were so glazed.

I pulled the bike around the back of the hotel and shut it off, then I found myself on the ground, the bike half on top of me, the back tire spinning in the air. My head hurt where my helmet had hit the ground, the only thing protecting me.

"Janet. Shit."

I heard Mick's voice, then felt him pull off the helmet, lift me into his strong arms, and carry me inside.

CHAPTER TWENTY-THREE

"I NEED TO TALK TO COYOTE," I MUMBLED.

Mick laid me on the bed, hands roaming my arms and legs, looking for injuries. "Shh. He's not here."

"I know. I need to find him. Or Bear."

"Love, what happened to you?"

He peeled off my wet jeans and shirt, then my bra and panties. I felt the large softness of a towel rubbed on my limbs, Mick drying me with thoroughness. The friction of the towel on my breasts and between my legs aroused me, but not enough to wake me up.

Mick kissed my face, my throat, my belly. The towel remained draped on my body, but Mick was draped there too, like the best blanket, his mouth a place of heat.

I didn't protest when he lifted my hips enough for him to slide into me and start to love me with slow goodness. The towel, still between us, absorbed our sweat in the hot afternoon. His whispers drifted over me along with his magic, drawing off my residual power, healing my body.

Sometime later, after he'd brought me to beautiful, dark climax, I drifted into exhausted sleep.

The shrill peal of a cell phone woke me. I jumped, finding the warm weight of Mick stretched beside me like a protective wall.

He reached down off the bed, plucked his phone from his jeans, and answered it. The strident tones of my grandmother filled the silence.

"Where is Janet? I need to talk to her."

Mick handed the phone to me without a word, not bothering to pretend we weren't in bed together.

"Grandmother?"

"Granddaughter, you need to get home. Right now. You, by yourself. Understand? I don't want to see that Firewalker with you. You know I don't like him."

I knew nothing of the sort. Grandmother had developed a fondness for Mick in spite of their rocky start.

"Right now. Do you hear me?" Grandmother's words grew distant from the phone. "Will you stop doing that?"

"Janet." Gabrielle's voice filled my ear. "Get here. It's important." She clicked off.

Mick took the cell back from me, his eyes changing from warm blue to black. He'd heard every word with his dragon hearing, not that my grandmother had bothered to keep her voice down.

"Someone's there with them," I said, and Mick gave me a nod.

"I got the not-so-subtle hint that I *should* come," he said. "How do you want to do this?"

I experienced brief moment of gratitude that Mick grasped essentials quickly without arguing. "I ride up alone." I traced his shoulder, where the line of dragon tattoo began. "You come covertly and back me up. And see if you can find Coyote. I still need to talk to him."

"You didn't tell me what for. What happened?"

I hesitated. *No one,* Coyote had said. Not even the man I loved best in the world?

Mick rolled up to sit on the edge of the bed, and reached for his clothes. I studied him as he dressed, his black hair that was wild and curly but not overlong, his square jaw, arms replete with muscle, very nice ass. A fine specimen of a man.

Mick didn't radiate the tightness of a person convinced he needed to prove himself. He carried himself easily, quiet until he was ready to strike. Because he knew he was strong and could easily hurt others, he was careful and gentle until the situation forced him to be otherwise.

I'd once seen him turn all his strength on me, and it had terrified me. No, it had nearly killed me.

I still hadn't quite recovered from that ordeal. What happened hadn't been Mick's fault, but when you see your loving boyfriend turn into a monster, it's hard to forget and move on.

Because I lay there inert, Mick opened my dresser, plucked out clean panties and bra and dropped them on top of me. "I think we're supposed to hurry."

I slid into the underwear. "Mick, I found the pot."

He stopped in the act of buckling his belt. His dark eyes widened, the black of the dragon still in them.

"Jamison had it." I filled him in on the events of the day, finishing with me taking the pot away from Jamison and how I'd had to fight to stop myself using it.

Mick's quietness left him, and the cold focus of the dragon pinned me. "Where is it now?"

"Nash has it."

He watched me a moment longer, then gave me a conceding nod. "Smart. Any signal it might give off to those looking for it will be absorbed."

"That's what I thought."

"Hmm." Mick stood there pondering, and my heart thudded in slow, painful beats. Mick was one person Nash would have a hard time besting. Mick's dragon fire wouldn't hurt Nash, but dragons aren't slowed down too much by bullets, and no human jail cell can stand up to fifteen tons of dragon bursting through its walls.

"I need to talk to Coyote," I repeated.

Mick patted me on the buttocks, gently pushing me toward the edge of the bed. "I'll see if I can find him. We really need to get that mirror fixed."

A non sequitur, but I knew what he meant. Journeying northward separately while keeping track of who was doing what would be easier if we could communicate via the magic mirror. Magic mirrors trumped cell phones every time. We each carried a piece of the thing anyway, in case it did wake up on its own. Sometimes that happened.

As we walked out of the private entrance of the hotel, heading for the shed that contained our motorcycles, Elena emerged from the kitchen door.

"Where are you going?" she asked me. "Don't lie."

"Many Farms," I said.

Elena's eyes narrowed, and she walked across the lot to us. "Trouble?"

Mick shrugged. "Probably. We'll find out when we get there."

Elena pulled off her chef's apron and dropped it to the ground. "I go with you."

"You can't," I said.

She put her hands on her hips. "Why not?"

"Grandmother told me to come alone, so I think I'd better appear to be alone."

"I'll ride with Mick then. That is your plan, isn't it? You go, and Mick sneaks in behind?"

"It's what Grandmother implied we should do."

"Then I go. With Mick."

Elena wore her stubborn look, the one that said she'd do whatever she damn well pleased, and we'd have to live with it. Elena wasn't just a middle-aged, bad-tempered cook. She had powers I hadn't begun to understand.

"Get her a helmet, Mick. I'll meet you up there."

I rose on tiptoe, kissed Mick on the lips, mounted my Soft-ail, and rode out.

I TRAVELED EAST OUT OF HOLBROOK ON THE 40 FOR ABOUT fifty miles, before turning north on the 191, a smooth road on rolling land, leading into the heart of the Navajo Nation.

I knew the rises and falls in this road by heart, the steep hills that dropped to tiny river valleys—the washes dry today—the T intersection in Ganado, which split into the road to Window Rock to the east and the highway on to Chinle to the left. I turned left, zipped around the new roundabout a few miles west, and headed more or less straight north.

As I crested the next big hill, a wide valley opened to my right, a vista of variegated hills rising to the mountain range behind it. Beautiful Valley, it was called on maps, and I'd always agreed. My heart lightened when I saw it, because I knew that in another thirty miles or so, I'd be home.

A storm hung out over the mountains east of Chinle and Canyon de Chelly, the sky black, a gray curtain of rain sweeping over the ridge toward the highway.

Today I was almost oblivious to the beauty that surrounded me as I hurried northward. Almost. This land was in my bones. No matter what the crisis, I was part of this place, tasting it, living it, feeling it.

I slowed to drive through Chinle, with its inhabitants—human, equine, bovine—wandering the roads. A friend of Jamison's, filling up his truck at a gas station, recognized me and waved, and I waved back but kept on going. Rude of me not to stop and say hello, but my worry about Grandmother drove me on.

I rode into the small town of Many Farms at dusk, the storms now behind me. The dying sun lit the broken clouds fuchsia, golden, and brilliant orange, and illuminated the stark sandstone butte north of town.

I made sure to raise my hand in greeting to those I passed as I rode through, and to travel at a reasonable speed, so no one would guess I was hurrying home in a panic. I didn't want half the town following me to see what was wrong at Ruby Begay's place.

I wasn't worried as much for my Grandmother and Gabrielle, who were very good at taking care of themselves. But unless my father had gone to Farmington with Gina, he'd be there in the middle of whatever was wrong.

I prayed to every god in the universe that he'd gone to Farmington, but that hope died as soon as I turned onto the narrow track that led to the house and saw his pickup there.

I killed my engine, parked, and left my helmet on the back of the bike.

Our long, low-roofed house looked quiet—which was highly unusual. Usual was one or more of my nieces playing in the yard, whatever aunt had come to visit arguing with my grandmother in the kitchen. My dad would be out tinkering with his truck, and these days Gina would be either helping him or sitting on the porch putting together the jewelry she made and sold.

Today no doors or windows were open, and I spied no movement inside the house.

I walked up to the front door without being challenged. I'd have sensed dragon aura loud and clear, and I didn't, so I knew neither Drake nor Colby was the source of the problem.

I did sense Gabrielle's aura, the bright, sharp edges of it. Whoever had managed to enter the house would have had to get past her as well as my grandmother. That didn't bode well.

The mystery was solved when I opened the door and walked inside.

My father and Gina Tsotsie sat side by side on the living room sofa. My father looked angry and so did Gina. Gina was a large woman, built along Bear's lines, a little younger than my father. She shared his quietness, and they said nothing at all when I entered.

My grandmother, wearing her traditional skirts and blouse, stood in the opening between kitchen and living room, her cane planted in front of her. Gabrielle had turned one of the kitchen chairs backwards and sat straddling it. She was the only one who looked interested instead of angry, the only one who didn't project an aura of fear.

I'd met the man who stood in my living room once before. He was about the same height as my small-statured dad and had neatly trimmed salt-and-pepper hair. He wore a designer business suit with a silk tie, polished top-of-the-line shoes, and eyeglasses with tiny diamonds on the temple pieces. Behind the glasses, his eyes held the coldness of a thousand winters.

Emmett Smith. Also known as the ununculous, the most powerful mage in the world, and the man Pericles McKinnon wanted to topple from his throne. In my house.

I directed my words at Gabrielle and my grandmother. "You let him *in*?"

"He walked in," Gabrielle said. "Watch this."

A ball of Beneath magic manifested inside her fist. Gabrielle never worried about tearing apart the fabric of the world if her Beneath magic rippled out of control—she just let fly.

She hurled the ball at Emmett. The magic hit a barrier around Emmett, which shimmered for a moment like a sci-fi special effect, then the Beneath magic whipped around him and hurtled back toward Gabrielle.

Gabrielle caught the radiant ball like an outfielder grabbing a pop fly. She clapped her hands around it, and the Beneath glow dispersed.

Her eyes shone, and she breathed a little faster. "Isn't that cool?"

No, it was terrifying. Emmett Smith had figured out how to shield against Beneath-goddess magic.

"I told you that when we met again, Stormwalker, it would be an interesting day," Emmett said. "My research turned up that you had a half-goddess sister and a grandmother who is master at Diné earth magic, so I've spent the time since our last meeting honing my defenses against such things."

I studied him, finger to my lips. "While you're stuck behind that barrier, can you do any magic of your own?"

"He can," Gabrielle said. Her voice went somber. "He did."

"Is anyone hurt?" I looked at my father in alarm, but he shook his head.

Gina answered me. "He beat Gabrielle's body against the floor. She tried to stop him coming inside, and he picked her up with some kind of spell and hurled her down. Repeatedly." Her anger radiated into her aura, overwhelming her fear.

Gabrielle didn't look bruised or bloody, but her dark eyes held a bright gleam. Too bright. "It was awesome," she said.

I swung to Emmett. "You touch my sister again, I won't care how many craters I make in the world when I kill you."

Gabrielle's smile widened. "Aw, Janet. That's sweet. Can I help?"

Emmett adjusted his glasses. "This is touching, but what I came here to get is the pot. Bring it to me, and I'll think about letting your family live."

I put myself between him and Gabrielle and folded my arms. "Leave my family alone, and I'll think about letting *you* live."

Emmett's smile widened, his eyes still as cold as all the ice floes in the Arctic. "Hmm, I knew this would be interesting. Where is the vessel?"

"I don't have it."

"But you know where it is. Call one of your minions and order him to bring it here."

"Minions." I looked at him, straight-faced. "Are you serious?"

"You're a powerful magical being. You might pretend you don't look down on those of lesser magnitude, but you do. You regard everyone below your power level as either useful or entertaining. Which one is the dragon?"

"Insulting me is not going to convince me turn the artifact over to you," I said.

Emmett's eyes widened. "You think I was trying to insult you? It's truth. It's how you think."

"No, it's how *you* think. You care only for power, not people."

"Not true actually, but I won't let you get around me by trying to figure out what broke my heart in the past. *The one vulnerability of the dark mage.* Is that right? What a cliché. I don't have any vulnerabilities."

I folded my arms. "So you call yourself a dark mage, do you?"

"I'm the ununculous," Emmett said patiently. "Neither dark nor light—I just *am*. Dark and light designations are for amateurs, for feel-good witches to write about in popular books about magic, which they spell with a *K*. Where *is* your dragon, by the way?"

"Not with me."

"I know that, but again, you know where he is. Don't play with words, Stormwalker. You're not good at it."

"I thought you wanted me to come alone."

"Yes, but I heard your grandmother's not very well-veiled plea for you to bring him along. I imagine he's hovering out there somewhere, going over tactics for how to extract you with the minimum number of casualties. Micalerianicum thinks like a general and always will. Doesn't matter how much you've softened him up by agreeing to marry him in the human way." He gestured to the silver and turquoise ring that clasped my finger.

I sent him a smile. "Are you trying to beat me down by stirring up my emotions about Mick? Talk about cliché."

Emmett laughed softly. "I'd never dream of it. Get on the phone, and have someone bring me the vessel. I want a look at it."

I didn't move. "If you take hold of that pot, every magical creature in the world will be after you, trying to wrest it from you. Do you want that kind of heat?"

"I'm the ununculous," he said without conceit. "No one will be able to take it from me."

"And as the ununculous, you can't afford to let anyone else have it. I held the thing—I know what it's capable of. I could have used it to best you if I'd wanted to."

"And you didn't?" Emmett looked me up and down. "You have remarkable restraint, Stormwalker. I salute you. But very stupid—you ought to have taken me out when you had the chance." He shook his head. "But you're right. I can't afford to let you keep it. I'm the best mage in the world, and I need to keep the most powerful toys for myself."

"And you're willing to risk me bringing the pot here?" I pointed at Gabrielle. "With her? You've tasted her magic. You know what it is."

Gabrielle nodded, face grave. "Big sis is right. I'm crazy. You can't know what I'd do with that kind of power in my hands."

Emmett took a handkerchief from his pocket, removed his glasses, and polished the lenses. With his glasses off, I saw that his irises were silver, like thin pieces of metal.

"You know," he said, "the only reason I didn't kill your entire family today is because you once helped me. Granted, you had no wish to help, and you endangered me rather badly in the process, but in the end, it was a help. Now I wish to assist you." He pinned me with a raw gaze that told me he didn't need the glasses to see. "That vessel is too dangerous to be loose, and you know it. You also know that I'm strong enough to keep it out of the hands of amateurs. I'll keep it safe for you."

"Sure you will," I said. "You know Pericles McKinnon? He wants your position. I imagine he'll be the first one after you once he knows you have the pot."

Emmett dismissed his archrival with the wave of his hand. "McKinnon, yes. I've met him. As a matter of fact, I told him that you had the pot and that I'd be coaxing you here today. I imagine he'll be here soon."

CHAPTER TWENTY-FOUR

"YOU DID *WHAT*?" I SHRIEKED.

I ran to the window, expecting a black cloud of evil to be boiling toward us. The sun was still setting, clouds bathed in last wild color, the land empty except for a neighbor's horse who'd wandered toward our house in search of more interesting grass.

I swung back to Emmett. "Why the hell did you tell Pericles?"

"To give you a choice." Emmett finished polishing his glasses and slid them back on. "You've met Pericles, that less-than-elegant mage with dreams of grandeur. Think about it. Would you rather give the pot to him, or to me?"

"That isn't the point!"

If Pericles knew I had the pot, or could at least bring it to our little house in Many Farms, and if he let that information slip—intentionally or not—we could expect trouble. Piles of trouble. The dragons had their collective ear out, so Drake would be up here, possibly Bancroft with him, definitely dragging Colby along to help with the dirty work. Entities more powerful and less inclined to reason than Drake might be here too, including Paige's Nightwalker.

I'd have a war on my hands.

And then there was Gabrielle. I hadn't exaggerated when I talked about the risk of letting her anywhere near the pot. I'd barely stopped myself using the thing to destroy every person who'd ever endangered or threatened me.

I'd stopped because I'd understood what I'd become if I did, and I didn't want to start hurting those who'd never done me harm. The threat of gods coming after me hadn't slowed me down at all.

Gabrielle didn't have the restrictions I'd learned to put on myself. Those restrictions let me have friends, a family who didn't shun me, and a relationship with a guy I loved. A normal life—well, normal for me.

Gabrielle, on the other hand, had been raised by an abusive dickhead, had abandonment issues out the ass, and professed not to care about being "normal." She'd calmed down a little under the tutelage of my grandmother, but I knew that any change I observed in her was Gabrielle's choice. If she thought she could go back to taking vengeance on anyone who'd ever hurt her—and get away with it—she just might.

If Pericles came here, with Emmett and Gabrielle already present, and Mick and Elena on the way—my beloved home could become a smoking sinkhole, even before I fetched the pot.

Emmett cleared his throat. "I don't see you making phone calls. You and your boyfriend don't have a way to communicate magically, do you?"

I didn't like the gleam of interest in his silver eyes. So far, I'd been able to keep quiet to Emmett that I had a magic mirror, and I wanted it to stay that way. Now the mirror shard in its chamois bag in my pocket made my leg tingle.

I slammed my focus out the window to the shed a little way from the house. That shed had replaced the one I'd burned

down as a kid, when my Stormwalker powers had first manifested. "Shut up, and let me think."

Pericles and any followers would be coming after me,
whether I liked it or not. What I had to do was make sure they
didn't come *here*.

I turned from the window. "All right," I said to Emmett,
raising my hands in surrender. "I'll get you the pot. But not
here. I'll have it taken to Chaco Canyon."

Emmett's well-groomed brows shot upward. "In the middle
of the desert in the dark? I'll get my shoes dirty."

"Janet," my grandmother said in the Diné language.
"Chaco is heavy with old magic. No telling what will happen
when you let loose something like *him* in it, let alone that
vessel."

"I know," I said. "But it's the only place I can think of that
can take the kind of forces he'll bring down on us."

"You know I speak at least a hundred and fifty languages,"
Emmett interrupted in Diné. "Including many Native American ones. But I agree with your assessment. Chaco has taken
great influxes of magic for millennia. A little tiff between mages
won't hurt it. But I'll still get my shoes dirty."

"You can buy new ones," I said. "Grandmother, I need to
use your phone."

~

"A MAGIC SHOWDOWN," GABRIELLE SAID WHEN I FINISHED
calling Nash. "This is going to be fun."

I ignored her for the moment to call Mick. Elena answered
Mick's phone, explaining that Mick was a dragon at the
moment. But she promised to give him the message.

"I have a message for *you*," Elena said before I could hang
up. "Cassandra called and said that a person named Rory is
trying to find you. He says to tell you he has the package you
ordered."

"Oh. Great. Thanks."

"What package, Janet?" Elena asked in suspicion.

"I'll tell you later," I lied. "Thanks."

I hung up and turned my back on the avidly listening crowd in the living room to punch in Rory's phone number. "You got him?" I asked when he answered.

"Of course I have him," Rory the slayer said. "Why else would I call? You still want him alive?"

The question was delivered in disbelieving tones. "Yes," I said. "Don't kill him. Stash him somewhere safe. Sheriff Jones will want to talk to him. And be careful. He's already murdered another slayer."

"Yeah, I know," Rory said testily. "It's going to cost you extra."

He hung up.

I replaced the phone on its hook and turned around to find the eyes of everyone in the house on me. Those of my family were disapproving or concerned, Gabrielle curious, Emmett amused.

"You done?" Gabrielle asked. "Can we go already?"

"You aren't going anywhere," I said firmly. "You're staying here with Grandmother and Dad in case anyone tries to double back here and cause more trouble."

"No way, Janet. I'm coming with you. I want to see this."

"And me." My grandmother gave me her mulish look. "Don't bother to argue. Start up your father's truck, and let's go."

"I don't want Janet leaving."

The quiet words came from my father. All of us, including Emmett, turned to him in surprise.

Dad had risen from the sofa, Gina with him. Now Dad let go of Gina's hand and moved to stand in front of me.

My father, Pete Begay, was an inch or so taller than me. In his early fifties, his hair was still midnight black, and his face bore few lines. He carried himself with a straight posture, without shame, but he kept himself to himself.

I'd spent many days and nights in companionable silence with this man while we'd driven out under the stars, or searched for stray sheep, or repaired his truck. I'd always felt a silent but strong bond between us, no words necessary.

Dad rarely said out loud what he truly thought. He'd always lived in a houseful of women with strong opinions—first Grandmother and his sisters, then Grandmother and me, and now Grandmother and Gabrielle. No one but me had ever asked for his thoughts or advice, so my father had stopped bothering to give either one.

Now he faced me, his mouth set in a stubborn line.

"Dad," I said softly. "I have to."

"No, you do not." His frown deepened until furrows appeared on either side of his mouth. "Mick can take care of this for you. I am tired of wondering when someone will come and tell me you are dead."

I glanced at Gina, but she'd backed away from the conversation, remaining on the other side of the small room.

My heart ached. I knew how Dad felt, because I equally feared such a phone call about him. I lived in terror I'd receive a call like the one today, informing me that my family—especially my dad—was in danger because of me. Or one that told me someone had figured out how to kill Mick. Even dragons aren't indestructible, and now that he'd mentioned dragonslayers, I had that to worry about too.

But I couldn't send Mick out there alone to face Emmett and Pericles, and who knew who else, even with Nash and Elena to back him up.

"I can't," I said. "Mick is strong, but his magic is different from mine. He'll need me for this."

"Your grandmother has told me what the pot does. It fills you up with power, but when it is drained, it will try to take yours to build up its own."

"Really?" I thought about how the splinters of pottery had detached themselves from the pot and flown at Nash at first. Jamison had said the same thing happened to him, except the shards had cut Jamison's flesh while the pot lent him power. Maybe the fragments dragged in power the same way, then poured themselves back into the pot.

"So the legend goes," Emmett said. "But a very strong mage such as myself can resist the drain."

"Huh," Grandmother said. "You think so? Janet, you never told me he was this arrogant."

My father said nothing, his focus on me.

I looked at the man who'd been my anchor, the only person in my life who'd loved me in spite of what what and who I was. He'd loved my mother, who'd lured him into an affair only so she could produce me. Pete Begay, when he found himself saddled with me, had decided to take care of me, where a lesser man might have dumped me onto the mercy of the world.

I owed Dad my life, my gratitude, my respect, my love. Which he had. All of it.

"I have to," I whispered.

Something had taken me to Chaco Canyon four mornings ago—it seemed a lifetime ago now. Had it been the vessel? Or the place itself? I had to know.

"I have to," I repeated, my voice steadier.

My father was never one to show his anger. No matter how much trouble I'd gotten myself into as a child, he'd never raised his voice at me.

He was good, however, at expressing disappointment. He'd inherited that from my grandmother.

He stared straight at me now, his eyes showing a deep sadness that cut me. He wasn't hurting me on purpose, because he didn't believe in making people feel bad, but I knew his sadness was real.

My father walked past me and to the back window, where he stood looking out at the desert beyond. His shoulders went up the slightest bit as he took a long breath, then down as he let it out.

Gina said nothing to me. She sat again on the sofa and watched us with her dark-eyed placidity.

"Are you finished?" Emmett asked.

"Meet us there," I said to Emmett. "I'll have the vessel."

"No," Emmett said, his lips curving into a humorless smile. "I don't trust you, Stormwalker. I want to be next to you every step of the way, even if I have to ride in a pickup truck."

I DROVE. I DIDN'T TRUST GABRIELLE BEHIND THE WHEEL OF anything, and I wasn't about to let Emmett drive my dad's pickup, so I slid into the driver's seat and started the truck. Emmett squeezed into the cab with me, Grandmother between us, and Gabrielle climbed into the pickup's bed. Gabrielle waved to everyone we passed on our way out of town, making no secret about us leaving.

I continued north on the 191, almost to the Utah border, then took the 160 east to Farmington, heading south again through New Mexico to the turnoff to Chaco Canyon. The journey took hours, and it was solidly dark when we reached the narrow road to the ruins.

The truck bumped and jounced down the winding road, the sky black with bulges of clouds on the horizon and tatters of clouds overhead. Through gaps in the thinner clouds, stars clustered in a thick smudge.

I had never feared the night, a time of intense beauty. What I feared was the layers of magic and old auras at the end of this road, and who or what we'd find waiting for us.

I drove past the entrance to the visitor's center, now closed, and around on maintenance roads past the ruins. My dad's sturdy truck, used to washed-out back roads, soldiered on.

Something huge rose in the headlights and slammed into the front of the truck. Gabrielle screamed, and I hit the brakes.

Grandmother and Emmett did little more than inhale sharply. Emmett opened the passenger door, balanced himself on the doorstep and pulled himself up to look over the top of the truck. Wouldn't want to get his precious shoes dirty getting out to see what was wrong.

"It's nothing," he said after a moment. "Just a dead coyote."

A dead coyote.

I set the parking brake, scrambled out, and ran to the front of the truck. Lying in the dirt, illuminated by our headlights, was a large coyote, bloody and definitely dead. Its head was half cut off, and entrails snaked out of its belly.

I fell to my knees beside it. The corpse stank, as though it had been out here a day at least. This animal hadn't run in front of our truck—someone had hurled him there.

"Coyote?" While the beast was covered in blood, it was giant for its species, and I was pretty sure the face, still intact, was Coyote's.

"This isn't time for your weird games," I shouted at him. "Come back to life already. I need you!"

Gabrielle stopped at my side, her motorcycle boots a match for my own. "You all right, sis? It's dead."

"He's Coyote." I shook the body. "Come on. Wake up."

The beast shimmered. Gabrielle drew back, but I didn't take my hand from his bloody body.

When mist cleared, Coyote the man lay on the ground. A deep gash cut through his neck, now coated with dried blood, and his belly lay open and pathetically exposed.

"Stop this," I babbled. "I need you."

Coyote opened his eyes. As when I'd found him dying behind the railroad bed, his dark irises were filmed over, and I knew he couldn't see me. "Bear," he said.

"I know. You explained about your bizarre ritual. But I need you. I have the pot. Or will have."

"You must destroy . . ."

"I know that. But how do I destroy it? *Tell me.*"

"Bear . . ."

"She knows?" Tears spilled down my cheeks. "Coyote, stop this, and get up."

Gabrielle bent to me, her hands on her knees. "Give him a break, Janet. He's dying."

"No, he isn't." I shook Coyote's shoulder. "Tell me what to do."

"Bear." He covered my hand with his. His strength, even in this state, nearly crushed my fingers. "Love you, girl," he said, and he called me by my spirit name—the name known to no one but my father and me. Gabrielle didn't hear it, because Coyote whispered it straight into my mind.

The word gave me a burst of strength. Coyote's form shimmered again, then the hand holding mine relaxed, and Coyote vanished.

I shuddered as I rose to my feet. Gabrielle remained staring down at the spot where Coyote had lain. "Well, that was weird."

I turned away in silence and got back into the truck. Gabrielle climbed into the bed again, and I drove on.

"He's dead then," Emmett said.

"Yes."

"Hmm."

"Shut up." I took the truck down a slippery track and stopped at the bottom.

The moon thrust itself out from behind the clouds and bathed the valley in subtle light. The rocky outcrops to either side of us became stark silhouettes.

One of the roads to nowhere, built for the gods, seemed to stretch toward the pile of clouds on the horizon. Lightning licked the clouds, flashing them purple and gold before the world faded again to black.

A figure stood at the foot of the road just inside the circle of my headlights, like a tall, upright monolith in open ground. At first I thought a bear stood there, a giant grizzly up on its hind legs.

As I got out of the truck, I saw that it was Bear. She was in human form, with a bearskin wrapped around her body, the dead bear's face forever fixed in a carnivorous snarl. Under the skin she wore flowing skirts like my grandmother's and her usual silver and turquoise jewelry. She'd tied three hawk's feathers in her black hair.

Her bangles, rings, and necklace caught the moonlight as she raised her hands, throwing the reflection at us in wide bands. The stone knife she'd used to slay Coyote hung on her belt, the aura of it thick and black against her otherwise clean silver.

"What the hell?" Gabrielle had stopped by my side.

Emmett, who'd gotten out of the truck in spite of the dirt, adjusted his glasses. "Bear goddess. Interesting."

Grandmother was walking toward Bear, her stick tapping the earth. She stopped about ten feet in front of Bear who watched us, her dark eyes quiet. "Did you know we were coming?"

Bear said nothing. I'd never seen her like this, not in her goddess persona. She'd always appeared to me as the large, rather placid Indian woman in her old-fashioned dress and jewelry, ready with her gentle strength and good advice—her hunting of Coyote with the knife notwithstanding.

Now she radiated power, the aura of her stronger even than the aura of Chaco itself. I felt her strength and her compassion, but also a power beyond measure, plus the crushing knowledge all deities had that they were far stronger than any creature on the earth.

She, like Coyote, had lived in the worlds before this one, the Beneath worlds, out of which the first men and women had climbed. She'd been one of the gods who'd sealed the Beneath worlds behind them, trapping the more evil gods and goddesses—my mother being one of them—inside.

But though Coyote and Bear and others had thus protected the world from the evils of Beneath, that didn't mean the gods who'd stayed in this world were wholly benevolent. They had their good sides and their frightening sides.

I was starting to get frightened.

Bear watched me as I stopped next to Grandmother, both of us sensing we shouldn't move closer.

"Stormwalker," Bear said. Her rich contralto rolled across the valley. "I've come for my vessel. Bring it to me."

CHAPTER TWENTY-FIVE

"*Your* vessel?" I asked in surprise, though Grandmother didn't look astonished in the least.

"I created it," Bear said, her voice filling the spaces around us. "I've come to take it back."

"And do what with it, exactly?" I asked. "Destroy it?"

"No."

Emmett and Gabrielle came up beside us—Emmett must think hearing this worth the dust on shoe leather. "A vessel fashioned by a Native American bear goddess?" he mused. "My price just went up."

"Price?" Grandmother scowled at him. "I thought you wanted it for yourself."

"I was speaking figuratively. Let me put it this way—the price for me helping you keep it away from her."

"You can't let her have it, Janet," Grandmother said, ignoring Emmett.

"Why not? I certainly don't want Emmett or the dragons getting their hands on it."

"Gods can't be trusted," Grandmother said firmly. "Even friendly ones. What *she* thinks is right to do with it might destroy half this world. She's originally from Beneath, remember? She doesn't have good, solid earth magic to ground her."

"Hey, *I'm* from Beneath," Gabrielle said hotly.

"Exactly my point."

I took a step forward, trying to shut out the distractions. "What do you want the pot for?" I asked Bear.

She fixed a gaze on me like the power of seventeen suns. "For? Why must things be *for*, human child?"

"I'm trying to understand why you didn't destroy a thing that dangerous a long time ago. It tried to turn me into something I didn't want to be. If I'd kept resisting it, I'd have died."

"Because you are human, Stormwalker. Though god blood beats in your veins, you are held to the earth, as is your sister. Humans are too weak for my vessel. The shamans who decided to destroy it in lava many years ago were unable to throw it away, so I took it from them and hid it. But it uncovered itself eventually, and so your Nightwalker's friend found it."

"You're going to hide it again?"

"Bring me the vessel, Janet."

"Janet." Another rumbling voice assailed me, one I was relieved to hear.

Mick walked out of the black shadows of the canyon walls, Elena with him. Mick was dressed, so he must have had Elena carry clothes for him, but the aura of his dragon flight was pungent—the familiar taste of fire and smoke wrapped up in the music of his name.

I tried not to hurry as I went to meet him. "Did you bring him?" I asked in a low voice.

Mick took my hand. "He's coming."

Elena wore her usual look of disapproval. "The Nightwalker insisted on accompanying us."

Ansel walked shakily out of the shadows, as though he'd been waiting until summoned. He folded his arms over his lanky body, his sandstone-colored Sedona T-shirt making his skin even starker white.

"This was my fault," he said. "I want to put it right."

I didn't agree with him, but Elena broke in before I could answer. "Whatever you do, don't give the vessel to the goddess."

"So Grandmother advised me."

"Ruby is correct. The bear goddess has infinite power, maybe more than Coyote himself. She made that vessel to contain some of her extra power so she could hold onto her shape and live more easily in this world. But she didn't know how to temper her strength. She gave it to shamans of a tribe, trying to help them. They found that the pot enhanced their magic, but the magic built to dangerous levels, and then the pot, made to siphon off excess power, sucked it all back out of them until they were dead. Mortals simply can't handle those kinds of forces."

Made sense from what Jamison had told me, and what I'd experienced. "How do you know all this?" I asked Elena.

"Bear told me."

I blinked. "She told you? Why didn't she tell *me*?"

"I don't know. Maybe she likes my cooking."

Elena shut off her stream of information then and walked away to be with Grandmother, leaving me with Mick and Ansel, Mick still holding my hand.

Elena's irritability aside, I agreed with her and grandmother that Bear shouldn't have the pot until we understood more what she'd do.

Ansel unfolded his arms. "I'm only here because one of these people has Laura. I'm not leaving until I find her."

He moved away from us and the rest of the group, his Nightwalker speed carrying him out of sight into the shadows before I could ask him to stay.

I squeezed Mick's hand. "We could go," I said softly.

We could fly away from here, to another continent or a remote island to lie in the sun or in a cool-sheeted bed together.

We could leave god magic, ancient pottery, and power-hungry mages to themselves.

Mick wanted to. His eyes flicked from black to the deep blue I'd fallen in love with.

I looked from him across the space of ground to Grandmother and Gabrielle, in a cluster with Elena, taking themselves apart from Emmett. My family.

As a child, my grandmother had been hard on me. I realized much later she'd been hard because she'd known I possessed powerful magic, more powerful than the earth magic she'd inherited from her shaman ancestors. She'd been afraid, I understood now, that I'd turn out to be an evil being like my mother, or at least arrogantly powerful like Emmett.

Now Grandmother had taken in Gabrielle, born of our goddess mother and an Apache man who'd been weak and cruel. Gabrielle was a handful of trouble, but Grandmother was teaching her and protecting her as she'd taught and protected me.

They were my family. Vulnerable. Here because of their own stubbornness, but here. To help me.

I swung Mick's hand. "Afterward? You and me? Beach?"

He sent me a sinful look that licked heat through my body. "I have the perfect place in mind."

Knowing Mick, it would be remote, quiet, and romantic, and we wouldn't resurface for days.

I let out a sigh. "Let's survive this first. We need a plan."

Mick grinned. "You brought us here without a plan? What am I going to do with you, sweetheart?"

"My plans always screw up. You know that. I hoped you'd have some ideas."

Mick studied the group with cool calculation. "Kill Emmett, kill Pericles if he comes. Tell Nash how to destroy the pot and have him do it for us."

"That sounds easy and dragon-y. What about Bear? She's insisting we bring the pot to her. I'm betting she's responsible for making my motorcycle carry me out here in the first place, so I'd get curious. Or maybe she planned to talk to me, but Officer Yellow got in the way. The mirror said a person hadn't been responsible, but Bear's not a person, she's a god." I let out a breath. "Would you fight her? I don't think we can."

"I've fought gods before." Mick studied Bear, who still stood patiently in the moonlight, the bearskin around her looking almost alive. "But with Bear, I was thinking about using reason."

"Good luck with that." Gods would listen to reason, true, but you never knew how they'd twist your reason to their own purpose. They might nod and agree with you, then walk away and carry on with whatever they'd planned in the first place.

Headlights broke the night, a vehicle winding down the canyon road. I couldn't tell at this distance what kind of vehicle, but I knew that Nash had come.

"We'd better decide fast," I said.

"We defend Nash from physical attack," Mick said. "He's our primary objective. When the others exhaust themselves trying to keep each other from the pot, then we disable them and decide what to do with it."

"What about if dragons join in?" I asked, looking up.

Mick snapped his attention to the sky. Two giant silhouettes blotted out the starlight, both with wings spread. One dragon was midnight black — Drake — the other fiery red — Colby, still under compulsion to obey.

Drake's fire streaked down and caught Nash's black F250. The impact lifted the truck a few feet into the air before dropping it again, the entire truck engulfed in incandescent flame. Dragon fire was magical, so it couldn't hurt Nash directly, but it could incinerate the truck he was in, or push it over the edge of the road into the canyon.

I started running. Mick didn't follow, and before I'd made it halfway to Nash, Mick shot into the air on colossal wings. He headed for Drake, his cry of challenge splitting the air.

Nash kept on driving, despite the fire dancing through his pickup. He was not going to be happy about this. He loved that truck.

Once Nash was on flat ground, he pulled onto empty dirt, leapt out, and started squirting the pickup with a fire extinguisher. Gabrielle broke away from Grandmother and ran for him.

I doubled my speed as Beneath magic glowed around Gabrielle, but when she reached the truck, the wash of Beneath magic she released only put out the fire.

Nash shut down his compact fire extinguisher and stood with it hanging from his hand. Perspiration streaked his face, and his jeans and sweat pants were singed and soot-stained. "Thanks," he said to Gabrielle.

"Where's Maya?" Gabrielle asked.

"Not here," Nash answered curtly. Maya was not a fan of Gabrielle, who had once taken Nash hostage. "I wasn't going to bring her to a meet like this."

"Did you have to lock her in a cell?" I asked.

"Yes."

I grinned. "Can I watch when you let her out? Please?"

Nash gave me a withering look. "Why the hell did you ask me to bring this thing to you? The dragons followed me the minute I left town."

I should have figured Drake was clever enough to realize that Nash was the logical person to watch over the artifact. Drake had probably commanded Colby to keep tabs on him.

"It's time to decide what to do with it," I said.

Gabrielle looked puzzled. "You're not going to destroy it, are you? Something like that would be useful."

"That's exactly why."

Gabrielle pretended to pout. "What, you still don't trust me?"

"No."

She laughed and put her arm around my shoulders. "You are so smart."

Grandmother was hobbling toward us, Elena at her side. Emmett continued to face Bear, who stood calmly, waiting.

Except that now two men faced Bear. The second was Pericles McKinnon.

How he'd gotten here, I didn't know, but he was a good mage, and I'm sure he had plenty of tricks in his repertoire. Emmett adjusted his glasses to look the other man up and down.

"They won't wait long," Grandmother said. "Whatever it is you're going to do to stop this, you'd better do it now."

"I'm not going to do anything," I said.

"You can't let either one of them touch that vessel. They'll unleash forces too large to handle, not to mention they'll try to kill every one of us. Yes, the pot will drain them, but they can do a world's worth of damage before then."

"I don't intend to let anyone grab the pot, Grandmother. I'll protect it with everything I have." I lifted my hands. "But if so many people want it, they can fight it out. I'll be over here protecting my friends and family."

Grandmother's eyes narrowed. "What about Bear?"

"I think she can take care of herself."

Bear hadn't moved. She watched the two mages size each other up, but she did nothing, said nothing. She, like me, waited to see what happened.

Above us, the dragons circled one another, shooting warning jets of fire whenever any of the three got too close to the others. Dragon battles were so deadly, Mick had told me, that dragons didn't fully engage unless they had to. For now, they were watching, wary, Mick keeping himself between the other two and Nash.

The clouds on the western horizon slowly moved our way, coming down from the Chuska Mountains and thickening as they went. The thunderheads drove dust before them, lightning curling under the clouds. I felt the storm's fiery tingle awaking the earth magic in me.

"Letting the mages and dragons fight each other might release powers this valley can't contain," Elena said. "We'll be caught in the backwash."

"But we are four of the most powerful women I know," I countered. "Between us, we can protect ourselves and Nash from anything they do."

In theory. I knew Gabrielle was strong, but I didn't know how close Elena had to be to her pool of shaman magic to use it, and I still had no idea how Grandmother's magic worked. She had a vast well of earth magic in her, which is where I'd come by my Stormwalker ability, but I had never seen her in action.

"I like this plan," Gabrielle said, sliding her hands into the back pockets of her jeans. "Whoever wins the free-for-all will be weak, and we'll just kill him."

"*You* aren't killing anyone," Grandmother said. "We talked about this."

Gabrielle shot me an appealing look. "See what I have to put up with?"

"Could everyone please shut up and let me think?" I stuffed my hands into my own front pockets, finding the chamois-wrapped piece of magic mirror. "Nash, will you bring it out?"

Nash looked up from checking the ammunition in his Glock. "Why?"

"You don't have to hand it to me. In fact, please don't. But uncover it."

Nash scowled, but he reached into the truck's cab and retrieved the leather-wrapped pot from the seat. He set the bundle on the hood, opened the drawstring, and peeled back the bag.

His null magic so absorbed the pot's field that Emmett and Pericles, still eying each other, didn't look our way. The dragons didn't break their focus on one another either. Even

I couldn't feel anything from the pot, which was fine with me.

Moonlight picked out the sharp outlines of the bear, the tortoise, and the jagged lightning. I wondered why Bear had chosen the tortoise and lightning. I'd love to sit down with her and ask her how she'd designed the pot, and even more importantly, why she hadn't told me she'd made it.

The light danced on the figures, which seemed to move themselves. Around and around they went, bear chasing tortoise, chasing lightning, chasing bear.

I blinked. The background now showed new figures, emerging under the moon's silver glow. I couldn't quite make them out, but they interspersed with the others, adding to the chase, the motion making me dizzy.

"Janet?" Gabrielle asked. Her tone didn't so much hold concern as it implied, *What are you going crazy about this time?*

I shook myself. The figures on the pot abruptly stopped, again becoming the still outlines of bear, tortoise, and lightning.

I took the shard of magic mirror from its bag. Even in the white moonlight, it was dark, holding secrets in its heart.

I moved as close to Nash as I dared, then I tossed the shard of magic mirror directly into the pot.

CHAPTER TWENTY-SIX

Nothing happened. I hadn't thought it would. If Nash could cancel out something as powerful as the artifact, he'd cancel out the mirror, and any magical interaction between talismans as well.

Nash peered into the pot. "Why did you do that?"

"Keep it in there for me, will you?" I said. "And let's go have a talk with our mages."

As soon as Nash stepped away from the pickup, pot wrapped again and tucked under his arm, Drake peeled away from Mick and went for Nash.

He didn't care that the rest of us were two feet away from him. Dragon fire boomed around us, and Drake came down at our little group, huge talons curled and ready to strike. Dragon fire might not be able to hurt Nash, but Drake could always pick him up and drop him somewhere out in the desert, then pluck the pot from his dead, broken body.

Elena grabbed Grandmother and dragged her out of the way of the flames. The two women ran back to Nash's truck, diving inside the cab. Gabrielle ran after them, scrambling into the truck's bed to stand, Beneath magic in her hands, to defend them.

Mick charged for Drake, forcing the black dragon to roll away and climb again, but as soon as Mick and Drake were out of the way, Colby attacked.

I knew Colby didn't want to, but under his sentence to play slave for the dragons, he went for Nash.

I pushed my awareness at the gathering storm, grounding myself with it while I drew on the Beneath magic within me. Without the pot trying to enhance me, I might be able to deflect Colby without hurting him too much.

Colby came on. I saw his huge dragon underside, giant wings, talons as large as my body, as he dove for Nash. Nash ran and then dropped and rolled, trying to reach an outcropping of rock for cover.

As Colby passed over me, I let fly my Beneath magic, right under his wing.

Colby screeched as he fell sideways, batting the air with the wing I hadn't zapped, the other one sweeping crookedly in reflex. He burst out with dragon fire, which I deflected with a Beneath-magic shield. Colby jerked, trying to rise into the air, but his injured wing caught the ground.

Dust boiled upward as the dragon hit, the fine grains of dirt flying through my shield to slice at my face. The Beneath magic kept out the magical, not the physical.

I ran for Colby. He raised his head, fury in his eyes. The anger was not for me, but for Drake, who still held him in thrall. Colby didn't want to attack me, and I didn't want to attack him, but neither of us had a choice.

"Colby!" I cried. "Turn human."

Colby had tricked Drake out of his chains once before. If Colby put himself under the sphere of Nash's null influence, Nash's negating field might be able to unbind him. It had worked the last time.

Colby gave me another look of pure rage. He got to his

dragon haunches, his wings sliding out smoothly despite the hit they'd taken, and he launched himself into the air.

Damn. I wouldn't put it past Drake to have added a compulsion spell that kept Colby away from Nash. Drake wouldn't let Colby trick him a second time.

Nash made it under the rock outcropping and scooted as far back under its shelf as possible. If Colby couldn't squeeze a talon inside there, Nash—and the pot—would be safe.

Colby decided to dive at the rock itself, spitting fire. I countered with my Beneath shield, and Colby shot for the sky again.

I didn't want to hurt him. I wished Mick had gone after Colby, because I wouldn't have minded pounding Drake a little. I was still pissed at him about my hotel.

High above, Mick and Drake tangled. Drake and Mick were matched in size, and both were experienced fighters. Fire streaked through the air, followed by dragon cries of fury and pain.

"This is your spectacular plan, Janet?" Nash yelled at me.

"You have a better one?"

Colby dove at us again, dragon fire bursting around the rocks and charring clumps of vegetation in a wide ring.

He came down for another pass. I stood up, balls of Beneath magic dancing in my hands, ready to stop him.

Spikes of light descended from the black of the sky like bolts of golden lightning. Colby shrieked and flapped out of the way. I looked up in amazement as a dozen tubes of light slammed into the ground like railroad spikes, enclosing me and Nash, still under the outcropping, in a golden cage.

Crackling power surged out of the tubes, making the hair on my arms stand up. Colby swooped down to study them, but he kept his flames to himself. Good thinking. No telling what these things would do if we threw more power at them.

Nash peered out at me. "What the hell?"

The fact that the magical lights didn't instantly disperse

meant that Emmett had calculated exactly how far from Nash's field of influence he had to place them. Colby was still above us —if Nash moved beyond the rocks to negate the spikes, he'd still be vulnerable to the physical threat of Colby.

More tubes surrounded the pickup with Grandmother and Elena inside, Gabrielle now sitting cross-legged on the top of the cab. Her laughter floated to me. "Wish I'd thought of that."

Emmett Smith looked at me, lenses of his spectacles shining in the residual light of the tubes. "Sorry, Stormwalker. I need you contained for a while."

He turned away without waiting for my answer and faced Pericles again.

Pericles was shorter than Emmett and squat of build, but as I'd learned when he'd lifted me over his head, his body was mostly muscle. Moonlight gleamed on his bald spot, and also on his eyes, which had gone white.

I never saw the fight begin. One moment the two mages still assessed each other, the next, Emmett was enveloped in a dense black cloud. I felt the edges of Pericles's spell twenty yards away, choking death meant to squeeze every ounce of life from its victim.

A glowing shaft like the ones that surrounded us slammed straight through Pericles. Pericles screamed, and the blackness lightened enough for me to see Emmett's glasses gleaming behind it.

The spike went right through Pericles, leaving a giant, bloody hole in the middle of him. But as the spike and darkness dispersed, Pericles's body closed with an audible snap, and the blood vanished.

He gave Emmett a vicious smile. "That all you've got?"

"I was going easy on you," Emmett said. "If you like, I'll let you live. We can meet to fight another day."

"Screw you. I'm not letting you get your hands on that pot."

"Ah, well. Don't say I didn't warn you."

Another shaft of light shot toward Pericles. Pericles deflected it this time, then the air around the two mages became thick with darkness, then mist, light, and blood—as they threw spell after spell at each other.

Splinters of their spells ricocheted and arrowed toward the rest of us. Many crackled to nothing against the glowing tubes, but the rest came at us like flying shards of glass. Nash unfolded himself from under the rock to step in front of them, letting his null magic cancel them out, and I deflected the others. At the pickup, Gabrielle swatted at the spell remnants with her magic, whooping and laughing.

Bear, who'd remained motionless throughout all this, suddenly raised her arms. She pointed both hands high into the sky and let out a screaming chant in a high-pitched voice, the kind achieved by the best traditional Indian singers.

The sound echoed up and down the canyon, bounced from the tall mesas along the river valley, and rang up to the stars. A small rumble shifted my feet, the merest vibration, the ground answering.

Bear was calling the spirit of the canyon, the thousands of years of life and people and what they'd left behind. Wind sprang from a circle around her, and I heard the first rumble of thunder.

She was awaking the canyon, and bringing on the storm.

I laughed. Bear went on chanting. Though she sang in a language I didn't know, the words took shape in my head.

She sang of the creation, of the first three worlds far beneath us, which had been filled with gods and magical beings. She sang about First Man and First Woman, about life emerging through the cracks in the world Beneath to this one, the fourth world, the world of light.

I knew the story, had heard it many times. Bear added to it the tale of the pot she'd shaped, fired, and imbued with god magic. As Elena had told me, she'd presented it to the shamans who'd lived in this canyon long before what now stood in ruins had even been built, then she'd left them. The shamans had tried to use the pot, but they'd become greedy for its power, and it had started to destroy them. Other shamans, drawn by the magic, had fought to possess the pot, and in a conflagration of magic, the entire tribe had vanished from the land.

The pot had lain hidden here in the places of the dead, undisturbed for years. Other tribes had come and gone, but they'd never touched the graves. Then new people came, digging up the land and stealing from the dead, selling the pottery and artifacts they found to those who paid vast sums of money for them.

Now Bear had returned for her vessel. She would use it to stop the mages and the evil, then she'd take it and go.

I stood, mesmerized, listening to her. So did Nash. Gabrielle had gone quiet, and Grandmother and Elena watched, motionless, from the truck.

Pericles and Emmett paid no attention. The air around them was thick and black but shot through with wild colors. I heard screams among the magic, sounds of agony as well as snarls of rage.

Bear chanted on, and the storm built. Its tingling consumed me, and I turned in a circle, arms outstretched.

"What are you doing?" Nash demanded.

"Storm," I said. "It's a big one."

"How big?"

"I'd say, take cover."

Nash let out a string of swear words. He crawled beneath the slab of rock again and huddled there, tucking the pot beneath him.

Bear's song went on. The mages fought. The dragons screamed and fired, Colby joining their battle.

Nash made no move to nullify the magic ring around us, even with Colby gone, and I was fine with that, because the barrier shielded us against the backlash from the mages' spells. Emmett wasn't being nice to us—when he was done with Pericles, he'd turn his attentions to us and the pot his barrier had protected. Very organized, was Emmett.

The storm came on. I smelled dust and dampness, and saw the wall of dust rising above the cliffs around Chaco Canyon to blot out the stars, the disc of the moon, and even the clouds themselves.

The dirt wall filled the horizon from end to end and rose a mile and more into the sky. It came fast, swallowing everything before it—buttes, the canyon walls, rocks, trees, and all light. It swallowed the sky itself, and the wind raged.

Haboob, such storms were called. They were thick, miles deep and miles wide, and could reach two miles high. Its winds blew everything before it—dirt and debris, which the desert had to spare, sand loosened by sudden rain after days of no rain. All gathered into one giant storm, and that storm poured down on us now without mercy.

The canyon whirled into darkness. Emmett's spell lights glowed feebly, and by them I could just see Nash hunkered under the rock five feet away. Nothing else.

I stretched out my arms and embraced the storm.

I'd been in bad dust storms before, but this one was different. Whether Bear's magic had called it, or the magic battle in the valley had enhanced it, or somehow it sensed the pot's magic, I didn't know. But I felt the demons in the storm, beings drawn to the magic, and to me.

I grabbed the winds. I heard my own laughter, wild and strong. I was free.

My body rose with the wind, but I felt no terror. I rose on the haboob's waves, and my Beneath magic, ironically, kept me grounded.

"Woo!" Gabrielle shouted from where she stood on the hood of the truck. "Look at Janet. Go, big sis!"

The demons in the wind fell back before me. I commanded them—they'd bend to my will. The storm was *mine*.

The mile-high wall went straight for the dragons. "Mick!" I screamed. "Get out of the way!"

Mick, my smart boyfriend, had already seen, already comprehended, and was already moving. He shot away in front of the storm, angling to the south and east, out of its path.

Drake went right after him. Colby hesitated, wings pumping the air, already hampered by his injury. I reached up with my magic and gave him a shove, and he flapped reluctantly away.

I turned with the storm toward Emmett and Pericles.

I hit them with two tunnels of wind, breaking their spells. Black, fragmented magic danced down the canyon, exploding against the walls in brilliant colors, like washes of fireworks.

Both mages swung to me. They were panting, sweating, covered in blood and dirt, Emmett's glasses broken.

They no longer wore the guises of ordinary men they showed to the rest of the world. I could see under their skins, the evil but beautiful things they truly were. They'd once been men, but the power they'd studied, or stolen, and hoarded for years had made them as cold and perfect as marble statues. Flawless. Deadly.

Emmett hissed. From his mouth issued a darkness so black that it sucked in and destroyed any color or light touched it. I knew death when I saw it.

I grabbed the wind, shaped it into an arrow, filled it with Beneath power, and shot the death out of the sky before it could touch me. Emmett's spell shattered like porcelain on concrete.

I'd never done this before. Usually, I drew on a storm's power—wind, lightning, rain, snow—mixed it with my natural magic, and let it out again.

This time, I was *inside* the storm. It was me, and I was it. I was flying, cradled in its power.

My awareness expanded with the storm. I stretched fifty miles across the desert, seeing the little towns and pueblos from here to the Colorado border. Sheep huddled together, worried shepherds among them. People rushed home and closed windows and doors, peering out at the giant wave of sand with frightened eyes.

The dragons fought south of here, almost to the slopes of Mount Taylor, which marked the traditional boundary of the Navajo lands. I saw Drake whirl to face Mick, then the two dragons began to battle, swiping with wings, claws, teeth, tails.

Colby reached them, but to my amazement, instead of attacking Mick, he turned on Drake.

I thought for a second that he'd managed to break his binding spell, but with my vision enhanced by my bath of magic, I saw the dark wires of the spell still wrapping him. He was fighting despite his bondage, helping Mick. And it hurt him.

Mick roared down at Drake, mouth open, claws ready to maul. Drake danced aside, but one of Colby's back feet managed to rake across Drake's chest, drawing blood. Drake fired at Colby, and Colby shot out of the way. Mick took advantage to get in a shot of fire across Drake's back.

Drake shrieked, his hide burning, but he whipped around and struck, full force of body and tail. Not at Mick—at Colby.

Colby couldn't dodge in time. He almost managed to dive out of the way, but Drake's long, barbed tail caught him under one wing.

The wing tore in a crackling of cartilage, and Colby rolled like a fighter plane shot out of the sky. Fire burst from his mouth as he fell and caught Drake on the belly. Drake screamed and winged higher, trying to let the wind put the fires out.

Mick was on Drake in an instant, but Colby plummeted from the heights, straight toward rocky ground.

I shot out a cushion of wind to try to help break his fall, but the problem with being part of such a huge storm was that its strength dispersed the farther I moved from its heart. The dragons were fighting on the very edge.

I slowed Colby's descent a little, but still he tumbled end over end until he crashed into tall grasses and rock. A billow of dust shot up from his landing place, then Colby lay still.

Mick saw, but he had Drake on him. My attention was jerked back to the canyon, to Pericles and Emmett, who'd both decided that the biggest threat they needed to take down was me.

I whacked away the tubes of light surrounding Nash's truck. As reluctant as I'd been to touch the tubes when they'd first appeared, I now dispersed them with a flick of my fingers.

"Grandmother!" I called. "Colby needs help."

Elena started the truck. "Where is he?"

I pointed, unable to explain. Elena gave me an annoyed look, but they were magical women—they'd sense the fallen dragon's aura and find him.

Gabrielle rolled off the truck and came to her feet as Elena drove away. "I'm not leaving. Bring it on, mages."

They did. I left the barrier up around Nash to protect both him and the pot from physical injury. He sat in the middle of it, arms around the pot, and watched.

"Can I dust them, Janet?" Gabrielle turned her face up to me. *"Please?"*

"In this case? Sure!"

She whooped, and I felt her burst of Beneath magic as she rose into the air beside me. She somersaulted once in midair, laughing. "And people say sisters don't do enough together."

The two mages faced us in silence. Whether they'd discussed working together or just realized it was expedient, they'd put aside their differences to tackle us. Emmett and Pericles locked hands, raised them, and each sent one half of a spell at us.

The spells combined into a furrow of darkness. My newfound clarity told me that the darkness was designed to get past our magic and rip into our bodies. Neither Gabrielle nor I was immortal. We could die, and with us, our power.

Gabrielle gleefully whacked at the spell with a shaft of Beneath magic, then she screamed. The darkness wound onto her magic like a sticky web and started crawling toward her outstretched hand.

I sliced down with my own power, not onto the dark web, but to Gabrielle's magic just above it, cleanly cutting off the white shaft. The web found itself wrapping around nothing and it drew back, pausing like an animal scenting the wind.

Then it reared up and it came for me. I flew upward, rolling out of the way as quickly as any dragon. I came down again, landing on the earth outside the barrier surrounding Nash.

The mage's web of darkness followed me down. I swatted it with a swirl of wind, but as it had done with Gabrielle, it tried to cling to my magic and follow my own power back to me.

I realized that I couldn't fight the spell itself—I had to fight the mages. I had to release myself from all the restrictions I'd put on my use of magic in the past year, and go for the end game.

I closed my eyes.

I might have been born with goddess magic deep inside myself, but fortunately for me, my father had come from a line of shamans who carried strong earth magics—powers bound to this world, not the worlds below.

Grandmother, by making sure my latent evil didn't destroy me from the inside out, had given me the strength to steady myself against the Beneath magic that threatened me every day. My father, with his silences and the quiet composure with which he approached all things, had shown me the value of patience and endurance.

Jamison, the man I'd fought so hard this afternoon, had taught me to calm myself, to meditate and control the impulses that raged inside me.

Then Mick, my first and only lover, had taught me spells to help balance and hone my storm magic into an efficient, controlled power.

I'd learned so much from them—family, friend, lover—and now their lessons let me hold the storm, center myself, and marry the storm with my Beneath magic.

I opened my hands and filled my palms with the winds. The web of dark magic still watched me, waiting for me to strike, but I ignored it.

Instead I gathered the dense cloud of dust and swept it around myself and the two mages, blotting out everything and everyone but us. I heard Gabrielle's snarl of frustration, but I didn't want to let her in here. She was strong, but not strong enough.

I couldn't see the mage's faces now, only the white shafts of their true selves. They threw another collective spell at me, this one designed to squeeze all the breath from my body and leave me flat.

I sent the winds into the spell to pull it asunder. As it shattered, I snaked the storm between the two men and flung them apart.

The mages fell, but were up again at once. They stopped trying to work together and just started throwing spells at me.

I laughed as I smacked down spell after spell. I left the ground again, laughing, joyous, pounding the two mages with the wild mix of my magic as quickly as they shot their spells at me.

Bear had stopped chanting. Through the dust, I saw that she now stood with her hands at her sides, her head bowed, the bearskin on her back shrouding her body.

I didn't have time to wonder what she was doing now. That is, until I felt the weight of the auras of the canyon.

The larger magics of Emmett, Pericles, Gabrielle, and the storm, had shielded me from the auras that usually drove me crazy. But now that Bear had sung to the spirit of the canyon —its collective aura—I felt them with a vengeance.

The auras swirled together like those I'd awakened from the artifacts in Richard Young's collection room. They gathered around Bear, joining together like a dark cloak around her. She'd tried to help them, she'd caused them sorrow, and now she'd come to awaken them and protect them.

I felt the crush of the auras start to weaken me. Bear was on their side, and I knew I'd be foolish to assume she was still on ours.

I had another worry. I was drunk with power, riding this wonderful storm, but storms don't last forever. This one would disperse when nature had finished with it, and I'd be left with a bad magic hangover and only Beneath power on which to draw. Beneath magic was strong, but these mages, especially together, were the equal of it. And with no storm to steady me, I might end up destroying the entire canyon.

I kept sending bursts of storm at Emmett and Pericles, and they shot things back at me—death spells, fire spells, ice spells, spells designed to eat my organs from the inside out, spells intended to separate my physical self from my magical one.

The last one made me cold, even as I kicked it aside. I hadn't realized spells like that existed.

The glow of the golden tubes flashed and went out. For a second, I had no idea what had happened, then I realized that Nash had approached one of the tubes of light and reached out to cancel its magics.

When it went down, all the others did too. Nash disappeared into darkness, but I saw his silhouette against my next burst of lightning.

Nash held his Glock in his hands, and he aimed it and shot Pericles straight through the heart.

CHAPTER TWENTY-SEVEN

PERICLES SHOUTED, STUMBLED, FELL.

I knew that a powerful mage like Pericles probably had spells to safeguard him from even a bullet in his heart, but the impact did slow him down. He dropped out of the fight, and now only Emmett remained.

Nash lined up another shot for Emmett, but Emmett shot a black spell that rushed at Nash like a javelin, and Nash took the impact straight through the gun. The spell vanished as it hit Nash's magic absorption field, but the shock made him drop the pistol.

I heard Nash curse as he lost the gun in the dark, but I had to turn my attention back to Emmett.

He knew some nasty magic. I hoped to all the gods that I could wring out of my body any spell that touched me, because with my heightened awareness, I saw that these spells could linger and affect my offspring.

The wild thought flashed through my head — *Can Mick and I even have offspring?* — when more immediate concerns interrupted me.

One was the auras surrounding Bear, which were now

spreading wide like the dust storm. The other was a crazed Nightwalker who rushed out of the shadows for the fallen Pericles.

Pericles started up—so Nash's shot hadn't killed him after all—but then Ansel was upon him.

"Ansel! Stop!"

Not that I cared at this point whether Ansel sucked Pericles dry, but I feared what Pericles's magic might do to Ansel. The blood of a mage could be deadly.

"Gabrielle, get Ansel!"

But Gabrielle wasn't where I'd seen her last. She was now in front of Nash, struggling with him for the leather-covered pot. Nash was trying to subdue her without hurting her, but Gabrielle beat on him with one fist while she tried to rip the pot from him with her other hand.

I couldn't do anything about her right now. The wave of ancient beings Bear had awakened engulfed Pericles and Ansel, swirling around them and blotting them from sight, then they took Emmett. And now they were coming for me.

I drew on my storm power, but found myself beating off streaks of darkness that dove at me like angry flies. The cuts on my face bled and stung, I lost hold of some of my power, and I hit the ground with both feet—hard.

I whirled and beat at the maelstrom, but the shards of auras slashed me as the ones that attacked Richard Young had, ancient things angry at the disturbance of their resting place.

I heard Nash shouting, but I was too busy swatting things to give him my attention. The storm started to die, dust and wind losing momentum as it moved on to another part of the desert.

Dimly, through the choking dust and dark auras, I saw Bear's hands go up. The pot, which Nash and Gabrielle still fought over, shot away from them and went straight for Bear.

She caught it without struggle. The pot glowed, the only bright point in the gloom. The animal patterns again chased each other and the lightning around the bowl. I clearly saw the tortoise morph into a coyote, who chased the bear, who chased the lightning, which chased the coyote.

Bear sang more words in her high-pitched voice, but these I didn't understand. The language was so ancient, it probably never had been heard in the world.

My feet left the ground again, but not by my doing. I dove for the earth, grabbing, but my fingers scrabbled in dirt, fine rocks and dried grass coming away as I was yanked upward.

I tumbled toward Bear, feet-first, a whirlwind sucking me to her. Gabrielle came as well, jerked from Nash's side, she screeching and swearing. Emmett slammed into me as he joined me, then Pericles struck me, then Ansel. Nash was the only one I didn't sense with us.

Gabrielle, Emmett, Pericles, Ansel, and I were squashed together into one mass. Pericles' blood was hot on my skin, and the stench of Nightwalker made me gag. Pericles was still alive, though, Ansel weakening.

We were pulled, painfully, inexorably, toward Bear. Her voice grew louder, filling the skies, and the auras swirled with us, binding us together.

The shape of a coyote rose behind Bear. He lifted his muzzle as she continued to sing, his huge face turning to the moonlight. There *was* moonlight again, a hole ripped through the clouds and my storm.

Coyote howled, not a mournful howl or the high-pitched yowling of a coyote, but a wailing song that blended with Bear's.

Coyote wrapped his arms around her, paws laced across her shoulders, not stifling her or hindering her, but joining her.

Bear and Coyote. Two of the oldest gods. Husband and wife. One.

The ring Mick had given me stung my finger. I held onto the magic of the turquoise and silver while the wild power around me threatened to batter me bloody.

We were dragged onward toward the shimmering pillar of Coyote and Bear.

Just before we reached them, the singing stopped, and a fierce weight crushed me into nothing.

I heard another scream, a voice familiar to me—not mine, not Gabrielle's, not Mick's. The voice, stronger than I'd heard it in a long time, wound up to a horrific shriek.

"Janeeettttttt! Oh, this is so not gooooooood."

Before I could react, the screaming cut off, and everything went dark.

MY OWN GROANS WOKE ME. I OPENED MY EYES.

I lay flat on my back in darkness, but it was natural darkness. Clouds filled the sky, blotting out the moonlight, and a steady rain fell.

I was soaked, muddy, and in pain. I licked water from my lips and tasted blood.

Something large, wet, smelly, and warm lay down next to me. A cold nose touched my face, then a hot tongue swiped across my lips.

"Ewww." I scraped my hand over my mouth. "What are you doing?"

In an instant, Coyote became a man—large, naked, and still wet. "Healing you," he said. "Coyote spit is clean."

"Yuck."

"I can keep on, if you want." He waggled his tongue.

"Gods, you are such a pervert."

Which, in my world, was terrifyingly normal.

"What the hell happened?" I asked.

"Bear activated the artifact, it did its thing, and she's gone."

"Gone." I tried to sit up, clutched my head, which hurt like hell, and tried again. I managed to become upright this time and sat unmoving, my head pounding.

I was still in Chaco Canyon. All was quiet, except for the rain and distant rumbles of thunder. No auras, no spells, no haboob, no Beneath magic. Just me laid out like I'd been on a three-week bender.

I saw bodies around me, each about ten yards from me and from each other. Nash's pickup and the dragons still hadn't returned.

"Where has she gone?" I croaked.

Coyote shrugged. "Who knows? She'll be back. When she's ready."

"What did you mean, the artifact did its thing? What did it do? Besides throw me across the valley?"

"What Bear made it to do. She put her power into that pot not only to keep herself stable, but to help and protect her people." He shrugged again, his large body with all its muscles slick with water. "But as well-intentioned as gods may be, our power is vast, and when it falls into the wrong hands . . . well, you saw what happened."

"We all went for it," I said.

"So she took back the pot and used it for what she'd really made it for. To keep the powerfully magical away from her people." Coyote's hand landed on my shoulder, his strength immense, but it was meant to comfort, not hurt. "She could have killed you—all of you. She chose not to."

"Oh." I said, my head hurting so much I wasn't sure waking up was a blessing.

"The pot sucked you into it," Coyote said. "Weird to watch. Then it spit you out again, along with your magic mirror. The pot didn't like it. Which might also be why you're still alive."

"Nice of Bear," I said. "And the pot."

Coyote gave me a serious look, then he laughed. "Yeah, you could say that."

I rubbed my head again, pain stabbing at my temples. The storm magic had been torn out of me, and I was jumpy. Being knocked out plus the blinding headache had subdued the aftershock a little, but I needed to get rid of my residual magic. I needed Mick.

Once I could see better, I realized that the body closest to mine was Gabrielle's. Coyote helped me to my feet, but I had to stand still a few moments, catching my breath and trying not to throw up, before I could hobble toward her.

Gabrielle lay facedown in the mud, her hands and hair covered with blood. Now that her magic had gone, she looked like nothing more than a young, helpless girl.

I crouched beside her and turned her over. Gabrielle looked even more helpless now, the blood and mud on her face creased with tears.

"I wanted it," she sobbed. "Why wouldn't he let me have it?"

I smoothed a tangle of hair from Gabrielle's face, but she jerked away and rolled to sit, drawing her arms around her knees. "Leave me alone."

"You don't need the pot," I said. "You're already so strong. What did you want it for?"

Gabrielle glared at me, her eyes swimming with tears. "To open the vortex, stupid."

I didn't need to ask her which vortex. Each of the vortexes that dotted this part of the world led to different parts of Beneath. The one near my hotel led to my mother's realm.

"Why would you want to?" I asked, keeping my voice calm.

"To see her. To talk to her. To find out why she doesn't want me."

The rain started to pelt down more earnestly. "Evil goddesses aren't nurturing mothers, Gabrielle. Trust me."

"She wanted *you*. You and your Stormwalker magic. All I got was a father who was a drunk."

"I know." I didn't say I was sorry. I *was* sorry for her, but saying so wouldn't help. Not with Gabrielle.

"Go away."

I stood up. Gabrielle hunkered down into even more misery.

I stuck my hand out to her. "Come on. We still have two mages and a crazed Nightwalker to deal with."

She stared at me with every ounce of hatred and loathing Grandmother and I had tried to ease out of her in the past six months. I thought we'd made some headway, but maybe not.

I kept my hand out. Eventually, Gabrielle's expression changed to one of mere sourness, and she let me help her to her feet.

"Can I kill the mages?" she asked.

"Depends."

Gabrielle didn't look mollified. I felt her fuming as we made our way through the rainy darkness to the other bodies.

I did feel bad for her. Our goddess mother had decided that because Gabrielle's father had no magic in him—he'd lied and told her he was a shaman—she wanted nothing to do with Gabrielle. I wasn't sure which was worse: our hell-queen mother wanting to rule the earth world through me, or being utterly rejected by her.

Nash hadn't been pulled in by the magic, or thrown down when Bear disappeared. He was sitting on the outcropping under which he'd hidden, his arms resting on his knees. He'd retrieved his gun and now held it loosely in one hand. I saw blood on his face, even in the dark, his black hair glistening with rain.

"You two all right?" he asked us.

I was stumbling, Gabrielle blood-streaked, but I knew what he meant. "After a hot bath and a good night's sleep, we will be."

"She means after a good night's screwing with Mick," Gabrielle said. She gave Nash a look I thought she'd stopped reserving for him. "How about it, Nash? There's plenty of motel rooms between us and Flat Mesa."

"No."

He said it simply and with strength. Nash had decided on Maya, and that was that.

Gabrielle's smile died, but she shrugged. "That's all right. I've decided that Drake is hot, and I've always wanted to do a dragon."

"Pick one without ice in his veins," I said.

"Like Colby? Mmm, not bad. Let me think about it."

I walked away from the bizarre conversation. I heard Nash jump down from the rock and follow me.

The next body I came to was Pericles. He'd reverted to looking like the short, muscular guy with the balding head who'd attacked me in the basement of Laura's store, except now his eyes were closed, his face wan. He also had a bullet wound in his chest.

Nash crouched down and checked him, then nodded at me. "He's still alive."

"Can I crush him?" Gabrielle asked, coming up behind Nash.

"No," I said.

"He tried to kill us tonight. Why not?"

I felt Gabrielle's magic building, and I put a hand on her wrist. "It's one thing to kill him in a fair fight, another to blast him when he's unconscious. It . . . would be wrong."

Gabrielle gave me an incredulous look, but her magic faded. "And you call *me* the crazy one."

Nash nudged Pericles with his pistol. "Hey. Wake up."

Pericles's eyes popped open. He took in Nash, the gun, and Gabrielle and me standing over him. He drew a long breath that ended in a cough and wince of pain. "The artifact?"

"Gone," I said.

Gabrielle smiled. "Too bad, so sad."

"You need an ambulance?" Nash asked him. "You took one in the chest. I don't care how magical you are . . ."

"No," Pericles snarled. He gave me a glare that boded me no good, then he vanished.

Nash rose to his feet and let out his breath. "One down," he said.

A voice floated faintly to me, one I hadn't heard in days. "Somebody? *Anybody*? Help me? Pleeeeeze?"

"What the hell is that?" Gabrielle asked.

The rain was starting to disperse, the moon reappearing through a torn cloud. Under its light, the valley floor glittered with rocks and quartz. One shard of mirror would be difficult to locate.

"Keep talking," I said. "I'll find you."

Nash looked around, pistol ready. "Who the hell are you talking to?"

"Who knows?" Gabrielle answered. "She's crazy. You get used to it."

"Please," the mirror sobbed. "Take me home. Oh, honey, I'm *so* scared."

I finally spotted it lying about a hundred yards to the east of where Bear had stood. The shard was silver and shining, no longer dark.

"Thank you," it gasped in relief when I picked it up. "Sugar-plum, you look *terrible*."

I closed my hand around the shard and turned to find Emmett Smith standing a foot away from me.

His glasses were bent, one of the lenses broken, but he'd shoved them back on and straightened his blood-soaked tie. Behind the ruined glasses, his eyes were clear and hard and held the intensity of a basilisk.

"You have a *magic mirror*," he said, voice ringing. "You bitch, you've been holding out on me."

CHAPTER TWENTY-EIGHT

THIS WAS NOT GOOD.

Emmett stood before me fully functional, while I was crackling with residual storm magic, exhausted, and had a headache from hell. All he had to do was kill me, and then kill Mick, and the mirror was his. At this point, I was pretty sure he could do it.

Emmett's aura was tough, like thick hide, bright white like Gabrielle's. He had no Beneath magic in him, but the earth magic he'd learned and stored filled every centimeter of his body. I felt that magic stir into a killing spell.

As Latin words started from his throat, I drew on the vestiges of the storm magic and my Beneath magic and channeled them into the mirror. But I knew it wouldn't be enough, not against someone like Emmett when I was this spent.

Just as Emmett let fly the spell, me desperately gathering my fading magic, several tons of dragon poured out of the sky.

One of Mick's wings caught Emmett and sent him tumbling to the ground. Emmett's spell went wide and missed me, to be caught in the gentle wind that played where Bear had stood. I redirected the last of my magic to the spell, sliced into it, and finished it off.

Emmett was on his feet, fists balled, readying another spell to blast Mick. And then Nash rose behind Emmett, pressing his pistol to the man's ear, his other arm wrapping around Emmett's waist. Emmett's spell, obliterated by Nash's null field, died before it formed.

"Leave," Nash advised him. "And don't let me find you around Janet or Mick again."

Emmett scowled, but I knew better than to think he'd obey Nash. Emmett would be back, now that he knew I had something worth his while. "Better start looking over your shoulder, Stormwalker," he said in his smooth, cool voice. "If you'll let go of me, Sheriff, I'll gladly go."

Nash kept his pistol trained on Emmett, but he eased his hold from around the man and took several steps away. Emmett straightened his tie again, then he vanished.

Mick had landed somewhere off in the darkness, and now he walked out of that darkness as a man covered in rain and streaks of blood. He came for me and lifted me off my feet, holding me against his hot, hard, wet body.

"Hey, baby," he said, his voice dark. "Miss me?"

Nash, two feet away from us, noisily re-holstered his weapon and cleared his throat. "Good to see you in one piece, Mick," he said. "Where the hell is my truck?"

ELENA CAME DRIVING BACK ABOUT THIRTY MINUTES LATER, steering Nash's F250 down the rutted road to the canyon.

While we watched them approach, Ansel rejoined us. He'd come out of the unconscious state the rest of us had been thrown into, and now he stood at my side, staring bleakly at the truck's approaching headlights. His eyes were normal, no blood frenzy, but I'd never seen him so morose.

Elena pulled the truck to a halt in the exact same spot from which she'd taken it. Colby, in human form, lay on his back in the truck's bed, a tarp over him. Drake, naked, bruised, and bloody, sat next to him.

I climbed into the truck and knelt next to Colby. Mick rested his arms on the truck's side and watched, concerned.

"Hey, Janet," Colby said, his voice weak. "I feel like shit."

Dragons are good at healing themselves, but sometimes it takes a while. Colby had been ripped into and then suffered a fall of several hundred feet. His injuries wouldn't be a quick fix.

Gabrielle vaulted over the side of the truck. "Aw, poor Colby. You look awful." Her voice went little-girl sugar. "And this itty-bitty, wittle binding spell can't be helping you, can it? I'll make it all gone."

Drake grabbed for her, but Gabrielle had already put her hand on Colby and let her magic surge.

Colby yelled as an arc of pure Beneath magic lifted his body from the truck bed and slammed it back down. He groaned in pain, but I saw the threads of the binding spell dissolve and disappear.

Colby took a deep, grating breath, and blinked. He raised his head and looked down at his body, then he blew out the breath and let his head drop back again. "Thanks," he said, his voice stronger. "I feel better already."

Drake's eyes narrowed as he began to chant the binding spell again, but Gabrielle seized his hand. "No, Drakey, don't do that. I might have to hurt you."

She clamped down on Drake's hand, and Drake winced.

"Tell you what," Gabrielle said. "Spend the rest of the night with me, Drakey, and maybe I'll let you put the spell back on him."

Colby raised his head again. "And that's fair, how?"

Gabrielle smiled at him. "You can join in, if you want. I'll heal you at the same time. It'll be fun."

Colby grinned with her. "That's more like it."

"Gabrielle." The voice was my grandmother's, the tone one she'd reserved for me on my most misbehaving days.

Gabrielle glared at Drake. "Now you've gone and gotten me into trouble."

She swung her leg over the side of the truck and slid down, moving to my grandmother's side, arguing as she went.

Drake raised his hand again, beginning the words to reinstate the binding spell.

"Don't," I said.

Mick only watched, but I sensed him tense, ready to fight. Drake lowered his hand but gave me a baleful look. "Colbinilicarium hasn't finished the terms of his sentence."

"He's been your slave for a while now," I said, "and he nearly got himself killed for you tonight. What did he do, anyway?"

Drake folded his hand in his lap and clammed up, his eyes telling me nothing.

Colby chuckled. "You really want to know? Okay, I might have stolen Bancroft's little black book."

I figured it might be something like that. Colby had once had a fling with the mistress of a dragon called Farrell, the head of the dragon council. That deed had landed him in plenty of trouble.

Bancroft was second-in-command of the tri-part dragon council, and headed the dragon compound in Santa Fe. Bancroft had never struck me as the playboy type—too cold—but then, neither had Farrell.

"That's it?" I asked.

"Well, I might have given a copy to his mate," Colby said.

"Oh, great. That can't have gone over well."

"And then I might have emailed copies to everyone in the book."

"Colby." Because the dragon population didn't contain that many females, all the women in the book were probably human. They probably also didn't know Bancroft was a dragon or about the other ladies in the picture. Bancroft must have had some fun after that.

"Crap on a crutch," I said. "Do all dragons cheat on their mates?"

"No!" Drake and Mick answered at the same time.

Colby laughed again, the laugh ending in a cough. "Bancroft's full of himself. He thinks he can do anything he wants. I showed him he couldn't. Thus, my punishment."

"I think he's had enough," I said. "Don't you, Drake? You don't think Bancroft was being just—I see it in your face."

"Perhaps not," Drake said quietly. "But he is my employer."

"Tell Bancroft that tonight Colby went above and beyond the call of duty for a dragon, and so I commanded you to free him." I gave Drake a smile. "If you don't, I can always talk to Bancroft myself, or I can let Gabrielle persuade you."

Drake glanced to where Gabrielle was arguing with my grandmother and Elena, and his face lost a little color.

"Fine." He stood up, his body gleaming like one of Jamison's sculptures. "I'll leave Colbinilicarium in your hands, and report that you and Micalerianicum forced the issue."

Without further word, Drake dropped out of the pickup, walked off into the desert, became dragon in the darkness, and winged away east.

"Aw, thanks, Janet," Colby said, reaching for my hand and squeezing it. "Now, how about a bed for the night? And some aspirin? I still feel like shit."

~

NASH AGREED TO DRIVE COLBY AND ELENA BACK TO MY hotel while I went to Many Farms with Grandmother and Gabrielle in my dad's truck, which had mercifully escaped damage. Mick gave me a long kiss and departed to fly Ansel home before sunrise.

I hadn't seen Coyote at all since he'd awakened me. He'd completely vanished, as usual. I didn't worry as much about him this time, as I drove away from the canyon, heading for the road that would take us to Farmington. He'd be back.

Gabrielle sulked through the long drive, which worried me a little, but Grandmother was perfectly serene. Gabrielle cheered up when we finally halted in front of the little house I'd grown up in, the lights in the windows a warm welcome.

Gabrielle ran inside ahead of us, while I waited to help Grandmother descend and make her slower way in.

"Janet was amazing," Gabrielle was saying to my father and Gina when we entered the house. "Did you see that dust storm? Janet rode it and made it her bitch."

"Gabrielle," Grandmother said disapprovingly.

"Then we kicked some dark mage ass," Gabrielle said, ignoring her. "It was awesome. They got away, but we'll get them another day. I'm hitting the showers. I stink. Bah-bye, Janet. Call me when Colby gets better."

I suppressed a shiver as she sauntered down the hall and slammed the door of the bathroom. Gabrielle and Colby—that would be trouble on the hoof. Or the wing.

Gods, Gabrielle reminded me of . . . me.

My father said nothing at all. He only watched me in silence while I fetched some water from the kitchen and Gina walked with my suddenly tired grandmother down the hall to her bedroom.

I came out of the kitchen. "Dad," I said. "I'm sorry."

He approached me without changing expression, but when he put his hands on my shoulders, his dark eyes were moist. "You do what you have to do, my daughter."

My dad has never been one to be overly demonstrative, but the way he squeezed down on my shoulders now conveyed his worry and also his love.

When he released me, giving me the lightest of pats, I also understood that he was making himself let me go.

I had a long ride ahead of me back to Magellan, so I finished my glass of water and prepared to leave. I could have crashed on the couch for the night, but I wanted my big bed, the safety of my warded and guarded hotel, and I wanted Mick.

I said goodbye to my father in our usual, understated way that spoke volumes, and left him.

Gina came out before I could start my bike. She glanced at the house where my father could be seen moving through the living room, then she leaned close to speak to me so her voice wouldn't carry.

"It's hardest on those who love the special ones. And you're special, daughter of my husband-to-be."

"I didn't choose this," I said, my throat tight.

Gina nodded. She was a bit like Bear, but she was human, and here. "He understands. Just love him."

"I do. For so long, he was the only one who believed in me."

"He still does," Gina said. "And I believe in him."

"Thank you."

I spoke in Diné, and Gina responded in kind. "Take care, daughter."

I rode away, unshed tears blurring my eyes, the storms in the distance rolling off to reveal the gentle night.

I rode quietly through Many Farms and back south on the highway through dark, beautiful Navajo lands to the flat plane of the I-40. The magic mirror, now awake, kept me company by singing.

MICK WAS WAITING FOR ME IN OUR PRIVATE QUARTERS, AND he started skimming off my clothes before the bedroom door even closed. He took me into the shower, washed me all over, made love to me against the wall, and carried me to bed.

He made love to me again, drawing off the lingering magic that still made my head ache, and healed me with soothing spells.

When I felt better, I loved him back with renewed energy. We wound up into climax together, erotic excitement spinning us higher and higher until we crashed back onto the bed, breathless and laughing. Then we spooned together under the sheet, Mick touching my body with gentle fingers, while I drifted to sleep, safe and warm.

I slept a long time the next day, not waking and rising until later in the afternoon.

I realized, as I had another shower then busily devoured a meal Elena prepared specially for me, that I still had problems to solve.

"Such as, where is Laura?" I asked Mick as he sat next to me in the kitchen. He folded his tattooed arms on the table as he watched me eat, as though he wanted to make sure I took every bite. "That's what started all this. Ansel still doesn't know, and Paige still has a bounty out on Ansel."

"We'll find her," Mick said with confidence. "When Ansel wakes up, we'll talk it over, and we'll figure it out."

"You don't have to worry about Laura," Elena said. She tossed a handful of onions into a sauté pan, the fragrance of onions and butter wafting toward us. "She's safe."

I blinked at her. "You know where she is?"

"Yes. She's staying with one of my friends up in Whiteriver."

Mick looked at her with as much surprise as I did. "In Whiteriver?" I got to my feet. "With one of your friends. Why the hell didn't you tell us you knew where she was?"

Elena gave me a slow look while she tossed the onions in the pan. "She asked me not to, and unlike some people, I can keep a promise. She turned up here about a week ago, worried about Ansel. She told me that a dark mage, or something worse, might be after her, and she wanted to warn Ansel. Well, I said, if a dark mage is chasing you, this hotel is the first place he'll look. So I drove her up to Whiteriver, and had her stay with a friend, another shaman. I didn't tell you, so that one of you wouldn't let it slip. I planned to fetch her back when the danger was over. We can go tonight, when Ansel is awake."

Finished, Elena turned her back on us to core and slice up a green pepper.

"Ansel was worried sick about her," I said. "You could have told him, at least? And it would have been helpful to ask Laura what she'd done with the real vessel."

Elena's knife went through the pepper in even strokes. "Ansel is a Nightwalker. How could I know whether he was worried for the woman's safety or wanted to kill her to protect himself? You found out what she'd done with the pot all on your own. Her part was finished, and I saw no reason to drag her back into danger. Now that I've had time to observe Ansel, I believe his feelings for her are genuine."

"Is that why you were guarding him so closely? To decide whether he had integrity?"

"Partly."

She went back to the pepper, which she finished chopping and threw into the pan. Oil hissed, the sound drowning out my, "Elena."

Elena totally ignored me. Mick and I exchanged a long glance, and he shook his head.

I supposed Elena had been right. If I or Ansel or Mick—or anyone—had known Laura's whereabouts, Pericles might have picked it out of us. Ansel had worried about her, but better he worry for nothing than Laura die because Pericles or Emmett had found her.

The kitchen phone rang. Elena cut into another pepper in silence. I waved Mick back as he stood to get the phone, heaved myself up, and answered it.

"It's Rory," Rory said. "I'm at the bar. We need to talk."

He hung up before I could say a word.

"Want me to deal with him?" Mick asked as I returned to the table. He'd heard.

"No." I shoveled in the last of my sweet corn tamales, drank some water, and wiped my mouth. "I want to do this myself." I gave him a brief kiss on the lips, one that promised much more later, and he let me go.

∾

RORY THE SLAYER NURSED A BEER AT A TABLE IN THE MIDDLE of Barry's bar. The Crossroads Bar was full this late in the afternoon, bikers from all over the southwest and into California liking Barry's place. This was neutral ground, by tacit agreement, no wars allowed.

Rory's crossbow hung from a hook on the back of his chair. I sat down facing him, folding my hands on the table.

"You owe me seven thousand dollars," he said.

I didn't flinch. "Where is Paige's boyfriend? The Nightwalker called Bobby?"

"Sheriff took him from me," Rory said, looking disgusted. "I made the mistake of telling your pretty hotel manager that I had him, and she called the sheriff. Sheriff came and got him, taking my Nightwalker safety box and all, saying he wanted to get Bobby for murder." Rory shook his head. "Arresting a Nightwalker for murder. Is he crazy?"

"Yes," I said. "But seeing as you don't have the goods, I see no reason to give you seven thousand dollars."

Rory reddened. "Don't even think about reneging on me."

"The Sheriff's department might give you a reward for bringing in a fugitive. If you ask nicely."

Rory glared at me. "You cheating bitch."

"While we're talking, I'm calling off the bounty on Ansel. Paige hired you because she thought Ansel had murdered her sister, and now it turns out her sister is fine and safe. So the hunt is over. Please spread the word around the slayer community that Ansel is not to be touched."

Rory listened first in surprise, then disgust. He shook his head. "It doesn't work that way, honey."

"No?"

"No. I don't just hunt for bounty. Nightwalkers shouldn't be allowed to live. When I find one, I kill him, bounty or no bounty."

"Change your policy," I said.

"Fuck you."

I leaned over the table to Rory, losing my smile and fixing him with my grandmother's best stare. "Listen very carefully. I want you to leave Hopi County today. Now, in fact. Don't come back here hunting Nightwalkers or anything else—ever."

"No, you listen to me," Rory said in the same tone. "I found that Nightwalker, I stashed him for you instead of killing him, and now you owe me seven grand. You give it to me, or you're the next body in the box."

Barry appeared at table, setting a cold bottle of beer in front of me and leaving his big hand on it. "Trouble, Janet?"

I gave him a sweet smile. "Nothing I can't handle. You have a fire extinguisher handy?"

Barry lost his answering smile. "Aw, shit," he said, and moved quickly back behind the bar.

"Fire extinguisher?" Rory asked.

"Yes. In case something goes wrong when I do this."

I was off my seat and had Rory's crossbow in my hand before he realized I'd moved. It was a nicely made weapon, engineered to fire with strength, but light, with a good grip and a smooth draw.

Rory grabbed for the crossbow, but I tossed it upward and blasted it with a tiny burst of Beneath magic.

The crossbow, though made primarily of metal, exploded into flames. The weapon burned merrily in midair for about

five seconds, then the fire vanished and the remains of the
crossbow dropped to the floor as a pile of ash.

Rory leapt from his chair. "Damn you, bitch. That cost a
me fortune." He yelled it, and then he went very quiet.

The explosion had jolted the attention of the bikers. Every
one of them drew, and every one of them cocked.

I turned to the room and held up my hands. "Easy, guys.
It's just me."

Though I was only the small Navajo woman who ran the
hotel across the parking lot, the bikers had come to treat me
with wariness, if not complete respect. Dangerous things
happened around me, and I knew dangerous people, like Mick.
They muttered, eased back on triggers, and sat back down.

"But you can do me a favor," I said to them. "This man here
is bothering me. I'd love it if some of you could escort him out.
And tell him never to come back. And if he does come back,
he's all yours."

There was murmuring, and laughter. Rory went pale.

I sat back down and sipped the beer Barry had brought
me. "I'd get out of here while I still could."

Rory gave me a final dirty look, but he knew when his odds
were bad. He walked out through the bar like he didn't give a
damn about the bikers, but I noticed that he walked fast.

Ten of the guys followed him. I set my beer aside, thanked
Barry, who was heading to the table with a broom to sweep up
the ashes, and departed.

When I emerged to the parking lot, I had the joy of
watching Rory the slayer speed off on his motorcycle toward
Winslow and the setting sun like all the hounds of hell were
after him.

~

MICK AND I ACCOMPANIED ELENA AND ANSEL TO
Whiteriver after Ansel awoke from his day sleep. Elena

borrowed Cassandra's car for herself and Ansel—and Laura, if she decided to return with them—while Mick and I rode double on Mick's Harley.

I loved this, snuggling into Mick's warm body as we raced down the open road under the stars toward the summits that made up Rim Country. The air turned cooler as we reached the higher elevations, then we made the turn at Showlow to take us south to the Apache reservation and Whiteriver.

Naomi had called me this afternoon while I filled in Cassandra on what had happened with the pot and tried to return to a little hotel business. Julie's hearing was still intact, Naomi said, sounding both hopeful and fearful of that hope. I couldn't tell her whether Julie's cure would be permanent. The talisman had vanished only last night, and perhaps its influence simply hadn't faded yet.

But the magic had originally come from Bear, and surely Bear wouldn't hurt Julie like that.

Then again, what had I truly known of the goddess? She'd been kind in her quiet way, but the power that had come from her last night had frightened me almost as much as any that emanated from my mother. Terrifying in a different way, but just as deadly. We would just have to watch Julie and see.

Elena's friend lived in a long and low trailer house set back among trees on the other side of Whiteriver. The yard in front of it was dark, but lights glowed from the small windows, and we heard a television playing.

Ansel was out of the truck before Elena even stopped it, his Nightwalker speed taking him to the little porch and up into the trailer. I heard a cry and the sound of something falling.

I hopped off Mick's big bike, dragged off my helmet, and dashed inside in time to see Ansel lifting a woman off her feet in a hard embrace. Laura looked much like her photo, with her athletic body, brown-blond hair, and pretty face, but now her smile beamed a joy that made her beautiful.

A small, plump Apache woman watched expressionlessly

from the kitchen as Laura hugged Ansel and kissed his thin face. The woman didn't acknowledge me, but gave Elena a nod and cast a brow-lifting glance at Mick as we crowded into the trailer.

"You're all right," Ansel said in his gentle, English voice, tears wetting his face. The tears were pink, mixed with blood —Nightwalker tears. "Love, you're all right."

Elena pushed past me, heading for her friend in the kitchen, but Mick wrapped an arm around me and tugged me back outside with him.

The night was quiet, crickets singing under the trees, cicadas calling, tree frogs chirping. In the distance, a coyote yowled then trailed off into a series of yips.

Mick walked me back to the bike, our footsteps muffled by fallen leaves. The weather was cool here, the breeze like a feather touch.

Mick leaned back on his bike seat and pulled me close, opening his legs around mine. Through the window, I could see Laura and Ansel still embracing, Ansel kissing her lips.

"Mmm," Mick said, his arms warm around me. "A Nightwalker and a human woman. That's going to be a challenge for them."

"Like a Stormwalker and a dragon?"

Mick turned me to him, hands on the small of my back. I touched his cheek, my turquoise and silver ring sliding against his unshaven whiskers.

"Something like that," he said.

We watched the two through the window, man and woman smiling into each other's faces, a moment of happiness.

"He must really love her," I said. "Ansel became the Nightwalker when he was with her, and instead of feasting on her blood, he fought off a dragon for her. Even the Nightwalker part of him cares for her."

Mick's eyes burned deepest blue. "The two-natured can love twice as deeply."

"So can the crazy woman with two magics tangling inside her. I won't even ask you what you were doing going off alone so often before all this started, or what you and my grandmother have been talking about in secret."

Mick didn't even look ashamed. "I thought you'd forgotten about that."

"I don't forget about anything when it comes to you."

"Mmm." Mick stared off into the distance, where trees sighed under the starlight. "I'll tell you when it's time. Let's just say I'm looking to our future."

I had no idea what he meant. That is, I had some ideas, but I didn't want to voice them, not now. For now, we had the night, and the cool mountain air, and the joy of Ansel's happy reunion.

Mick kissed me, his most effective way of silencing me. I let him, floating on the kiss to find and savor the peace of the moment.

Beyond the house, movement flickered in the trees. I thought I saw a large bear running after a giant-sized coyote, but I couldn't be sure.

End

BOOKS BY ALLYSON JAMES

AKA JENNIFER ASHLEY

Stormwalker
Firewalker
Shadow Walker
"Double Hexed"
Nightwalker
Dreamwalker
Dragon Bites

**Shifters Unbound
(Paranormal Romance
w/a Jennifer Ashley)**
Pride Mates
Primal Bonds
Bodyguard
Wild Cat
Hard Mated
Mate Claimed
"Perfect Mate" (novella)
(in the anthology, *Unbound*)

Lone Wolf
(gathered with Feral Heat in the anthology *Shifter Mates*)
Tiger Magic
Feral Heat
(gathered with Lone Wolf in the anthology *Shifter Mates*)
Wild Wolf
Bear Attraction
Mate Bond
Lion Eyes
Bad Wolf
Wild Things
White Tiger
Guardian's Mate
Red Wolf
Tiger Striped
(novella)
Midnight Wolf
Shifter Made ("Prequel" short story)
(gathered in print with *Hard Mated*)

ABOUT THE AUTHOR

Award-winning author Allyson James is a pen name of *New York Times* bestselling author Jennifer Ashley. Allyson has written more than 85 published novels and novellas in romance, urban fantasy, and mystery under the names Jennifer Ashley, Allyson James, and Ashley Gardner. Allyson's books have been nominated for and won Romance Writers of America's RITA (given for the best romance novels and novellas of the year), and several *RT BookReviews* Reviewers Choice awards (including Best Urban Fantasy, Best Shapeshifter Romance, and Career Achievement in Historical Romance), and Prism awards for her paranormal romances and urban fantasy.

More about Allyson's books can be found at the website www.jenniferashley.com (click on "Allyson's books" on the menu) or join her newsletter at

http://eepurl.com/47kLL

CPSIA information can be obtained
at www.ICGtesting.com
Printed in the USA
LVHW092232171019
634597LV00001B/210/P